"The more we wo‌ ‌
you will learn. K‌
you and enunciate when h‍ ‍

"Enough what when he speaks?"

"E-nun-ci-ate. To say something clearly."

Eli nodded, flustered he'd misunderstood Miriam.

She touched his face. Startled, he froze.

"Eli, do not be embarrassed. Even people with perfect hearing miss words."

Was his pain emblazoned there? The last thing he wanted was her pity.

He realized how he'd misread her when she said, "Your hearing loss is nothing to be ashamed of."

"I know."

"You say that. But you do not act that way. It will get easier." She smiled as if he were one of her scholars.

Was that how she saw him? That *was* what he was, but when she touched him on his arm to get his attention, he couldn't think of her as anything other than a charming woman.

She was his teacher—and his neighbor. Nothing else. He was being a fool. He wasn't going to invite more pain into his life. Not when he'd come to Harmony Creek to start over.

Jo Ann Brown has always loved stories with happily-ever-after endings. A former military officer, she is thrilled to have the chance to write stories about people falling in love. She is also a photographer and travels with her husband of more than thirty years to places where she can snap pictures. They have three children and live in Florida. Drop her a note at joannbrownbooks.com.

Rebecca Kertz was first introduced to the Amish when her husband took a job with an Amish construction crew. She enjoyed watching the Amish foreman's children at play and swapping recipes with his wife. Rebecca resides in Delaware with her husband and dog. She has a strong faith in God and feels blessed to have family nearby. Besides writing, she enjoys reading, doing crafts and visiting Lancaster County.

JO ANN BROWN

The Amish Suitor

&

REBECCA KERTZ

Her Forgiving Amish Heart

H HARLEQUIN®LOVE INSPIRED®

LOVE INSPIRED BOOKS

Recycling programs for this product may not exist in your area.

ISBN-13: 978-1-335-47012-6

The Amish Suitor and Her Forgiving Amish Heart

Copyright © 2019 by Harlequin Books S.A.

The publisher acknowledges the copyright holders of the individual works as follows:

The Amish Suitor
Copyright © 2018 by Jo Ann Ferguson

Her Forgiving Amish Heart
Copyright © 2018 by Rebecca Kertz

Printed in U.S.A.

CONTENTS

THE AMISH SUITOR   7
Jo Ann Brown

HER FORGIVING AMISH HEART   227
Rebecca Kertz

THE AMISH SUITOR

Jo Ann Brown

For Gary Rubin,
the "younger man."
A dear friend for longer than either of us
wants to admit!
Do you still remember the parade in Hop Bottom
with one marching band and nineteen fire engines?

Be strong and of a good courage,
fear not, nor be afraid of them:
for the Lord thy God,
he it is that doth go with thee;
he will not fail thee, nor forsake thee.
—*Deuteronomy* 31:6

Chapter One

Harmony Creek Hollow, New York

The bottle of spaghetti sauce at the top of the pyramid swayed.

The three bottles below it rocked.

The whole stack quivered.

Eli Troyer leaped forward and hooked an arm around his nephew. He yanked the six-year-old away from the grocery store endcap. Kyle let out a shriek. Whether it was shock or a forewarning, everyone within sight in the small grocery store froze.

But not the bottles. The stack began to crumble.

Just as the wall had.

Irrational terror swelled through Eli, clamping talons around his windpipe. He couldn't breathe. He couldn't move. Sounds erupted in his mind. The memory of an earsplitting crack from a wall that couldn't stand any longer. A man's horrified shout, a woman's scream, crashing stone, pain...silence.

Always the silence.

Knowing he had to protect the little boy, Eli put out

a hand in a futile effort to stabilize the bottles, to keep the display from crumbling. Too late. Just like before. In a slow-motion avalanche, the tower collapsed. He bent over Kyle, keeping himself between the little boy and disaster. Time escalated again when the first jar hit the concrete floor and shattered. The rest followed. Some bounced and rolled, but most exploded in a spray of marinara sauce. The sharp sounds resonated through his hearing aids as if he stood in a giant hailstorm.

Shouts, loud enough so he could hear them, though he couldn't pick out words, rang through the store. His fear faded into knowing he must deal with what had happened in Salem's only grocery store. He fought the yearning to flee as a different panic burst out in a cold sweat. After four years of staying out of the limelight, eyes were focused on him. It was the moment he dreaded, the moment he'd hoped wouldn't come.

Someone was going to talk to him. Ask him questions. Expect him to understand what they'd said and then answer.

What once would have been a snap now was torture. Since the retaining wall had fallen on him and his brother and sister-in-law, he'd asked God at least once a day why Kyle's parents had been killed and he hadn't. He'd survived, but most of his hearing had been lost, leaving him encased in silence.

Not just his hearing had changed that day. His whole life had. If the wall hadn't capsized, he'd be married to Betty Ann Miller. He hadn't been sure if her averted glances had been pity or if she was ashamed because she found herself walking out with a damaged man. Either way, he never walked out with her again, and she'd married someone else.

He avoided talking to people. Most when they saw his hearing aids raised their voices and spoke slowly as if that would have helped more. Before he'd brought Kyle north from their home district in Delaware, he'd known when to dodge chatty neighbors. The storekeepers near Dover had learned it was easier to let him point to what he needed and not engage him in conversation.

Ach, how he missed the simple pleasure of a chat. Now he mostly spoke to Kyle, who helped him with even the simplest interactions.

"Are you okay?" he asked his nephew.

The little boy, who looked like Eli's late brother with his bright red hair and freckles, nodded.

"What happened?"

Kyle shrugged and held up a box of brown sugar before going to stand by where the sugar was on a shelf. It was at least three feet from the endcap, farther than the little boy could reach. The motions were Kyle's way of telling him that he hadn't touched the bottles.

His mud-brown eyes widened, and he pointed past Eli.

Expecting to see an angry store manager, Eli squared his shoulders and prepared to strain what little hearing he had left to pick up the manager's words. He turned.

And stared.

On the other side of the broken bottles and splattered sauce stood two women and two half-filled shopping carts. An elderly *Englisch* woman cowered behind her cart and peered like a cartoon owl through glasses with bright green frames. The other woman stood in front of her.

Eli's breath caught as he looked at the pretty Amish woman. He hadn't attended a church service in Harmony Creek Hollow yet, because he and Kyle had just moved into the new settlement earlier in the week. But he guessed she was the sister of the settlement's founder, Caleb Hartz, because beneath her heart-shaped *kapp*, she had similar pale blond hair and intense jade green eyes. As well, she had her brother's impressive height.

Her apron and the hem of her dark purple dress, as well as her black sneakers, had been showered with spaghetti sauce. A dab highlighted her left cheekbone. Pink was returning to her cheeks, replacing the gray of shock.

Kyle grasped his hand tightly. They stood side by side when a harried *Englischer* wearing a bright red bib apron as the cashiers did rushed to him. The man, whom Eli surmised was the store manager because he wore a white shirt and tie, pushed past the crowd of shoppers toward the elderly *Englisch* woman.

"Okay…boy?" he asked, stopping to look at Eli.

Before Eli could answer, the elderly woman waved her hands, gesturing toward him and Kyle. He struggled to follow the conversation as Kyle's grip grew more constricting.

Guessing the old woman was accusing Kyle of causing the sauce bottles to fall, Eli said, "See here—"

The tall Amish woman—Eli thought Caleb had said his sister's name was Miriam—turned to help the older woman stand straighter. The *Englisch* woman was getting more upset, and Miriam bent to speak with her.

He opened his mouth, but Kyle tugged on his sleeve. When he looked at the little boy, his nephew shook his head. Did Kyle want him to say nothing?

Straining his ears, he tried to hear what was going on and why Miriam Hartz was getting involved.

* * *

"The boy didn't do anything." Miriam saw the shock on the faces of the three friends she'd come with to the Salem Market, but she wasn't going to watch in silence while a *kind* was falsely accused.

She guessed the little boy was Kyle Troyer, because she'd met the other *kinder* who lived along Harmony Creek. After the little boy and his *onkel* had arrived from Delaware, Caleb had gone to their house at the far end of the hollow, but she hadn't joined him. She'd sent a chicken-and-noodles casserole as well as vegetable soup and a few jars of the grape jelly she'd brought from Lancaster County. Caleb had said Eli wasn't talkative, but seemed determined to make a home for himself and his nephew.

She realized her brother had left out a few details. Details like how tall Eli was. She wasn't accustomed to looking up to meet anyone's eyes other than Caleb's, but when the newcomer's gaze caught hers, the startlingly blue eyes beneath his dark brown hair that was in need of a trim were a half foot above hers. Next to his left eye, a small crescent scar matched another on his chin. Neither detracted from his *gut* looks.

"You're wrong!" The angry woman's piercing voice broke Miriam's mesmerism with the stranger. She pointed a gnarled finger toward the scared little boy. "He's the one who did it!"

"Are you certain, Mrs. Hayes?" asked the dark-haired man who stood beside the woman. A name tag pinned on the red apron's bib showed he was the manager and his name was Russ. "You may not have seen clearly. You're wearing your reading glasses."

"I know what I saw!" Mrs. Hayes ripped off her

glasses and let them drop on a chain hanging around her neck and set another, more sedate, pair on her nose.

The manager hesitated, and Miriam thought he was going to listen to the old woman.

Every instinct told her to remain silent, but she couldn't. She wondered why Eli Troyer wasn't defending his nephew. The *kind* reminded her of Ralph Fisher, the little boy whom she'd thought would become her son. The two boys were close in age. Seeing the *kind* sent a wave of regret through her. She'd lost everything the day Ralph almost drowned. His *daed*, Yost, had put an end to their marriage plans, telling her the near tragedy was her fault.

She hadn't thought so because the little boy hadn't been in her care when he got into trouble. True, he'd been on his way to her house where she was going to watch him that afternoon, but she hadn't expected him to arrive until much later. Shouts for help from his friends had reached her, and she'd pulled the little boy from the pond and got him breathing by the time the ambulance arrived. The little boy had survived and was fine, though he'd had a lesson about showing off she hoped he wouldn't forget.

She hadn't expected praise for doing what anyone would have done. Nor had she expected Yost's anger and the repercussions and recriminations that followed. However, as time went on and others seemed to believe her ex-fiancé, she'd started doubting herself. No one else could blame her more than she did herself. She'd been a teacher for more than eight years and knew what trouble a six-year-old boy could find. Though she'd glanced out the window to watch for Ralph, she hadn't gone to meet him. Her prayers that God would show her if the mistake was really hers hadn't been answered, so she'd stayed away from *kinder*. In case Yost was right.

Her arms ached to hold the frightened little boy next to Eli and offer him comfort. But she couldn't let herself be responsible for another *kind*. Next time it might not be an almost-tragedy.

Still, she couldn't stand there and let a young boy be accused wrongly.

Those thoughts fled through her mind in a second. Stepping forward, she said with a gentle smile, "Ma'am, I think there's been a misunderstanding."

The manager glanced at her with relief. He was ready for someone else to try to reason with Mrs. Hayes.

The old woman wasn't in a reasonable mood. "That boy bumped me a few minutes ago and almost knocked me off my feet. I'm sure he did the same to the sauce."

"Did you see him do that?" asked a voice from the crowd of onlookers.

Mrs. Hayes glowered. "I didn't have to. He was running wild. That man—" She aimed her frown at Eli. "I don't know how you people raise your kids, but they need to learn manners."

"I didn't mean to bump her," the little boy said. "She stopped right in front of me. It was an accident."

"Wouldn't have mattered if I'd fallen and broken a hip, would it, boy?"

"Let's be thankful that didn't happen," Miriam said. "Why don't you let him help you load your groceries into your car? That way, he'll have another chance to say he's sorry."

The *kind* glanced at his *onkel* and made motions with his hands.

Looking from him to her, Eli nodded.

"I can help you," the little boy said, sticking out his narrow chest.

The elderly woman seemed to have second thoughts as if she'd just realized how young the *kind* was. "No, that's not necessary." She frowned at Eli again. "You need to keep a closer watch on your child, and both of you need to learn how to behave in a store." With a muttered comment Miriam didn't catch, she walked away, pushing her cart.

The manager stepped forward, careful to skirt the broken glass. He motioned for a couple of his teen employees to start cleaning up the mess. He apologized to her and to Eli, ending with, "Mrs. Hayes means well."

"I understand," Miriam replied.

Eli said, *"Danki."*

His voice was a rich tenor as smooth as warm molasses. She wished he'd say more, but he didn't.

When Russ offered to pay to have her clothing cleaned, Miriam assured him it wasn't necessary. She wasn't sure she'd be able to get the stains out, but she didn't want to hand her clothes over to a stranger. The manager insisted on giving her a discount on her groceries, and she agreed after realizing she'd become the center of attention in the cramped store.

"You, too, sir," he said to Eli.

Again, Eli didn't reply until his nephew tugged on his arm. *"Danki."*

He took his nephew by the shoulders and steered him to a cart farther back in the aisle. When he glanced at her again, their gazes locked. Did he want to say something to her?

For the third time, he said, *"Danki."*

The single word's warmth and the sincerity in his

voice swirled through her like a spring breeze after a difficult winter.

"You're welcome," she replied.

After he gave her a slight nod, he and his nephew walked away.

And Miriam let the air in her lungs sift out. She hadn't realized she'd been holding her breath, and she wasn't sure why she'd been.

"Are you okay, Miriam?" asked a soft voice from behind her.

As Eli and his nephew went around the end of the aisle and out of view, Miriam turned to her friend Annie Wagler. Annie, her twin sister, Leanna, and Sarah Kuhns had come with Miriam in the *Englisch* van they'd hired to bring them the three miles into Salem for grocery shopping. The other women were, like Miriam, in their midtwenties and unmarried. Each had come to the Harmony Creek settlement to join members of their families in making a new home. The twins lived with grandparents and their brother and his family while Sarah kept house for two brothers.

"I am. *Danki* for asking. I never expected so much excitement." She was babbling. She needed to stop, but her mouth kept moving. "Be careful. Glass is scattered everywhere."

"Bend down." Annie plucked a shard from the top of Miriam's *kapp*.

Annie was the complete opposite of Miriam. A tiny brunette doll instead of a female Goliath towering over everyone else as Miriam did. Annie possessed a sparkling effervescence that brightened every life she touched…which Miriam couldn't. Annie was honestly cheerful while Miriam had to struggle for every smile, though it'd been easier this morning while she and the other women rode in a white van driven by Hank Puente, who wasn't much taller than the Wagler twins.

While Annie handed the glass to a store employee, Miriam shook her apron and dress with care. She was shocked when several more pieces of glass dropped to the floor. When she washed her clothes and herself, she was going to have to take care not to get cut.

Sarah stepped forward. She was a couple inches taller than the twins, but had hair as red as Eli's nephew. She wore gold-rimmed glasses, which she pushed up on her freckled nose as she helped Annie and Leanna do a quick check to make sure there was no glass among the groceries in Miriam's cart. Other shoppers edged around them, staring. Not at the plain women, but at the mess. More than one *Englisch* woman asked if Miriam had gotten hurt.

Miriam was amazed how the incident had opened the door wider for them with their *Englisch* neighbors, who had watched the Amish newcomers with polite but distancing curiosity. When she mentioned that to her friends, Annie giggled.

"What's the saying? An ill wind blows no *gut*? I'd say it's the opposite today. *Gut* things are happening."

Annie saw the positive side of every situation, one of the reasons Miriam was glad they'd become friends. Annie's optimism helped counteract her own regrets at how her betrothal had ended.

As she moved her cart aside so the store employees could clean the floor, she saw Eli and his nephew checking out. She watched the little boy signal his *onkel* each time the cashier spoke to them. Comprehension blossomed when she remembered Caleb saying Eli wore two hearing aids. They must not be enough to compensate for Eli's hearing loss because he needed help from his nephew.

"Someone's curious about our newcomer," Leanna said.

"I'm more curious how long the checkout lines are," she replied.

With another giggle, Annie said, "She's not denying it."

Miriam shook her head and looked at Sarah, who was more serious than she was. They shrugged before separating to finish their shopping.

Ten minutes later Miriam was watching her purchases flow along the belt at the checkout. Coming into the small village to do errands had become more fun than she'd expected. Other than the spaghetti sauce disaster, but that would be amusing when she told her brother about it. She was glad she'd accepted the invitation to share a ride with the Wagler twins and Sarah Kuhns.

Hearing laughter, she grinned at Annie. The tiny woman was in a silly mood today. They were enjoying a respite from the hard work of making homes out of the rough buildings on the farms where they lived.

It hadn't taken long to get their groceries. The store had only three rows of shelves and was much smaller than the big-box store where Miriam used to shop at in Lancaster County. She hadn't gone with women friends then, but with Ralph.

Her happiness faded again at the thought of the little boy she'd believed was going to be her son when she married his *daed*.

"*Ach*, Miriam, where did you find those oyster crackers?" asked Annie.

"I think," she replied, "the crackers are in the middle aisle."

Telling her twin to stay with their cart, Annie sprinted away as if she were as young as the boy with Eli. Two men at the other register followed her with their eyes. Nobody could be unaware of the interest Annie Wagler drew from men, except Annie herself.

"That's forty-nine dollars and twenty-seven cents," the cashier said. In a singsongy tone that suggested she repeated the words many times each day, she asked, "Do you have one of our frequent shopper cards? You get a point for every dollar you spend. When you fill the card, you get twenty-five bucks off your next visit. If…" The woman paused. "Do you people use these sorts of cards?"

Miriam smiled at the woman whose hair was the same rich purple as Miriam's dress. After five months, *Englischers* around Salem still worried about offending the plain folks who'd moved into their midst.

"*Ja*… I mean, yes," Miriam said, wanting to put the other woman at ease. "We're known for being frugal."

"Squeezing a penny until it calls uncle, huh?" The cashier laughed as she pulled out a card and handed it to Miriam. "Bring this with you every time you shop."

"Thank you." She put the card in her wallet and pulled out cash to pay for her groceries. "Do you take checks here?"

"As long as they are local and have a phone number on them."

With another smile, Miriam accepted her change and helped the cashier bag her groceries. She put the grocery bags in her cart and walked toward the automatic door. As it swung open, she walked out. She watched a buggy leave the parking lot. It wasn't a gray buggy like the ones she was accustomed to, nor was it the shape of the black buggy Sarah's brothers had brought from northern Indiana. Though the departing buggy was also black, it was wider. It had to belong to the Troyers, because when she'd visited a cousin in Delaware, she'd seen similar Amish buggies.

Once their *Ordnung* was decided, everyone in the new settlement would drive identical buggies. Discussion had begun on the rules for their church district, but nothing had been voted on yet.

Hearing the store's door opening behind her, Miriam hurried toward the white van. Hank slid aside the door as she reached it. He reminded her of a squirrel with his quick motions and gray hair and beard. He wore a backward gold baseball cap as well as a purple and gold jacket, though the June day was warm. He'd explained the coat was to support the local high school team.

"Find everything you wanted?" he asked.

"And more."

"Ain't that always the way?" He looked past her.

Turning, she saw her friends approaching with their carts. Once their groceries were loaded with Hank's help, Sarah volunteered to return the carts to the store.

Miriam climbed in and sat on the rearmost seat. Leanna sat beside her, leaving the middle bench for her twin and Sarah.

After the van pulled out onto Main Street, they drove past several businesses, including a hardware store separated from the building next door by a narrow alley, a drugstore and several beauty salons and barbershops. Two diners faced off from opposite sides of the wide street. An empty area where a building had burned down five decades before was where a farmers and crafters market was held every Saturday. Miriam looked forward to being able to bring fresh vegetables to sell later in the summer.

They waited for the village's sole red light to change before turning left along East Broadway. Ahead of them was the old county courthouse, and the redbrick central school sat kitty-corner from it.

"*Danki* for asking me today," Miriam said with a smile. "I had a *wunderbaar* time and got some errands done, as well."

"We watched you having a *gut* time." Annie grinned. "Eli Troyer was intrigued with you."

"Don't be silly."

"Am I being silly?"

The other women shook their heads and laughed.

Deciding not to get caught in a game of matchmaking when she had no intention of making the mistake again of believing a man loved her enough to accept everything about her, Miriam said, "We should do things together more often."

"I agree." Leanna sighed. "I miss the youth group we belonged to several years ago at home."

"Here is our home now," Sarah said in her prim tone. "We've got to remember that."

Miriam wished Sarah would stop acting as if the twins were *kinder*. Maybe being around kids all the time, as Sarah was in her job as a nanny, made her speak so. Sarah needed to lighten up. Just as, Miriam reminded herself, she needed to.

"What shall we do for our next outing?" Annie's eyes twinkled. "We can be an older girls' club and have fun as the youth groups do."

Sarah nodded. "*Ja*, but I don't like calling ourselves 'the older girls' club.'"

"How about if we become a 'women's club'?" Leanna asked.

Annie shook her head. "Those are for married women. We aren't married. We're… What's the term? Not old maid. No. There's another one."

"Spinster." Miriam smiled. "Why don't we call ourselves the Harmony Creek Spinsters' Club? After all, a spinster is someone who helps take care of a home for her siblings and parents, which is what we do."

"I like it," Sarah said.

Leanna grinned as Annie jumped in with, "I like it, too. We'll be the Harmony Creek Spinsters' Club, and we can take turns choosing fun things to do together."

"Until we get married." Leanna wore a dreamy look. She was a romantic and devoured romance novel after romance novel.

Miriam wanted to warn her not to be so eager to make a match, but how could she when she'd been glancing out the window every few seconds, looking for a glimpse of the Troyer buggy? *I'm concerned if the little boy is all right.*

She chided herself for telling herself lies. She needed to listen to the advice she would have liked to offer Leanna. A desperation to get married could lead to dreadful mistakes. It was better to trust God's timing. Maybe if she'd done that, she wouldn't have jumped to accept the proposal of a man who'd seemed more interested, in retrospect, in having her raise his *kind* than anything else.

But no matter. She wasn't going to make such a mistake again.

Chapter Two

Kyle tugged on Eli's sleeve, trying to get his attention.

His nephew had been doing that for the past ten minutes while their buggy headed north along the main road that ran through the center of the village. They'd passed several fallow farms and newer houses on smaller lots.

Pulling his gaze from the road, he glanced at the little boy. Kyle swung his arm toward the horse, arching his brows.

Where are we going?

Eli sighed. He and the little boy, his only living relative, had developed their own sign language after the accident that killed his nephew's parents. Kyle had been a *boppli*, so for him, Eli's hearing loss was a normal part of his life. However, Eli doubted he'd get used to it himself. Hours of prayers, railing at God for the deaths of his brother and sister-in-law, had given him no insight into why the accident had to happen. Nor had pleading or bargaining. He didn't understand why the retaining wall his brother was building had collapsed.

What had Eli missed? He'd pointed out places where Milan needed to strengthen the wall, and his brother said he'd done as Eli suggested. Eli was a carpenter, unlike his brother, who'd seldom thought of anything other than his dairy herd.

Guilt rose within him like a river of fire. In retrospect, maybe he hadn't been as focused on the wall as he should have been. The day of the wall's tragic failure, too many of his thoughts had been about how he'd ask Betty Ann that evening to be his bride. He hadn't been sure she'd accept his proposal because he'd noticed her eyeing a couple of other guys, so nerves had plagued him. Distracted, he must have missed what brought the wall down on them.

When Kyle yanked on his sleeve, Eli wondered how long he'd been lost in thought.

"Let's go home," Eli said, checking the road before he made a U-turn.

The little boy frowned. Kyle probably thought his *onkel* had parted company with his mind.

And maybe Eli had because he'd driven out of his way to avoid having to see Miriam and her companions when their van zoomed past the buggy. It wasn't as if she'd strike up a conversation then. His efforts to avoid talking with his new neighbors had been successful so far, but church was the day after tomorrow. He couldn't avoid them there, though the *Leit* in Delaware had become accustomed to him and Kyle leaving right after the service and before the meal was served.

He wouldn't skip the gathering to worship together, but he dreaded seeing people bend toward each other to whisper as he passed. As if he were blind as well as almost deaf. More than once, he'd been tempted to shout that they could yell, and he wouldn't hear everything they were saying. He also hated the pitying looks aimed in his direction. Each one was a reminder of the expression Betty Ann had worn the first time she came to the hospital to see him after the accident. The first and only time she'd visited him there.

Would Miriam Hartz look at him the same way? The idea that such a lovely woman, who'd stepped in to defend a little boy she didn't know, would regard him as a victim of sorry circumstances twisted his stomach.

He was glad when Kyle demanded his attention again by pointing out sheep in a field they passed. He didn't want to think about seeing sympathy in Miriam's eyes.

God, give me strength.

He hoped this prayer would be answered before Sunday.

"Got a minute?"

On Saturday afternoon, Miriam looked up from her sewing machine.

Her brother walked into the barn that served as their home while he worked to make the farmhouse livable. The pipes in the house had frozen, and water spread through it, ruining floors and walls.

The barn was a single open space. Upon their arrival, she and Caleb had strung a web of ropes halfway to the rafters. Hanging quilts on the ropes had created rooms, including the private spaces where they slept. She'd placed rag rugs on the uneven floorboards to protect their feet from splinters. A propane camp stove allowed her to cook, and a soapstone trough became their kitchen sink. She and Caleb missed cakes, bread, cookies and everything else prepared in an oven. He'd picked out the double ovens he intended to put in the house. Until then, it was rough living, but with the doors and windows open, including the ones at either end of the loft, the space was comfortable at last. She'd thought they might become human icicles during the coldest days of the winter.

Turning off the sewing machine that got its power from a car battery, she made sure the half-finished purple dress was folded before she stood.

"What do you need, Caleb?" she asked.

"A favor." He sat at the table in the center of the open area. "Please hear me out before you give me an answer."

"Of course." She slid onto the bench facing him.

"I received a letter yesterday from the local school district. They'd written it at the request of the state education department."

She clasped her fingers together on the table. "Why?"

"They're concerned our *kinder* haven't attended school the minimum days for the school year."

"Mercy Bamberger has been homeschooling her two, and Nina Zook taught her four *kinder*."

"But there are four other families with *kinder* in our settlement. The state insists they attend the minimum number of school days."

"Do they have a suggestion of how we should do that?" Her brows lowered as she said, "If we'd had a school here, by now our scholars would be done so they can work on their families' farms."

"They suggested—and the local school superintendent, Mr. Steele, agreed—we hold school here for the next four weeks. That would take us to the middle of July, so the older scholars would be available to help with the harvest. At the end of the term, the *kinder* would be tested to make sure they'd learned what's mandatory for their ages."

She leaned toward him. "I thought our schools were independent of interference from *Englischers*."

"They are, but as you know, the *kinder* need to attend for a minimum number of days." He gave her a small smile. "I'm sure I can talk Mr. Steele into not having the testing, as long as I assure him the scholars will be in school for four weeks."

"That sounds like a *gut* idea. We've got about ten *kinder* of school age, I'd guess."

"Nothing you can't handle."

"Me?" she managed to choke out past her shock.

He didn't look at her as he said, "I sort of volunteered you because nobody else in the settlement has been a teacher."

"What about Mercy or Nina?"

"Mercy has her hands full with her foster son, and Nina is going to have her new *boppli* any day. You're our best choice to oversee the school."

Like everything else her brother did or said, it made complete sense.

But teaching? *Kinder* who'd be put into her care for six hours each day? She stared at him. How could Caleb ask such a thing of her? She'd come to Harmony Creek to escape the murmured accusations she couldn't be trusted with *kinder*.

"It's for only four weeks, Miriam," he said. "By the time school starts in the fall, Nina has said she'll take over until we can find a teen girl to teach. Just four weeks."

"All right, I'll do it." What else could she say? She had to help keep the new settlement from getting off on the wrong foot with their *Englisch* neighbors.

"And I need you to do one other thing for me."

"I thought you said *one* favor."

"I guess I should have said one at a time."

She laughed with him. As hard as Caleb was working to make the settlement a success, he must be learning, at last, that he couldn't do it all himself. Though he continued to try.

"We're having a school built, so we'll be ready to go in the fall," he said. "It'll be between our farm and Jeremiah Stoltzfus's. There's a level piece of ground with not too many trees that will be perfect. We've hired a carpenter."

"What do you need me to do?"

"He's never built a school before, and you know what's needed."

"Our schools are pretty much the same."

"*Ja*, the ones in Lancaster County are. But schools in Indiana sometimes have two rooms and two teachers."

"Is that what you're planning on here?"

He shook his head. "The majority of our families are from Pennsylvania, so we're building what we're used to." His cheeky grin returned. "And one room is cheaper than two."

"True." She couldn't believe she'd agreed to be responsible for almost a dozen *kinder*.

"Will you work with him on the project?"

"Of course."

"*Gut*." He pushed himself to his feet, came around the table and gave her a quick hug.

"Who's going to build the school?"

"Eli Troyer." Her face must have betrayed her shock, because Caleb added, "I know it'll be a challenge to work with him."

She hadn't mentioned yesterday's incident at the grocery store to Caleb, because she'd been so busy she'd forgotten until after her bedtime prayers. "His nephew—"

"Shouldn't be around more than any other kid."

Hating the sympathy in her brother's voice, Miriam loved him at the same time for worrying about her. He did understand. She'd wondered whether Caleb would have invited her to join him in northern New York if circumstances in Pennsylvania had been different.

"Having kids around seems to be a given." She was shocked at the bitterness in her voice. She wasn't angry with her brother, but she was dubious of being in charge of the scholars. What if one of them got hurt?

Caleb's face lengthened with dismay. "If you don't want to—"

"I said I would, and I will."

"*Danki.* We should have the school done before the month is over. This weekend we're going to get the walls up and the roof on. Eli will cut in the windows and doors and finish the interior." This time her brother misjudged her hesitation because he went on, "I realize Eli has trouble hearing. I speak slowly, and he gets most of what I'm saying."

She thought of how his nephew seemed to be helping him comprehend what was being said. "How bad is his hearing? Really?"

Caleb shrugged. "Enough to be frustrating to him, I'd guess."

With a wave, her brother left.

She stared after him. If he'd told her first that she'd be working with a man who had a *kind* the same age as Ralph Fisher, would she have agreed to assist with the school? She wasn't sure.

Eli was paying more attention to Miriam than he was to their temporary bishop Wayne Flaud, who'd come to oversee the service at the farm owned by the Kuhns brothers. How had Miriam reacted when Caleb told her that she'd be working with him? Had she been as astonished as he'd been?

Those were questions he couldn't get answered unless he asked her. He wouldn't put her in an embarrassing situation.

She was as lovely as he'd recalled over and over during the past two days. Her eyes weren't sparking as they had when she'd defended his nephew. Seated with the other young women who'd been at the grocery store, she looked at her clasped hands or the bishop who spoke at one end of the benches that faced each other. He could re-create her eyes' rich green shade. Even while sitting, she towered over the women around her. He was amazed such a tall woman could be so graceful in every motion.

And, when he'd thought nobody would notice, he'd been watching her every motion since she'd stepped out of her brother's buggy.

The bishop's voice, raised as he asked everyone to pray, intruded into Eli's thoughts. As he moved to kneel, facing the bench where he'd been perched, his eyes cut to her again.

He got caught, because his gaze connected with hers. For a single heartbeat before she turned to kneel. It'd been enough for him to confirm she'd been surprised by her brother's suggestion they work together. He didn't see dismay, though.

Lord, please make this collaboration a gut *one so the work we do together is a reflection of the hopes of this settlement.*

Keeping his prayers focused on the future was the best way to avoid thinking about the past and another pretty woman who'd dumped him like yesterday's trash. He glanced at his nephew beside him. He owed his brother and sister-in-law a huge debt for failing to protect them, and he intended to repay it, in part, by raising their son as they would have wanted.

Eli kept reminding himself of that obligation as the service came to an end. He needed to make a comfortable home for the little boy and earn a living to put food on their table. Once he finished, he'd look for more work.

As he'd done in Delaware, he made an excuse to avoid staying for the meal. If he met his neighbors one by one, he'd be able to get to know them well enough to guess what they were saying. In a crowd of almost thirty people, picking out individual voices and words was impossible.

Kyle looked disappointed as he glanced at the other *kinder*, but he didn't protest.

Eli draped an arm over his nephew's shoulders, surprised again at how much the little boy had grown in the past year. He'd inherited the Troyer height, and if he kept shooting up as he was, he'd be taller than Eli by the time he was a teenager. When they reached their buggy and Kyle climbed in, the little boy leaned forward and grabbed onto the sleeve of Eli's black *mutze* coat.

Astonished, Eli asked, "What is it?"

Someone talk to you.

"Who?"

The little boy pointed in the direction they'd come.

Eli's next question went unasked when he saw Miriam standing behind him, about ten feet away. By herself. Her friends were putting food on the tables set in the grass. Knowing he shouldn't be paying attention to such details, he couldn't help noticing how Miriam's dress was the exact green of her eyes. Her white *kapp* glistened as light sifted through the heart-shaped top, and her apron of the same shade seemed to glow in the sunshine.

She said something as she walked toward the buggy.

He assumed it was a greeting because she gave him a polite smile.

"I know Caleb wants us to work together," he said.

She blinked, and he guessed she'd expected him to chat about the weather or the church service before getting to the subject of the school. She couldn't know how difficult it was for him to make small talk.

"Ja," she said.

So far, so good.

"Miriam, I want to say *danki* for what you did at the store."

"You already…"

He hoped she'd said something about him previously thanking her for helping Kyle.

"It means a lot to me for someone to come to my nephew's defense as you did."

"…little boy, and he…nothing wrong." He was surprised when Miriam peered past him and into the buggy.

"Looking for something?" he asked. Too loudly, he realized when she winced.

After four years he should be used to that reaction

from people when his voice rose with the strength of his emotions. He wasn't.

"I was...no matter."

Or at least that was what he thought she said as she stepped aside as Kyle jumped out of the buggy and gave her a big grin. Her expression grew uncertain and wary.

Of his nephew? Why?

Unsure how to ask that, he said, "I don't know if Caleb told you my nephew is living with me. His name is Kyle. He'll be one of your scholars. School starts next week, ain't so?"

When she forced a smile, it looked as if her brittle expression could shatter. She seemed to shrink into herself, acting as if she were allergic to Kyle and him.

He thought again about how she'd jumped to his nephew's defense at the grocery store. Why had she changed from that assertive woman—too assertive, many would say, for a plain woman—to a meek kitten who acted afraid of her own shadow?

"If you want to play ball with the *kinder* for a few minutes, Kyle," he said, "go ahead. Just come when I call you."

Kyle punched the air and ran off to join a trio of other boys and two girls near his age.

Knowing he should keep an eye on his nephew, though there were plenty of adults around, Eli couldn't stop his gaze from shifting toward Miriam again and again. She stared at Kyle and the other *kinder* as if they were a nest of mice about to invade her home.

Shock rushed through him. Why would Miriam Hartz agree to teach the settlement's *kinder* if she didn't like kids? Hadn't Caleb told him that she'd been a teacher in Pennsylvania? He had missed something,

something her brother said or she did. No Amish woman who stood up for a little boy as she had displayed such an undeniable distaste for *kinder*. Why had she cringed away from Kyle?

As she noticed him appraising her, she said something he didn't hear and hurried toward the house and her friends. He'd better figure out her odd actions if there was any chance of Miriam and him working together successfully. He wished he knew where to begin looking for an explanation for her peculiar behavior.

Chapter Three

Miriam stood by the window offering the best view of the rolling foothills of the Green Mountains at the horizon. When she'd first arrived at the Harmony Creek farm, the hills had been a sad gray brown. The bare trees had grown thick with leaves and bushes until the hills looked as if they were covered with tight green wool.

Closer were the neat rows of her gardens. Caleb had rototilled two beds for her as soon as frost left the ground. She put in seeds and the immature plants she'd started in the cold frame. The simple wooden box topped by glass acted as a miniature greenhouse. Using it added to the time the plants could grow, which was important when the growing season in northern New York was short. Now in June, the plants were thriving in the earth.

With a chuckle, Miriam tossed her dust rag on the table and checked that her simple blue kerchief was in place over her hair. Why was she inside on such a beautiful day? School was starting at the beginning of the week—the reason why she'd been trying to get her weekly chores done today—so she wouldn't have as much time to enjoy her garden.

She glanced around the large space with its quilt walls. The ones hanging as "bedroom doors" had been pulled aside to let air circulate. It was strange to live in a place like this one, but it was beginning to feel like home.

As she walked outside, she thought of how truly blessed she was. She had *gut* friends, including those in the Spinsters' Club. She laughed. So far she hadn't shared the name and their plans to enjoy outings together with anyone else. She wondered what the reaction would be. Though she'd considered mentioning it to Caleb, she hadn't. He was so solicitous of her, and she wondered if he would think she'd lost her mind amidst her desolation about the canceled wedding.

The grass beneath her bare feet was as soft as the breeze making loose strands dance around her face. She curled her toes into the grass and drew in a deep breath as she watched Comet, their dappled-gray buggy horse, rolling like a young colt in the pasture. He was taking advantage of the day as she was.

Pausing to pluck a couple of weeds out of the flower bed to the right of the barn door, she glanced at the battered farmhouse. It was two stories high, but the roof dropped low over eyebrow windows. Caleb had replaced missing slats on the roof and installed drywall inside the house. Because he'd had to remove everything to the studs, he'd asked her to redesign the first floor. She'd made the kitchen bigger and added a mudroom and laundry room with a door to the yard, so it'd be easier to take laundry out to the line that ran from the house to the biggest barn. He'd put a movable wall between the two front rooms. That way, when it was their turn to host church, the wall could be shoved against the kitchen wall, making enough room for the *Leit*.

The outer walls would be painted white, and he'd agreed the shutters should be the same dark green as the shadows beneath the pine trees. The barns were a worn red, and he'd have to repaint them, too, but for now he was concentrating his scarce free time on the house.

Miriam admired the buds on the daylilies. They soon would be blooming. She planned to transplant her perennials along the front porch, and the best time for moving daylilies was August. She could wait longer to shift the daffodils she'd found in the woods. For the first two days after she brought the bulbs closer to the house, a groundhog had dug them up. She'd convinced the irritating burrower to leave them alone by dousing the flowers with a liberal amount of chili powder mixed with water. The strong scent had kept the animal away…at least so far.

She squatted by the flower bed and went to work. Less than five minutes later, she heard buggy wheels rattling toward the barn. Wondering who was coming, she gathered the weeds she'd pulled. She tossed them onto the compost pile before she walked around the barn's corner. If someone was looking for Caleb, she'd have to admit she wasn't quite sure where he was. He'd had a long list of errands to do in Salem and in Cambridge, about ten miles to the south.

She stopped in midstep, surprised when Eli climbed out of the family buggy. Why hadn't he said anything yesterday about plans to stop by?

Her breath caught when his nephew hopped out behind him. The little boy looked around with the candid curiosity of a six-year-old, and he pointed to Comet. The horse wasn't a common color for buggy horses. If the little boy went into the pasture and frightened him, it could be—

Stop it!

She scolded herself for looking for trouble where there might not be any. She wanted to stop reacting to the sight of a young *kind*, thinking of things that could go wrong, but she couldn't. Kyle reminded her of Ralph Fisher. Both were spindly and all joints as their elbows and knees stuck out from their thin limbs while they grew like cornstalks.

Eli had noticed her dismay yesterday after the church service. Nobody else had, not even her friends in the Spinsters' Club. She needed to keep her feelings to herself to halt the questions from beginning again—such as why a teacher hated kids. She didn't hate them; she loved them. Because she loved them, she didn't want to be the one to put any in danger.

"Gut mariye," Eli called.

She waved to him and his nephew and waited for them to cross the yard to where she stood. A siren sounded from the main road, and she flinched.

Kyle did, too, and scanned in every direction to see what sort of emergency vehicle it was.

Eli kept walking as if nothing had happened.

How bad was his hearing?

It wasn't her business. However, the teacher in her was curious how he'd managed to get by with only his young nephew to clue him in. A few quick tests he wouldn't know were going on would tell her the extent of his hearing loss.

"I brought plans for the school," he said when he reached her. "Do you want to see them?"

"Ja." She didn't nod to confirm what she'd said. "Seeing them is a *gut* idea because you want my help, ain't so?"

His dark brows dropped in concentration. He must have heard some of what she'd said and was trying to piece it together. Wondering why he didn't ask her to repeat what she'd said more slowly, she sighed. Even her *grossmammi* had resisted help for years because of *hochmut*, but pride did nothing to help her escape the ever-narrowing walls of her world as her hearing continued to fail. Nor would it help Eli.

She spoke to Kyle. "There's chocolate pudding in the fridge. Go ahead and help yourself to some. Have some with a glass of milk, too, if you want."

"Can I, *Onkel* Eli?" he asked.

More confusion fled through Eli's eyes, but he nodded when the little boy made motions that must have conveyed the question without words.

Miriam bit her lip to keep from saying sign language had limits because it could be understood by a limited number of people.

When the little boy skipped to the door and disappeared inside, she saw Eli's distress before he could mask it. Didn't he realize that, with Kyle beginning school, he needed to learn a different way to communicate? He wouldn't be able to depend so much on the little boy.

"Let me show you the plan I sketched for the school," Eli said, motioning toward the barn.

Was he hoping to head inside where his nephew could give him hints about what was being said?

"It's such a nice day, ain't so?" She sat on the cement ramp's edge. It would be used to bring equipment into the barn, once it was no longer their home. "Let's go over what you've got out here."

She thought he'd object, but he opened a large sheet of paper and spread it across the ramp beside her. He stood so close, each breath she took was flavored with the scents of his laundry soap and bleach. Unlike her brother's, his white shirt pulled over his head and had a stand-up collar. The tab front closed with four small buttons. Beneath the cotton, the shadows of the muscles along his brawny arms drew her eyes.

She looked away. Eli Troyer was too handsome for her own *gut*. She wasn't Leanna Wagler, believing in the possibility of a storybook hero coming to sweep her off her feet and carry her off to a *wunderbaar* life.

"What do you think?" he prompted, looking at his drawing. "It's a rough sketch, but it should show you what I'm planning. Feel free to tell me changes you think will make the school better."

She looked at the page. It was far more than a rough sketch, she realized. He'd marked out on the floor plan how the desks for the scholars and another larger one for the teacher would be set. He'd drawn the interior walls as if she stood in the room and looked at each one. It allowed her to see where he intended to place the blackboard and the bulletin boards. A generously sized storage closet was in a back corner.

He pointed to the narrow rectangles in the walls. "Those are windows. The bigger ones with the dotted lines showing the space for each to swing open and closed are the doors. What do you think?" He tilted his head toward her.

All air vanished as she found her nose so close to his that the piece of paper would have barely fit between them. She couldn't move or blink when she raised her gaze to meet the blue-hot heat in the center of his eyes. Every emotion within him was powerful and uncompromising.

Somehow she gathered enough air to ask, "Do you have a pencil I can use? I want to make a small change."

"Ja." He groped in his pocket and pulled out a short ruler.

"Pencil," she repeated as she pantomimed writing. Once he'd looked away, she drew in a deep breath.

What was wrong with her? She couldn't remember feeling like that when she was with Yost, and she'd been in love with him.

When a pencil was placed in her hand, she realized she'd drifted away on her thoughts. She kept her eyes lowered and squared her shoulders before bending over the page. The sooner she was done with reviewing the plans, the sooner she could put space between her and Eli.

"I think there needs to be another window on either side of the door." She drew what she wanted on the drawing.

"What are those?"

"Windows." She gestured toward the barn. "Windows."

"I know what you meant." He shook his head. "Windows suck heat out of a building. If there are more windows in the school, you'll be using a lot more propane to keep the building warm."

"Two small windows won't make much difference."

"I've been a carpenter since I was fourteen, and

I've learned a lot in those seventeen years. One thing I learned is that extra windows means needing more fuel to keep the space warm. No more windows."

"But—"

"You can't change facts, Miriam, no matter how much you want to."

"The fact I know is *kinder* work better in a sunny place than one filled with shadows." She folded her arms in front of her. "My brother trusts me to know what to do. That's why he's having me work with you to design the school."

He frowned, and she wondered if he'd understood what she said. She realized he'd gotten a bit of it when he said, "*Ja*, sunshine and shadows. Like in a quilt."

"I'm going to talk to Caleb about this," she said.

At her brother's name, comprehension dawned in his eyes. "Discuss it with him if you want." He shrugged. "He'll tell you the same thing I have."

She looked away. "He'll agree with me." She added the silliest thing she could think of. "He does about blue flamingos."

When she got no reaction from Eli to her challenging words, she stood and walked behind him as if looking at the sketch from another angle.

"I will be celebrating when he agrees with me," she said.

Again no reaction.

She clapped her hands.

He glanced over his shoulder and frowned. "Why did you do that?"

His question proved he could hear sounds, which was more than her *grossmammi* had been able to in the three years before she died.

"I told you." She smiled.

Her expression unsettled him. His gaze turned inward, and she guessed he was trying to figure out what she might have said. The silence stretched between them, a sure sign he couldn't guess what she claimed she'd told him.

"Oh." He gathered himself and said with calm dignity, "If you've got no other comments about the school…"

As he bent to get the piece of paper, she cupped her hands to her mouth and called out, "I've got lots and lots of comments. I want to paint the floor yellow and the walls purple. I want—"

He spun and stared at her before she could lower her hands. Wide-eyed, he demanded, "What are you doing?"

She met his accusing stare. "Testing you."

"Pestering me? *Ja*, that's true."

"No!" She frowned at him. "Testing. With a *t*." She sketched the letter in the air between them.

"I'm not one of your scholars. You don't need to test me to find out what my reading ability is."

Folding her arms in front of her, she gave him a cool smile. "That's not what I was checking. If you want, I can teach you to read lips."

"What?"

She touched her lips and then raised and lowered her fingers against her thumb as if they were a duck's bill. "Talk. I can help you understand what people are saying by watching them talk."

When he realized what Miriam was doing, Eli was stunned. A nurse at the hospital where he'd woken after the wall's collapse had suggested that, once he was healed, he should learn to read lips. He'd pushed that advice aside, because he didn't have time with the obligations of his brother's farm and his brother's son. Kyle had been a distraught toddler, not understanding why his beloved parents had disappeared.

During the past four years he and his nephew had created a unique language together. Mostly Kyle had taught it to him, helping him decipher the meaning and context of the few words he could capture.

"How do you know about lipreading?" he asked.

"My *grossmammi*." She tapped one ear, then the other. "…hearing…as she grew older. We…together. We practiced together."

Kyle came outside and rushed to them when Miriam gestured. He wore a milk mustache, and chocolate pudding dotted his chin.

When she bent to speak to him, too low and too fast for Eli to hear, the little boy nodded and took the tissue she handed him. She motioned toward Eli as she straightened.

Wiping his mouth and chin, Kyle faced him. *Learn to read talking. What's that?* The puzzled boy looked from Miriam to him at the same time he made the rudimentary signs he used to help Eli understand others.

"I can help." She put her hands on Kyle's shoulders. "Kyle…grows up. Who will…you then?"

Who would help him when Kyle wasn't nearby? He was sure that was what she'd asked. It was a question he'd posed to himself. More and more often as Kyle reached the age to start attending school.

"How does it work?" he asked.

"You watch my lips. We start with simple words. It is how my *grossmammi*... I learned."

Watch her lips? Simple? He would gladly have spent days watching her lips. His gaze was drawn to those rose-colored curves too often. Now she was giving him the perfect excuse to stare at them...

He shook his head.

"You...no help?" she asked, and he realized she'd confused his refuting of his own thoughts as an answer to her kind offer.

Before he could answer, Kyle pulled on his sleeve and motioned, *Help you. Her help you.*

As his nephew pointed at Miriam and then at Eli, Kyle's signals couldn't have been clearer. Kyle wanted Eli to agree to the lessons.

Not for the first time, Eli thought about the burden he'd placed on Kyle. Though Eli was scrupulous in making time for Kyle to be a *kind*, sometimes, like when they went to a store, he found himself needing the little boy to confirm a total when he was checking out or to explain where to find something on the shelves. If he didn't agree to Miriam's help, he was condemning his nephew to a lifetime of having to help him.

That wouldn't have been what his brother would have wanted. Milan and his wife, Shirley, had expected their son to play with friends and go to school and learn to assume responsibility for the family's farm. The farm had been sold so he and Kyle could start over by Harmony Creek, but he could ensure his nephew had the chance to be a kid. Was Miriam the way God was answering his prayer for help? If so, he needed to agree.

"All right," he said. "You can try to teach me to read lips."

She gave him a nod and a gentle smile, not the superior one he'd worried she'd flash at him. "…next Monday. You and Kyle—" she pointed at his nephew and at him, matching Kyle's motions "—supper. After we eat…"

"All right."

"Tell me."

For a second he was baffled, and then he realized she wanted him to repeat what she'd said so she could be certain he'd grasped the meaning of her words. His confusion became surprise. Why hadn't he considered such repetition was an easy way to avoid mistakes?

"You invited Kyle and me to supper," he said. "After the meal, you'll start teaching me to read lips."

"Gut," she said as his nephew held his fingers in an okay sign. Satisfaction sparkled in her cat-green eyes as if she'd enjoyed a bowl of cream. "Be prepare…work."

He hoped he wasn't going to prove to be an utter failure as he'd been with helping his brother make sure the wall was safe. Miriam seemed so confident she could teach him. He didn't want to disappoint her when she was going out of her way to help him.

Kyle threw his arms around Miriam and gave her a big hug. He grinned, and Eli realized how eager the *kind* was to let someone else help Eli fill in the blanks.

"You'll have a *gut* time at school, ain't so, buddy?" Eli asked, trying to cover his trepidation at losing Kyle's help.

Kyle tensed. *No go. Go later.*

Eli knelt in front of his nephew. "You'll be fine. You're going to enjoy school."

When Miriam nodded and said something, Kyle looked dubious.

The little boy shook his head. *Stay together. Eli and Kyle. No go now.*

"You'll be fine," he repeated. "The day will go so quickly you won't realize it because you're having fun with learning and your new friends."

Kyle touched one ear, then the other.

It took every sinew of strength Eli had not to flinch. That was a signal he hadn't seen the little boy make often, but he knew what it meant. Kyle was scared something bad would happen, as it had to Eli and his parents.

"It'll be okay. Miriam will be watching over you so you don't have to worry about getting hurt, ain't so?"

He raised his eyes toward her, expecting her to confirm his words. Instead, Miriam eased out of the little boy's embrace, her smile gone. She said something, but Eli didn't get a single word. She rushed away, vanishing into the barn where she lived with her brother.

What had he said wrong? One minute she'd been working to convince Kyle that going to school was something he wanted to do. The next she was fleeing as if a rabid fox nipped at her heels. Was it the thought of being with the scholars? Again, Eli found himself wondering why anyone who was so uneasy around *kinder* was going to be the settlement's teacher.

He didn't have time to figure it out. He needed to calm his nephew. "Looks like we're both going to start school next week," Eli said, patting him on the back.

Kyle gave him a distracted nod and kept staring at the door Miriam had used. Why was he acting as oddly as she had?

Had what Miriam said upset the little boy?

"What did she say as she was leaving?" he asked

as he tucked the page with the school drawing into his pocket. "Did you hear what she said?"

He nodded.

"What was it?"

The little boy started to open his mouth, then clamped it closed. Shaking his head, he ran to the buggy and climbed in.

Eli sighed. Kyle had heard something he didn't want to repeat. It'd happened a few times before, and Eli had discovered how useless it was to badger the little boy again to help him understand. Kyle always found a way to avoid answering him.

But Eli now did have one answer. He wasn't going to come to regret his decision to let her teach him lip-reading.

He already did.

Chapter Four

Drying her hands, Miriam crossed the barn toward the open door at one end. The *beep-beep-beep* announced the delivery truck from the lumberyard backing toward where a dozen men and boys waited in eager anticipation. The school's concrete foundation had been poured and given time to cure. Now they would work together to build walls and rafters. Once they had the skeleton in place, Eli would install shingles, clapboard, windows and doors before he finished the interior.

Spending time with Eli while he finished the school wasn't going to be easy. Having his nephew hanging around was going to add to the stress, but she needed to get used to it because other *kinder* would be coming to the barn for school on Monday.

And, in the fall, though she wouldn't be the teacher, the *kinder* would arrive every day to the school right across the road from her house.

Her heart contracted with the pain that never went away. *Ach*, how she'd longed for the family she thought she and Yost and Ralph would be! Even if the Lord hadn't blessed her and Yost with more *bopplin*, they would have had the three of them.

Then it was all gone.

Tears welled into her eyes, but she dashed them away. Crying for what was impossible was absurd.

She'd been blessed when Caleb invited her to come with him to help build a new settlement. Their parents and four older siblings, who were well established in their lives, had remained behind in Lancaster County. God had brought her to this point. He must have a reason for it. She must have faith that someday she would understand, and she would be able to accept why her joy had been torn away.

"Gut mariye," called the irrepressible Annie as she peeked past the front door. "Anyone home?"

"Komm in!" Miriam was glad to push aside her uncomfortable thoughts.

Dwelling on the past was useless. Dreaming of the future was more fun, but just as useless. She needed to concentrate on the present where she'd found three *wunderbaar* friends.

It was time to put sorrow behind her. She had to believe God had something better for her, something she couldn't even imagine yet. Wasn't that what faith was all about? Believing God would get her through the rough times?

Annie bounced into the barn followed by her twin. "Are you ready for a Harmony Creek Spinsters' Club meeting?"

"I'm ready to enjoy a visit from you anytime. Are you here for a meeting?"

"Of course not." Leanna rolled her eyes as she untied her bonnet. "Sarah had to work today. But the men are

having a work frolic, so we decided we should, too."
She put a basket on the table. "It was Annie's idea."

"Why am I not surprised?"

"Because you know I have *gut* ideas?" Annie asked.

"No, *that* would be a surprise," her twin teased with
affection. Motioning after she set two more bags on the
table, she added, "*Komm* here, Miriam, and see what
we've been able to dig up."

Miriam wasn't surprised when the twins began to
unload schoolbooks and stack them on the table. Each
grade level was printed with a different color cover,
and she saw they had several for most grade levels. She
already had the teacher's editions. Caleb had packed
them, figuring someone would use them along Harmony Creek. She wondered if he'd assumed he could
persuade her to teach again…at least temporarily.

She tapped her cheek in thought. "We'll need work-
books. I wonder where we can order them."

"Is there a bookstore in the village?" Leanna asked.

"Not that I've seen, but Caleb may know where one
is."

"Or go to the library and order the books from a
computer there." Annie's eyes twinkled.

"I'm not sure the bishop would approve." Miriam
sat at the table and began to sort the books out by
grade. "Maybe Sarah could ask Mrs. Summerhays if
she knows where we can place an order without using
the internet."

Since her arrival from northern Indiana, Sarah had
been working as a nanny for the Summerhays family,
who lived almost two miles east along the road toward
Rupert, Vermont. There were four *kinder*, two preteens
and two much younger *kinder*. Sarah told them it was

what *Englischers* called a blended family. The parents had been married before. Miriam didn't know if death or divorce had led to the *daed* and *mamm* remarrying, and she didn't ask. She assumed Sarah knew, but her friend wouldn't carry tales about the family's private business.

Leanna opened a textbook and turned the pages. "Here's the address for the publisher. If Mrs. Summerhays doesn't have a suggestion, I can write to the publisher and ask how to order more books. In the meantime, the scholars may have to share."

"A *gut* lesson for them," Annie said. "And the lesson for us is that the men working on the schoolhouse are going to be grouchy if there isn't food waiting for them for dinner."

They laughed and got to work unpacking food from the baskets. Squeezing cold casseroles into the small refrigerator along with the dishes Miriam had prepared, they set the hot selections on the table atop towels so the wood wasn't scorched. More food would be arriving soon.

"Mercy promised to make nachos," Miriam said as she handed several more glasses to Annie.

"Your neighbor is Hispanic, ain't so?" Annie asked.

"*Ja*, but she told me she learned to make nachos from her adoptive *mamm*. Her adoptive *Mennonite mamm*."

That brought more laughter as they worked together.

"Before the others get here," Annie said, "we need to plan another event for the Harmony Creek Spinsters' Club." She giggled. "I love getting to spend time with you. What does your brother think of it, Miriam?"

"I haven't said anything to him about our club." Her

embarrassment faded when she saw the uneasy expressions on the twins' faces. "I guess you haven't, either."

"It sounds as if we're desperate to be married," Annie murmured.

"Or have given up." Leanna clasped her hands in front of her. "I believe there's a man out there who will fall in love with me."

"All you have to do is not be looking for him, ain't so?" teased her twin. "Isn't that what you say the heroines in your romance novels do?"

Color burnished Leanna's cheeks. "I know those are just stories, Annie. I like reading them."

"I do, too." Annie's face became almost the same shade as Leanna's. "But if the right man comes along…" She sighed. "I don't want to lose this friendship."

"Once a member of the Harmony Creek Spinsters' Club, always a member, ain't so?" Miriam laughed, so glad she could let her worries slide away at least for a short while. Between the *kinder* coming for lessons and having Eli across the road day after day, in addition to teaching him to read lips, *not* thinking about those hurdles was a blessing. "We could rename it—"

"No! Don't change its name." Annie leaned forward with clasped hands. "Please!"

"But if none of us has told anyone—"

"The next one we come up with could be worse." Annie shuddered.

Again, they shared a big chuckle.

"If you'd let me finish…" Miriam waited until they were listening again. "I suggest we rename our older girls' group the Harmony Creek Spinsters' and Newlyweds' Club."

Leanna brightened. "That's perfect."

"Do you have something to share, little sister?" asked Annie as she winked at Miriam. "Big plans for the fall?"

Taking pity on the younger woman, Miriam put her arm around Leanna's shoulder. "I thought brothers were awful about picking on their sisters, but I think Annie takes the cake."

"Did I hear someone say cake?" called a deep voice from the door.

Miriam started to turn to motion to her brother to come in, but her eyes were caught by how pale Leanna's face became.

The young woman clamped her lips closed, but her gaze followed every motion Caleb made as he sauntered into the room and greeted them. When he spoke to Leanna, color erupted anew into her cheeks.

Could Leanna have a crush on Caleb? And did he look and smile at Leanna a bit longer than he did Annie? Caleb had been gone in the evening a lot lately. Was he walking out with Leanna?

Coming to her feet, Miriam knew she shouldn't be speculating on such private matters. A couple who was seeing each other didn't make that fact public until their intentions to marry were published two weeks before their wedding.

"You don't have an oven here, do you?" asked Annie.

He shook his head. "And I miss baked goodies." He winked at Miriam.

Her brother didn't like anyone outside the family to know he was a far better baker than she was. She could make tasty food, but he managed to create treats that were delicious and spectacular-looking. She understood his reluctance to share his skills with others. Few plain men spent time in the kitchen unless necessary.

"I wanted to give you a head's up," Caleb continued as he snatched a cookie off the tray the twins had brought. "We'll be ready for dinner in about a half hour. Will that work for you?"

"Certainly." Miriam smiled. "Do you want to eat at the school or here?"

"We're going to set planks on sawhorses out in the yard. That way you can serve from here. Does that work for you?"

"Perfectly."

The other women nodded.

As her brother hurried out to continue working, Miriam noticed Leanna wasn't the only one watching. Her twin was, as well. Were they both interested in her *gut*-looking brother, or was something else going on?

Miriam didn't have time to puzzle out an answer as two more women came into the barn, carrying additional food for the midday meal. As they worked together to have the meal ready for the laborers across the road, she didn't have a chance to think of much of anything but the tasks at hand.

It was an excellent beginning.

Eli straddled the ridge board at the roof's peak as if it were a horse. Looking at the level stretched out before him, he smiled. The bubble in the center glass of the lengthy tool was exactly in the middle. He held his right thumb up. Those who'd been working on the school cheered.

Handing the level to LaVon Schmelley, who'd moved into the hollow from Pennsylvania a month or so before Eli and his nephew arrived, Eli reached for his hammer as he waited for the first sheet of plywood to be slid toward him.

LaVon squinted through his gold-rimmed glasses as he handed off the level to someone standing on the ground and guided the large sheet into place. Eli nailed the top into place with an air-powered nail gun. LaVon used a regular hammer on the bottom.

The other man grinned and said something Eli didn't catch; LaVon pointed to the ground. Eli looked down.

Caleb and Jeremiah Stoltzfus, whose farms shared a common border, motioned toward them. Eli couldn't guess what they were trying to communicate. When LaVon edged to the ladder while the other men put aside their tools and walked across the road, Eli guessed it was time to eat.

His stomach rumbled at the thought and tightened with anxiety. He hesitated while the men began lifting plywood on top of sawhorses. From where he sat, he could see Miriam working with a half dozen other women to arrange chairs around the makeshift tables.

He groaned, wishing he had some excuse not to join the communal meal. Unlike on church Sundays, he couldn't slip away. He was needed to oversee the afternoon's work. A quick glance at the ground warned he couldn't use needing to get more supplies as an excuse for why he couldn't sit with the rest of the workers while they ate.

Taking a deep breath, he climbed down. He took his time switching off the nail gun and the air compressor. Without its low rumble, he caught staccato hints of voices and laughter. No specific words, but he guessed the atmosphere was casual and cordial. He wished he could feel that way, too.

Pausing to wash his hands at the hand pump set between the barn and the dilapidated house, Eli walked to where a generous assortment of food was arranged on planks that would be used on the school's roof and walls. Drawing in a deep breath of the aromas, he helped himself to a variety of casseroles, a couple rolls and apple butter. Conversation buzzed like a swarm of maddened bees, and he picked out a few words. Enough to let him know most of the discussion was about the progress on the school.

He smiled. That he could talk about, though he wished Kyle was there. His nephew was *gut* about clueing him in to the specifics of anyone's comment.

Taking a seat at the end of one makeshift table, he said silent grace before digging into his food. It was as tasty as it smelled. He'd learned that bending over his plate and appearing completely focused on his meal kept others from trying to draw him into the conversation.

He couldn't keep himself from looking at where Miriam sat at a nearby "table." She was chatting with her friends, and they laughed with an ease that suggested they'd known each other their whole lives. He remembered when it'd been simple to be around people and enjoy their company, but that seemed as if it were part of someone else's life.

Suddenly, she looked in his direction.

And caught him watching her.

A piece of roll stuck in his throat, and he fought not to cough. It would draw everyone's attention.

Miriam will help you learn to understand others better.

He couldn't deny the truth, but spending time with her might only increase how often she invaded his thoughts. A bad idea. He couldn't see any outcome other than her dumping him as Betty Ann had or her trying to shower him with compassion. He didn't want either, especially the latter because he'd come to equate compassion with pity.

When Caleb called out what must have been a jesting comment because everyone laughed, Eli chuckled, too, though he had no idea what Caleb had said. He relaxed when he realized the topic was how he was looking to establish himself as a carpenter. Questions were fired at him, and he kept nodding, hoping he wasn't committing himself to something he didn't have the skills to do.

"…more pie?" asked Miriam as she held a plate out in front of him.

The aroma of baked apples flavored with cinnamon and nutmeg made his mouth water. He took the plate. *"Danki."*

"You…doing well."

"Ja, you'll be moving the scholars into the school before you end your summer term."

Her smile wavered as it did whenever he mentioned her teaching the *kinder.* Curiosity tugged at his tongue, urging him to ask the obvious questions.

He didn't.

If he started probing into why she acted as she did, she might do the same to him. He didn't want to talk about the tragedy…again and again as he'd had to in Delaware.

"You…rest doing a *gut* job," she said before she put another piece of pie in front of a man who'd been cutting two-by-fours.

In spite of himself, Eli's hand paused between the plate and his mouth while he watched the other men's gazes following Miriam. That wasn't any surprise, because she was lovely. What *was* a surprise was the swell of something distasteful when she wore a brilliant smile as she answered a man on the other side of the table.

Jealousy.

For the time she was spending with the others? Or for how easy it was for them to talk with her?

Or both?

Lord, help me focus on what's important for me and for Kyle.

It was a prayer he needed to keep in his heart every hour of every day.

Yet, it was impossible to look away when Miriam set a plate in front of LaVon, who was sitting across from him. She said something to the other man, but her gaze locked again with Eli's.

This time she didn't look away like a frightened rabbit. She met his eyes. The bits of voices he could discern faded as he became lost in the connection between them. Every instinct told him to tear his gaze away. He didn't.

Was it confusion he saw on her face? Was she as baffled and uncertain about this invisible bridge that spanned the distance between them?

Eli had no time to puzzle that out because she looked toward the other end of the tables. Just as everyone else did. Belatedly, he copied the others' motions.

Caleb had risen to his feet. He was smiling as he spoke, but Eli caught only two words.

"Fire department…"

He didn't know what else Caleb had said. Whatever it was must have been important because the other men were sitting back, considering Caleb's words. Eli waited for one or more of them to ask questions so he could discover why Caleb had mentioned a fire department.

"Volunteers…?" asked LaVon.

"Ja." Caleb smiled as he sat again and folded his arms on the table. When Eli strained, he picked out the words, "With more houses… Harmony Creek…more volunteers. We're here during the day. That…*gut* for the department."

Eli understood. Or hoped he did. The local fire department was looking for more volunteers, especially those who were at home during the day. From what he'd learned about Salem, most people worked in other towns, some driving more than thirty miles each way. A fire during the day would get out of control without enough volunteers to fight it. The arrival of the Amish who worked on their farms was the perfect solution to the quandary.

"Interested?" asked Caleb as he looked in Eli's direction.

"Ja. I volunteered in Delaware." He wished he hadn't jumped on the chance when he saw Miriam frown in his direction.

He understood what she didn't say. Kyle had told him about the sirens that had sped past on the main road, the ones Eli hadn't heard when he went to talk to Miriam about the schoolhouse plans. No wonder she looked puzzled that he was volunteering to be a firefighter.

As if she'd voiced her doubts, Caleb said, "We…pagers." He held up a small device before hooking it onto his belt. "They alert…and we go."

"Okay with Wayne?" asked Jeremiah.

"Ja," Caleb said.

Everyone began talking at the same time, and Eli

couldn't pick out more than an occasional word. Rising, he carried his plate to where a tub was filled with soapy water. He put it in and headed back to work.

He halted, almost rocking off his feet to keep from running into Miriam. She stared at him, silent.

"If you think," he said, deciding to speak plainly, "I can't be a firefighter because of my hearing loss, think again. Nobody can hear much of anything when a fire is roaring."

Her eyes narrowed. "But you need…hear if the fire… unexpected turn."

"If the fire goes in a different direction?" When she nodded, he added, "You sound as if you've had experience with a bad fire."

"How many of us haven't?" She glanced at the barn that was the Hartz family's home. "Lightning and barns…no mix."

"I don't know how bad lightning will be along our creek. I'd expect bolts would head straight for the water." His eyes swept the hills and mountains edging the horizon before focusing on her. "We're sited low compared to what's around us. That should keep us protected."

"Unless the storm is right over us."

He gave her a grim smile. "Looking for trouble means finding it. I'd rather have faith God will send the storms around us. It's not our place to tell Him what to do, ain't so?"

When he saw her flinch, he realized he was being too inflexible. She was concerned about his safety. He should appreciate that, and he did. But when she stood so close he had trouble thinking only about his nephew and their future.

"When…lessons…?"

She was asking about him learning to read lips. He wanted to tell her he'd changed his mind, that he was willing to go on as he had. He'd gotten by four years without the skill.

"Is Monday night still okay? *Komm* to supper," she said. "Lessons…after…" Not giving him a chance to answer, she walked away to help clear the table.

His gaze followed her until he realized others were watching him watch her. Turning on his heel, he strode toward the school's framework.

Miriam might be able to teach him to read lips, but he'd learned a tough lesson from his ex about trusting women. It was one he'd be a *dummkopf* to forget.

Chapter Five

Miriam stood in the barn door as she had in the Lancaster County schoolhouse door when she'd been the district's teacher. She didn't have a bell to ring, but the moment she'd opened the door, the boys and girls began running across the yard toward her. She hadn't guessed they'd be eager to spend summer mornings doing schoolwork.

The day was humid, so maybe they preferred sitting inside to working in the fields or weeding in the garden. The big barn, which had been so cold during the winter, seemed resistant to letting heat in. For that, she was grateful.

She silently counted as she greeted each *kind* coming through the door. Ten students. Half the number she'd had in Lancaster County, and most of the scholars were between the ages of six and nine. That would give her more time with each group while they concentrated on doing the work the state education department deemed necessary.

Caleb was discussing the need for end of term testing with the local school superintendent. Miriam hoped her suggestion that each scholar do a special project would be acceptable rather than requiring the *kinder* to take day-long tests in the middle of July's heat. Her brother intended to share that plan with Mr. Steele at their meeting next week.

"Find a seat at the table," Miriam said with the best enthusiasm she could gather.

Her hands shook as she walked to one end of the table where she'd set a whiteboard Caleb had found for their impromptu classroom. She hoped the *kinder* wouldn't notice her trembling fingers, and, if they did, they'd think she was nervous about teaching.

Ten young faces looked in her direction. Her heart swelled with affection for the little ones who were the future of their new settlement.

She could do this. She could keep them safe for six hours each day. Each *kind* was being picked up that afternoon. Their parents had agreed to come to collect them, so she'd confirm which routes the *kinder* would take to and from the school. That way she could keep an eye out for them in the morning and make sure they left in the proper directions in the afternoon. Knowing she was watching might keep a few of them from getting into trouble as Ralph and his friends had.

"Shall we start our morning with a song and a prayer?" she asked.

As the scholars replied with enthusiasm, she thanked God for the routine that had served her well in the past. She sang with the *kinder*, loving the sound of their treble voices brightened by their smiles. In spite of everything, she was grateful for a chance to spend time with them. She was sure, with His help, she could get through the next four weeks. Then she'd hand the teaching job over to Nina and find a way to be busy every morning and afternoon in a part of the house that didn't have a view of the school or the *kinder*.

Cutting herself off from the scholars would break her heart. But if Yost had been right and she couldn't be trusted with kids, it was for the best.

The next evening Miriam took the warm strawberry pie Mercy Bamberger held out to her and thanked her in *Englisch* and *Deitsch*. Mercy, who lived on the farm next door, gave her a grateful smile. Her neighbor was struggling to learn the language so she could become a full member of the community when she was baptized in the fall. In addition, the woman, who'd been raised as a Mennonite, worked to understand the High German used at the Sunday services. She was making *gut* progress, and her *kinder* were speaking *Deitsch* as if they'd used it their whole lives.

"Are we the last ones to get here?" Mercy asked as her daughter and son went to join the other *kinder* who were kicking a ball around the far end of the barn.

Once the discussion on their new *Ordnung* began, the youngsters would take their game outside between the barn and the house, out of the way of buggies driving into the farm. Caleb had looked at Miriam with sympathy when she made that suggestion. Though her brother was well aware of everything that had been said in Lancaster County, he'd never questioned her assertion that she hadn't realized she was supposed to watch Ralph before he arrived.

He'd been the only one.

Shaking those thoughts from her head, Miriam said,

"No, you're not the last. Eli and Kyle haven't arrived yet."

Why, when he'd been understanding about the near-tragedy in Pennsylvania, had Caleb been oblivious to her frustration when he'd shifted the settlement's weekly Tuesday meeting to tonight? She was supposed to start teaching Eli to read lips tonight, but he wouldn't want to begin the lessons when so many others were gathered in the barn.

Nor did she want to teach him while they had an audience. Her *grossmammi* wouldn't have cared who was there. She'd been so eager to learn. Eli was suspicious of the whole process and didn't think it would help him much. She wasn't sure why he was reluctant. If their situations had been reversed, she was certain she'd want to try anything and everything that might help her "hear" again.

"Paul will be disappointed to hear that," Mercy said, drawing Miriam out of her thoughts. "He was looking forward to seeing Kyle."

Miriam nodded. The two boys spent every possible minute together at school. "It's too bad they live at opposite ends of the hollow."

"They'll be able to get together when they're older and know to watch out for cars along the road."

As if to emphasize Mercy's words, wheels squealed around a turn in the road outside the barn. Everyone stopped talking and exchanged uneasy glances.

"Maybe we should talk to the sheriff sooner rather than later about how fast cars go along this road," Sarah's brother Menno said with a scowl. "I know you want to wait until you've had a chance to discuss this with Wayne, Caleb, but someone's going to get hurt or killed."

As she set the pie on the table with the other food brought by the members of the settlement, Miriam watched her brother debate with himself. He was distressed when *Englisch* teens drag-raced and when their parents drove too fast. The road with its curves and hills and dips made it impossible to see far ahead. But he was bothered more by everyone looking to him as if he was the bishop. The settlement needed to ordain two of the married men to become their first minister and deacon. Those men would then oversee the *Leit*, but that wouldn't happen until the communion service in the fall.

When Eli and Kyle walked in, Caleb looked relieved that he didn't have to answer right away.

The boy grinned and waved in Paul's direction. Miriam wondered if anyone else noticed the odd motions the boy made to his *onkel* before Eli nodded, and Kyle skipped across the barn to join the other *kinder*.

Menno called, "Eli, did you see the speeding car?"

She held her breath, eager to discover how much he'd understood. When he took his time to reply, no one else seemed to think it was unusual. Many plain people had developed the habit of answering every question after what *Englischers* in Lancaster County called "an Amish pause." Perhaps it was another reason Eli had been able to function with his severe hearing loss for so long.

"Cars," Eli responded. "Two of them. They were racing. Praise the *gut* Lord we'd already turned onto your lane, Caleb, when the cars came around the corner. If we'd been on the road..." He didn't finish.

He didn't have to. Every plain person understood

the peril of a collision between a car and a buggy. The results were almost always the same. There would be damage to both vehicles, but the passengers in the buggy had only a thin layer of fiberglass and wood between them and a steel-reinforced car. The *Englischers* might be injured if they hit the horse, but the plain people were often killed.

Jeremiah sighed. "Menno, I think your suggestion about contacting the authorities right away has a lot of merit."

Miriam watched everyone turn to Caleb. She admired how he'd shouldered the burden without complaint, but he seemed more weighed down every day. She wished there was something she could do to help him. Maybe—and she looked to where Eli had found a seat among the other men—teaching Eli to read lips would help. Eli was a man who considered his thoughts before he spoke. Such a man would be able to ease Caleb's load.

There was a single empty chair among the women who'd brought their mending and other sewing to do while the men debated. As soon as she sat, she realized Eli was in her line of sight. She couldn't move as her friends exchanged mirthful glances. Later she'd explain to them—again!—that she wasn't interested in Eli, other than as her student.

Don't be false with yourself, cautioned her conscience.

She realized she'd flinched in response to that thought when Annie leaned over and whispered, "Are you okay?"

"Ja." Miriam offered her friend a smile.

It must have been believable because Annie nodded

and grew quiet as the *kinder* hurried outdoors and the men began their meeting.

The topic was buggies. Or it was supposed to be, which was why Miriam was surprised to hear Caleb say, "That's why my sister has been concerned about where the scholars travel to and from the school."

Had someone complained about her questions to the scholars' parents earlier? If so, why hadn't they spoken to her? She would have been happy to explain, though she wouldn't have shared why she was concerned.

Eli's gaze caught hers, erasing the distance between them. He shook his head.

What did he mean? It was odd to be trying to figure out what he was attempting to communicate rather than the other way around.

When he gave her a smile and a wink, she almost gasped. How could he be so bold when everyone was around them?

Then she realized nobody else had paid attention to her and Eli staring at each other…for how long?

Two youngsters ran into the barn, one holding out a bloody finger. She jumped to her feet and rushed to get her first-aid kit. In quick order she had the two boys, who were among the oldest in her makeshift school, seated while she tended to the finger as well as the other youngster's scraped knee. She stepped aside when their *mamms* came to comfort them.

And her eyes locked again with Eli's. Had he been watching her the whole time? A startling warmth swept over her. Not embarrassment, but something sweeter. Something she'd vowed not to feel again. She didn't want to be drawn to another man, especially one with a *kind*.

She looked away. She must not put herself into another situation where she would prove to be a disappointment to someone she cared about.

While Miriam returned to her chair among the other women, Eli turned to look at the gathered men. They'd drawn chairs closer for the discussion. He was relieved the women wouldn't join the conversation. Otherwise, he would have had to swivel to try to catch what they said. It was difficult enough to guess which man would speak next.

"Tonight's topic for our *Ordnung*," Caleb said, "is buggies. Color and style."

Eli wasn't surprised Caleb wanted to start with an item that was vital to the identity of the settlement. Because families had come from multiple districts and states, there were different types of buggies in use. Eli's from Delaware was black and squat. LaVon Schmelley drove one with the bright yellow top that was used in western Pennsylvania. Sarah's brothers had a black Indiana buggy. The rest of the ten families living in the new settlement drove the gray-topped buggies seen in Lancaster County.

Deciding on the new settlement's buggy style wasn't simple. Once a unanimous decision was made and the bishop concurred, the families driving nonconforming buggies would have to purchase new ones. Each could cost $5,000 or more.

Menno suggested that they continue to drive their current buggies until after the crops were harvested in the fall. Each farm could put a share of their crop profits into a central fund to purchase buggies for those families who would need new ones.

"Once we know how many we'll need to replace," Eli said, "we might be able to work a deal because we'll be ordering more than one. Selling the ones we don't need could help raise the funds, too."

"That's true." Caleb glanced around the circle before his gaze settled again on Eli. "…buggy maker?"

Why hadn't he kept his mouth closed? Now he was part of the conversation, and Caleb, being the fair man he was, intended to keep him included.

Before Eli could figure out what to say when he didn't understand the question, Menno asked, "Sarah, didn't you… Mr. Summerhays…connection to the horse racing in Saratoga?"

She nodded, looking up from the shirt she was mending.

Menno turned to the men again, making it easier for Eli to hear him. "Mr. Summerhays is the man my sister works… He and his business partners own…racing horses. The…harness track…small-wheeled vehicle… sulky. Someone builds…sulkies. Why couldn't…buggies?"

As the others continued to discuss the issue, Eli looked at where the *kinder* were again playing with a ball in a corner. They must have returned inside after the two were hurt. He was glad to see they were far enough away from the area Miriam and Caleb used for their home, so there wasn't any chance something would be broken.

Someone tapped on his arm, and Eli returned his attention to the conversation. What had he missed?

As if he'd asked that aloud, Caleb said, "Eli…your buggy."

Eli had no idea what Caleb wanted to know. Was he

asking about Eli's buggy or had he been talking about something else altogether?

"A moment," he said as he waved toward his nephew. Trying to piece together what everyone was talking about was impossible without help.

Kyle handed another *kind* the ball he was holding and trotted toward Eli. When the boy exchanged a glance with Miriam, Eli didn't have to guess to know what they were thinking. Miriam's expression was sympathetic and Kyle's resigned.

Guilt surged through Eli as the boy stopped beside him. He was torn. He wanted his nephew to have a chance to play like the other kids, but without Kyle's help, he'd be lost. If he'd started lipreading lessons with Miriam by now… But he hadn't, and he needed the boy's help.

Eli was able to follow the conversation better with Kyle's assistance. No one asked why he'd brought his nephew into their circle. Several times he caught Kyle glancing wistfully toward the far corner. The guilt gnawing at Eli grew.

When a decision was reached on the color and style of the buggies to be part of their *Ordnung*, Eli wasn't surprised. Most of the families drove gray buggies, so it'd be easier for the community to help pay for replacement buggies for the few families who didn't. Eli surprised himself by entering the conversation again to say instead of selling the nonconforming buggies, they find someone to strip them and turn them into open buggies teenage boys drove during their *Rumspringa*.

When the meeting broke up after dessert and *kaffi*, Eli went to where Miriam was gathering paper plates and cups. The families were using disposable dishes until they could purchase enough china and flatware for the whole settlement on a church Sunday. His buggy might be reconfigured into a bench wagon to move the supplies from house to house every other week. Few changes would be necessary, because the axles were wide enough to support a vehicle that would hold plenty of benches and dishes.

"Is...wrong?" he heard Miriam ask.

He shook his head. "No. Why do you think there's something wrong?"

"You're frowning."

"Just thinking." He explained how his buggy could be put to use.

She gave him a faint smile. "Tell Caleb about... It... *gut* solution."

"Ja." Without a pause, he asked, "When can we begin lipreading lessons?" He couldn't forget the glance Miriam and Kyle had thought nobody else had noticed.

"It's late tonight."

"It is."

"Tomorrow...ain't so?"

Praying he'd understood her, because it wasn't easy concentrating on listening to her when he couldn't stop wondering if her skin was as smooth as it appeared, he replied, "Tomorrow is *gut*."

Relief blossomed in her pretty eyes, and he was amazed. Why was she determined to help him? He was pretty much a stranger.

Then he saw her turn to smile at Kyle. A genuine smile, and Eli wondered if she'd offered to help him because of his nephew. And why that made him relieved and hurt at the same time.

Chapter Six

When he heard Eli and Kyle were coming to the barn
the following evening, Caleb had told Miriam he'd be
willing to stay instead of painting the kitchen in the
house. He was eager to get to work, because he wanted
the house ready for them to move into as soon as possible. Neither of them wanted to spend another winter
in the drafty barn. Jeremiah had offered to help him
tonight. The two men also, she suspected, would be
talking about removing the fences along their shared
property lines, so they could work the small fields more
efficiently. The fewer times the teams had to turn at
the end of each row, the more quickly the field could
be plowed and harvested.

Miriam had urged her brother to work on the kitchen
as he'd planned. She didn't need to be chaperoned. After
all, the little boy was coming along with his *onkel*. She
was glad because Kyle needed to learn, too, so he could
help Eli practice.

She wasn't sure if Eli would be willing to have his
lesson if Caleb was present. She'd seen his respect for
her brother, and, though he had no reason to, Eli was

disconcerted whenever he must admit his hearing loss was worse than others guessed.

That was what she kept telling herself as she waited for the Troyers to arrive. Yet, she couldn't ignore the truth. She was looking forward to spending time with Eli and having a chance to know him better.

He fascinated her. She sensed there were depths to the man he refused to allow anyone to see. Discovering what he hid could be foolish because she might, at the same time, reveal too much of what she wanted to put behind her. What would he think if he found out her betrothal had been broken after a *kind* had almost died because of her inattention?

Eli was so protective of his nephew, and, if he learned the truth about what had happened to Ralph, he might decide to pull Kyle out of school. That could create problems for Caleb with the *Englisch* school district. She must keep her past in the past so it wouldn't interfere with the future of the settlement…and her slow-growing friendship, if it could be called that, with Eli.

The aroma of fresh *kaffi* wafted through the barn as Miriam put chocolate chip and oatmeal-raisin cookies on a plate. She'd gone to the twins' house to make the cookies earlier. She'd set some aside for Caleb. Her brother missed having an oven as much as she did. Maybe more. Though he never spoke of it beyond their family, Caleb had been taught to bake by their *grossmammi*. As a boy, he'd hurried to finish his chores so he could assist *Grossmammi* Hartz in the kitchen.

Miriam smiled. The stove with double convection ovens had been delivered by a large truck earlier. Caleb had been as excited as the scholars at recess.

"Guten owed." Eli walked in, followed by his nephew.

Their expressions were wary as they took off their straw hats. She must make them feel comfortable straightaway, though she wondered why the boy was as leery of these lessons as his *onkel*.

"Guten owed," she replied and motioned toward the table where the scholars sat during the school day. "You can put your hats on a chair. Caleb moved the pegs we have been using to the house. Help yourself to some cookies. *Kaffi*, Eli?"

She was no longer surprised he looked at his nephew before he answered. She'd seen he had a greater difficulty hearing women's voices than men's. She wasn't surprised because her *grossmammi*'s hearing loss had been much the same.

"Ja," he said finally.

With a smile, she looked at the boy. "I've got lemonade, Kyle, but you probably don't want that with cookies. Milk?"

The boy nodded.

She went to get drinks for them and a glass of milk for herself while they sat beside each other at the table. With a smile, she set a cup in front of Eli and the milk by Kyle's clasped hands. She retrieved her own glass before sitting on the bench facing them.

"Shall we begin?" Miriam asked, knowing how Eli struggled, even with Kyle's help, to engage in small talk.

Both Troyers nodded as Kyle reached for a cookie.

Miriam took a deep breath. She recalled the simple techniques she'd learned at the beginning of her training with *Grossmammi* Hartz. She could still hear the first words spoken by the instructor, an *Englisch* woman who was almost as old as her *grossmammi*.

"You are learning to read lips," the instructor had

said. "It would be easier if the people around you learned, too. That is not going to happen. That is why you must find a way to function in any situation."

"How can I help my *grossmammi*?" Miriam had asked.

"Start by not using contractions or complex sentences. Follow the kiss rule by keeping it short and sweet." She'd smiled. "Kiss and lips go together."

Miriam remembered blushing, which brought laughter from the older women. But she hadn't forgotten.

She tapped her lips, drawing Eli's gaze toward them. "It is time to begin."

"Okay." His tone was dubious.

As if he was enthusiastic, she began to outline what she intended to teach him. She spoke slowly but not with exaggerated enunciation. Eli needed to learn to communicate with people who were talking normally. She would increase her speaking pace as his skills grew.

She began by pointing to common items and naming them. Eli and Kyle repeated them after her. She told Eli to look from her to Kyle as each of them took turns speaking. Following a conversation among multiple people was a tough skill to become proficient in, so she wanted him to practice right from the beginning.

Eli was more patient than she'd expected. That told her how desperate he was to be able to understand those around him. She hoped his resolve didn't falter as the lessons went on.

"Some words are confusing," Miriam said after refilling Eli's cup and Kyle's glass. "Like bat and pat." Making a pair of wings with her hands, she flapped them. "Bat." She tapped the table. "Pat. See? They look the same on the lips."

"Ja," Eli replied. "But if I can't understand such simple words, how can I learn the more difficult ones?"

She laughed. "The difficult ones are easier to understand because they are unique. See? No other word looks quite like *unique* when spoken." She repeated the word twice more.

"*Unique* is unique. Is that what you're saying?"

When she smiled, Kyle giggled and reached for another cookie.

"You must have a mirror in your house," Miriam said after taking a sip from her own glass.

Eli nodded. "*Ja*, I've got one for shaving."

She didn't look at the strong line of his jaw as she imagined him drawing a razor along it before he swept soap suds from his skin. Many times she'd seen her brother perform the daily task. Yet, the thought of Eli doing the same sent a warm shiver of something delightful through her.

Hoping he couldn't guess the course of her thoughts, she said as if she had nothing more on her mind than their lesson, "You should practice in front of the mirror."

"Practice what?"

"Reading lips."

"My own?"

"*Ja*. Put the mirror on the table while you and Kyle are eating. Prop it against something. Watch your lips move as you speak to him. *You* know what you are saying. Learn how your own words look. It will help you recognize the same words when others say them."

He didn't reply, and she could see he was trying to puzzle out what she'd said. She halted her immediate instinct to repeat herself. If she did without waiting for him to ask, she wouldn't be helping him.

"That makes sense," he said.

"But?"

"But what?"

"That is what I am asking you. You sound as if you are unhappy that I made a *gut* suggestion."

His eyes widened, and he shook his head. "I didn't mean that. My reaction didn't have anything to do with you. Just with me. I should have thought of doing these exercises myself."

"Why?"

Again, he looked at her, baffled. "I don't understand what you mean."

"I mean, why are you rebuking yourself for not figuring out what it took experts a long time to?"

"It's been four years since I could hear well." His mouth grew taut, and his eyes cut to the boy beside him before guilt washed over his face.

Instead of answering him, she smiled at his nephew. "Kyle, will you take these extra cookies to the house? Caleb and Jeremiah are there, and they would like a snack."

"Can I take some for me?" the boy asked.

"Two more."

He grinned, jumped from the bench and hurried out with the plate. She hoped the cookies would survive his eager lope across the yard.

Eli stood. "Where's he going?"

"To the house." She reached across the table and tapped a finger against his arm. When he focused on her, she repeated her answer before adding, "I sent him over there to Caleb and Jeremiah because I could tell you did not want to talk about when Kyle's parents died. Not while he was sitting right here."

"No, I didn't." He frowned. "How did you know?"

She motioned for him to sit again. When he had, she said, "It is another part of what you need to learn. You can get clues to what is being said by watching what people say with their motions and expressions."

"What?"

Realizing he hadn't caught enough of her words to comprehend what she was saying, she replied, "Body language. Do you know what that is?"

"*Ja...* No, not really. I've heard people mention it, but I don't know what they were talking about. Sorry."

"You do not need to apologize. I did not know what it was until I started helping my *grossmammi*." She smiled. "Not by name. I did not realize what I was sensing without realizing it." Getting up, she folded her arms and raised her chin. "Can you tell what I am feeling if I stand like this?"

"Proud?" he asked.

"Try again."

"Angry?"

"Closer." She gauged his expression and posture to make sure she didn't push him until frustration made him give up. After letting him guess two more times, she said, "I am defiant, an emotion you know well, because you refuse to accept your hearing loss."

He rubbed his chin between his finger and thumb as he considered her words. "And I look like that sometimes?"

"More often than you would guess. Crossed arms are a signal the person wants to keep you at bay. Raising your chin means you refuse to be moved by anyone else's words."

His eyes brightened, a sure sign he understood. The next few poses he identified immediately. Each correct answer seemed to add to his confidence, as she'd hoped.

This might work. She realized how uncertain she'd been about helping him.

And how pleased she was that she could.

The clock on the wall beside the sink chimed nine times, and Eli was astonished more than two hours had passed since he and Kyle had arrived at the Hartz farm.

He stood. "*Danki* for taking the time with me tonight, Miriam."

"I am glad I can help. Tomorrow evening at the same time?"

"So soon?"

"The more we work together, the quicker you will learn."

He couldn't argue with that logic. He'd be a *dummkopf* not to take advantage of her willingness to help him become adept at reading lips. "I'll talk to Mercy and see if Kyle can go over to their house tomorrow evening."

"Kyle needs to come, too, at the beginning. He must learn to face you and enunciate when he speaks."

"Enough what when he speaks?"

"E-nun-ci-ate. To say something clearly."

He nodded, flustered he'd misunderstood her.

Before he could lower his head or look away, she put one hand on either side of his face. Startled, he froze. He hadn't expected her to be so brazen. He could sense every inch of her skin against his as if it were his own. A warmth coursed over his cheeks, teasing his arms to slip around her, pulling her closer.

Her words shattered the daydream. "Eli, do not be

embarrassed. You missed one word I said. Even people with perfect hearing miss words."

"Not all the time like I do." He tried to shake aside the cloying image of her in his arms. He must concentrate on what she was saying.

"True, but you will learn. You will miss less then."

"You make this sound like it will solve everything."

She lowered her hands and put them on her waist in the pose of a *mamm* about to scold a *kind*. "Are you feeling sorry for yourself? Or are you trying to make me feel sorry for you?"

"Neither. I don't want pity."

"You understood everything I said."

"Because I caught enough to know what you were saying."

Not moving, she said, "And how I am standing gave you a clue, ain't so?"

"*Ja.*" Wonder slipped into his voice. "*Ja*, it did. Is it really that easy?"

"For simple situations, *ja.* You have got a lot to learn before you can function well at a group event like when the men get together to discuss our new *Ordnung.*"

"I hope I do better at the next meeting."

"You have six days to practice what you have begun to learn." She continued to speak slow enough for him to figure out what she was saying.

If everyone would speak at that speed…

That was a futile wish. Hearing people—himself included before the accident—never thought about how fast they spoke. To expect them to change was foolish. Instead, he needed to master the skills Miriam was willing to teach him.

"Six days isn't long," he said as he realized the enormity of the task ahead of him.

"It can be long enough to master the basics. It is up to you how you want to look at this challenge."

He reached for his straw hat he'd set on a chair behind him. "The real problem I've got is trying to follow a conversation that jumps from one person to someone else, because I can't guess who's going to be talking next. It was extra hard because I couldn't see everyone's face."

"You should have asked everyone to move so you could see."

"I didn't want to make trouble."

"What trouble would it be to move a chair?" When he didn't answer, she came around the table and put a hand on his arm. Warmth spread from where her fingers touched his skin, but her attention was on his face.

Was his pain emblazoned there? As he'd told her, the last thing he wanted was her pity.

He realized how he'd misread her when she said, "Eli, your hearing loss is nothing to be ashamed of."

"I know."

"You say that. You do not act that way. It will get easier." She smiled as if he was one of her scholars.

Was that how she saw him? As a student? That *was* what he was, but when she touched him, even with a motion as commonplace as putting her fingers on his arm to get his attention, he couldn't think of her as anything other than a charming woman.

She was his teacher! That and his neighbor. Nothing else. He was being a fool. He wasn't going to invite more pain into his life. Not when he'd come to Harmony Creek to start over.

"It will get easier," Miriam said again when he didn't answer.

"Really?"

"Really. Eli, you want this. You will learn." She smiled. "Just as Mercy is learning to speak *Deitsch*. It may be slow, but it will be worth the time you spend practicing."

"I hope you're right." He caught sight of a short silhouette near the buggy he'd left between the barn and the house. Kyle was returning. The other shadow with him must be Caleb.

Eli needed to leave, though it was tempting to stay and chat with Caleb. For too long, his only company had been Kyle. He loved the little boy, but it would be a true blessing to have the opportunity to speak with another adult. But lingering to talk with Caleb would be, he had to admit, simply an excuse to spend more time with Miriam.

"*Danki* again," he said, walking toward the door. He turned to face her. "Sorry to run like this, but I've got meetings for prospective jobs tomorrow."

"Are you taking Kyle with you? He is welcome to stay here whenever you need someone to watch him."

"That's kind of you when you've got the scholars here five days a week. I'll try to arrange to do my business during the time he's here at school, but that may not always be possible."

"Especially with *Englischers* on fast time."

He nodded. Plain families didn't set their clocks forward an hour in the spring and turn them back in the fall. That meant they had to be aware of the hour's difference in the summer when they went to an *Englisch* store or had a *doktor* appointment.

"But if Kyle is here, will you be able to get the gist of what is being discussed in your meetings?"

Trust Miriam to see beyond the facade that fooled everybody. When he looked into her gentle face, he saw honest curiosity. As if he was just like everyone else. He wondered if she knew how much of a gift that was.

"I will do my best."

"No one can ask more." A smile tugged at the corners of her lips. "Just remember. It is okay to ask someone to repeat what they said."

"*Danki*, Miriam." How many times was he going to repeat that tonight? He needed to go. Now! "I'll practice as much as I can."

"*Gut*. I will see you tomorrow when you drop Kyle off for school and tomorrow evening for your next lesson."

He put his hat on his head, but before he could leave, her fingers curved along his face as she turned his face toward hers. She lowered her fingers, but the resonance of her touch lingered on his skin as he stared at her lips. Her oh-so-kissable lips. They were moving, but instead of watching them to determine what she was saying, he imagined them against his own.

With a gulp he was certain could be heard throughout the hollow, he bid her good-night and left while he still could keep himself from kissing her. If Caleb thought he was being terse as Eli collected his nephew and got into the buggy, he didn't say anything.

Eli looked back as he drove toward the twisting road.

Miriam stood in the doorway. To greet her brother or to watch the buggy leave? He didn't want to know the answer.

Chapter Seven

Eli was rising from the breakfast table in his sunny kitchen the following Tuesday morning when he saw someone at the back door. It opened, and Caleb stuck his head in.

"Busy?" he asked.

"No, *komm* in," Eli called, hoping his practice for the past week on what Miriam had been teaching him would allow him to understand what the settlement's founder had to say. He'd spent an hour with Miriam each evening and done more work after he came home. To be honest, he was tired of looking at his own mouth in the mirror, though—and again he had to be honest—he couldn't imagine getting tired of watching Miriam's.

Heat rushed through him when Caleb walked into the kitchen. To have such thoughts of his friend's sister… He hoped Caleb wasn't as aware of body language as Miriam was. Otherwise, his friend might guess how often Eli's thoughts centered on her.

"*Kaffi?*" he asked, hoping his voice didn't sound as raspy as it felt in his tight throat.

"Sounds *gut*." Caleb glanced at the table where Kyle

was wiping the last of the butter and syrup from his plate with a folded pancake. Turning to Eli, he said, "I hope I am not interrupting your breakfast."

Miriam must have told her brother not to use contractions so it'd be simpler for Eli to make out what he said. He appreciated Caleb's efforts, though Eli guessed it would be difficult for everyone, including Miriam, not to use them. Eli hoped soon he'd be able to read lips well enough so it wouldn't matter.

"I'm done." He grinned at his nephew, happy he'd caught enough of what Caleb had said. "Kyle eats more than I do. I don't know where he puts it."

"Into growing bigger, ain't so?" Caleb laughed.

His nephew grinned as if Caleb had given him a compliment. Eli smiled. Boys at Kyle's age started having growth spurts. Just as Eli and his brother had when…

Pain surged through him. His brother hadn't been the easiest person to get along with, because Milan had always been very sure of his opinions. On the other hand, he'd stood up for Eli whenever someone picked on him. Milan had said more than once that was how it should be. He'd claimed that older brothers had to be smarter so they could look out for their younger brothers.

But it should have gone both ways. Eli should have checked the wall in spite of Milan's reassurances it was fine. If he had, his brother and his sister-in-law would be around to watch their *kind* growing and changing from a toddler into a sprouting boy.

"…a few minutes of…time," Caleb said.

Eli pulled his attention back to the other man as he finished filling a cup with steaming *kaffi*. He needed to watch Caleb's lips to know what his friend was saying. It would be simpler if Miriam's brother spoke more slowly, but Eli was the one who needed to adjust to the "fast time" speaking of the world around him.

"Sure." He hoped Caleb had asked to speak to him. It was the obvious thing for Caleb to say upon his arrival. "Let's take our *kaffi* into the living room. That will give Kyle time to wash before I take him to school."

The boy grimaced, but his nephew loved spending time with the other *kinder* and Miriam at the temporary school. Kyle did his kitchen chores without complaint when it meant they'd soon be hitching the buggy and heading toward the Hartz farm. Any other time, his nephew made sure Eli heard and witnessed his annoyance at having to do what he called "girls' work." Eli had made the mistake—only once—of reminding his nephew they didn't have girls in the house. Kyle had suggested that could be resolved if Eli would get married.

He almost snorted at the thought. Who would want to marry a man who had lost his hearing in the accident that had claimed his brother and sister-in-law? An accident Eli should have been able to prevent. If he couldn't save his own family, how could any woman trust him?

Not wanting to become mired in self-pity, Eli led the way into the front room. His living room was simple, even by plain standards. A sofa that had seen better days and an antique rocker with a propane floor lamp were arranged on the bare floor. He'd sold their furniture except for the rocker, which his *grossdawdi* had made for *Mamm* to use to rock her *kinder*. It'd been in Milan's house, and Eli had brought it along because Kyle had sat in it for hours after Milan's and Shirley's deaths. The boy had retreated there when he was sad or upset for more than a year.

Eli had found the sofa and the battered table in the kitchen at a secondhand dealer south of Salem. He'd uncovered two beds and a desk with one leg shorter than the others in the dealer's crowded barns where everything was stored haphazardly. After cleaning the furniture, putting a new leg on the desk and painting the headboards on Kyle's bed and his own, the pieces barely resembled the ones he'd dug out of the barns.

Caleb chose the rocker, so Eli dropped onto the sofa. The thick cushion hid how the springs were almost worn out.

"What brings you by this morning?" Eli asked.

After taking a sip, Caleb made a face. He reverted to his usual smile, but Eli wasn't surprised. Miriam's *kaffi* was far superior to his own, which was why he looked forward to having a cup or two during their lessons.

"Volunteers…fire department… Chief is happy…" Caleb set his cup on the floor beside him and sat straighter so he could face Eli. Had Miriam told her brother to look at Eli while talking to him, or had Caleb gotten into the habit when visiting with his *gross-mammi*? Asking someone to look directly at him was a request, she'd reminded Eli more than once, he needed to be comfortable making. "The chief is having training on Saturday. Will you be able to attend?"

Eli grinned. He hadn't heard every word Caleb had spoken, but he'd been able to piece enough together by watching the other man's lips.

"Ja."

"The local fire department is really grateful to have so many volunteers from the Harmony Creek settlement."

"That's no surprise." As they'd discussed before, the plain farmers—and Eli, whose work must be within ten miles so he could get there each day with the horse and buggy—would be nearby during the day. *"Ja,"* he repeated. "I'll be there on Saturday."

He focused on Caleb's lips as the other man spoke. *"Gut."* He handed Eli a piece of paper with a name and number on it. "Call him." A flush rose up Caleb's face. "Or why don't I let him know you're coming when I call with the final list of who can go?"

Eli realized anew Miriam's advice to gauge someone else's stance and expression was more important than he'd guessed. Between Caleb's ruddy cheeks and how his gaze shifted away, Eli knew the other man was embarrassed at suggesting Eli use a phone. Since the accident, the few times he'd had to make a call, he'd had Kyle listen and relay to him what was being said.

"I appreciate that, Caleb. *Danki.*" He took a drink of *kaffi* and grimaced. It hadn't improved with age since he first started it around 5:00 a.m.

"The chief is looking forward to meeting you and Jeremiah because you've got experience working with a volunteer fire department." Caleb faltered, then said, "I told him about your hearing loss, and he said your experience is more valuable to him and the department than how much you can hear."

Eli nodded, grateful to Caleb for handling the uncomfortable topic. Now he had to prove only his fire-fighting skills to everyone else.

"Don't worry about Kyle," Caleb went on. "I'm sure Miriam will be glad to watch him while you go to the training. She thinks a lot of him. She says he's very *gut* during school." He grinned. "Something she can't say about all the scholars. The younger Bowman boys have tried her patience every day."

Eli recalled her expression when, after that first lesson, she'd offered to watch Kyle. She'd been generous to offer, but he sensed she preferred not to have *kinder* underfoot beyond the school day. "Before I bother your sister, I'll check with Mercy. She's been asking for Kyle to come and play with her *kinder*. Let me see if she's willing to have Kyle on Saturday. If Mercy and the kids are busy, I'll ask Miriam."

"That sounds like a plan." Standing and picking up his cup, but not taking another drink, Caleb went into the kitchen. He set the cup in the sink, then reached into his pocket. "Here. Chief Pulaski asked…pager to each of our volunteers. Just…look it over and be ready with questions on Saturday."

"It beeps when there's an emergency?"

"*Ja*, and they vibrate. We…hear them over noise… machinery."

"*Gut.*"

After telling Kyle to enjoy his day at school, Caleb left to deliver the other pagers.

Eli gestured for Kyle to grab his lunch box so they could leave, too. Herding the boy out of the house, Eli took a quick glance at the kitchen clock beside the stove. He needed to run into the village and get supplies for finishing the school. He should be done with it by early July. Would Miriam be glad to get the scholars out of her makeshift schoolroom and into the new building? Most likely.

In the buggy, Kyle stared at the pager peeking out of Eli's pocket. His nephew tapped him on the arm, and as soon as Eli looked at him, asked, "How old do I have to be before I can get one of these?"

"A few more years at least."

"After I am done with school?"

He nodded, not wanting to say no fire department was going to let a fourteen-year-old join as a volunteer. As he turned his attention to the road, keeping to the far right in case a car came past, he was grateful Kyle had heeded Miriam. The boy had gotten Eli's attention before he began talking.

When they reached the Hartz farm, Eli walked Kyle to the barn. The *kind* could have gone alone, but the chance to speak—even for a few minutes—to Miriam was too enticing to resist.

His steps slowed as he approached the barn. Miriam wore the brittle smile she did every morning when she welcomed the scholars. The *kinder* didn't seem to notice, or maybe they thought that was her normal smile.

Eli knew better. He'd seen her true smile. It glowed in her eyes and lit her face, easing the sadness hanging over her like a cloud that never dispersed. Again, he wondered what sorrow plagued her. Was it as appalling as his own?

That evening Eli and Kyle walked into the barn again. Caleb greeted them before picking up *The Budget* and walking into one of the "rooms" that had quilts for walls. He lowered the quilt serving as the door. Light from a lamp appeared around the edges along with the sound of the pages rattling as he opened the newspaper.

Eli appreciated Caleb giving them privacy for tonight's lesson. Having someone witness his stumbling attempts to grasp everything Miriam said would be embarrassing. No matter how many times she told him he shouldn't be ashamed of his disability, he couldn't shake that reaction whenever he messed up and couldn't get the gist of a conversation.

When Kyle rushed over to Miriam, chattering non-stop, Eli hung back. His nephew couldn't hide his delight at seeing his teacher again. Eli hadn't seen that big grin since… He couldn't remember the last time Kyle had been so giddy with happiness. The boy's smile broadened more when Miriam squatted so their eyes were level as she listened to whatever Kyle was saying too swiftly for Eli to catch it.

An odd sensation roiled through him. An unpleasant sensation that again felt too much like envy.

Nonsense! He couldn't be envious of his nephew, who was so comfortable with Miriam and brought out her genuine smile.

But he was.

He wanted to be the one she welcomed with joy. He longed to be able to gaze into her grass-green eyes and see a glow that was only for him.

As she came back to her feet, Eli pushed that distressing thought out of his head. He'd learned his lesson—or he should have—about how sweet smiles quickly could become pity.

Miriam took Kyle's hand, and they walked to the table. They sat and looked at him, clearly baffled about why he was hesitating to join them.

He took his seat. He should be grateful either his expression hadn't revealed his thoughts or Miriam's keen eyes hadn't noticed it while she talked with Kyle.

The lesson went as the previous ones had with her drilling him on different words and asking him to show his progress with Kyle's help. He stumbled more than once as he attempted to keep his mind on his task.

"Watch my lips." She frowned when he failed to respond properly to what she'd said.

He was tempted to tell her he'd been doing that far too much, and that was the reason he couldn't focus. He nodded, not trusting his voice. It might give away the thoughts he shouldn't be having.

Caleb emerged, put the folded newspaper on the table and shot his sister a sympathetic glance. He announced he needed to go next door and asked Kyle if he wanted to come along to see his best friend. The boy eagerly agreed.

Eli knew Caleb's offer was a ploy to prevent any further distractions. It didn't help. Once Eli and Miriam were alone, he found his concentration wandering more. Not only did he want to watch Miriam's lips, but he also couldn't keep his gaze from admiring her pert nose and high cheekbones. He noticed for the first time a few faint freckles there.

He wondered what else he could learn about her at the same time he kept his pain hidden so he didn't have to watch her warm smile change to disgust as Betty Ann's had.

"Keep practicing," Miriam said wearily. It was obvious Eli had other matters on his mind tonight. She hoped he hadn't decided he'd learned enough. He'd made great progress, but still had a lot to learn. "Do not get discouraged. You have hit a plateau. It happens with a new skill. You will break through again soon."

"I'm sure you're right." He stood. "I should head over to Mercy's and get Kyle." He gave her an uneven grin.

"I'm glad he had a chance to play with Paul. I know you want him here so he can learn what I'm learning, but he needs time to be a *kind*."

"I agree. A youngster must have responsibilities so he or she can learn what they need to know, but they also have to have time to play and explore and learn on their own." Rising, she sighed. "If they do not get it, they may do something stupid and get themselves into trouble."

"Do you believe that?"

"Ja."

He was amazed. "Why do you look at *kinder* so negatively? I thought you liked them."

"I do, but as their teacher, I must be prepared for whatever they think up. I pray nothing bad happens. If it does, I can be of more help if I know what they might do."

"But if you look on the positive side, you can still be prepared."

"I do not know how. I know I must be ready for whatever could happen."

How could she explain to him how a little boy had nearly died because she hadn't paid enough attention? If she'd considered the many ways a little boy could get into trouble beforehand, she could have halted him from going into the pond in the first place. She wouldn't make the same mistake with Kyle, but without revealing the truth, she couldn't reassure Eli. She prayed he'd trust her as much as she wanted to trust herself.

"I guess I worry too much about the scholars," she said, glad to speak the truth.

"I don't think anyone would want it any other way, though no *kind* wants to be smothered by too much attention. They need to have elbow room to explore and learn."

"Within limits."

"I agree. As Kyle's *onkel*, I have a duty to him as you do for the scholars."

She came around the table. "Before you go, I need to ask you one thing. Kyle asked me today if I would talk to you about him staying after school to play ball with the other boys."

"No."

She was shocked by his terse answer. After his comments about how she was being too protective of the *kinder*—*smothering* was the word he'd used—he was acting that way himself.

Eli reached for his straw hat. "It's my duty to rear my brother's *kind*. I don't take that lightly. As soon as school is out, Kyle needs to come to the schoolhouse where I can keep an eye on him. I'm sure you understand."

She didn't, but she should be grateful she'd be watching out for one less *kind*. Yet, when she thought about the disappointment on the little boy's face each time he couldn't stay and play ball with the others, she understood how important it was for Kyle to feel like he was a part of the community of the settlement's *kinder*.

However, Kyle needed to obey the rules Eli set. Having those rules was a parent's duty. To keep a *kind* safe and out of trouble as well as teaching the skills a youngster would need to be a vital part of the community when he or she became an adult.

"I will send him across the road after our lessons

are done," she said before she half turned so she didn't have to look at him as she spoke the unpleasant words.

"You think I'm wrong."

"It is not my place to say whether you are right or wrong."

When his broad hand settled on her shoulder, she almost jumped out of her skin. She hadn't thought he'd touch her when they stood in the barn's doorway. If someone happened to see...

Bringing her to face him, he said, "I can't read your lips if you're not looking at me."

"I am sorry." She was, because she'd forgotten the very first lesson she'd taught him and Kyle.

"What did you say when you were turned away?"

"That I should not judge what you are doing. Kyle is your nephew, and you know what he needs better than anyone."

Grief swept across his face, but vanished as fast as it'd appeared. "*Danki*, Miriam. I'll see you tomorrow."

"You will?" A silly question, because he always dropped Kyle off for school before heading across the road. She was letting herself become bemused by his brilliant blue eyes and curiosity about what thoughts were hidden behind them. That was foolish. Hadn't she—seconds ago—been irritated by how curt he'd been while dismissing her request on his nephew's behalf? And now she was losing herself in a fantasy of spending time with him.

She wasn't a teenage girl, waiting for the boy she had her eye on to ask to take her home after a singing.

She was far wiser than that young girl, or so she'd believed. Now she wasn't so sure.

Eli wasn't a callow young man who looked at the world with eager eyes. He'd suffered too much of a loss.

As he bid her good-night and walked out to collect his nephew, she blinked back tears. She was sad for Eli and herself and all they'd lost.

And all they could never have together.

Chapter Eight

Laughter sounded outside the barn as Miriam was drying the last dish from Saturday's midday meal. Not just any laughter, but Annie Wagler's distinctive laugh that was impossible not to join in with.

Wearing a broad smile, Miriam went to the door and greeted the other members of the Harmony Creek Spinsters' Club who were carrying cardboard boxes. She was delighted to see Sarah with the twins. The redhead must have the day off from working as a nanny.

With the sun shining, the June day wasn't too hot. Bees swarmed through the shrubs, looking for flowers they hadn't visited. In the distance she could hear the lowing of cows and a soft tinkling sound.

"Hear that?" asked Annie.

"It sounds like a bell." Miriam stepped aside to let her friends into the barn.

"From Leanna's new goats." Annie smiled at her twin. "She plans to make goat milk soap *and* goat milk cheese to sell at the Salem farmers market later this summer."

"You're going to be busy." Miriam chuckled. "Or busier."

Leanna wagged a finger at her. "Look who's talking. We've heard Caleb finished your kitchen, and it was the final room he had to do before you could move in."

"Not quite. The upstairs needs to be painted."

"So you're using both floors?" asked Sarah.

"No. Not right now."

"Then the house is done." Annie's tone dared anyone to disagree with her. "Done enough for us to help you move your things from here to the house."

"Now?"

"Do you know a better time?" Leanna dimpled. "You don't have to teach today, and Caleb is at the firefighter training with the other men. We can take your household items over and have them put away in the cupboards before the men bring in the furniture."

Sarah added, "You do so much for others, Miriam. Let us do this for you."

"Because we're going to anyhow." Annie's laughter drew everyone into her *gut* spirits.

Miriam didn't answer, because she realized whatever she said wouldn't have made any difference. Her friends had decided upon the perfect frolic for a quiet Saturday, and she was grateful for their help with a chore she hadn't been looking forward to.

No one was surprised when Annie gave each of them instructions for their tasks. She worked as hard as the rest of them did, maybe harder, because she toted many of the heavier boxes they packed to the house herself.

Miriam began to unpack in the kitchen and admired its soft tan walls. Caleb had added new cupboards to the ones he'd been able to salvage from the original kitchen. Once he'd painted them white, they looked as if they'd always been hung together. The propane refrigerator was a generous size, but the centerpiece of the kitchen was Caleb's double wide stove with its massive ovens. He had plans for using it, though he hadn't shared them with her yet.

By four, they had moved about half of the portable items from the barn to the house. Miriam grinned as she served her friends lemonade from a pitcher stored in the new refrigerator. She led the way out to the porch. Sitting on the steps because the chairs remained in the barn, she scanned the horizon.

Mountains rose to the north, west and east. To the south, the river valley was edged with distant hills. Caleb had been excited when he found farms for sale edging the north side of Harmony Creek, and now that she lived here, she understood why.

"Pretty, isn't it?" Sarah asked nobody in particular.

Miriam smiled. "Caleb says when the leaves start turning in the fall, it's as if someone melted a box of red, orange and yellow crayons along the hillsides."

Sipping her lemonade, she took a deep breath and glanced at the road where a silver car drove past at a reasonable pace. She recognized it as belonging to the farm next to the Kuhnses'. When the driver waved out the open window, Miriam waved back.

"He's not there, you know," Sarah murmured.

"He?" repeated Miriam, wondering what she'd missed.

"Eli." Before Miriam could ask what her friend meant, Sarah went on, "We've noticed how you avoid looking at the schoolhouse. I thought you were helping Eli make sure everything is in the proper place."

Miriam tried not to flinch as Sarah patted her shoulder in silent commiseration before putting down her empty glass and heading back toward the barn for another box. She *had* been using any excuse to keep from checking the school's progress. Since her last conversation with Eli, when he had refused to let Kyle join the other scholars for an after-school softball game, she hadn't spoken to him. He seemed to agree, because he hadn't come back for lipreading lessons.

She was sure it was for the best. When they'd been alone the other night, she'd lost herself in imagining what it would be like to be in Eli's arms. She'd been shown how dangerous for her equilibrium it could be to spend time with him.

Caleb had asked what was wrong and why she wasn't working with Eli any longer. She'd given him a shrug because she wasn't sure. Maybe Eli believed he didn't need further lessons. He'd caught on quickly, but there was more she could teach him. Things like refining his skills so he was more comfortable with a group of people.

"I'm supposed to help him if he's got questions," Miriam said, realizing her friends were waiting for an answer. "And I do, when he's there. He's at the training session today with Caleb and the other men."

"He's going to be a firefighter?" asked Annie, her eyes wide.

Miriam nodded. "Caleb tells me that Eli is an experienced firefighter. He volunteered in Delaware."

"Surely that was before he lost his hearing."

Leanna frowned at her sister. "Annie, you don't know anything about being a firefighter. It's something Eli must be able to do, or he wouldn't be attending the training today."

"I'm sorry. I shouldn't have said that, but I'm surprised he can work with the others without being able to hear them." She rushed to catch up with Sarah, who was at the barn.

"Forgive her," Leanna said. "She speaks before she thinks." Chuckling, she added, "And I think too much, and I don't speak before the conversation has moved on."

"It's already forgotten," Miriam reassured her friend. "Annie asks so many questions because she cares about everyone and everything. And to tell you the truth, there have been a bunch of times that I've been glad that she's asked questions I wanted to know the answer to."

"Me, too."

Miriam thought that would be the end of the uncomfortable subject of her spending time with Eli, but as her friends were about to leave, Leanna took her aside and apologized again for her sister's comments.

"Don't worry," Miriam said. "I've forgotten about it." *Just as I wish you three would forget about there being anything between Eli and me. He's made it clear he doesn't want that.*

"I'm glad." She glanced at the nearly finished schoolhouse. "And I'm glad you're helping Eli with the school. It'll make teaching much easier for the next teacher."

"Like I said, I offer help when he asks. Otherwise, I don't want to get in Eli's way. He doesn't need an audience when he's working. If he gets distracted, he could get injured."

Leanna's smile turned soft. "You do care about him."

"Don't read any extra meaning into my words."

"I don't have to. Your expression says it all." She

hugged Miriam before her twin came toward them with Sarah not far behind.

Not wanting the conversation to turn to Eli again, Miriam said as the four of them walked back into the house and into the kitchen, "*Danki* for helping today."

"It was fun," Annie said. "We'd like to have another frolic, if we could. Can we join you while you're teaching school one of these days?"

"You want to help me with the scholars?"

"*Ja.*" She smiled. "It'd give us a chance to get to know the *kinder* better. These kids are like we were when we thought that being with an adult was boring."

"You're blessed to be able to spend so much time with the girls and boys." Leanna glanced around the kitchen and sighed. "It's like having a huge family of your own."

"A family who goes home at the end of the day so I only have to cook for Caleb and me," Miriam joked to keep a wall between her heart and the anguish of losing her chance to have the family she'd loved. When a pulse of pain didn't thud through her, she was astonished.

Maybe it was because she was having fun with her friends, and the grief that had been her unfailing companion for months was beginning to dull. Would it stay like that? If someone had asked her before, she would have denied her anguish would diminish.

Whatever the reason, she was grateful for the temporary reprieve.

"*Ach,*" sighed Leanna. "I wouldn't mind if I had two dozen to cook for each day if I could have a family of my own."

Annie watched her twin walk out of the kitchen. For once, Annie wasn't smiling. As if to herself, she said,

"I wish Leanna wouldn't obsess about getting married. I'm afraid she's going to become so desperate to get wed that she'll agree to any proposal that comes her way."

"Even if it's not Caleb asking?"

"Caleb?" Annie's eyes grew big.

"I saw how Leanna looked at him the nights we've met to discuss the rules for our new *Ordnung*. She seems taken with him."

For a long minute Annie said nothing, and Miriam could tell her friend was taken aback. How could Annie have failed to notice how her sister had reacted each time Caleb spoke, whether he was in the midst of the debate about buggies or the use of solar panels?

"I guess I was paying too much attention to the discussion," Annie replied at last. "I've been praying she doesn't do something stupid like ask someone to marry her without waiting for him to ask."

"Why do you think she'd do that? Leanna is sensible. Why wouldn't she wait for the man to ask her?"

"She tried that before, and he asked someone else."

"I'm sorry to hear that. She must have been heart-broken."

"She was because she hadn't realized he was walking out with the other girl while bringing Leanna home from singings." Annie's mouth tightened. "I tell her that any man who does such a thing doesn't deserve her, but she believes the only thing that will mend her heart is getting married herself."

"That's so sad."

"I know." She drew in a deep breath and then sighed. "I keep praying she'll find someone to marry for love not for revenge."

"I'll pray for her, too. A marriage based on vengeance can't be happy."

"*Danki*, Miriam." She squeezed Miriam's hand before heading toward the door. As she was about to leave, she paused and turned. "Please don't think Leanna is foolish."

"I'd never think that."

"She needs to prove to herself that she's worthy of being loved."

"All she has to do is open her eyes and look at her twin."

Annie smiled faintly. "She wants more than a sister's love."

"But she's blessed to have you worried about her."

"And I'm blessed to have her." Annie started to add more, but halted when Sarah called her name.

Miriam waved goodbye before opening one of the last boxes they'd toted from the barn. She put the pots and pans in the lower cupboards to the right of the big stove. On the left, she planned to store baking pans and casserole dishes.

Her eyes were caught by a motion beyond the window over the double sink. Two little boys raced out of the woods. Her heart swelled as she thought about Ralph and his buddies, but reality hit. It wasn't Ralph, the boy she'd loved almost as much as his *daed*.

Maybe more, she admitted.

Again, she was disconcerted by her own thoughts. Could that be true? Could she be more like Leanna than she'd guessed? Wanting a family so much she'd been willing to marry a man who could provide her with one...even if she didn't love him as much as she did his *kind*?

As she opened the door, she smiled at the two boys loping toward her.

"Kyle! Paul! Does Mercy know you are over here?"

Both boys nodded before Kyle said, "You're moving into the house, ain't so? Can we help you carry stuff?"

"The more hands, the better." Crooking a finger toward them, she said, "*Komm* with me. I'll show you which boxes you can bring over to the house."

In the barn, she selected boxes that were light enough for the boys to heft without hurting themselves. Setting them together, she said, "If you can take these to the house, it'll be a huge help."

As if it was the best game ever invented, the boys carried the boxes to the house. Miriam rewarded them with icy glasses of lemonade, which they swallowed in one gulp. She refilled the glasses, and the boys drank more slowly.

They handed her the empty glasses and bid her goodbye. Paul rushed out the door, and she smiled. It would appear the boy had one speed—fast.

Kyle paused in the doorway. "Will you talk to *Onkel* Eli again about me playing ball after school?" Before she could answer, he hurried to add, "He lets me hang out with Paul, so why won't he let me play with him and the other boys after school?"

"I don't know."

"Didn't you ask him?"

"I did, but he just said that he wanted you to come over to the school as soon as we're done with lessons. You should ask your *onkel* why he feels that way. Maybe he'll explain his reasons to you." *Though I don't know why he wouldn't tell me.*

"Will you ask him again for me?"

She wanted to say no, but the entreaty on Kyle's face halted her. "Let me think about it." It wasn't a promise or a direct no. She hoped it would be enough for the boy.

It was. He grinned and skipped out, heading toward Mercy's farm.

She closed the door and leaned against it. Raising her gaze upward, she said, "God, You keep putting Eli in my path. I know You must have a reason, and I wish You'd share it with me."

Eli looked across the table at Miriam the following Tuesday evening and sighed. Tonight's lesson, his first in the house instead of the barn, hadn't progressed as he'd hoped. It'd been over a week since his previous lesson, and he could see that she was wondering if he had practiced at all during that time. He considered telling her how much he'd comprehended during the firefighter training, but bragging about that would border on *hochmut*.

Kyle sat in the living room, looking at a picture book about farm animals. More than once, he'd glanced into the kitchen. He'd come into the kitchen only when Miriam offered him a piece of cake, the first one baked in the new oven. As soon as he was finished, he'd gone back to his book.

The boy had been on edge all day, though he hadn't said why. Eli was curious what was on his nephew's mind, but he didn't press the *kind* to explain. Kyle's *daed* had become introspective at times, and nothing Eli had done would convince Milan to talk one second sooner about what was bothering him. Maybe Kyle was the same.

"I understand you are frustrated," Miriam said.

"You've got no idea how much."

"*Ja*, I do. Remember I learned lipreading because my *grossmammi* needed help. I know it is not easy. Eventually, you will be able to read lips almost as easily as you once heard words. I am sure of that."

When she stood, he did the same, knowing it was the signal that the lesson was over. He should've looked away, but he couldn't pull his gaze from her graceful steps and the gentle sway of her dark purple hem as she went to the sink to put their cups in to soak.

He bid her a good-night and left with Kyle and the book Miriam told him he could borrow. Eli wanted to let her faith in him sustain him until he made another breakthrough. Maybe he should have told her about how he didn't have to remind himself with every encounter to be aware of body language. It was becoming almost second nature to him.

Why could he function well with everyone else but stumbled during his lessons with Miriam?

The question kept Eli awake too long and followed him to the new school the next morning after he dropped Kyle at Miriam's house for the boy's own lessons.

He had to stop during the day when yawn after yawn interrupted his work. He needed to concentrate twice as much as usual to make sure the moldings around the windows—including the extras Miriam had insisted on—were straight. Measuring multiple times, he pulled off two pieces and realigned them so they were level.

By the time Kyle arrived midafternoon, Eli felt as if he'd worked a full week, though he'd accomplished less than half of what he'd planned. His exhaustion didn't prevent him from noticing how the little boy shuffled into the school as if on his way to be punished.

"Did you have a *gut* day at school?" Eli asked.

The *kind* nodded, but didn't look up.

"What did you study today?"

He shrugged.

"Kyle, look at me."

His nephew regarded him with tear-filled eyes.

Before Eli could ask what was wrong, the crack of a bat and cheers came from the other side of the road. The scholars were playing a game of softball before heading home to help with evening chores. Every instinct urged him to relent, but how could he work at the schoolhouse when his nephew was out of his sight? Going to school was one thing. The state required it, and Eli didn't want to get their new settlement in trouble with the authorities. As well, Kyle was being watched by Miriam. She wouldn't be able to oversee the *kinder* as closely while she finished her daily household tasks and made supper for her brother.

Kyle sighed.

"I was honest with your teacher. I need your help here." Was Eli trying to convince himself or the boy the half lie was the whole truth?

"I know." The *kind*'s head was down, and he scuffled his feet across the floor, every step broadcasting how angry he was at being thwarted from joining his friends for the game.

When Eli suggested Kyle play with the marbles they'd picked up in Salem on their last visit, the boy acted as if he hadn't heard. Eli took his nail gun and moved to the molding for the back door beyond where the teacher's desk would be placed. He tried to work, but the quiet in the building was appalling, even for a man whose world was blanketed in silence.

He turned to see Kyle standing by a window Eli had finished. His nephew stared out, hunger on his young face. Eli knew the little boy was watching the *kinder* in Caleb's yard. The sharp sound of another ball against a bat exploded, and Kyle stood on tiptoe to watch the batter run the bases as the other team scrambled to stop the ball and throw it in to prevent the home run.

Eli sighed. Miriam had been right about the importance of body language when he couldn't see someone's face. Just by observation, he could tell what someone else was saying.

And what they weren't saying.

Kyle's muteness spoke more clearly than the little boy could. He didn't want to play marbles all alone. He wanted to play with the other *kinder*, to be part of something bigger than himself.

Instead of protecting his nephew, Eli was breaking his heart by keeping him from doing what the rest of the *kinder* could. That wouldn't have been what his brother would have wanted.

It was time to admit he'd made a mistake.

"I'll be right back, Kyle," he said, disconnecting his nail gun from the air compressor and setting it on the floor.

Either the boy didn't answer or Eli didn't hear him.

Crossing the road, he edged around the improvised ball field where a new batter was getting ready to swing. He headed toward the house. He opened the door and called Miriam's name.

"Eli!" She walked into the kitchen from the living room. Her blond hair was covered by a black kerchief, and she held a wet rag. A bucket on the floor by the front windows showed that she was washing them. "Are we supposed to have a lesson this afternoon?"

"No."

"Are you looking for Caleb, then?"

He shook his head as he closed the distance between them. "No." His eyes took in the splatters of water that created small dark circles on her dark green dress. A single strand of blond hair had slipped from her bun and hung draped over her right ear. Soapsuds curved along her cheek where she must have pushed her hair back. His fingers itched to follow the same path across her face, caressing her soft skin.

To keep from giving in to the impulse, he said, "I want to talk to you about Kyle."

Miriam dropped the wet cloth in the sink and faced Eli. "That is *gut* because I want to talk to you about him, too. I realize I have asked you about letting Kyle stay after school to play ball with the other *kinder* and you have given me your answer."

"*Ja*, but—"

"But you are wrong, Eli! That boy needs to spend time with his school friends."

"I know, and—"

Again, she interrupted with, "It is important for a *kind* to learn more than what is in books. He needs to discover about what it means to be part of a team. That teaches him the importance of community and how we must depend on each other as well as upon God."

"Miriam—"

"Let me say what I've got to say, and then I'll listen to what you have to say. Kyle has become more droopy each day. You must have noticed, too."

"I have."

"You're too overprotective." She realized she was using contractions, but couldn't halt herself as her tone became heated. He wouldn't hear that. She folded her arms in front of her and narrowed her eyes, wanting him to understand her fervor as she spoke on his nephew's behalf. "I know you want to keep Kyle safe. Every adult wants that for *kinder*, but one thing I have learned is if you don't give a *kind* a bit of freedom, he or she will take it anyhow and get into much bigger trouble."

She had to struggle to get the last few words out. Yost had vacillated between being too protective and too indifferent to his son. At first when she began walking out with Yost, he'd insisted upon knowing where the boy was every minute of the day. Later, he had handed that duty over to her and berated her when she didn't smother Ralph as he had. His final words to her, after Ralph's near-drowning, had been a furious, "I told you so."

She didn't want Eli to make the same mistake. Though the two men were different in many ways, if Eli continued to stifle Kyle's natural exuberance, his nephew was going to act as thoughtlessly as Ralph had.

Eli cleared his throat. "I should tell you before you go any further, what I wanted to talk to you about."

She lowered her eyes. Were Annie's outspoken ways rubbing off on her?

"I wanted to tell you," he went on, "that I've changed my mind. If you'll assure me that you'll keep a close eye on the *kinder* while they're in your yard, I'm willing to let Kyle join the games after school."

Shock blocked every word she could think of. Finally, as he began to smile, she asked, "Why didn't you say so right from the beginning?"

"You didn't give me a chance."

"True." Her cheeks grew warm. "I am sorry about that."

He chuckled, and his eyes lit with *gut* humor. It was an expression she savored each time he smiled. "No need to be sorry. You couldn't have guessed I was willing to change my mind. Let's try it for next week and see what happens."

"Just a week? Okay." She laughed when his mouth dropped open. "Did you think I would not agree?"

"You've got as much work as the rest of us, and you've taken on teaching the scholars."

"Someone had to."

"But nobody else did except you. Are you always this willing to put aside what you need and want for others?"

"I try to be now."

"Now? Did something happen before?"

Miriam berated herself. How could she make such an obvious reference to the past when Eli was making it clear he was letting Kyle stay after school because he trusted her with his nephew? If he knew the truth…

No, that must never happen.

Chapter Nine

"Let's go to the Fourth of July parade and carnival in Salem together!" Annie's eyes sparkled as she cut tops off the strawberries she and Leanna had picked that morning at a nearby farm. They'd come home with enough berries for each member of the Spinsters' Club to make shortcake for supper.

"It's supposed to be a fun, family-oriented celebration," her twin added.

"And the money raised at the carnival benefits the fire department."

"Having a *gut* time and helping the firefighters. What could be better?"

"Did you hear there's going to be an auction? A cake auction!"

"We spinsters will have to donate cakes, ain't so?"

"Ja!"

Miriam grinned as the twins continued talking at the same time. Neither she nor Sarah attempted to interject a word. Not that they had a chance. Somehow, each twin seemed to understand everything the other said, even when their words bounced off one another as they did while they made and discarded plans so quickly Miriam couldn't keep up.

"It must be a twin skill," she whispered to Sarah after she went to check—again—on the scholars who would soon be finishing their after-school ball game.

"They say one twin always knows what the other is thinking." Her grin revealed her dimples. "It must be true. Otherwise, they'd be as confused as we are."

Annie broke off the conversation with her sister to ask, "What are you two talking about?"

"We could ask you the same thing," Miriam said.

The twins shared a bewildered glance before Leanna replied in a tone that suggested she had no idea why they would have to ask, "We're talking about our next Spinsters' Club outing. We want to go to Salem for the Fourth of July celebrations. Let's go together! What do you say?"

"I can go," Miriam said, cutting more of the big berries into pieces and putting them in a bowl. Her fingers and the knife were stained with the luscious-smelling juice, and her mouth watered at the thought of having the berries for dessert later.

"Me, too." Sarah reached into one of the plastic buckets for another handful of berries.

"You don't have to work on the Fourth?"

"Just in the morning to get the *kinder* their breakfast. Both parents are home for the week, so they don't need me to stay after lunch." She smiled. "My brothers are looking forward to me making an extra cake for them while I bake one for the auction, but it won't take long."

"The parade starts around 6:00 p.m." Annie grinned. "Let's hire Hank's van to take us in and find a great place to watch the parade. Then we can go to the carnival. The dessert auction is scheduled for around eight o'clock."

"Exactly when everyone realizes they missed dessert before the parade." Miriam laughed. "That's the perfect time. The firefighters should make a lot of money by having cakes and other goodies to bid on."

She sidled once more to the window and looked at where the boys and girls were done playing for the afternoon and had stored the equipment in a wooden box by the barn door. As they began to head for home, she returned to cutting strawberries.

"Eli changed his mind about letting Kyle play, I see." Sarah wiped bright red juice off her cutting board before it could stain the counter.

"He's trying to be a *gut daed* to the boy, and he saw how much Kyle wanted to play." She didn't say how she and Eli had debated the topic multiple times before he acquiesced. Nor did she mention how nervous she was with having to keep an eye on the *kinder*.

As long as the scholars played where she could see them, she let them choose whichever games they wanted. A couple of the older boys had started to slip away, and she'd insisted they stay with the other *kinder* or go home and not play after school for the rest of the term. She guessed their plans had been no more mischievous than exploring the woods behind the barn, but she refused to relent. Kyle's probation week—as well as her own—was almost over, and everything had gone well.

"It's settled, then? We're going together to Salem?" Leanna stacked the empty buckets together to take home.

Everyone agreed enthusiastically as they divided

the strawberries, and Miriam found her smile wouldn't budge from her face. Spending time with her friends would be relaxing and fun. Just what she needed while she prayed Eli would let his nephew continue to participate in the ball games for the last week and a half of school.

With his tool belt slung over his shoulder, Eli walked from the schoolhouse to the other side of the road where Kyle sat beneath a tree. Eli had asked his nephew to wait there each day, because Eli hoped there would be a chance to talk with Miriam.

Hearing female laughter coming from farther along the road, he saw the Wagler twins and Sarah Kuhns walking toward their families' farms. Had they been at Miriam's? If she had company, would she have remembered to keep a close eye on the *kinder*?

Kyle must have guessed his thoughts. "Don't worry. Miriam checked on us every few minutes like she said she would."

"That's *gut* to know."

Whatever he'd planned to say next melted away in his mind as he saw Miriam walking toward them. He'd never seen another woman who could make everyday steps appear as if she were floating on a cloud. There was a lightness about her that drew him to her, but that cloud could become stormy without warning. More than once, he'd considered asking her what darkness from her past clung to her.

He hadn't. Asking her to reveal the truth opened himself to speaking of the tragedy that shadowed his and Kyle's lives.

"How is the work going at the school?" she asked.

Curious what was in the covered plastic bowl she carried, he said, "I'm hoping you and the *kinder* can move in after the holiday. That way you'll be able to give it what the *Englischers* call a beta test before school begins in September."

"A beta test? Isn't it something to do with computers?"

"I think so, but what I mean is if you find any problems with the building, I'll have time to correct them."

That faint cloud misted across her face. "You haven't found other work yet?"

"It'll come. I trust God has a plan for me." Wanting to bring back her smile, he said, "And speaking of plans, have you thought about attending the carnival on the Fourth of July?"

"I'm going with my friends. We decided this afternoon to go together."

"Then I'll see you there."

"*Gut.* Caleb tells me the parade attracts a lot of spectators, but the route along Main Street and to the carnival grounds is long enough so there are plenty of places to watch it."

"That's what I've been told, too."

Her smile again became as bright as the sunshine. "You're doing much better with your lipreading and comprehension."

"I've had a *gut* teacher." He was pleased when her cheeks turned a deeper rose and her eyes glowed. "You've made a difference in my life. A big difference. I should have thanked you before."

"You don't need to thank me."

"I know, but I'm grateful how much easier my day-to-day life has become. There are still a lot of things

I miss when I can't see someone's lips. However, I'm learning there's no shame in asking the person to repeat what was said."

"Gut." She held out the bowl. "The Wagler twins picked strawberries this morning and shared them with us. There are more than Caleb and I can eat. Would you like them?"

Kyle cheered his excitement before Eli could reply and held his hands out for the plastic bowl.

Eli put out his arm to block her from giving the strawberries to his nephew. "We've got to run into Salem. Can we pick them up later?"

"Of course. They'll be waiting for you."

He wanted to ask if she would be waiting for him, too, but halted the words before they could form. Instead, he said, "Let's go, Kyle."

"Can Miriam come with us?" He kept his face turned toward Eli, a sign Kyle didn't want a single word he spoke missed.

"Do you want to drive into Salem with us?" Eli asked.

Seeing her astonishment, he wondered if asking her to ride in his buggy had been too blunt. Not that the invitation could be construed as romantic when they would be accompanied by a six-year-old.

He was so sure she'd refuse, it was his turn to be shocked when she said,

"I need to get mayonnaise. We're out. Let me put your strawberries in the house, then I'll meet you at the school."

"That sounds *gut.*"

As Eli walked toward the school with Kyle, he admitted having time with Miriam should be far more than *gut.* He glanced at his grinning nephew. The boy was as happy as Eli was to have Miriam join them for the drive into the village.

Or was the boy giddy about something else? Like matchmaking?

Eli shook those questions out of his head. He was being ridiculous. Kyle was focused on his friends, school and softball.

Making sure no sign of his errant thoughts were on his face, he had the buggy ready by the time Miriam came across the road with a black bonnet covering her *kapp*. As soon as they were settled inside the buggy, Miriam sitting on Kyle's far side so Eli could see them at the same time, they headed toward the village.

Not that Eli or Miriam had a chance to talk while Kyle gave them a play-by-play recap of the ball game. When Miriam mentioned one of the long hits before the boy could, Eli realized Kyle was right. She was watching the *kinder* closely.

They were driving into the village, past old farmhouses and Victorian houses, before Kyle was finished. The traffic was light, so Eli held the reins loosely. He trusted Slim to go along the road without much supervision because they'd traveled that way enough times for the horse to know the way.

He glanced at Miriam. "I can drop you off at the grocery store before I do my errands, if you'd like."

"I…"

He couldn't catch the rest of her words. "Your bonnet is shading your face."

She untied her bonnet and placed it in her lap. "Is this better?"

"*Ja*. It seems I've still got a lot to learn."

"If you can't see someone's mouth to watch their lips form words, you can't read them. It's as simple as that."

"I guess it's always going to be a challenge."

"It will be," she said, "but how we face challenges reveals who we truly are. If we've got faith that God has a reason for putting those roadblocks in our way, then we can't help but realize each lesson we learn is one He wants us to discover."

As they passed the brick central school set on lush green lawns, Eli had to pay more attention to the traffic. A milk tanker rumbled past, but Slim didn't pay any more attention to it than the smaller cars. *Kinder* stopped playing and pointed as the buggy drove by. When Kyle waved to them, the youngsters couldn't hide their envy at him riding in it.

"I can get out here," Miriam said when they stopped for the red light at the intersection of Main Street and Broadway in the village. "Where do you want to meet?"

"I'll meet you in the parking lot at the grocery store in half an hour. Okay?"

"Ja." She climbed out of the buggy and crossed to the sidewalk.

Eli heard Kyle sigh beside him as Miriam strode along the street, her bonnet again in place.

"I like her," his nephew said. "A lot."

"I know."

"Do you like her, *Onkel* Eli?"

"Of course. She's our neighbor."

"And our teacher."

"True." Eli gave Slim the command to move when the light turned green.

"Do you like her a lot, too?"

He wouldn't lie to his nephew, but knew how *kinder*

talked among themselves. He didn't want his name or Miriam's to be fodder for speculation.

"Kyle, look at the gas station and see if there's a place we can pull in next to one of the pumps."

As Eli had hoped, the request diverted the boy, who scanned the busy gas station on the opposite corner. Kyle pointed to an open pump in the center of the three rows.

Curious—and shocked—glances came in their direction when Eli stopped Slim by a gas pump. As he climbed out of the buggy, the man pumping gas on the other side stared so hard it looked as if his eyes were in danger of searing their imprint into the side of the buggy. Conversations faded to silence as Eli walked around the buggy and opened the back. He felt each look aimed at him, but he pretended he didn't notice as he took out two plastic gas containers.

He checked the pump and saw he could pay after he got the ten gallons the red containers could hold. Setting the pump to regular, he opened the containers. He stuck the nozzle into the first one and listened to the gas splash into it. Once he'd filled it, he repeated the process with the second container.

"I didn't think you Amish used gas," said the man on the other side of the pump, who drove a bright silver truck. A little girl, who couldn't be more than four, had her head stuck out the window and she was staring at Eli, Kyle, the buggy and Slim.

"I need it for the air compressor that runs my power tools." He put the nozzle into place and screwed the lids onto the containers. "It won't run on oats like my vehicle does."

The man grinned, then laughed as Eli hefted the

containers into the buggy. "That's a good one. I wasn't sure Amish made jokes. You always look so serious."

"We make jokes, sometimes really bad ones."

That brought more laughter, and the little girl asked if she could pet Slim. After checking with the man who was probably her *daed*, Eli nodded. She squeezed past the pump. Eli halted her from running right at the horse.

"Horses don't like to be surprised," he said.

Lifting her, he let her pat the horse's nose. Slim, who was accustomed to Kyle and other *kinder*, accepted the attention as his rightful due. The little girl giggled with delight as Eli handed her to her *daed*, who thanked him.

Eli left Kyle with instructions to move the buggy if a car was waiting for gas, then went inside to pay. The store was cramped and filled with every kind of soft drink and candy bar Eli had ever seen. He ignored the treats as he thought of the fresh strawberries he and his nephew could enjoy tonight. Giving several bills to the cashier, he waited for his change.

"I thought I was seeing things," the older man said as he opened the register. "A horse and buggy in the gas station? I wouldn't have believed it if I hadn't seen it with my own two eyes." Handing Eli several coins, he added, "That's a nice-looking family you have. Saw you by the light before you came over here."

Eli was puzzled. He hadn't imagined anyone describing his nephew that way. Then he realized the man assumed Miriam was Eli's wife.

He hurried out of the gas station, but he couldn't move fast enough to get ahead of his thoughts.

Nice-looking family you have.

A family? Of his own?

After assuming responsibility for Kyle, he hadn't

thought of building a family beyond the two of them. At least, not until he met Miriam Hartz. The warmth in her eyes when she looked at him suggested she might have feelings for him beyond being his teacher. Even when that gentle heat became a vexed flame, there was a softness in the way she treated him and Kyle.

"Where to next?" Kyle asked.

"The hardware store. I need to get a gallon of black-board paint."

His nephew wrinkled his nose at the thought of lessons being put on the blackboard in the fall.

Eli chuckled and drove the buggy onto Main Street. He parked it about halfway along the street near a thin tree between the road and the sidewalk. He could trust Slim to stay without being tied, but there was more traffic along Main Street than the horse was accustomed to. He lashed the reins around the tree as Kyle jumped out and peered into the alley where grass grew in the middle, showing it wasn't used much. Together they walked up the three steps to Rossi's Hardware's front door.

Opening the door, Eli led the way into the shadowed interior. Instantly, he was transported to Kent County and the small shops where he used to buy supplies for the farm with his *daed* and brother. Those stores had displayed wares on every available surface, too.

He wasn't surprised when the worn floorboards, wider than any a modern sawmill could cut, creaked. Made dim with the dust left by hundreds of footsteps before his, they rippled like some great creature had dragged its claws along them.

Kyle wandered away to look at the tools and parts held in wooden barrels and on shelves and pegboards.

A few glass cases were scattered among the stacks of rubber boots and fishing poles and other equipment.

The paint was at the rear of the store, so Eli headed that way. Using blackboard paint instead of slate saved money and time, though slate was quarried only twenty miles to the north and east. Maybe the settlement would decide on a slate chalkboard later, but for now he'd paint one behind the teacher's desk.

Finding what he needed, he carried it to a long wooden counter that must have been in the store since the business opened. He set it by the register and nodded to the heavyset man there. The man with a full head of bright white hair was Tuck Rossi, the store's proprietor.

"Did you find what you want?" Tuck asked in his booming voice.

"I did."

Tuck rang up the paint. "Is this for the school you're building in the hollow?"

"*Ja*. I mean, yes."

"You're the carpenter?"

Eli nodded as he paid for the paint.

"Do you make furniture?"

Or at least that was what Eli guessed Tuck had asked. The man talked fast, faster than most of the plain folks. But Eli seemed to be getting most of what the hardware store owner was saying. Not once had Tuck given him that peculiar glance that warned Eli that he'd made a complete mess of "translating" what someone else said.

"No, I do rough and finish carpentry, but I've got a neighbor who builds furniture. I can give you his name, if you're interested."

"*Onkel* Eli makes cabinets for kitchens and bathrooms, too," Kyle said with a grin as he came to stand by the counter.

"That's good to know." Tuck pulled a pad of paper from under the counter. "Write your contact information there. Your neighbor's, too, if you don't mind."

Eli did, wondering if he should have contacted the hardware store earlier to let folks know he was looking for work.

Tuck took the pad, glanced at it and nodded. "This is good. Some people around here don't want to drive almost an hour to Glens Falls to order cabinets. Once they find out you're around and willing to work on kitchens, you'll have more jobs than you can handle."

Thanking Tuck, Eli took Kyle's hand. They put the paint in the buggy.

Miriam hurried along the sidewalk toward them. She swung a bag by her side, and she smiled as she neared.

What would it be like to have a beautiful, kind-hearted woman like her for his own? A lovely wife and precious *kinder*, a true part of his life, not a dream he barely dared to have any longer.

Pain slashed him. That happiness had been almost within his grasp before his mistake—whatever it had been—had caused a wall to collapse and crush his hopes. He'd been careless once, and he didn't trust himself not to make the same horrific error again, no matter how hard he tried.

"We may get wet," Miriam said as she reached the buggy.

When she glanced at the sky, he saw a storm off to the north. It wouldn't hit the village, but it might come close to Harmony Creek.

Kyle again sat between him and Miriam as they

headed home. Eli was grateful for his nephew's babbling about what he'd seen at the hardware store. That
way Eli didn't have to make conversation with Miriam. How could he say anything when his wayward
thoughts might burst out? She might consider him just
another of her scholars. She was nice to him, but she
was with everyone.

You should be glad, he told himself, but he wasn't.

After dropping Miriam off at her house and collect-
ing the strawberries, Eli continued toward the far end of
the hollow. They'd gotten home without any rain, and
the storm was heading east into Vermont.

"Look!" cried Kyle, almost standing.

Eli put out an arm to keep the boy in his seat, but
stared in astonishment at their home. The big oak had
fallen between the house and the barn. The storm's
winds must have toppled it. The top branches had
clipped the roof of the house, ripping off shingles. Two
windows on the second floor were shattered—one in
his bedroom and the other in Kyle's. Debris was scattered everywhere, leaves, branches and pieces of wood
that looked as if they would crumble if touched. Where
the tree had broken, decayed wood was visible along
the trunk.

In addition, the road to the barn was blocked. He
couldn't drive his buggy inside or put Slim in his stall.

Turning the buggy wasn't easy at the narrow end of
the road, but Slim seemed as eager to get away from the
damage as Eli. Kyle, for once, was silent as they drove
in the direction they'd come.

The tools Eli needed to fix the house were at the
school. He hoped Miriam would watch Kyle while Caleb

and more of his neighbors helped him clear away the broken tree.

Miriam threw open the front door as they got out of the buggy. "Eli! Why are you here? Did you forget something?"

Kyle pushed past him and threw his arms around her. For the first time Eli was envious of his nephew as the boy embraced his teacher, talking nonstop about the damage at the end of the hollow.

"A tree?" she asked, looking over Kyle's head to Eli for confirmation.

Behind her, Caleb appeared, his face drawn with anxiety. "Has something happened, Eli?"

He answered them at the same time by explaining what he and Kyle had come home to find.

"I didn't guess the wind would be that strong at your end of the creek," Caleb said.

"The tree has a lot of rot on one side. I don't think it took too much wind to knock it over."

"If you had been at home and Kyle out playing..." Miriam shuddered and again he had to fight the yearning to draw her close so he could comfort her. "Thank the *gut* Lord it happened while we were in town."

"I'll head over to the Kuhnses' sawmill," Caleb said. "They've got a couple of chain saws." He paused. "What about the roof? Will you need a tarp?"

"*Ja*, and plywood to put over the broken windows. There are pieces left over at the school."

"Use whatever you need." He rushed out the door to alert their neighbors.

"Miriam, will you watch Kyle?" Eli asked.

"For as long as you need. *Komm* for supper." She

gave him a weak smile. "We'll have strawberry short-cake, then you and Kyle can stay here tonight."

"You don't have room for guests."

"We'll make room."

He knew better than to argue when she stood with her hands at her waist and her chin had that determined line. And he was grateful his nephew wouldn't see the inside of the house and the full extent of the damage until after it was cleaned up.

His nephew grinned. "Will you read me a story and tuck me in at bedtime?"

She faltered as if the air had been drawn out of her, and her expression fell into what had to be regret or grief. Her arms wrapped around her middle in a pro-tective pose. For a second. She straightened again. By sheer will, if Eli had to guess.

"We'll see," she said, and he wished he could bet-ter discern her tone. "Lots to do before then, ain't so?"

"But I can't wait to find out what happens to the boy and girl in the story you've been reading at school. Do they get down from the top of the mountain?"

She wagged a finger at his nephew, once again self-assured and playful. "Letting you hear before the oth-ers wouldn't be fair, would it?" With a laugh, she urged him to put the strawberries away so they stayed fresh.

As Kyle went to put the bowl in the refrigerator, Eli found himself lost in Miriam's eyes again. He stepped forward and cupped her cheek. He ran his thumb across her lower lip. It was as silken soft as he'd imagined while he'd stared at her mouth during their lessons… and other times, too.

The slamming of the refrigerator door brought him to his senses. He dropped his hand and hurried outside.

Only when he reached the schoolhouse and was searching for pieces of plywood to cover the broken windows did he realize she hadn't halted his questing touch. He grinned. Maybe she felt something more for him than friendship. He intended to find out.

Chapter Ten

Miriam waited while her three friends edged past her and stepped out of Hank's van. She climbed out into the cloying heat and turned as the retired farmer called out to them.

"You said you wanted me to pick you up at the carnival grounds at nine." He rubbed his fingers against his chin. "Are you sure you don't want to stay and watch the fireworks?"

When Annie shot a glance at her, Miriam wanted to sigh. She understood more and more how much Caleb wished someone else would step forward to be the settlement's leader. Somehow, though she didn't know when or how or why, Miriam had been made the leader of the Spinsters' Club.

But Annie should understand why Hank was confused. Miriam had become so used to having Hank in their lives that she'd forgotten Hank, as an *Englischer*, used daylight saving time.

"You're right, Hank," she replied, not bothering to explain the simple mistake. "We're going to want to stay for the fireworks."

"They're scheduled for around nine thirty, but sometimes they don't get started until around ten. I'll be getting there a little before that to find a good place to watch. There's a dead-end street close to the carnival grounds. I should be able to find a parking space on it later in the evening. Look for the van after the fireworks. It should be easy to find. I'll let you know if I have to park somewhere else." He looked past them. "There's got to be ten times the number of vehicles in town today than usual."

And twenty times as many people as she'd ever seen before, Miriam realized as she and her friends crossed at the stoplight so they could stand in front of the library to watch the parade. Or that was where they'd planned to stand. It was obvious between the crowd gathered there and the raised table where two men and a woman were seated, it wouldn't be a *gut* place for her and her friends to view the parade.

The handwritten signs on the chairs announced the people at the table were judges. She wasn't sure what they were going to judge, but she heard spectators talking about floats in the parade.

Annie said, "It was nice of Hank to ask us about staying for the fireworks."

"Because he wants to watch them, too." Leanna winked at Miriam.

Her twin made a face. "Why didn't he say so?"

Miriam shrugged. "Who knows why men do any of the things they do?"

She regretted the words as soon as she spoke them, because the other three women stopped and regarded her with curiosity.

"Is something wrong? I thought you and Eli were

getting along well," said Leanna, ever the romantic. "He and his nephew have been over at your house most evenings, and you invited them to stay with you and Caleb until their house was safe to live in again."

"You know why they've come over in the evening. I'm teaching Eli to read lips."

Annie tapped her own. "Read my lips." She made a loud, smacking sound. "Kiss me, my darling."

Heat rose up Miriam's face and the twins began to giggle when an *Englisch* woman regarded them as if they'd lost their minds. They must be if they were discussing such things on the sidewalk where anyone could hear. Though they spoke in *Deitsch* among themselves, the teasing tones and the laughter spoke the truth in any language. And there were *Englisch* words interspersed, words they'd learned first in *Englisch* or had no real equivalent in *Deitsch*.

"They haven't been at the house the last couple of nights," Miriam said. "Eli's cleared away enough of the downed tree so they could get to the house. He's already made temporary repairs. Caleb said it was a real blessing nothing was badly damaged."

"Or no one." Sarah took Miriam's hand and squeezed it, the motion speaking more loudly than any words.

Aiming a smile at her friend, Miriam motioned with her head along the street. She kept taking surreptitious glances in every direction as she walked with her friends. Had Eli and Kyle arrived yet? They'd spent two nights with her and Caleb, and she hadn't had a chance to talk to Eli since then. Kyle gave her updates every day on the repairs his *onkel* had completed, and she guessed Eli would be back to work at the schoolhouse tomorrow to finish up the last few things before the scholars could use it.

Her skin tingled when she recalled how Eli's fingers had caressed her cheek before slipping along her lips. If Kyle closing the refrigerator door hadn't interrupted, would Eli have kissed her? Would she have let him?

She sighed as she thought of her reaction to his nephew's simple request for her to read to him and tuck him in. Eli had taken note of it. She was grateful he'd refrained from asking her why she'd acted as she had. Otherwise, she would have had to spill the past she wanted to put behind her for *gut*. But she couldn't forget the joy of putting Ralph to bed at her house when Yost had been too far away to get home before the boy's bedtime. It had happened more and more as their wedding day approached, but she'd seen it as a chance to spend extra time with Ralph. She'd also wanted to be supportive of Yost's business that had, for reasons he'd never explained, required him to be away several nights each week.

But cuddling the little boy and listening to his prayers and reading him to sleep had ended along with her betrothal.

Miriam shoved those memories away. Today wasn't for letting the past swallow her again. It was for enjoying a celebration with neighbors, both *Englisch* and plain.

Where were Eli and Kyle? She saw no sign of them.

Sweat bubbled on her forehead as they continued along the street. Maybe she should have worn her black bonnet, but the brim wouldn't have offered much of a reprieve from the sun in the cloudless sky. She breathed a sigh of relief when she stepped into the shade from the trees between the sidewalk and the road.

Finding a cool spot, she stood by her friends and waited for the parade to start...and for Eli to arrive.

Eli led his horse into one of the empty bays in the old firehouse. He saw two other buggies parked out front, one of them LaVon's bright yellow one. Miriam and her friends had arranged for the van to bring them into Salem. Had others done something similar? He hoped more people from the new settlement would come to enjoy the evening. Kyle had told him for the past few days the *kinder* had discussed nothing other than the parade and upcoming carnival. As the events began after milking should be done, a tradition from a time when *Englischers* worked the small farms that surrounded the village, the other families along Harmony Creek should be arriving soon.

Looking at his nephew, who was rocking from one foot to the other in his excitement, he grinned. Kyle must have checked the clock in the kitchen every five minutes, waiting for when they would leave for the village.

Eli motioned for his nephew to follow him toward the street. The parade's start time was still almost a half hour away, and Kyle wasn't the only one excited about it. Other *kinder* raced along the sidewalks edging the road and the parking lanes that were wide enough for two cars.

Or one big tractor and a flatbed trailer, he realized when he looked north along Main Street and saw the equipment parked in front of the small, red building. It had been built as a movie theater decades before and now served as a *doktor*'s office. A small structure that appeared to be made out of cardboard and construction paper sat in the middle of the flatbed where hay bales had probably been stacked a few days ago.

Two popcorn wagons, their silver sides glinting in the sunshine and the aroma of butter and salt the best advertisement of their wares, were parked on opposite sides of the street. Lines snaked away from them as people waited to buy popcorn, peanuts and other treats.

Eli sensed the curious glances aimed at him and his nephew. Unlike the *Englischers*, who were dressed in shorts and casual T-shirts and baseball caps, they wore dark brown broadfall trousers, light blue shirts and their straw hats. He nodded to people he recognized from doing errands in the village and smiled at others.

"Have you ever seen so many people?" Kyle asked as he held tightly to Eli's hand so they didn't get separated in the crowd clogging the sidewalk. "Everyone in the county must be here. Maybe the whole state."

"And beyond." He was amazed at how easily he discerned what his nephew was saying. Miriam had been correct. Before he had begun lessons with her, he'd already been reading lips without being aware of it.

Kyle bounced on every step as they headed south toward where there were some open places among the crowd where they could get a *gut* view of the parade. The stoplight at the intersection of Main and Broadway was being ignored while two county sheriffs directed cars and pedestrians. Other officers would halt traffic going through the village while the bands and floats followed the parade route toward the carnival grounds on Archibald Street.

They found a spot close to the bridge over White

Creek. As Eli glanced at the shallow water flowing between two stone walls, he thought of the stories he'd been told about how a hurricane a few years before had turned that trickle into a torrent. Water had spread out more than a quarter of a mile across the village, turning Broadway, the street that became the road running past Harmony Hollow, into a raging river. Dozens of homes had been damaged.

Tonight the creek flowed innocently beneath the bridge. A few fish darted through the clear water. When Kyle noticed them, he leaned against the concrete wall and stood on his tiptoes.

Eli resisted the urge to warn him to be careful. He couldn't be overprotective, but kept glancing toward his nephew until someone tapped Eli's arm.

His heart jumped. Hoping Miriam was trying to get his attention, he turned to see a tall, thin *Englischer* with a graying mustache and a navy baseball cap with a bright B in the center.

Boston Red Sox, Eli translated. The baseball team in Boston was another subject that transfixed Kyle.

"Are you the Amish carpenter?" asked the man. "Eli Troyer?"

He nodded. "That's me."

"Tuck Rossi over at the hardware store said you were looking for work. Do you have a business card?" The man didn't give him a chance to answer before going on. "My wife has been reminding me that we need to do something about our sagging sunporch. Is that something you could take care of?"

"I can tell you once I've had a chance to examine the porch."

"Can you stop by soon?" The *Englischer* grinned. "I'm John Osborne, by the way."

"How about the day after tomorrow in the morning?" It was the best time for Eli because Kyle would be at school.

John agreed so eagerly Eli guessed the porch must be in dire condition. Getting the man's address, which was close to where the carnival was being held on Archibald Street, Eli shook John's proffered hand before John went across the street to where an elderly woman and a bunch of *kinder* stood. When the youngsters greeted John with enthusiasm, Eli guessed they were John's *kins-kinder*.

"Who was that?" asked Kyle as he pushed away from the bridge to move to where he could see the parade.

"A man who may have a job for me."

The boy's eyes widened. "And you were able to talk to him without me?"

"*Ja*. I've learned a lot from Miriam."

Kyle stared at the ground and mumbled something.

When Eli was about to ask him to repeat it, a siren blared so loudly he couldn't miss it. He put his hands on his nephew's shoulders, ready to pull him back if a police car raced along the empty road.

It inched along the street instead. It must be the signal that the parade was about to begin. People around him clapped and cheered and called joking remarks to the two officers, who waved through the open windows.

Moments later the car was followed by a group of teenagers dressed in black trousers and white shirts with purple and gold scarves around their shoulders. They were playing a variety of musical instruments. He guessed they were the band from the local high school. He didn't recognize the song, but the band played it with enthusiasm as they marched with heads high. Several of the younger students were out of step, but the spectators cheered as they went past.

"You know what, *Onkel* Eli?" asked Kyle after tugging on his sleeve to get his attention.

"What?"

"We need to get some drums." He made motions with his hands as if he held drumsticks. "I could play them while you play your harmonica. It would sound great!"

"Definitely loud." He hadn't unpacked his harmonica since their arrival in the new settlement. Was this Kyle's way of saying it was long past due? Ruffling Kyle's hair, he said, "Look! Here comes the Salem Volunteer Fire Department."

The boy was enchanted by the antique horse-drawn pumper being pulled by two men in old-fashioned turnout gear and bright red T-shirts. The firefighters had buckets attached to their trousers, and they tossed candy to kids on both sides of the street. Kyle joined the others running to collect pieces of hard candy and gum.

Eli smiled when his nephew offered a toddler boy a share of what he'd gotten.

The little boy grinned and selected a few pieces.

"What do you say?" his *mamm* prompted.

He assumed the *kind* said *danki*, because the woman smiled.

"Stick with me." Kyle puffed his thin chest out as he ruffled the *kind*'s hair as Eli had his. "We'll get more the next time." He pointed to his mouth where one of his upper teeth had fallen out that morning. "I'll give the sticky ones to you cuz my other tooth is loose."

Caught between being delighted at how much of the conversation he could understand as he looked from one person to another and his nephew remembering his lessons about sharing and helping others, Eli accepted the thanks the *Englisch* lady gave him.

"How cute is that?" asked Miriam as she stepped forward.

How long had she been standing nearby? Not long, he guessed, because Kyle waved in excitement when he saw her. As he had before, he rushed over to embrace her. The boy showed off the candy he'd picked up and motioned for her to help herself.

Eli didn't catch what Miriam and his nephew said to each other because their heads were bent together. He guessed she'd urged Kyle to enjoy his bounty. It wasn't easy to think about anything else when he had a *wunderbaar* excuse to look at her pretty features. Not just her lips, but her twinkling eyes and the gentle curve of her high cheekbones. Even with the heat, she managed to look fresh.

When Kyle saw a tractor and flatbed wagon approaching, he hurried to where the little boy was waiting for him. They grinned as candy flew off the float. Some things about the size of Kyle's fist were tossed, as well.

Kyle picked up one.

"You can have it," Kyle said as he handed the small red plastic tractor to the littler boy.

The *kind* beamed and jumped up and down with his excitement. He gave Kyle a big hug before spinning to show the toy to his *mamm*.

"That was very kind of you, Kyle," Miriam said.

"He's an *Englischer*, and it was an *Englisch* tractor," the boy replied with a youngster's logic.

The little boy tugged on Kyle's arm. When Kyle

looked at him, the *kind* smiled and said something Eli couldn't hear.

Miriam tapped Eli's arm. When he looked at her, she smiled. "Kyle's little friend said T-A-N-K E-W."

Eli chuckled along with her as the little boy went to stand beside his *mamm*. "They create a language all their own when they're little."

Kyle pointed at another trio of fire trucks rolling in the middle of the street. They were from three different nearby villages. He'd heard of Cambridge and Greenwich, but not Argyle. Each vehicle was met with shouts and cheers. When they blew their sirens or honked their resonant horns, he wasn't surprised Kyle and the little boy and half of the other spectators put their hands over their ears. The sound blared through his hearing aids, but he didn't turn them down. He didn't want to miss a moment of the excitement.

"Kyle told me that you're about finished repairing the house," Miriam said as the trucks rolled past.

"The roof didn't take long to repair, and the tree's been cleared away. Plenty of *gut* firewood for next winter."

She gave an emoted shudder. "I want to enjoy summer before I think about cold weather again."

"Agreed." He couldn't halt the thought of holding her close on a cold winter night. Sitting by the stove in his house on the simple sofa he'd rescued from the used furniture dealer, he'd put his arm around her shoulders and invite her to lean her head against him. They wouldn't have to talk. Just being together would make him happy.

As it did now.

He was saved from his own fantasy by the arrival of the next float. It was filled with *kinder* and decorated to look like a dairy barn. Two teenage girls wore lacy gowns, and two younger ones were dressed in black-and-white and had horns on their heads. The latter he guessed were supposed to be cows that belonged to the other boys and girls who wore overalls and straw hats.

Farmers, he was sure.

That was confirmed when he saw the sign on the side of the decorated hay wagon. The two in the fancy gowns were that year's Washington County Dairy Princess and the runner-up to the title. The girls waved, and the younger *kinder* threw more candy toward the spectators.

Again, Kyle took the little boy by the hand and helped him gather up pieces. They giggled together and compared what they'd gotten.

A bigger boy reached around the little boy and snatched the candy out of his hand. The *kind* began to cry.

Kyle stepped toward the boy, then paused. He glanced over his shoulder at his *onkel*.

Eli said nothing. Kyle knew the importance of not getting into fights. He'd been taught he must turn the other cheek and avoid any violence, no matter the circumstances. Still, his nephew needed to make such a decision himself.

The taller boy stuck out his chin as if daring Kyle to hit him. The nearby adults looked on in shock.

By Kyle's sides, his hands started to curl into fists. He halted himself and turned to the little boy. Holding out his right hand with several types of candy to the *kind*, he yelped when the bigger boy grabbed Kyle's candy, too, and then laughed.

That laughter disappeared when a man in a deputy sheriff's uniform stepped forward and grabbed the boy by the shoulder. The deputy was such a broad man, the boy who'd taken the candy seemed puny in comparison.

"Did I see you steal candy from these boys?" the deputy asked. Without giving him a chance to answer, he growled, "Give it back and apologize."

"Sorry," mumbled the boy as he handed Kyle the candy.

Kyle gave it to the little boy as the deputy ordered, "Say it louder."

"Sorry," repeated the boy, kicking at a loose stone. It skittered onto the road.

Kyle stepped forward and looked at the tall deputy. "Sir, he can have my candy if he wants it."

The deputy was speechless, and other people around them looked even more astonished.

"I've got plenty," Kyle continued, and Eli realized his nephew had mistaken the man's amazement for hesitation to accept the offer from a *kind* he didn't know. "If he wants it, he can have it."

"But he was going to steal it from you and that little guy," said the deputy.

"I know, but it's important we forgive those who trespass against us." He looked at the boy who was half a head taller than he was. "If you want my candy, you can have it." He held up his left hand and unfolded his fingers to reveal five pieces.

The boy took one, then a second piece. "Thanks."

"Your boy?" asked the deputy, looking at Eli.

"Ja." It wasn't easy to keep his pride with Kyle out of his voice. He hoped God would forgive him for the burst of *hochmut*.

"You've taught him well."

Eli nodded his thanks, and the deputy walked away, herding the boy ahead of him.

When another float came by and balloons floated out to be batted among the spectators, Miriam gave him a smile that seemed to reach inside him and soothe the pain that had been his companion for the past four years. He didn't notice when a balloon bounced off his head or Kyle's laughter as he hit it to someone else. All he saw was her smile.

"The policeman is right," she said. "You have taught Kyle well."

"I've tried."

"And succeeded. I've worked with *kinder* since I was sixteen, and not many of them—whether plain or *Englisch*—would be so forgiving and generous. Kyle is blessed to have you in his life." She took his hand and held it between both of hers. "And so am I."

When she released his hand and began to laugh as she looked at where Kyle was again helping the littler boy gather a collection of candy and small toys, Eli wished he had an excuse to touch her again. He was determined to find a way before the night was over.

Chapter Eleven

Miriam was glad she and Eli held Kyle's hands as they walked in the middle of the street. No vehicle traffic was allowed on the route the parade had followed. With the rush of people, she wondered how anyone could have gone in the opposite direction.

Though only one side of the street had a sidewalk, people walked on both, tramping through front yards, as well as down the road. Every front porch was filled with celebrants who'd had great seats for the parade that passed right by their homes. American flags flew from almost every house, and some were decked with bunting. Decorative banners hung at the front of about half of the houses with appliquéd pictures of balloons and puppies and summer scenes.

Behind the houses, Miriam saw the flat wagons used for floats parked out of the way. Tissue paper and streamers fluttered in the evening breeze, and pieces that had escaped from chicken wire and staples bounced along the ground.

"Be careful there," called a woman.

Miriam looked at the porch to her right. Two *kinder*

were trying to edge past a trio of tables where cakes, pies and plates of cookies were arranged. How many guests was the family expecting?

She got her answer when another woman stopped at the bottom of the steps and held up a cake topped by coconut frosting. The woman with the cake apologized for being so late with her contribution to the cake auction.

Scanning the tables, Miriam smiled when she saw the donations from her friends in the Spinsters' Club. Annie had made a cake that looked as stunning as something Caleb might have made. Sarah's wasn't as fancy, but the bright green frosting made it stand out. Leanna had sent a heaping plate of chocolate chip cookies.

Caleb had delivered all the goodies earlier in the afternoon before crowds made it impossible to navigate with a cake in each hand. She walked toward the porch to admire the variety and quantity of cakes. There must be almost two dozen arranged on the table.

"Which one is yours?" asked Eli when he came to stand beside her.

"That one," Kyle said before she could answer. He pointed to a round cake with grape jelly as well as buttercream frosting. "I'm right, ain't so?"

She was astonished, and as she nodded, she could tell Eli was, too.

"Don't be surprised," the boy said. "That's the same grape jelly you sent to us the day we arrived."

"Kyle," Miriam said, putting a hand on his arm when she saw Eli struggling to understand what the *kind* had said. "Slow and simple, remember?"

His nephew nodded and spoke slower. "It is the purplest purple I've ever seen." He looked at her. When she smiled, he looked as proud as if he'd been the grand marshal of the parade.

"In all your six years?" asked Eli.

"*Ja*. I have eaten lots and lots of jelly sandwiches." His grin widened. "Lots and lots and lots."

"Which is why you're growing like a weed." Eli tapped the top of his nephew's straw hat. "This is going to be even with mine soon."

The boy grinned.

"Aren't you a firefighter?" the woman on the porch asked Eli.

"*Ja*. Yes, ma'am, I am."

"Good. You're here just in time. We need to get the rest of these donations to the carnival for the sweets auction."

Miriam grinned as Eli looked at her and arched his brows. He didn't say anything to her as he climbed the two steps and asked, "How can I help?"

"Wait right there." The woman called to two younger *Englisch* women who'd been chatting on the other side of the porch.

As they walked to the table, they admired Eli, though they looked away if his eyes shifted in their direction.

Miriam despised the twinge of something unpleasant in her middle. She didn't like how the women were boldly ogling Eli and how he politely smiled in return. She was glad when the older woman returned with two cut-down cardboard boxes.

After putting two cakes in each box, she set the wider one on top of the other. She held them out to Eli.

"Here you go," the woman said. "Thank you for helping, young man."

Kyle laughed at his *onkel* being addressed as a young

man, but couldn't hide how much he wished he was old enough to tote a box himself to the carnival.

They continued along the street with Kyle walking a couple of steps ahead to clear a path for Eli and the cakes. When Miriam glanced back, she saw several other firefighters waiting to help with delivering the desserts to the carnival grounds. She smiled as the two young women flirted with them as they had with Eli.

She shouldn't have gotten upset over the flirts. Eli hadn't invited it, and the young women obviously were just having fun.

Grant me the wisdom to see the truth, Lord, not what I fear is happening. I will try to hand my fears to You, so I can come to see how infinitesimal they truly are.

"Are you all right?" asked Eli as he looked at her.

She hadn't realized she'd stopped while sending up her heartfelt prayer. "I'm doing fine. Let's go. I can't wait to see what you firefighters have devised for our entertainment tonight."

"I know what you mean." He winked at her and continued along the street. "I can't wait, either."

She matched his steps while anticipation bubbled through her as she looked forward to the evening to come. It was going to be *wunderbaar*.

The carnival grounds consisted of a half dozen white buildings. One was almost as large as the first floor of Miriam's house, but the others were narrow and only wide enough to hold two or three people. Open squares built of narrow boards were set in the center between the smaller buildings. Cars were parked in surprisingly even rows on the grass along with three buggies. Smells of hot dogs and hamburgers and sweets reached out to lure them into the carnival.

Eli was astonished how many people had come to the carnival grounds. The few permanent buildings housed games for *kinder* and adults who were young at heart. A long line was in front of the open area where players could test their skill at sinking a miniature basketball in a small hoop. When someone managed to make a basket, shouts resounded over the music from a deejay.

Once he'd delivered the boxes to the biggest building where the cake auction would be held in a few hours, he set off to explore the carnival with Miriam and Kyle. He wasn't sure which of them was the most excited to be there. As they walked around, trying not be separated by the eddies of people, they looked in the booths.

"They're all skill games," Miriam said with a big grin. "Putting a ring around a bottle top or tossing a coin on a dish or breaking a balloon with a dart. I didn't expect that." Laughing, she added, "I didn't know what would be here, so everything is a surprise."

"So you're not going to try to win a goldfish by tossing a Ping-Pong ball in a bowl?"

She laughed again. "Caleb has been talking about getting a dog, and I can see the dog lapping water out of the poor fish's bowl."

Kyle grabbed his arm. "Look, *Onkel* Eli. That man is saying anyone can win a stuffed toy by knocking over three burlap cats. Can I try?"

"It won't be as easy as they make it sound," he warned.

"But I throw *gut*." He puffed out his thin chest. "I've pitched twice at school."

Putting his arm around his nephew's shoulders, he

said, "You can try it once. There are other games I know you'll want to play, too."

Kyle rushed to the firefighter who was manning the booth and gave him two quarters. As the firefighter, one Eli hadn't met yet, handed three baseballs to the boy, he asked, "Who's going to throw?"

"Me!" Kyle grinned and bounced from one foot to the other. He dropped one of the balls, but Miriam snagged it before it could roll far away.

While Kyle took his place to throw, Eli introduced himself to the other man. They watched, along with Miriam, as Kyle drew back his arm to throw the ball at the stuffed burlap cats set in a pyramid on a narrow shelf.

The boy grunted as he hurled. The ball bounced off one cat, which rocked but didn't tumble off the shelf. The next two balls sailed over the uppermost cat.

Kyle didn't say anything as he shuffled aside to let the next thrower have his turn.

Eli debated between consoling his nephew and saying nothing. He wasn't sure which he should do.

Beside him, Miriam didn't seem to have any qualms. "That first throw was *gut*, Kyle."

"It didn't knock the cats over."

"No, but you did hit one. If you'd been throwing in a ball game, that would have been a strike."

"It would have been, wouldn't it?" The *kind* perked up. "Who wants a stuffed dog anyhow? I'd rather be a *gut* pitcher."

Eli smiled at Miriam over the little boy's head. She was *wunderbaar* with *kinder*, and she would be a great *mamm* someday.

No, he wasn't going to think of the future. He wanted to enjoy the evening.

Had he missed his chance, he wondered when Miriam excused herself and went to talk to her friends? He couldn't monopolize her time, though the bare light bulbs hanging from wires strung from booth to booth and across the center didn't seem so bright and festive when she walked away.

Taking Kyle by the hand, he went with his nephew to the next booth. It was identical to the previous one, except there were three pyramids of empty vegetable cans. Two air guns rested on the board across the front of the booth at the perfect height for a teen to rest an elbow on while firing. A wooden crate waited for young *kinder* to use.

"Try this, Kyle." Eli paid Chief Pulaski, who was in charge of the booth, then handed an air gun to the boy. "Aim at a can. One at a time."

Kyle climbed on the crate before taking the air gun with the piece of cork stuck into the barrel. He hefted it to his shoulder and leaned his elbow on the edge of the booth.

Eli held his breath as the boy did before squeezing the trigger. The small chunk of cork hit the empty can, knocking it off the others. He did the same with his second shot, but the third one missed.

"Good shooting, young man," Chief Pulaski said. "You need to have your uncle bring you to the gun safety course at the courthouse as soon as you're eight years old. You'll learn to handle guns and have a chance to shoot them."

"Can I?" Kyle asked, his eyes glittering like the stars appearing in the sky.

"Ask me again when you are eight," Eli said, taking the gun and handing it to the chief. "Until then, no guns for you. Except if you want to visit this booth again next year."

Kyle's grin was almost too wide for his young face when he took the plastic whistle the chief held out to him.

"Go ahead," the older man said. "Try it out and make sure it works."

The boy put the whistle to his lips and blew. Its shrill squeal silenced the people around them.

"Are you trying to convince the firefighters to get rid of their sirens and give you the job?" asked Eli.

"He's loud enough," the chief replied. "Better put it in your pocket, son, and save it for when you get home." He winked at Eli. "That way, you'll disturb only a few people at a time."

Eli laughed, though the shrill sound had been intensified painfully by his hearing aids. Taking Kyle's hand again, he continued around the carnival, which seemed to be growing more crowded by the minute.

When they passed a roped-off area where a girl was walking a horse around in a circle with a small *kind* on its back, Kyle said, "Next year let's bring a horse and give rides."

"We don't have a saddle horse."

"Yet. We're going to get one, ain't so?"

"Ja." He smiled at his nephew, knowing how much the boy missed riding their neighbor's pony in Delaware. "Once we build another stall in the barn, we'll start looking around for a pony."

Kyle shook his head. "A horse. I'm getting too big for a pony."

"Let's see what we can find." He turned to see Miriam and her friends strolling toward them.

His nephew raced toward her, edging around people and managing not to bump into anyone. When Kyle showed her the whistle he'd won at the shooting booth,

Eli didn't have to see his face to know he was telling her everything about the experience.

Sarah, Annie and Leanna greeted Eli with smiles when he joined their group. Though he saw the curiosity in their eyes as they looked from him to Miriam, none of them asked any questions.

When Annie invited him to join them for the cake auction, he agreed…a few seconds after Kyle gave his enthusiastic answer. His nephew grinned at him, and Eli wondered if the boy had picked out the cake he wanted his *onkel* to bid on. If it was the one Miriam had made, that was sure to cause talk, but the funds were going to the fire department and he could put up with *gut-*natured teasing.

The women found a spot off to the left of the building where they would have an excellent view of the auctioneer, who was the assistant fire chief Robert Quartermaine. The firemen called him "Q" not because of his name, but because, as they'd told Eli, the assistant chief was as bald as a cue ball.

Miriam motioned to him and Kyle. "Don't bid on my cake. I'll make you one if you'd like. Buy someone else's cake, so you can sample something different."

Eli nodded, wondering if she'd made the offer to keep from putting them in an embarrassing situation. He told himself to stop looking for ulterior motives. She was being nice, and he should appreciate that and enjoy her company.

Now *that* was a plan for the evening.

Miriam gazed at the overhead lights and the moths dancing around them. Everyone and everything was having fun at the carnival. Walking through the crowd that hadn't diminished though it was getting late, she took care her cotton candy didn't get bumped. The sticky froth would cement itself to clothing or hair.

She smiled when Eli and Kyle walked toward her. The two were deep in conversation. Kyle continued, she noticed, to make the same type of motions he had before Eli began reading lips. A habit? She wondered if the boy realized what he was doing. When she had the opportunity, she'd speak to Eli about it. Not in front of his nephew, because she didn't want to embarrass the *kind*.

They paused to look at the ground, and Miriam watched how Eli pointed out something to the boy. Anyone seeing them together couldn't fail to notice the strong bond between the tall, broad-shouldered man and the little boy. In the stark light from the bare bulbs overhead, glints in Eli's hair were almost as bright red as Kyle's ginger hair.

Eli stood straighter, and his gaze found hers over the people walking between them. He walked toward her, his eyes glowing with the special warmth that urged her to believe in love again. Knowing she was risking her heart, his smile and easy gait dared her to throw caution aside.

When he stopped in front of her, he asked, "Have you been having a *gut* time with your friends?"

"Ja." It was the truth. There was no reason to tell him that, even while she was walking around with the other members of the Spinsters' Club, she'd watched for any glimpse of him and his nephew.

Kyle skipped to them. "What's that?"

"This?" She smiled. "It's cotton candy and my weakness. I can't resist it." She offered the column of spun sugar to Kyle and then to Eli.

They each took a small piece. When his nephew's eyes widened as they savored the sweetness, Eli reached into his pocket.

"How much is it?" he asked.

"A dollar," she replied.

He handed four quarters to Kyle. "Meet us here as soon as you get your cotton candy."

"Danki," the boy shouted over his shoulder as he ran toward where the spun sugar was being sold.

"He said—"

He interrupted Miriam. "I guessed what he said."

"You're getting much better at reading lips and body language."

"I'm trying."

She offered him another bite of the cotton candy. When he looked at his fingers that were already stained blue, he shook his head with a grin. He did sample a small piece of Kyle's pink cotton candy when the boy came back to them.

A man followed him. She realized it was Lyndon Wagler, who was a couple years older than his twin sisters, Annie and Leanna. With him was his son, also named Lyndon but called Junior. He and Kyle sat next to each other during school.

Miriam picked at her cotton candy as Lyndon talked to Eli, and Kyle showed off his whistle to his friend. She could wander away and find her friends, but she didn't because she wanted to spend more time with Eli.

"We're going fishing in the morning," Lyndon said. "Junior is wondering if Kyle would like to spend the night tonight and go with us."

Junior added, *"Komm* over, Kyle. We'll have a lot of fun, and *Daed* says we can cook the fish we catch."

When Kyle hesitated, Miriam was bewildered. She'd expected Kyle to leap at the chance to join his friend.

"That sounds like fun," Eli said. "Go if you'd like, Kyle."

"I can stay and help you understand what's going on," Kyle said.

"I'm fine. Go and have fun. If I need help talking to someone, Miriam will help me."

The boy hesitated, an odd look on his face, and then nodded before he walked away with Lyndon and Junior.

Watching them, Miriam said, "Kyle has had too much responsibility for too long." She put her fingers to her lips, but lowered them as she added, "I didn't mean to criticize."

"You aren't saying anything I haven't thought," Eli replied. "That's why I wanted him to go and have fun."

"You're a *gut onkel*."

"And you've got blue lips." He laughed. "Someone would think you were freezing to death."

Teasing each other, they walked to where people were gathering to watch the fireworks that would be shot off in the next half hour. Eli knew an excellent place to view them and asked her to go with him. She agreed, stopping long enough to let her friends know she would meet them at the van later. She hoped Eli didn't notice the knowing grins the other young women exchanged.

Eli led her past Hank's van. The driver was standing beside it, bending another man's ear. Not slowing, Eli walked to the end of the street and the cornfield beyond it. The young stalks of corn stood higher than her knees, a *gut* sign according to farmers' old adage of having corn be "knee-high by the Fourth of July" in order to get an abundant harvest before the first frost.

A fire engine was parked at the edge of the field. He called a greeting to his fellow firefighters. They were leaning against the engine in nonchalant poses, but they'd leap into action if a firework fell to the ground and ignited the grass.

She enjoyed talking with Eli as they waited for the show to begin. The street behind them became thick with spectators, and she was glad he'd suggested finding a spot when he did. Anticipation became almost tangible as the clock ticked past the scheduled starting time, but nobody complained.

Then with a *whoosh* and a *boom* that rattled the windows of the houses along the street, the first rocket exploded into shades of red, white and blue.

"Wow!" Miriam gasped.

Eli turned down his hearing aids as he said, "You're supposed to say 'Oooo' first, then 'Aaaah.'"

She looked at him, then at the sky as another explosion, this one bright white, scattered the darkness. "I didn't know there were rules."

"I didn't, either, but Kyle informed me today that was how I was supposed to react when the fireworks were set off." He paused as another thud followed an explosion that looked like a giant, golden weeping willow in the sky.

Too soon the show was over. Everyone clapped and shouted before turning to return to their cars and homes. The Fourth of July celebrations were over for another year.

When Eli didn't follow the others, Miriam asked,

"Do you need to help with cleanup at the carnival grounds?"

"That's scheduled for tomorrow. The new guys are expected to put in a few hours." His voice softened as he said, "I know you're planning on going home with your friends. But I'm headed that way, too, and if you'd like, you can ride with me. The evening's been too much fun to let it end now."

Her heart did a pirouette in her chest. "*Ja, danki.* I'd like that."

He smiled, and she was sure every bone inside her melted. Oh, she was getting in way too deep! *It's just a ride home with a friend.* She was trying to delude herself. And failing big-time. She was thrilled to imagine sitting beside him in his buggy as they drove through the humid night.

"Slim is at the old firehouse next to the library. It's far enough away so the fireworks shouldn't have spooked him." He readjusted his hearing aids and held out his hand. "Shall we go and see how he's doing?"

She started to put hers in it, then paused. "Before we go, I need to let my friends know so they do not wait and wait for me by the van."

"Your Harmony Creek Spinsters' Club friends?"

Fire erupted up Miriam's face as Eli grinned. In the streetlight's glow, she could see his eyes twinkling. She resisted her urge to cross her arms in front of her and meet his gaze. He'd become too skilled at reading body language, and she didn't want to give him any clue to her embarrassment.

"How do you know that name?" she asked in a careful tone.

"Menno heard his sister talking with the Wagler

twins, and one of them mentioned the four of you had started a frolic group called the Harmony Creek Spinsters' Club."

"The name is a joke."

"I guessed that, but it's a joke I like because I have never seen your cheeks so rosy before."

"You can't see that at night."

"I can imagine it." He ran a crooked finger along her left cheek. "And I can feel it."

Aware of how many people lingered along the street, she lowered her head, though his touch was beyond delightful. She went to the van, but only Hank was there. She asked him to tell her friends she had another ride home. He nodded and returned to his conversation. She was relieved she didn't have to see her friends' smiles that warned her they were planning to tease her the next time they were together. At least Eli wouldn't witness it.

Together they strolled back the way they'd come. When Eli took her hand, Miriam moved a half step closer to him. A few other people walked toward Main Street, and none of them paid any attention to her and Eli.

Moonlight streamed along the street as they headed north hand in hand. Cars went by, but the sidewalks were growing deserted beneath the bright moon and scattered stars. They stopped to collect Slim, who nickered a greeting at Eli's arrival. He hitched the horse and climbed into the buggy to sit beside her. Was he as aware as she was of how nothing was between them, not even his nephew?

By the time they reached the edge of the village, the only sounds beyond the peepers were the rattle of the wheels and the clatter of Slim's horseshoes on the asphalt. Eli reached out and took her hand, drawing her along the seat to him. Leaning her head on his shoulder, she gazed at the stars poking through the darkness above the mountains.

The buggy slowed to make the turn onto the road along the creek. When he drew in the horse, stopping them, she asked if everything was all right.

Instead of replying, he contracted his arm to tilt her toward him. His fingers beneath her chin brought her face toward his. He gave her no time to protest, though she couldn't have imagined uttering a single word as she looked into his moonlit face. He slanted his mouth across hers. The enthralling sensation of his lips on hers banished every thought but of the moment. As his lips thrilled hers, her fingers slid to curve around his shoulders. She clasped her hands at his nape, and he showered kisses across her cheeks until she laughed with joy.

He drew back enough to say, "You taste as sweet as cotton candy."

"Because I had some, remember?"

"No, that's not what I meant. Maybe I should have said cotton candy tastes as sweet as you."

He claimed her lips again, and she welcomed his kiss, for once not caring what she was risking.

Chapter Twelve

Eli woke smiling. The memory of the buggy ride home last night was as *wunderbaar* as his favorite dream, but it'd been real. For so long he'd imagined holding Miriam to his heart. When it had happened, she'd been more splendid in his embrace than he'd been able to guess. He'd given her another kiss when he dropped her off at her house. It had whetted his yearning for more kisses.

He wondered when he could ask her to go for a ride with him again. Would tonight be too soon?

Sitting, he stretched to switch on the propane light atop his bedside table. He yawned as he got up and dressed. Staying out late with a pretty girl and then rising early in the morning to do chores was something that had seemed easy when he was a young man.

But he wasn't old. He'd turned thirty-one a few months ago. Yet, in some ways, it felt as if he'd lived a complete lifetime in the past four years since his brother's death. He couldn't remember the last time he hadn't felt the weight of his obligations pressing on him. He needed to be a *gut* member of the new settlement's *Leit*, to rear Kyle and to do his best for anyone who hired him. He'd been able to forget all that while he held Miriam in his arms.

By the time Eli finished getting ready for the new day, he realized he was whistling. He couldn't remember the last time he'd done that. He didn't stop as he started *kaffi*. He broke two eggs into a cast-iron pan and began scrambling them. Making bacon, he put it on a plate while he fried toast. He spooned the scrambled eggs over the toast and carried the plate to the table. Pouring a cup of *kaffi*, he took milk out of the refrigerator and put both beside his plate that looked so alone on the big table.

He realized it was the first time he'd eaten breakfast without Kyle almost since the boy was born. As he bent his head to say silent grace, he added a prayer of thanks that God had brought Kyle a *gut* friend. He looked toward an eastern window. The sun was rising, and the boys should be having fun fishing on such a pleasant morning.

Eli drove with Menno to the carnival grounds to help his fellow firefighters empty the metal barrels that had served as trash cans. He found coins that had either fallen out of someone's pocket or skittered off one of the low platforms where quarters had been tossed at glasses and bowls. By the time he finished just before midday, he'd collected almost ten dollars, which he gave to Chief Pulaski to add to the firehouse's coffers. Others picked up change, too, increasing the profits for the carnival.

He left Menno at the Waglers' farm and went to his own. As he did each time he drove in, he glanced at the stack of firewood from the tree that had crashed into the house. He was grateful the repairs had been quick and that all the materials he needed had been available at Rossi's hardware store.

His stomach growled as he put Slim out to pasture. Going into the house, he considered what to have for his noon meal. He decided on a peanut butter and jelly sandwich with the last jar of Miriam's grape jelly.

He was about to take his first bite when the door opened. He grinned as Kyle walked in. "Did you catch a lot?"

"No." He grimaced. "Nothing was biting except mosquitoes."

"The cortisone is in the medicine cabinet upstairs. It'll take away the itch."

"I know."

Though Eli couldn't hear the boy's tone, it was easy to tell something more than a fruitless fishing trip was bothering Kyle. He looked as downtrodden as he had last night at the carnival grounds before he left with his friend. Was whatever had upset him last night still nettling him today? The boy's shoulders slumped, and he didn't meet Eli's eyes. More than once, he shifted as if he didn't want Eli to make out what he appeared to be muttering.

Eli gave him a chance to voice his distress while he made a second peanut butter and jelly sandwich. He put it and a handful of chips on a plate and set it in front of the boy. His nephew took a couple of bites and broke the potato chips into tiny pieces on his plate and moved them around with his fingertip.

Abruptly, Kyle pushed back from the table and ran into the living room.

About to call after him with a reminder Kyle needed to bow his head and share with God his gratitude for the meal before he left the table, Eli halted when he saw the little boy throw himself into the rocking chair so hard it almost tipped over.

Kyle gripped one of the vertical slats on the back and leaned his head against the rest. He didn't say anything. He didn't move. He stared at the wall.

Something had happened.

Something bad.

Eli stood, then paused to aim a prayer at God. It was an apology for being as remiss as his nephew at not showing his gratitude. However, most of his wordless prayer was asking God to give him the right words to help Kyle. The last time he'd seen his nephew sitting in the rocker like that was during the weeks after Milan and Shirley were killed. Then Kyle had spent hours in the chair, rocking and saying little.

He took one step toward the living room before the kitchen door opened.

Miriam carried in the cake she'd promised last night to make for them. She greeted him, but her smile faded when he didn't return it. Looking past him, he knew the exact moment when she saw Kyle curled into a ball, clinging to the chair. Dismay dimmed her eyes and stiffened her shoulders.

She set the cake on the table and untied her bonnet. Looking at him, she arched her brows in a silent query.

He raised his hands, palms up, in a shrug before walking to the rocker. Putting his hand on the top of the chair, he asked, "Won't you tell me what's wrong, Kyle?"

For a long minute Kyle said nothing. He bounced to his feet, his fingers curled into fists by his sides as they had during the parade. Not angry fists, but frustrated ones Eli realized when his nephew wailed, "Why did everything have to change?"

"I thought you liked living here in Harmony Creek."

"I do, but—" He hung his head.

Miriam said, "Your *onkel* can't hear you if you don't look at him."

Again Kyle hesitated, then his head jerked and his shoulders went back. He stood as stiffly as if he'd been turned into a statue. Tears filled his eyes and hung on his lashes.

"Living here isn't the only thing that's changed! We've changed. We used to be a team. You and me. That's what you've told me. Over and over. You said that you and I would always be a team."

"And we are. We always will be." He swallowed hard. His nephew's words pummeled him like a blow to the gut.

"No." His voice broke. "Not like we used to be. You don't need me anymore."

"What?" He should say more, but words deserted him.

"You know what everyone says. I'm glad you do, but you don't need me anymore. You've left me behind." He sank into the rocker. "Just like *Mamm* and *Daed* did."

Eli was struck speechless as Kyle rested one arm on the chair and wept. That his growing proficiency with reading lips would make his nephew feel abandoned had never crossed his mind. He'd thought Kyle had come to terms with Milan's and Shirley's deaths better than Eli had himself. The boy hadn't. He somehow had managed to hide his pain. Did Kyle believe as others did— including Eli—that his parents' deaths must be Eli's fault? Eli had dared to believe the boy didn't understand the depths of his guilt. Perhaps Kyle had been hiding that truth, too. A fresh flood of guilt washed over him until he felt as if he was going to drown.

"Are you okay?" Miriam mouthed, standing so Kyle couldn't read her lips.

He shook his head.

"Can I help?"

How he wanted to say *ja*! As he opened his mouth to release the truth he'd been withholding from her, the words wouldn't come. He couldn't bear the thought of her looking at him with disgust as he told her how he'd failed his brother. Others had done that, but others weren't the woman he was falling in love with.

He had to tell her. Just not when Kyle's pain seemed greater than his own.

"Help him," he said silently.

Miriam put her fingers on his arm and nodded.

Everything he'd said to the boy had been wrong. Maybe Miriam could do better. He prayed so. Once this crisis was past, he had to tell her the truth about the day Milan and Shirley had died. He trusted her with Kyle. Now he needed to trust her with the truth.

Miriam took a steadying breath. She couldn't let either Eli or Kyle down. Their bond, which had seemed unbreakable, was so fragile. They'd lost much the day Kyle's parents died. Severing the connection between them would be a tragedy, too.

She knelt by the little boy, but didn't touch him. "Kyle, Eli hasn't left you behind."

He didn't look at her. "He doesn't need my help anymore."

"Maybe not with understanding what others are saying, but he needs you in other ways. He's got this farm to take care of along with his carpentry work. Who helped him paint the chalkboard at school?"

"Me." The admission was reluctant.

"You help him in more ways than anyone can count."

"*Ja.* I help, but he doesn't need me."

She had to try something else before he stopped listening to her. "Kyle, look at me please."

Slowly, he did. His face was streaked with the trails of his tears.

"Eli does need you," she said, holding his gaze with her own. She chose every word with care, knowing the impact each could have. "Eli is here because of you. If you hadn't helped your *onkel* as you did, he might have given up."

"*Onkel* Eli doesn't give up." He glanced at Eli.

He put his hand on the boy's shoulder. "Miriam is right. Without your help, Kyle, I couldn't have imagined coming to Harmony Creek and joining this community. If you didn't help me practice, I wouldn't be able to read lips as well as I do."

"Is that true?"

As he gave his beloved nephew a gentle smile, he said, "I'll never lie to you, Kyle. No matter what happens, you can depend on me to be honest with you. There will be times when you may not like what I'm telling you. You might get angry or be sad, but you can be sure what I'm saying is the truth."

The *kind* said nothing for almost a full minute, then nodded. "So we are a team?"

"*Ja.*"

Kyle stood. "Can I have my sandwich and some new chips?"

Eli nodded. Kyle went into the kitchen and to the table. Once he was eating, Eli took Miriam's arm and steered her toward the front porch.

She went with him. No chairs offered a place to sit, and he leaned one shoulder against an upright. She clasped her hands in front of her, feeling shy with him as she never had before. Easily she could have slipped into his arms.

"Danki," he said.

"For what?"

"For convincing Kyle that he and I are a team."

She smiled. "I was telling him what anyone can see. You two have become two parts of a whole."

"Hole?" Before she could answer, he gave her a wry grimace. "You mean whole as in complete, ain't so?"

"Ja. That's one of those words where you have to figure out what's being talked about by the context. It'll get easier with time."

"Or not, but I'm going to learn how to deal with it and not berate myself for not understanding everything the first time."

She took a step toward him. When he reached for her hands, she put them in his. She laced her fingers among his and gazed at his strong face that could be so tender.

"Do the same with Kyle," she said. "Learn how to deal with him and don't berate yourself if you don't understand him the first time." A giggle slipped past her lips. "And as soon as you learn something about him, he'll change. Keep telling him how important he is to you, so he knows it deep within his heart."

"As I should keep telling you how important you are to me?"

"Ja," she said as he drew her nearer. She rested her

cheek against his chest and drank in the scents of his clothing. Her heart beat with the rhythm of his, and she couldn't imagine anywhere else she wanted to be.

He wasn't Yost. She could trust him to know she wanted the best for him and Kyle.

Couldn't she?

The first day back to school after the three-day holiday break was hot and humid. The *kinder* grew restless and had trouble concentrating on their lessons. In part, it was because they were in their new school building. The furniture had been moved in the afternoon before, and Miriam had spent an hour last night after supper hanging bright posters to add color to the white walls.

Deciding she was wasting her time—and the scholars'—by trying to teach them, she sent them outside for an early dismissal. Tomorrow, if the weather was fair, she would take them for a walk in the shady woods where they could learn about the variety of trees and look for signs of animals.

She glanced out the windows at where the scholars were playing softball. At the same time, she gathered the information she needed to write a final report on the impromptu school session. First, she compared what each *kind* had completed to the lessons in the syllabus. Almost all were ahead of where she'd prayed they'd be at this point.

God, danki *for putting a love of learning in their hearts.*

The Schmelley twins were the only ones lagging. She needed to talk to LaVon about them. In many ways the boys seemed younger than their six years. Many multiple births were complicated by the *bopplin* needing months in a hospital neonatal unit before coming home. A teacher she'd met in Lancaster had talked about being in a similar situation with her scholars. She said she'd read somewhere a *kind*'s age for judging skills, physical and mental, should be counted from the day he or she came home from the hospital, not the day they were born.

How long had the twins been in the hospital? With their *mamm* taking several weeks to recover from an infection, they probably had been kept longer than usual so LaVon could prepare himself for taking care of a sick wife and two newborns.

The twins had made enough progress, however, to satisfy the *Englisch* school superintendent. She bent to start writing the report she would give Caleb to deliver to Mr. Steele, who'd agreed, at long last, testing was unnecessary when school would be starting again in a few weeks. At that point the new teacher must begin keeping a record of the number of days school was held. That way if the *Englisch* district asked, the community could show they'd met the requirements of the state board of education.

Her pen faltered. A new teacher? Handing the job over to someone else was a sad thought, though Miriam had been so reluctant to take on the task of teaching a few weeks ago. She'd enjoyed her time with the scholars, and except for a couple of the boys who pushed her limits about the rule to stay in sight, the *kinder* had been well behaved. Eli had stopped checking on her to make sure she was keeping Kyle safe after school.

She could ask Caleb what he thought about her continuing on in the fall as the teacher. If he agreed that it was a *gut* idea, he then would speak on her behalf with the *daeds* who served as their school board and discover if they were interested in her keeping the job for a full year.

A flash of lightning brightened the school before vanishing. A thud of thunder swiftly followed. She glanced outside to see roiling clouds contorting in the sky. She hadn't noticed them building while working on the report. The storm was close, too close to let the scholars play ball or walk home along the tree-lined road.

Miriam half ran to the door and shouted for the *kinder* to come in at once. A gust of wind swept her words away. She picked up the bell by the door and rang it hard. As one, the scholars, who'd been so engrossed in their game they hadn't noticed the oncoming storm, either, whirled toward her. She motioned for them to hurry inside.

They ran toward her as another bolt struck somewhere farther south in the valley. Herding them through the door, she urged them not to stop to put the bats and balls away. That could wait until after the storm passed.

As she turned to tell them to take their seats, she gasped. Where was Kyle?

She didn't realize she'd spoken the words out loud until a boy said, "He went after the ball."

"Where?"

"It was hit into your yard. He went to get it."

Wishing this once Kyle hadn't offered to be so helpful, she strode to the door and opened it. She shouted his name over the rising wind, which whipped her skirt around her knees.

He must have heard her, because he paused and waved to her.

"Forget the ball!" she yelled and pointed at the darkening sky.

Looking in curiosity at the clouds, he didn't listen. Instead, he ran into the road just as a speeding car careened toward him.

Chapter Thirteen

The door crashed against the wall as Miriam rushed onto the school's porch. From the raised position, she could better see the car coming around the curve at a rapid speed. The driver wouldn't be able to see the boy until the last second. It'd be too late. He couldn't stop the car in time.

She called Kyle's name, but again, the wind stole her voice. Why had God sent a storm now?

She tried to run, but her legs felt like tree trunks, heavy and connected to the ground.

"Kyle!" she screamed, his name tearing out of her throat.

He turned in the middle of the road, staring at her in shock because she'd never raised her voice to the scholars before.

His motion and surprise freed her from her paralysis. She took several giant leaps forward, stretched out, grabbed his arm and yanked him back onto the grass. They fell to the ground as the car zipped by. It slowed for a second as if the driver was deciding whether to check if they were okay, then took off even faster.

The other *kinder* rushed from the building, alerted by her shriek.

Lifting the boy, Miriam ran to the school. She ordered the scholars inside. She held Kyle close as she followed them into the classroom. Was he trembling or was she? Maybe both at the thought of how close he'd come to being struck by the car.

She set him down, making sure he was steady before she released him. It took every bit of her flagging strength to tell him that they would collect the ball once the storm was past. Her knees barely held her as she walked to her desk and asked the scholars to sit at theirs. A sticky dampness on her right shin warned that she must have scraped it. She hoped she wouldn't bleed through her dark sock. That would upset the *kinder* more.

"Let's study our spelling words," she said as if nothing out of the ordinary had happened.

The scholars reached into their desks, then froze as lightning flashed and a gust of wind battered the school. The windows rattled again as the building shook with a rumble of thunder that exploded like the fireworks had on the Fourth of July.

It was followed by a louder crack. Through the windows on the right side of the school, she saw a tree shuddering by the road to her brother's farm. Suddenly, it toppled. *Kinder* shrieked, but their voices were muffled by the tree hitting the road so hard the branches bounced and slapped the asphalt a second time. Many shattered and were tossed by the wind toward the school.

"Stay in your seats," she ordered when several of the youngsters stood. She started to add more, but a motion on the other side of the school caught her eye.

Who was out in the rising storm? Had whoever it was lost his or her mind?

Before she could go to the door, it opened. Eli blew in along with leaves and broken twigs.

"Get away from the windows!" He hurried to each group of *kinder* and pulled them into the center of the room. "The wind is getting worse by the minute. We need to find shelter. Right away!"

When Miriam blanched, Eli knew she understood the severity of the storm surging into the hollow. The mountains that protected the valley from the most vicious storms had captured one and weren't letting it escape. He'd seen a few tornadoes in Delaware, and the damage they'd done had been horrific.

Were there tornadoes in northern New York in July? He had to assume it was possible. Even if the storm didn't get that bad, the furious winds were going to cause destruction.

"Shelter?" asked Miriam. "Where? Hiding under the desks won't make them any safer if a window shatters."

Wind slammed into the school again as if to emphasize her words.

"We can't get to the house," Eli said, though even the youngest *kind* must know that. "And we're too exposed in the school with so many windows. We'll have to ride out the storm in the storage closet."

"Impossible."

"There's plenty of room."

She shook her head. "It's filled with books and supplies for the fall."

"We need to clear it out." Yanking the closet door open, he wanted to groan. The space that had seemed so spacious when he'd been building it was now crammed with boxes.

He grabbed the first one and shoved it into her hands. She passed it along to one of the older *kinder* as she told the younger scholars to push the boxes out of the way. As the storm moved closer, he motioned the youngsters aside and set the boxes wherever he could reach. Miriam shifted them into haphazard piles, so he could keep pulling more out of the closet.

It felt like hours, but it couldn't have been more than three minutes before the closet was empty. As he stepped back from the doorway, Miriam sent each small *kind* in with a bigger scholar. Not one complained when she told them to hold on to each other as they squeezed into any available space. In the light of the nearly constant lightning flashes, their faces were bright with terror.

As soon as the *kinder* were inside, Eli asked, "What are you waiting for, Miriam? Get in!"

"Only if you do."

"Trust me. I will!" Putting his hand at the small of her back, he steered her into the closet.

She fit, but he wasn't sure if he would. When she reached past him and grabbed the door, pulling closed, he heard the *kinder* gasp as they were pressed more closely together.

"It'll pass soon," he called over the screeching wind. "Then we can unpack ourselves."

He couldn't tell if they heard him. Two of the youngest *kinder* were crying, hiding their faces against older scholars. Kyle, near the back, looked scared. Once the storm finished funneling down the creek, Eli would console him.

The door jerked from his hand. He grabbed for the knob and missed. Wind swirled in, as if trying to sweep them out like a broom finding dust bunnies beneath a bed. He saw papers flying about the schoolroom. Had a window broken? An outer door blown open?

He didn't wait to find out. He pulled the door closed and locked his hands around the knob. It fought to escape him.

Would the building hold together?

Dear God, let it withstand the storm.

If it failed—as the wall on Milan's farm had failed— he would be to blame for every injury or worse that happened. Just as he'd been when his brother and sister-in-law had been crushed because of whatever mistake he'd made.

But he'd been extra careful with the construction of the school. Putting in more nails and supports than were necessary, wanting to guarantee nothing would cause the building to collapse. He'd done everything he could and more, but what if it wasn't enough?

A shiver ran along him. It wasn't his place to guarantee anything. It was God's. Though he had faith God had guided his hands and his decisions during the building of the school, the final outcome was known only to God.

When a slender arm encircled his shoulders, he realized the shifting *kinder* had brought Miriam to stand right next to him. She held Kyle and two other smaller scholars tight against her other side. He took one hand off the door, and his arm went around her waist, holding her to him. If these were to be his final moments, he wanted them to be with her.

"We'll be fine," she said, gazing at him so he couldn't

miss the words her lips formed. "You built the school. We'll be safe here."

He expected her to add an "ain't so." She didn't, and when he met her earnest gaze, he saw she believed each word as if it were engraved in stone. For her to have such faith in him...

He didn't deserve it, but he craved it. If she believed in him, maybe—just maybe—he could begin to believe in himself again.

No! That would lead to the same arrogance that caused him to ignore the mistakes in the wall's construction.

Something struck the school. Everything shook. There was a scream even he could hear, but he wasn't sure if it was the wind or the *kinder*.

He grasped Kyle by the sleeve and yelled for the scholars to hold onto each other. He doubted that would help if a twister was ready to pull the school apart.

Then the only sound was rain. Had the storm moved on, or was it a lull?

Everyone seemed to be holding their breaths and straining to hear what was going on beyond the closet. When he looked at Miriam, she nodded in response to his unspoken question.

He pushed the door open and stepped out. Papers crackled beneath his feet. Every surface in the room was covered in a thin layer of white. The chalkboard was plastered with papers. The whiteboard Miriam had brought to the school had been tipped over, markers strewn everywhere. He wondered how long it would take to sort out everything.

But at least the scholars hadn't been tossed around, too. Eli went to the back door. It was ajar and rocked in the remnants of the wind. He closed and latched it. The windows were intact, though they were so covered with bits of green it was impossible to see through them. The front door had withstood the storm.

Miriam led the *kinder* from the closet while Eli went outside. She urged them to thank God for bringing them through safely. Saying his own grateful prayer, Eli looked around.

A big branch had hit the porch and was shattered into pieces no bigger than matchsticks. One of the porch railing posts was cracked. Otherwise, the rail was secure. Two boards flapped at one side of the building. The corner piece holding them in place must have been torn off.

"The school rode out the storm well," said Caleb when he arrived and picked his way through the downed branches. "If you hadn't insisted on those extra nails in the roof boards, the whole roof might have been ripped off."

"I wanted to keep the *kinder safe.*"

Caleb clapped him on the shoulder. "The *kinder* and their teacher, ain't so?"

"When I worked on it, I hoped, as the rest of the builders did, anyone who enters the schoolhouse will be safe," he said, acting as if he didn't understand what the other man was saying.

That was the last chance Eli had for conversation the rest of the day. While parents came to collect the scholars and see them home, many returning to help clean up, he listened to reports of damage. Shingles had been torn off, and another tree blocked the road in front of the empty house next door to the Waglers' farm. The faint sound of a chain saw announced someone was at work removing it.

A large Town of Salem truck stopped beside the tree in the road between the school and Miriam's house. Four men and two more chain saws were soon cutting the giant tree into smaller pieces and stacking them in front of the school. The supervisor said they'd return to collect the wood, but Caleb told them that wasn't necessary. The Kuhns brothers would drag it to their sawmill. The *Englischer* smiled, relieved, that was one task he could strike off his long to-do list. The storm hadn't spared any section of town. The *gut* news was nobody had been gravely hurt.

Eli tossed a branch on the tall pile behind the stack of wood. The smaller ones and leaves would have to be raked. The scholars could do that in the morning when the grass was drier.

A plastic glass of lemonade was held out to him, and he seized it, downing the contents before he realized Miriam had handed it to him. She filled the glass again from the pitcher she carried along with a tower of glasses. Before he could thank her, she rushed to offer someone else a refreshing drink. She flitted from one person to the next like a busy bee in a field of flowers.

He sipped to make the lemonade last longer and sat on the school's porch by the steps. He'd replace the cracked rail tomorrow before he went back to work shoring up the Osbornes' sunporch.

When Kyle plopped down beside him, Eli ruffled his nephew's hair. "Pretty exciting day at school today, ain't so?"

"Ja." He took a deep drink of his own lemonade, then jumped to his feet as Miriam walked toward them.

Eli noticed dried blood on one of her black socks.

Had she hurt herself while clearing away the mess in the schoolyard?

Kyle paid no attention. He started to give her a hug, but she waved him back with a smile until she'd put the pitcher and remaining glasses on the porch.

She held out her arms, and Kyle threw himself into them. Over the *kind*'s head, she smiled at Eli.

"I was saying to Kyle," Eli said as he stood, "that it was an exciting day at school."

"Too exciting," she replied. "I'm so glad you were here to help with the *kinder*."

"You could have saved them by yourself."

"I would like to think so, but…"

Kyle interjected, "You would have, Miriam. You saved me *twice* today."

"Twice?" Eli asked.

Miriam started to reply, but the excited boy burst in and told how, when he'd gone to retrieve the ball, she'd pulled him out of the road before a car could run him over.

With every word, anger rose in Eli. He'd listened to Miriam's reassurance his nephew would be safe, and she'd let him run into the road when a car was barreling toward him.

Kyle wasn't finished with his tale, but Eli interrupted to demand, "Why weren't you watching him, Miriam? He could have been killed. I thought I could trust you to protect him. You didn't!"

Her face had become a sickly gray. She lowered her eyes.

"She did!" Kyle stamped his foot so hard the boards reverberated beneath Eli's boots. The boy yanked on his sleeve and threads snapped. "*I* went after the ball.

Miriam called to me to come inside, but I didn't listen to her. I kept going after the ball. It's my fault. Not hers."

A rational part of Eli's mind urged him to listen to Kyle. Instead, he grabbed the little boy's hand and strode down the steps. He looked at Miriam. She hadn't moved.

She must regret not keeping better track of the boy. But the thought of what could have happened, how he could have lost the last member of his family, ached inside him. It laid another thick layer of guilt to silence his foolish heart that told him he hadn't been wrong to trust again or to love again when he'd thought it would be impossible to find someone who would accept both him and Kyle.

The boy protested as Eli steered him toward the buggy. No matter what his nephew said, Eli must not do anything to risk the *kind* again. Dissolving into angry tears as they drove away, Kyle didn't look at him.

And Eli didn't look back.

Chapter Fourteen

Eli slowed his buggy in front of the school on the last day of school. His nephew slid out and loped toward the building, not waving goodbye as he used to.

"Kyle?" Eli called.

Reluctantly, the boy stopped. Eli thought he wouldn't face him, but Kyle did, his right hand in his pocket. His expression wavered between hurt and anger. He'd worn that expression for the past week since he'd admitted the day after the storm that he feared his *onkel* would pull him out of school.

Eli had considered it, but the trouble that could cause the settlement had halted him. And what would he have done with his nephew while he was rebuilding the Osbornes' sunporch? The boy was helpful on a job site, but Eli wasn't sure how *Englischers* would feel about a *kind* there. It was important to get this first job right, so others would offer him work.

"Don't forget," Eli said. "I'll pick you up after I get done with my meeting this afternoon."

"I know." Kyle's tone was petulant.

"Don't head home by yourself and no ball games."

"I know." The boy's shoulders hunched, and he stuck his other hand in a pocket, too. It was as if he'd grown into a rebellious teen in the blink of an eye.

Then Kyle spun and ran toward the school.

Sighing, Eli rested his elbows on his knees. How could life turn from *gut* to horrible this fast?

His mind was mired in exhaustion. He hadn't slept much for the past four nights, thinking of how he'd reacted to the news a car had nearly run over his nephew.

Or, according to Kyle, how he'd overreacted.

Kyle was so furious with him that for a day, he'd refused to look at Eli while speaking. Eli had insisted, and the boy obeyed, but hadn't said much other than to repeat Miriam had done nothing wrong. She'd saved his life. Hadn't Eli noticed the blood on her leg? Kyle was sure that had happened when she risked herself to pull him out of the road.

Eli had seen the blood on her black sock, but she wouldn't have been hurt if she'd been keeping a closer eye on a rambunctious boy. He wanted to believe Kyle, but his nephew was a *kind*. He didn't understand that in spite of Miriam saving him, she'd allowed her attention to be drawn away in the first place.

His nephew didn't know how Eli had made a promise by his brother's casket to keep the boy safe. If Eli had done that instead of letting Miriam persuade him to go against his best instincts, nothing would have happened.

He couldn't explain to Kyle that he was angrier at himself than he was at either Miriam or the boy. He'd been shown what could happen if he forgot his promise...even once.

The school door opened as Kyle reached it. When Miriam stepped out, Eli's breath caught in his throat.

His arms could almost feel her soft curves in them. She didn't move as the distance between them dissolved until he could almost believe that if he reached out, he could take her hand. And he wanted to. He ached to pull her close and breathe in the fresh scent of her hair and savor her fingers' light caress as they uncurled along his face or wove through his own fingers.

His heart urged him to go to her, to tell her that he didn't want what they shared to come to an end like this. To tell her that he loved her as he had no other woman. As he would never love another woman.

But his duty to his late brother halted him. He'd never guessed a pledge made in *gut* faith could destroy his hopes for love.

As soon as Miriam said the day was over, the scholars rushed toward the door. The enthusiasm that had been with them at the beginning of their unplanned term was gone. In the aftermath of the big storm, the air had been wiped clean of humidity. The *kinder* wanted to be outside, enjoying the freshness.

The special school session was finished.

Just like any dreams she'd had about her and Eli. Those were gone almost before they'd begun.

Should she have defended herself when Eli accused her of being careless? How could she have done that when Eli was right? She should have kept a closer eye on Kyle. She'd said she would, and then she had let herself become distracted...as she had the day Ralph had almost drowned.

In each case the boys had survived thanks to her, but they shouldn't have been in such dangerous circumstances to begin with. She closed the door and walked to her desk to finish the report on the term. It was just as well she hadn't spoken with Caleb about applying to teach during the new school year.

Her breath hitched as she sat and stared at the page. The words blurred. What would she do with the rest of her life?

She looked at the small package on the desk. She'd offered to take it to the post office after school because Caleb had a long day in the fields and planned to meet with the other men after supper to discuss the clothing issues they needed to define for their *Ordnung*. Running errands was something she could do to help, but eventually Caleb would marry, and he'd have someone else to oversee his household. Where would Miriam live then? Maybe one or more of the other members of the Spinsters' Club would find a small house somewhere to live together.

The jesting name no longer seemed funny. It sounded lonely.

"Miriam?"

Surprised by Kyle's voice, she looked up from her clasped hands on the desk. She'd assumed he'd left with the other *kinder*.

Again, she'd failed to keep track of the boy. In spite of her broken heart, she hadn't learned a thing.

She stopped rebuking herself when she met Kyle's eyes. They were dull with unhappiness, and hints of red suggested the little boy had been crying. She hadn't seen any tears on his face while the scholars were inside, but she thought about how, after the *kinder* were released, he hadn't joined in the last game before their shortened vacation. He'd been standing by the tree with

Mercy's son Paul. She'd seen Paul pat Kyle on the shoulder. Had the little boy been crying then?

Her heart threatened to break anew. She stood and walked around her desk. Taking his trembling hand, she led him to a desk. He sat at it, and she pulled out the chair of the next one.

Lowering herself to the tiny seat, she asked, "Is Eli coming to get you, Kyle?"

"Ja."

"At Paul's house?" The two boys had walked there after school each day since the storm. They left right after school was out, not staying to play ball.

"Paul has something he has to do this afternoon, so I decided to stay here with you, which is *gut* because I want to—that is, I need to…" A flush climbed his face.

"Do you want to talk to me about something, Kyle?"

He nodded, drawing his lower lip beneath his one upper tooth that hadn't fallen out yet.

"Go ahead," she urged.

He opened his mouth but clamped it closed again as if he didn't dare to let words escape. As if he was frightened by the strength of his own emotions.

Ach, how she wanted to draw him into her arms and tell him she shared his dread. Every word she'd said since the day of the storm had been the wrong one. Either an evasion from the truth or an attempt to deny what she felt. She avoided any conversation that might turn to her and Eli and how she'd failed him. Her brother and the members of the Spinsters' Club were giving her time to tell them what was bothering her in the wake of the tempest, but she wasn't sure how long their patience would hold up.

"Sometimes it's hard to say what is inside of us,

ain't so?" She had to stop fretting over her own problems and help the *kind*, if she could, with whatever was bothering him.

He nodded, staring at the toes of his scuffed shoes as he swung his feet against the chair legs.

She leaned forward to where she could catch his eyes. "When I find it hard to say what I'm feeling, I know there's only one thing to do. I have to say it. Once I do, I feel better."

"Really?"

"Ja," she replied, but glanced toward the door as if she'd heard someone outside.

She couldn't meet the little boy's eyes any longer. Would he see how guilty she felt about giving advice she hadn't taken for herself? Or was she seeking a bit of his courage to enable herself to face the truth that she'd destroyed any affection Eli might have had for her? Not that she could blame him. Yost had acted the same way when she messed up. But she had been sure she'd learned her lesson and would be extra careful with *kinder*, particularly with mischievous little boys. Maybe she had, but not well enough.

"Miriam?"

Again, his tiny voice, barely more than a whisper, shredded her thoughts.

"Ja?" she prompted.

"Why is *Onkel* Eli mad at me?"

She smiled gently at him. "He's not angry with you. He's angry with me."

"He *is* mad at you," Kyle asserted, "but he's mad at me, too."

"Why do you think that?"

"He's acting strange."

"Maybe he has something on his mind." *Something like how disappointed he is in me.*

The boy shook his head with the certainty of a six-year-old. "He's had stuff on his mind before, and he never acted like this. He has a hard time hearing, but he used to be *gut* at listening. He hasn't been listening to me—really listening—since we've moved here." He propped his elbow on the desk and his chin on his palm.

"I'm sure he's listening to you the best he can." She was surprised how right it felt to defend Eli, though he hadn't given her much of a chance to explain what had happened the day of the storm. What could she have said? That she'd made the same mistake of trusting a *kind* who had his mind set on a course of action? "Remember? He has to concentrate on reading lips. It isn't easy for him."

"No, he isn't listening!" Kyle gave her a frown, which made him look more like his *onkel* than ever. "Will *you* please listen to me, Miriam? *Onkel* Eli thinks I'm upset with him."

"For what?"

"For selling my *daed*'s farm."

Miriam hesitated. If she said the wrong thing, she could cause more damage. "Why do you think that?" she asked, deciding to let the little boy lead the conversation that was going in a very unexpected direction.

"I heard talk back in Delaware about what a shame it was *Onkel* Eli got rid of the farm when families in our district had to move out because there aren't farms available." His forehead ruffled with his puzzled expression. "I didn't understand that because he sold it to the son of one of our plain neighbors."

Little pitchers have big ears.

She suspected the little boy had misconstrued the conversation, but she didn't want to complicate matters by saying that. Instead, she patted Kyle's shoulder as he leaned his chin on his hand again. "You know there's an easy way to clear this up, don't you?"

"*Ja*. If I give *Onkel* Eli a gift, he won't be angry with me anymore."

"You don't need to get him a gift. He knows how much you care about him."

He shook his head. "I'm not sure if he does, but he'll believe me when I give him something I know he wants. After he's happy with my gift, I can tell him that I know he sold my *daed*'s farm because he wanted the two of us to have a new and better life here." He rubbed a knuckle against his eye, but tears welled out and trickled down his round cheek. "He thinks he's hiding it, but he's sad about the day *Mamm* and *Daed* died." His mouth tightened. "He believes the accident when the wall collapsed on them was his fault."

"Why would he think that?" she blurted.

The boy had to have misheard again. She didn't—couldn't—accept that Eli had had anything to do with the tragedy other than as a victim. He was the most cautious person she'd ever met, watching out for any possible contingency that would be dangerous. His work on the school had saved them from being hurt in the storm. He watched over Kyle, almost stifling the little boy. How could anyone so careful imperil his family?

Or, her mind argued, *is he anxious because of the error he made four years ago?* He battled a deep-seated pain. Because of his failure to see the wall was unsteady before it toppled?

"*Onkel* Eli believed what was said by people who were mean to him at the funeral."

"Weren't you too young to remember it?"

"I remember bits. How everyone was sad. How it was a sunny day, but then there was a thunderstorm. I also remember hearing people say those mean people who blamed *Onkel* Eli were *Mamm*'s cousins. They said her cousins needed to be forgiven because they'd lashed out in pain. What does that mean?"

How often had Eli's neighbors spoken bluntly because they knew he wouldn't hear what they were talking about? They'd failed to realize Kyle was standing there, soaking up everything they'd said.

"It means," she said to answer his question, "those people said things they shouldn't have. That their grief kept them from thinking straight or knowing their words would have painful repercussions."

Pride slipped into his voice. "*Onkel* Eli turned the other cheek as Jesus said we're supposed to. He refused to argue with them." His shoulders slumped. "But he believes they were right. Others—a lot of others—didn't believe the wall falling was *Onkel* Eli's fault. Maybe he didn't hear what our neighbors kept saying."

Miriam had grown numb with shock as Kyle's explanation added layer after layer of additional heartache for Eli. She must say something. The boy was looking at her, hoping she'd confirm his words, though she'd never met any of the people he was referring to.

"It's likely he didn't hear your neighbors," she said, responding to the most innocuous thing Kyle had said. "You know as well as I do your *onkel* missed a lot of what was being said around him before he began to read lips." Again, she spoke with care, not wanting to cause Kyle distress at the reminder of how independent Eli could be.

"I wish he'd learned a long time ago."

She felt her own shoulders ease a bit at the boy's words. He'd set aside his hurt at not being indispensable to his *onkel*.

But could it be true Eli's inattention to the wall-building project had led to the disaster? She stiffened again. From the first day she'd met Eli, she'd sensed he was carrying a heavy burden. For him to believe he'd caused the deaths of two people who were so important to him would place an unbearable weight upon his soul. No wonder he yearned to shield Kyle from even a faintest hint of danger.

Unaware of her thoughts, the youngster went on, "Some folks said it was *Onkel* Eli's fault, because he was the one who knows construction and should have seen the problem before the wall fell. Others insisted my *daed* must have made a mistake somewhere along the way and hid it from *Onkel* Eli. Our bishop warned folks to keep their opinions to themselves because the only One who knew the truth was God." Kyle looked at her with wet eyes. "The bishop wouldn't have said it if it wasn't so, ain't so?"

Again, she didn't answer right away. When he began to squirm in the seat, she said, "It's true God knows every event in our lives and every thought in our heads and every beat of our hearts. Bishops are honest, just as they ask us to be when they urge us to tell the truth, and we try, but sometimes it's not easy."

"I know, but some people seem to like lies better than the truth."

"Maybe they don't know what they're saying isn't true."

Kyle stuck out his chin in an obstinate frown. "They had to know *Onkel* Eli wouldn't do anything to hurt someone else."

"Of course he wouldn't."

Tears rushed into her eyes, and she turned away before Kyle could see them. The boy was upset. He didn't need to have her pain added to his. She'd thought he was oblivious to the real reasons his *onkel* had insisted he no longer stay after school, but Kyle had known better than she had.

Her first instinct was to sit on the porch and wait for Eli to arrive. Would he listen to her when she told him how sorry she was for his pain, or would he refuse to acknowledge her sympathy and forgiveness? Would he walk away…for *gut* this time?

That Eli had dared to trust her showed the depth of his feelings for her, because he didn't trust anyone else, not even himself. And she'd let him down, as she had Yost.

But it was different. Yost had been growing distant in their last few weeks as a betrothed couple. When he'd come to the house, there had been undeniable tension in the air. Not just between Yost and her, but between her betrothed and Caleb. Her brother had refused to explain why he didn't want to be in the same room with the man she planned to marry. Though Caleb had comforted her, she'd sensed his relief that she would never be Yost's wife.

She hadn't ever figured out why the onetime friendship between Caleb and Yost had soured. She must have been too focused on spending time with Ralph to see what had happened. Or had she been like Kyle, witnessing exchanges she somehow couldn't understand because she didn't have the facts and attempted to fill in the blanks herself?

Not once had she defended herself against Yost's accusations. She couldn't imagine Eli doing such a thing; yet his silence was worse. She had to think of a way to ask how she could regain his trust.

"Will you take me today?" Kyle asked.

Miriam blinked as if waking from a deep sleep. "Take you? Where?"

"Will you take me to the hardware store?" Impatience laced through his voice.

"Why do you need to go to the hardware store today?"

He stood and regarded her with an expression that conveyed without words that he was wondering if she'd lost her mind. "I told you. I want to get *Onkel* Eli a gift, so he knows I'm not mad at him. They've got a hammer there that I know he'd like to have." Reaching into his pocket, he pulled out a small plastic bag filled with coins and a collection of glass marbles. "Won't you help me buy him a gift to make him be happy again?"

Her gaze cut to Caleb's package on the desk. If she waited for Eli to finish his day's work and return to Harmony Creek, she wouldn't get to the post office before it closed. She had to go into Salem, but she couldn't leave the little boy by himself at the school.

"Okay," she said, "but we must leave a note for your *onkel*."

His brow furrowed, and she thought he'd protest. Then he nodded with a grin.

Miriam wrote a quick note on the whiteboard in blue marker. It let Eli know that Kyle was with her and they'd gone into town. Eli was sure to notice the bright blue letters when he walked into the school to look for his nephew.

"Let's go," she said. "We need to be quick, so we're back before your *onkel* gets here." She held out her hand, and he took it.

As they went down the steps, Kyle gasped. "I forgot my money!"

She sent him to get it while she hitched the horse to the buggy. Kyle ran into the schoolhouse and returned wearing an even bigger grin. He grabbed her hand and talked on and on about how *wunderbaar* it was going to be to give Eli a special surprise. How it was going to make everything all right again.

She wished she had his faith that a heartfelt effort would close the chasm between Eli and his nephew. If she did, maybe she could find a way to do the same for her and Eli. Maybe it was still possible to return to the time when being in each other's arms was the most important thing in the world.

Chapter Fifteen

"Do you know where the hammer you want is?" Miriam asked as she opened the door to the hardware store on Main Street. The cool dusk inside was a welcome relief from the bright sunshine making shimmering waves along the sidewalk. Steam rose from the hot concrete. The sprinkle that had fallen on their way into the village hadn't relieved the humidity. Rather, the air seemed heavier than before the spotty rain.

She needed to hurry Kyle because she'd left in the buggy the few groceries she'd bought after stopping at the post office. The buggy was parked in front of the grocery store at the only hitching rail in the village. One was planned near the library, but the work hadn't been completed.

Not that she would have used it because the grocery store was closer to the hardware store. More dark clouds were gathering in the northwest corner of the sky, so they needed to finish their errands and get home before the storm broke.

Kyle had been eyeing the clouds, and she was sure he was thinking—as she was—about the tempest that had swept over the school. But he wouldn't be remembering Eli's strong arms holding her close as he protected her and comforted her. The memory was bittersweet, but she couldn't change what had happened after she'd believed the worst of the storm had passed.

"*Ja*, I know where the hammer is." Kyle called a greeting to Tuck, the man behind the counter.

She guessed Tuck was the owner, so she returned his smile.

Kyle didn't give her a chance to say anything. He was almost hopping in his excitement at buying a gift for his *onkel*. He'd been as patient as possible while they stood behind two other customers at the post office and then went to the grocery store. He couldn't wait a second longer.

Taking her hand, he led her around bins and racks of items for sale to what must have at one time been a separate store because there was a door to the street in the other half of the store. Three lawn mowers and a snowblower blocked it. Two tents, one put together, were set in front of the machines. She wondered how long it'd been since that door was opened.

She slowed herself and Kyle before they could run into an *Englischer*. The dark-haired man who wore denim overalls stepped aside, dropping a roll of chicken wire.

"Excuse us," she said.

He nodded and smiled as Kyle slipped past him and continued toward where the hammer he wanted was waiting. "Someone's in a big hurry, isn't he?"

"He is."

"Boys at that age seem to have two speeds. Fast and faster."

Glad the *Englischer* was kind, she gave him room to pass with the chicken wire before saying in *Deitsch*, "Kyle, apologize please."

Kyle did as the man walked toward a long counter with a modern register at one end. Then the boy focused on a pegboard where hand tools were displayed. There were more varieties of screwdrivers than Miriam had guessed existed. Manual ones and battery-operated ones and electric ones. Fortunately, there were fewer choices for the hammers.

"Which one?" she asked.

"That one! Right there!" He looked at her with a smile that revealed his lone top front tooth was getting loose enough to hang at an angle.

She reached for one with a black handle, but he shook his head.

"The one beside it," he said. "The green one."

She smiled as she lifted the hammer he wanted from the display. She handed it to him and watched as he examined it.

For a very short moment, she'd dared to dream this sweet little boy would become her son when she married the man raising him. A man she was ready to give her heart to for the rest of her life. Once again her hopes had been foolish. More foolish than in Lancaster County. At least then Yost had asked her to marry him. Eli had said nothing of them having a future together.

"Do you think *Onkel* Eli will like it?" Kyle asked.

"I'm sure he will because you got it for him." The words were automatic, and she scolded herself for putting her own sorrow before his excitement.

"Maybe he'll let me use it sometimes."

"Maybe."

She glanced over her shoulder as the front door opened. Two men walked in, but moved to a different section of the store. She put out her hand to make sure Kyle didn't take it into his head to go and see what they were doing and almost run into them, too.

"Let's pay for this," she said. "I want to get back before we end up soaked."

He held out his bag of change. "I've got eight dollars and forty-three cents. That's enough, ain't so?"

Looking at the board where the prices were listed, she nodded, though he was a couple of dollars short. She hoped she could slip the store owner the extra money without Kyle noticing. The boy was staring at the hammer, fascinated, so it shouldn't be hard to make up the difference. She could always ask Kyle to separate his money from his marbles. That would keep him from seeing her add to his total.

"It'll be fine." She smiled at him, admitting to herself she hoped the gift would persuade Eli to listen to her as well as to Kyle.

She whirled at the sound of a bitten-off curse and a shriek. Glancing toward the door, she saw a silhouette vanish out the front door into the eye-searing sunshine. She noticed that before her eyes focused on two men by the counter. One wore a black ski mask, the other, shorter by almost a head, wore a bright green one with a garish face on it.

Something glinted in one man's hand.

"He's got a gun," Kyle moaned beside her, clutching her skirt in terror.

"Don't anyone else move!" snarled a man whose voice was higher pitched than Tuck's. "This is a robbery!"

"What do we do?" Kyle whispered.

Pulling him to her, she answered, "Don't move and pray hard. Harder than you ever have."

Eli strode past a field where beef cattle grazed in complete indifference to the storm coming toward the hollow. A pile of sawdust had grown into a mound beside the busy sawmill.

The Kuhns brothers had set up the mill in an open-sided building near the woods behind their barn. Instead of tending to a crop in the fields, they were using the summer to cut lumber from the trees they'd felled in the woods higher on the hillside. In the winter they planned to sell Christmas trees from the lot that had been on their farm when they bought it. The Amish didn't put trees in their houses and decorate them, but selling them would help the family make a success of the farm.

Stone ridges cut through most of the fields, so they weren't good for much but grazing and lumber. He'd heard the brothers were thinking of starting an apple orchard, but the trees needed to grow between three and five years—depending on what variety the brothers planted—before bearing fruit. The Christmas trees, meanwhile, would provide a comfortable income for the family.

Eli winced and covered his ears as he walked into the open-sided building. The shriek of steel and belts as the saw sliced through an oak log was blistering when augmented by his hearing aids. He turned them down before he took another step. It shouldn't take him long to get the boards he needed to finish the Osborne project and to start his next one.

He smiled. The job offer had come less than two hours ago, an *Englischer* who lived a few doors away from the Osbornes. It was a bigger project, a complete kitchen renovation. He wanted to bring Jeremiah Stoltzfus in on the project, because the *Englischer* had talked about having a corner table with raw edges to match the rustic decor they were planning for the whole house. That would require a skilled woodworker like Jeremiah.

His smile broadened when he saw Jeremiah standing with three other men by the saw. Jeremiah was examining a length of wood that had been sliced off a log. It was thick enough for a tabletop, so Eli guessed his neighbor would soon be shaping it into one of the beautiful pieces of furniture that had caught the attention of *Englischers*. Rumor suggested more than one interior decorator from New York City had traveled almost two hundred miles north to arrange for Jeremiah to make furniture for picky clients in the city. No wonder the man who'd hired Eli had been so pleased when he'd mentioned the idea of having Jeremiah contribute to the kitchen project.

The men yelled greetings before returning to their shouted conversation. Over and over as he walked toward them, he noticed how they asked whoever was speaking to repeat himself. Just as Miriam had told him, nobody seemed bothered by the request.

He could understand every word spoken. Being able to "hear" others when they couldn't hear him was bizarre. Miriam's lessons on lipreading and body language allowed him to understand what two men on the other side of the saw were discussing.

It took three tries before Jeremiah understood that

Eli wanted his assistance on a job in Salem. Smiling, Jeremiah agreed to go with him tomorrow and bring designs to share with his new clients.

Eli thanked him and turned to leave. He was late getting Kyle at the school. Knowing he should have stopped on his way to the sawmill, he realized he owed his nephew and Miriam an apology for being late.

And for so many other things.

After praying for God's guidance, he was trying to accept he couldn't change the past and letting it destroy his present and future was going against God's will. He owed forgiveness to so many, including those who had accused him of carelessness. He hoped Kyle would accept his apology for refusing to listen to the boy.

But most of all, he needed to ask Miriam to forgive him. Kyle had insisted she hadn't been to blame for his being almost hit by a car. She had saved him. Rather than listen to the facts, Eli had let past events propel him into making unfounded accusations. He didn't want to think of what would happen if she forgave him but wanted nothing more to do with him.

A hand grasped his arm. He looked over his shoulder to see Caleb behind him.

"Can we talk somewhere quiet?" Caleb bellowed.

Eli nodded and followed his friend out of the sawmill. Turning up his hearing aids once they'd put distance between them and the shrill machinery, Eli leaned one shoulder against a tree and waited while Caleb turned to face him.

"This isn't easy to say," Caleb said, rubbing his hands.

"Then spit it out and be done with it."

"*Ja*, that's *gut* advice." He met Eli's eyes. "Miriam was upset after the storm. It wasn't the danger you'd faced. It was something much more painful to her. Do you know why?"

He wasn't going to lie. "I do."

"Will you tell me?"

"She didn't?"

Caleb shook his head. "Miriam is a private person at the best of times. When she's upset, she becomes more closed. You may have noticed that."

"I have."

"What happened?"

It didn't take Eli long to explain, saying nothing to excuse his part in what had occurred.

With each word spoken, Caleb's face crumbled more. He shook his head and sighed. Not that Eli could hear the sound, but he recognized the rise and fall of Caleb's shoulders.

"I was afraid something like that had happened," Caleb said. "No wonder she was so shattered."

"We've had differences of opinion before, but she never reacted as she did then."

"I'm sure she didn't." Caleb gnawed on his bottom lip, and Eli could see he was debating with himself. "What I'm about to tell you can't go any further."

"Gossiping isn't something I do, even when I could hear well."

"*Gut*, because what I've got to tell you isn't something that should be spread around. Miriam has already had to deal with half-truths and outright lies spoken by people who should know better." Taking a deep breath, he said, "Before we moved to this settlement, Miriam was set to be married."

"She was?" Eli was stunned. Not once had she given him any hint she'd been serious about a man in the past.

"To a widowed neighbor of ours. Yost Fisher. I was surprised when she told me that they were planning to marry. I thought Miriam could see he was only looking for someone to oversee his house and take care of his son, nothing more."

"Love is blind, so they say."

"And they are right." Caleb gave him a crooked grin. "Miriam was in love. Not with Yost, but with his six-year-old son, Ralph. The two of them seemed to be meant to be together. That was why I urged her to take the teaching job for the summer. She loves being with *kinder*."

"They adore her, too." He thought of how his nephew looked for any excuse to spend time with Miriam. Even when he was supposed to be playing with friends, he sought her out. "Why did she seem hesitant about taking over the school for the summer?"

"Because Ralph nearly drowned. Miriam saved his life."

"Thank God He put her in the right place to help the boy. But what does that have to do with her being unsure about being around kids?"

"The boy's *daed* blamed her for the boy getting into trouble in the first place." Caleb's mouth tightened into a thin line. "Yost, who should have been keeping an eye on the boy, was, as I learned later, with another woman several districts from where we lived."

"What?"

"He'd been seeing her for quite a while. He left his son with Miriam when he had to go away on what he called *business*."

"But he was spending time with this other woman."

Caleb nodded. "Miriam never found out about what

Yost had been doing. He made sure of that by proclaiming it was Miriam's fault for what happened to the boy instead of being grateful. He never took an ounce of blame himself because he didn't bother to make sure Ralph got to our house. How could he...?"

Eli hung his head. He didn't need to see Caleb's expression to know he'd be a hypocrite if he condemned Yost Fisher. Like the man he'd never met, he'd accused Miriam of endangering a *kind* when, instead, she'd kept Kyle from being hurt.

Fingers tapped on his arm, and he looked up.

"Miriam said you can't hear everything," Caleb said, his face taut with distress, "unless you're looking at the person talking."

"True."

The other man had more to say, and he didn't intend for Eli to miss a single word. "You've got to understand, Eli. What Yost did broke her heart...and her spirit. I wasn't sure if she'd heal." He gave a terse laugh. "She wouldn't have if she remained behind when I came here. People who should have known she'd never do anything to endanger a *kind* started to believe, when she didn't defend herself, that maybe Yost was right."

"Did you?"

"No." His smile was sad as his gaze turned inward with memories of what must have been a terrible time for the whole Hartz family. "But I know Miriam always would wonder. That's why I asked her to be the teacher for our summer school."

"So you devised the plan for having the scholars return to school?"

Caleb shook his head. "No, that wasn't my doing. The minimum days of school had to be taken care of, but as soon as I heard that, I jumped at the chance to show my sister that we trusted her with the *kinder.* She'd started to believe it again."

"Until I accused her of not watching over Kyle and the other scholars as I believed she should have." He didn't make it a question. He and Caleb knew it was the truth. "Even if she'd been watching the scholars every second, she still wouldn't have stopped Kyle from going to get the ball. She tried, and he didn't listen. She did all she promised to do." His voice broke in his throat. "And she saved his life. I let my fear for him make me do the stupidest thing I could have."

Pushing off the tree, Eli left without saying where he was going. Caleb knew, too, that it was long past time for Eli to tell Miriam he'd made a big mistake and he was sorry.

But an hour later he still hadn't had a chance to apologize. She wasn't at home nor at the school, though he guessed she'd been earlier because a quartet of colorful posters had been rehung around the room. Kyle must have been with her then because Eli could see erased words on the whiteboard where his nephew liked to write, but the boy was gone, too. He hoped Kyle was with her.

As he drove toward his farm at the far end of the hollow, Eli stopped at the Waglers' farm. Neither twin nor anyone else there had seen Miriam or Kyle that afternoon. He didn't bother to visit the Kuhnses' farm because Sarah wouldn't be home during the week.

Maybe Miriam had gone to visit her at the Summerhayses' house. Would she have taken Kyle with her? It was possible. Eli recalled there was at least one *kind* in Sarah's care who was about his nephew's age.

Turning around, he drove toward the main road. He saw Mercy waving to him as he passed her house. He slowed the buggy. Maybe Mercy had seen her and Kyle.

As the buggy rolled to a stop, he realized what a change Miriam had made in his life. He never would have, after the wall's collapse, considered instigating a conversation. Instead, he would have scurried away like a frightened woodchuck hurrying into its den.

Mercy came to the road. To his question, she nodded. "I saw her drive past about an hour ago. She had Kyle with her. They stopped, and said they were heading into town for an important errand." She smiled as she wiped her hands on her apron. "She said if I saw you to let you know that she'd left you a note at school."

He started to say he hadn't seen any note, then thought of the partial words on the whiteboard. Had it been the message left by Miriam? But if so, who had erased it?

Mercy tugged on his sleeve, and he looked at her. "Kyle had an errand at the hardware store today. She told me to tell you he'd explain when they got back."

"They went into the village?"

"As far as I know, *ja*."

"*Danki*, Mercy." He drove away slowly so he didn't raise a cloud of dust to choke her.

The creek road had never seemed so long, but when he got to the main road, he drew in his horse. Chasing her and Kyle into Salem was *dumm*. What was he going to do when he found them? *Ja*, he and Miriam needed to talk, but what he had to say to her he didn't want to say in the middle of a crowd of *Englischers*. Or among their Amish neighbors. The private conversation that was long overdue could wait until she returned home.

He should head to Caleb's farm so he would be there when she and Kyle got back.

Hearing a rumble of thunder to the west confirmed his decision. Miriam would stay in Salem until after the storm was over. He'd be a *dummkopf* to continue to town while he and his horse got soaked. Another glance at the sky told him he should have time before it reached Harmony Creek to hurry to the Hartz farm and put Slim in their barn.

Eli was about to turn the buggy around when a county sheriff's car sped past in a blur. It was followed moments later by a state police vehicle.

The pager at his waist buzzed.

Looking at the code, he saw it was a request for all available firefighters to rush to the firehouse. Was there a fire in Salem? Or was it in a nearby town, which meant sending Salem's firefighters and equipment to work with the local department to put out a major fire?

"Go," he shouted to Slim as he slapped the reins on the horse's back.

Startled, Slim broke into a near run.

Eli pulled Slim to the right as more emergency vehicles—both state police vehicles—zipped past. The buggy rocked. Not from the cars speeding by, but from a gust coming out of the storm. Thunder cracked nearby. He ignored the storm as he raced the buggy toward town and the firehouse.

He hoped he'd be in time.

Chapter Sixteen

When Eli reached the intersection in the heart of the village, he was shocked to see traffic being rerouted along West Broadway toward the post office. Nobody—not even pedestrians—were being allowed to go north on Main Street.

He glanced at the sky, but saw no dark smoke to indicate that there was a fire. What was going on?

As he reached the intersection, a man in a sheriff's uniform held up his hand. "You can't go through."

"I'm a volunteer firefighter, and we've been called in."

The deputy sheriff motioned to another man. The older man wore a state police uniform. He asked what the problem was. He barely glanced in the buggy's direction, keeping his attention on the deputy.

"Let him through," said the state policeman and walked to where he'd been standing by a length of yellow tape that crossed the street from one corner to the other. He didn't pay attention to the lightning and thunder that were getting closer by the second.

"Stay as far left as you can at the intersection," the

deputy said. "We need to keep the intersection clear for emergency vehicles to come through."

"What's going on?"

"A robbery."

He must have misread the officer's lips. "What did you say?"

"A robbery." He hooked a thumb toward the northern end of Main Street. "Someone is robbing the hardware store."

Hardware store? Mercy had said Miriam was taking Kyle to the hardware store.

He scanned the street. He didn't see Kyle's bright red hair or a white *kapp*. Where were they?

Pulling his buggy beside the library across the street, he lashed Slim's reins to a planter. He glanced up the street at the array of police cars, with lights flashing. Nobody was going to let him through there.

The alley by the hardware store! Could he sneak in that way? He jogged toward the rear of the soda shop on the corner. Looking between it and the tiny antiques store next door as lightning danced in the sky overhead, he frowned. The way was blocked by several high fences, plank and chain-link. He kept going away from Main Street. Past the stone church was an open lot with a large stone to mark where a fort had stood during the Revolutionary War.

He almost let out a cheer when he saw a clear path to the alley between the hardware store and the diner. He squinted through the dim light, but saw nobody there. Forms moved stealthily on the far side of the hardware store. If he could slip past them, he would come out on Main Street.

Keep Miriam and Kyle in Your hand, Lord, and if it's Your will, let me get to where I can help them.

Using the plank fences to shield him from any eyes, Eli slipped into the alley. Sounds were distorted by the close walls, but he guessed someone was using a bull-horn to communicate with the thieves.

He stepped out of the alley, sidling to his left to blend in with the handful of people standing on the diner steps and watching the police officers. Eli listened as a man related in a frightened voice how he'd escaped out the door seconds after the robbers entered.

"Anyone else in there?" Eli asked.

"Yep. Tuck is." The man gulped. "And I saw a woman and a kid."

The world seemed to tilt, and Eli grasped the iron rail by the steps. Could that be Miriam and Kyle?

"Do you know who they are?" someone else asked before he could.

The man nodded, his eyes wide with terror. "They must be one of those Amish families that have moved into the hollow by Harmony Creek. The woman had on a thin white thing on her head. Like those women wear."

Eli dropped to the step. Eyes riveted on him and his plain clothing. He saw mouths moving and concerned expressions, but he couldn't take in a single word. He'd never understood what it meant not to be able to catch his breath...until now.

"Don't do anything stupid," the taller man with the black ski mask said as he waved a gun between Tuck, who was behind the counter, and Miriam and Kyle, who still stood by the tool wall. "Give us the money, and we'll go. Nobody gets hurt."

"All right, all right." Tuck raised his hands over his head as he edged toward the register.

"Listen to them," Miriam whispered to Kyle, whom she kept behind her.

The shorter man growled something in their direction, and Miriam clamped her lips closed.

When the bell on the cash register rang, the sound echoed through the silent store. It was followed immediately by the scream of a siren coming along the street. Tires squealed as one vehicle, then another, came to an abrupt stop in front of the hardware store.

The two thieves exchanged an anxious look at the same time Miriam and the man behind the counter did. Would the thieves realize the futility of continuing or would the arrival of police make them more desperate?

She must make sure the little boy obeyed. "Kyle?"

No answer.

"Kyle?" she whispered, a bit louder as she prayed her voice would be lost in the screech of more sirens.

Again, she got no answer.

Risking a glance over her shoulder, she saw no sign of the little boy. Her heart exploded into her throat. Where was he? How could she protect him if she didn't know where he was? No matter what Eli thought, she held tightly to her vow to keep Kyle safe.

She couldn't draw attention to herself. Without moving, she scanned the sections of the store she could see. A door at the back was ajar. Had it been that way before? Maybe Kyle had seen his chance to escape and had taken it. She hoped so.

As the two men debated, she heard a soft rattle near the open door. Kyle? Why hadn't he fled? There must be an exterior door for deliveries. Was it locked? She didn't dare to keep looking, not wanting the men to notice her interest in the half-open door.

Suddenly, the two men came along the counter and ran toward the back door. She took a step to follow, but was shoved aside. She hit the floor hard and stared in horror as the men rounded the counter.

With a shout, the shorter man collided with the other thief.

"Watch out!" the man in the black ski mask shouted.

The shorter man growled a curse and shoved his fellow thief. "You watch out. Don't run into me."

"I didn't. You bumped into me. Let's get out—" He screeched as he lost his balance on marbles strewn across the floor.

Kyle's marbles?

Miriam held her breath as the thief's shoulder hit a display of keys, knocking it off the shelf. Blank keys flew in every direction. She took the opportunity the chaos provided to look toward the door that was ajar. She saw Kyle peeking out around it. She motioned him to hide.

Too late.

The shorter man caught Kyle by the sleeve and dragged him into the store.

"I'll show you what happens to little boys who get involved in something that's not their business." He raised his gun toward the *kind*.

Kyle's grin vanished along with every bit of color in his face. Tears flooded his eyes that locked with Miriam's.

She didn't stop to think. She jumped to her feet and between Kyle and the gun. Shouts came from everywhere as she shoved Kyle behind a stack of paint cans.

At the click of the trigger, she prayed the bullet wouldn't hit her or the boy.

Protect him, Lord! Eli needs him.

Everyone in the street froze at the sound they'd prayed they wouldn't hear coming from the hardware store.

A gun firing.

The noise vibrated through Eli's hearing aids and into his heart. The two people he loved most were in that store.

He raced forward as rain began to fall in a torrent. Arms surrounded him like a net, keeping him back. He tried to push them aside. He had to see what was happening in the store.

He had to!

Police ran up the steps, ramming the door open. They carried pistols and long guns.

Eli's gut cramped. Miriam or Kyle could be hit by a ricocheting bullet.

Someone appeared in the doorway. A flash of lightning flickered off white organdy.

Miriam!

Tearing himself away from those trying to hold him back, Eli rushed up the steps. He grabbed her hand and swung Kyle, who stood beside her, into his arms as if he were still a toddler. Racing down the trio of steps, he pushed past the cops heading into the store. He ducked into the alley between the two buildings. He held Miriam against the wall of the diner and stepped between her and the street.

He set Kyle on his feet before looking for any sign of injury on the boy and Miriam. She was clutching the bricks on the wall as if she could drive her fingertips into them. Her face was the color of her *kapp*. She released the wall to put her arm around Kyle as he leaned against her. They stared straight ahead, fear imprinted on their faces.

But he didn't see any blood on them as rain poured down. Had the shot missed them? Had it hit someone else? He'd find out later. For now only the two people in front of him mattered.

"Are you hurt?" he asked.

"We are okay," Miriam said, but her lips trembled so hard he barely could understand what she was saying.

"Are you sure?"

She clasped his face between her hands. "Read my lips, Eli. We—both Kyle and I—are fine."

"But I heard—" He choked on the words.

Kyle tugged on his arm. When he looked at the boy, he was astonished to see his nephew grinning as if he'd just been on the greatest adventure.

"*Onkel* Eli, you should've seen Miriam! The thief aimed his gun at me. She jumped in front of me. Right in front of that guy's gun." His eyes glittered with excitement, and Eli wondered if his nephew was enhancing the tale. "She wasn't scared. Not a bit."

"I was terrified," Miriam said, her voice quavering. "If the taller thief hadn't hit the shorter one's arm and caused the shot to go astray, we might be dead."

"You saved him," Eli said as, in the street, police officers were putting handcuffs on the thieves. He ignored them.

Miriam did, too. "I told you I'd do everything I could to make sure nothing bad happened to him."

"And you did. *Danki*, sweetheart." He tipped her lips

beneath his and kissed her so she understood he meant exactly what he was saying.

By the time the police had hustled the thieves away and interviewed Miriam and Kyle as well as Tuck, the storm had passed. They'd been invited into the diner where the owner put complimentary bowls of hearty soup in front of them. Miriam and Eli sat at a table while Kyle joined Tuck at the counter, who was discussing the merits of the pies on display.

The boy had apologized for erasing the message on the whiteboard at the schoolhouse. He'd wanted to keep his gift a complete surprise.

Miriam put down her spoon after a single bite. "Eli, I need to tell you—"

"I need to tell you…" Eli began at the same time. "Go ahead."

"I need to tell you about what happened before I came to Harmony Creek."

He shook his head. "I know what happened. Caleb told me today."

She lowered her eyes. "You know you were right not to trust Kyle with me."

"Don't." He put a finger to her lips. "Don't say another word about that. Ever. If Yost Fisher couldn't see the obvious fact you saved his son, why do you think he could see anything else? All you did wrong was to believe a man who shifted his guilt onto you." He folded her hand between his as he added, "I'm sorry I did the same."

"I should have told you about all of it before now."

"Just as I should have told you before now about why the wall fell at my brother's farm."

"Which Kyle tells me you believe was your fault, though it wasn't." She explained what the little boy had told her he overheard.

He didn't reply for several minutes. At last, he said, "I should have listened to Kyle. Just like I should have listened to you, but I refused to believe anyone who told me my brother didn't follow the instructions I gave him for building the wall. I told myself they were trying to make me feel better when I had lost so much."

"I told myself the same thing when others seemed to believe Yost's accusations. People I respected. If they believed it, why shouldn't I?"

"Because we didn't want to think people we loved would think poorly of us. As poorly as we thought of ourselves for failing to be perfect. It's time, my sweet one, to stop worrying about what others think of us and do what we know is right." Raising one hand, he curved it along her cheek. "I asked you to watch over Kyle, and you have. Will you watch over something else for me?"

"What?"

"My heart. *Ich liebe dich.*"

"You love me?" she whispered.

"Ja."

"And *ich liebe dich.*"

"Will you—"

Kyle's voice rose over Eli's. "Oh, no!" cried the boy, jumping off the stool and running to their table.

"What's wrong?" Eli asked.

"I left your gift at the hardware store."

Eli gave Miriam the lazy smile that delighted her. "Don't worry. We'll get it, but first, Miriam, would you give me a gift, too? Would you give me your hand in marriage?"

"Ja!" Kyle announced before she could reply. "She'll marry you, and we'll be a real family at last."

She laughed. "I couldn't say it any better than he did. *Ja*, I'll marry you, Eli, and I'm going to stop caring about what others think of me when I know something is right."

"Marrying me?"

"Nobody will doubt that is right." She leaned across the table and kissed him.

When Kyle cheered, the other patrons joined in.

But she heard only the sound of Eli's heart beating with hers, a thrilling melody they'd share for the rest of their lives.

Epilogue

"Miriam, where are you?"

"Coming." She hurried up the stairs of the old farm-house at the far end of the hollow. The house where Eli and Kyle lived. Soon the house would be her home, as well. She stepped into a simple bedroom set close between two dormers and looked through the doorway at the precious people who already had become part of her family.

Eli gave her a warm smile as he took her hand and sat her on the side of Kyle's bed. The little boy was scrubbed, his hair damp from his shower. Cute blue pajamas were bright against his white sheets, but matched one of the colors of his crazy quilt.

"Ready for your story?" she asked.

"Ja." The *kind* wiggled in excited anticipation. "Tell me the story about the day you got chased by the bees."

"You've heard that one a dozen times," Eli said with a laugh.

"But I like the faces Miriam makes when she tells it."

"How about the rest of the chapter in the book we've been reading?" Eli winked at Miriam, and happiness swirled within her heart. "I don't know about you, but I can't wait to hear what happens to the boy and the missing kittens."

"He's going to find them." Kyle rolled his eyes. "You know that, *Onkel* Eli."

"But how? Isn't that the question?"

Miriam leaned forward and patted the little boy's shoulder. "We'll finish the chapter tonight. Remember? Books on school nights and tall tales other nights."

"Okay." Kyle nestled against his pillow. "Are you going to read to us in school tomorrow, Miriam?"

"I plan to." She'd been asked to stay on as the school's teacher for another year. Though it wasn't common for a married woman to teach, she'd continue after she and Eli took their vows. By the time next fall rolled around, she would hand the school over to someone else and focus on making the creaky old farmhouse a comfortable home.

As she read, she kept looking at the man standing in the doorway. He was watching her face. Not to read her lips, he'd told her, but because he enjoyed looking at her and knowing they'd be together for the rest of their days.

She finished the chapter, then listened while Kyle said his prayers. She blinked back happy tears when Kyle asked for a blessing for "*Onkel* Eli and *Aenti* Miriam."

Tucking in the *kind* and giving him a kiss on the forehead, she stepped aside to let Eli do the same. After they'd wished the little boy sweet dreams, she followed Eli down the stairs, which were too narrow for them side by side.

He paused at the bottom and took her hand as they walked out onto the front porch. He didn't release it as they sat together on the swing he'd installed the previous week.

With her head on his shoulder and his arm around hers, they rocked together and gazed at the stars.

"Our wedding plans will be published this Sunday," he murmured against her *kapp*.

She glanced at him. "I know. I can't wait."

"Neither can I." He brushed his lips against hers. "Because I know there's nobody I trust more to keep my heart safe."

He kissed her again, and she knew he could read on her lips how much she loved him, too. It was a message she intended to share with him as often as possible.

* * * * *

HER FORGIVING
AMISH HEART

Rebecca Kertz

For Judith E. French, my dearest friend and the sister of my heart. You touched my life in ways you'll never know. Thank you for everything. Our friendship of nearly thirty-six years has meant a lot to me. May you rest in peace, dear Judy. I love you.

Whoso findeth a wife findeth a good thing,
and obtaineth favour of the Lord.
—*Proverbs* 18:22

Chapter One

❧

Late spring, Lancaster County, Pennsylvania

She felt the first drops of rain as she steered her horse-drawn open wagon home after a visit to her friend Mary. Leah Stoltzfus sighed as she reached under the carriage seat for her umbrella. She probably should have headed home hours ago, but it had been so nice to spend time with Mary, who'd fallen in love and married Ethan Bontrager before moving into the house her husband owned in New Holland two years ago.

The light drizzle turned into a shower as Leah pushed open the umbrella while she continued to steer her horse. The patter of rain on fabric was soothing, and she smiled as she made a left turn. She was still miles away from home, but the downpour didn't bother her. Until suddenly the wind picked up, so strong that it turned the umbrella inside out, ruining her rain covering beyond hope. She cried out when a gust tore off her prayer *kapp*. She tried to catch it, but it was a lost cause. When a sharp clap of thunder followed a bright flash of lightning, she knew she was in trouble. She needed to find a safe place to wait out the storm. She sent up a silent prayer that the Lord help her to find shelter soon. She had been terrified of thunderstorms since being caught in a severe one as a young child.

Yoder's General Store loomed ahead as if the Lord had provided in Leah's time of need. Relieved, she pulled into the parking lot and tied up her horse before she ran to the front entrance. Thunder rattled the building's windows as she tugged to open the door, but it wouldn't budge.

Locked! A flash of lightning made her flinch. The rain spilled down in buckets now, and the air temperature dropped quickly. Soaked, she hugged herself with her arms as she tried to keep calm. The wind gusted and blew the rain sideways while lightning continued to flash and was followed by horrific crashes of thunder.

Feeling desperate, Leah leaned her face against the window to peer inside and caught a tiny flicker of light from the back room. *Thanks be to God!* She hurried around to the rear entrance and hammered on the door with her fist. She waited for someone to come, her heart racing wildly as she tried not to shrink with fear every time there was lightning and thunder. She pounded again. *Please, Lord. Please, Lord.*

What was she going to do? Worried about her horse, she turned to leave.

The door flew open behind her. "Leah?" a male voice roared above the wind. "Is that you?"

She spun, then stared at the man who gazed at her from the open doorway. Henry Yoder. The last person she'd expected to see—and the last man she wanted anything to do with. He unsettled her. He'd once been her cousin Isaac's best friend, until he'd betrayed him.

"I have to go." She gasped. A boom of thunder made her duck for cover, her arms shielding her head.

"Leah." His voice was soft and near. "Come in from the rain." He captured her arm gently and pulled her into the store.

Leah was tempted to stay, her fear momentarily getting the better of her. Then she met Henry's gaze and closed her eyes, debating. Storm versus Henry Yoder. She bucked up as she made the choice to rein in her fear. She sprang out the door.

"Leah!" he shouted as he came out after her.

She halted and met his concerned gaze. "My mare."

Understanding brightened his blue eyes. He nodded. "We'll put her in the storage barn. I'll get your buggy."

She shook her head, refusing to allow him to see how frightened she was. "I'll get it."

Their gazes locked. Henry stared at her, then inclined his head. "I'll meet you over there." He gestured toward the large pole-barn structure behind the store, then rushed out into the blinding rain after shutting the door behind him.

Water streamed in her eyes as she ran to her buggy. Her horse was antsy, shifting nervously as she whinnied. Concerned for the animal despite her fear, she took the time to stroke the animal's neck. "I'm going to get you inside where it's safe, girl."

After one last pat, she lifted a leg to climb into the vehicle, slipping on the wet wood before she managed to get seated. Leah grabbed the leathers and steered the horse toward the Yoders' outbuilding. Her heart gave a lurch when she saw that Henry had dragged open the two huge doors for her. He stood back and waved her into the building, but as she urged the mare closer, he grabbed hold of its halter and led her horse inside. The interior of the structure was dark except for the brief flashes of lightning that lit it up. Leah waited until he maneuvered her vehicle in as far as it could go before she let go of her tight hold on the reins and climbed down. Henry waited for her at the rear of the buggy.

"'Tis a little noisy, but she will be safe here," he said. Rain plastered his dark hair to his head. Rivulets of water ran down his handsome face and his clothes were soaked, but he didn't seem to mind. "Come on. Let's get back to the store."

Leah opened her mouth to refuse, to tell him that she would wait with her wagon inside the building, but then she closed it and nodded. She couldn't be rude to Henry after he'd come to her aid. Besides, she wasn't going to let the man see her as anyone other than a strong-minded individual who wasn't fazed by anything. *Especially by him.* Bright lightning flashed, followed by a thunderous boom. She gasped. *Except by thunderstorms.*

A bright white bolt shot from the sky, and there was an explosion as it hit something in the distance. "Come on!" Henry urged. "Let's go now before things get worse." She was shocked, conscious of the warmth of his fingers when he caught her hand and tugged her with him as he ran.

Aware of Leah's hand in his, Henry hurried to safety. The storm was a doozy. It had been a long time since he'd seen one this bad. He pulled open the door, tugged her inside, then shoved the door shut against a gust of wind.

"Are you *oll recht*?" he asked when he saw how hard

she was breathing. Her eyes refused to meet his as she inclined her head. A crack of thunder made her flinch, and he reached for her and eased her away from the door. He flipped on the light in the storage room and urged her inside.

She glanced at him with alarm that told him she was as afraid of him as she was the storm. Hurt, he hid his reaction and softened his expression. "'Tis safer here," he explained. He gave her a crooked smile. "No windows."

Understanding flickered in her eyes and he was glad to see her relax.

She shivered. He realized that she was cold, soaked through like he was. "I'll be right back," he said. He hurried to the front of the store. Behind the counter hung a quilt made by his mother. His *mam* had hoped to sell it, but with the Amish as their main customers there was little opportunity for a sale, so it hung high on the wall simply as a decoration. Henry reached up, slipped it from the wall rack and returned to the storage room. He caught sight of Leah, off guard, hugging herself with her arms. She was bent forward as if she could shield herself from the raging storm outside.

He felt a painful lurch in his chest as he studied her without her knowledge. Wet blond hair, the bluest eyes and prettiest face he'd ever seen, Leah Stoltzfus was something to behold even as clearly upset as she was. He longed to pull her into his arms to comfort her, but from the look on her face when he'd answered the door, he knew she wouldn't welcome his hug. She'd wanted to flee when she saw him and he understood why. Years ago Leah's cousin Isaac and he had befriended some young *Englishers* during their time of *rumspringa*. Late one night, while Henry waited for Isaac to join them, Brad Smith and his English friends had spray-painted graffiti over the exterior of Whittier's Store. When Isaac had arrived on the scene, Brad had shoved a can of spray paint into Isaac's hands, then dragged Henry with him as he fled while the sound of police sirens echoed in the distance. Brad had warned Henry against telling the authorities who was responsible and promised retribution against him, his family and Isaac if Henry did. This new side of Brad had terrified him, and so Henry had kept his mouth shut and allowed his best friend to take the blame. Isaac had stayed silent and suffered because of it. Henry had waited too long before he'd finally come forward, confessed before the church congregation and asked for forgiveness. The community had forgiven him and so had Isaac. But given her cousin's suffering because of Henry, and the fact that Leah had avoided him ever since, he didn't think she had forgiven him.

Henry sighed with disappointment before he eased back to where she couldn't see him. He made a loud sound to give her warning of his return. With the quilt draped over his arm, he entered.

"Here," he said as he approached. He tried unsuccessfully not to be offended when she instinctively backed away. He exhaled loudly. "Leah, 'tis just something to warm you."

Her eyes flickered as she saw what he held. "I'm sorry." He saw her swallow hard. "I… I'm not exactly fond of thunderstorms." She seemed surprised by her admission.

He smiled as he moved closer, relieved that she didn't withdraw as he draped the quilt gently around her shoulders. He gazed at her and she stared back. The room was small, and he could see her fear of the storm in her pretty blue eyes, hear it in her heightened breathing, although he could tell she was struggling to fight it. "Are you warmer now?"

"Ja, danki." She glanced away.

"I don't bite, Leah."

Her head came up and anger lit her expression. "You think that's funny?"

Holding her gaze, he shook his head. *"Nay."* He was glad to see her angry and less afraid.

"How long will this storm go on?" she complained after another clap of thunder reverberated throughout the store.

"Are you asking me for an answer?" he quipped with amusement.

He felt happy when Leah narrowed her gaze at him. Anger was so much better than fear. She'd endure the storm better if he continued to taunt and tease, keeping her fury alive.

"What are you doing out in the storm anyway, Leah?" he asked.

"I was—" She stopped. "What business of it is yours?" she snapped.

Henry shrugged. "None, I guess. I'm just curious." He leaned casually back against a stack of cardboard boxes filled with merchandise. "Doesn't seem smart to venture out in a storm so far from home."

She opened and closed her mouth several times, clearly trying to come up with a retort. Her lips firmed. He hid his pleasure when her eyes shot daggers at him. "It wasn't storming when I left this morning for New Holland," she replied through tight lips.

"You went to see Mary and Ethan Bontrager."

She looked shocked. "How did you know?"

He was starting to feel uncomfortable with his wet hair and soaked clothes. "I know that you and Mary are friends and Mary married Ethan, then moved to New Holland."

She looked horrified. "How do you know who my friends are? You've not been coming to church services or any Visiting Sundays!"

"*Ja*, but I'm friends with Isaac."

"Isaac and you are spending time together?" She gasped.

He had to stifle his own spark of anger. "*Ja*, your cousin has forgiven me as the other members of the community have." He paused. "Except for you."

Her eyes widened as she gazed up at him. She was obviously at a loss on how to respond. He detected a flash of remorse in her eyes before she looked away. The fact that she didn't deny it hurt. "I forgave you," she mumbled, looking away.

Skeptical, he pushed away from the boxes. "I'm going to check outside. See how the storm is doing." He hoped it would be on its way out, for it hurt to endure Leah's judgment of him. He strode out of the storage room toward the back entrance. He opened the door and released a sharp breath when he saw the pouring rain. He detected a brightening in the sky that told him the worst of the storm has passed. The distant rumble of thunder confirmed it. The thunderstorm had moved on, leaving only rain. The wind had left as quickly as it'd blown in.

Henry shut the door. He wasn't eager to return to the storage room. He'd lived with the guilt of what he'd done long enough. He didn't need Leah Stoltzfus reminding him of his past mistakes. He still felt bad enough as it was. He moved to the window to stare at the rain until it slowed, then finally stopped.

Henry was gone a long time. It shouldn't bother her but it did. Leah listened and realized that she could no longer hear thunder. The small room where she stood had muffled the storm and she felt less frightened. Or was it her fury at Henry that had caused her to forget the storm?

Should she wait for his return? She closed her eyes. She wouldn't blame him if he didn't come back. She'd been awful to him, and she felt bad about it.

He and Isaac talked about me? And just like that her anger returned. She closed her eyes and prayed. Anger was a sin. She needed to fight it.

'Tis not right to be angry or deliberately cruel to a man who helped me when I needed aid most.

She didn't know how to deal with Henry Yoder—or any man for that matter. She'd never had a sweetheart, never had any man's attention and her at nearly twenty-four years of age.

Leah closed her eyes. Resigned to being an old maid, she would choose her own future. She ran her fingers across the multicolored quilt that Henry had given her. The pattern was lovely, the stitches neat and even. She always appreciated good craftsmanship. One day, she'd open a craft store where she'd stock quilts just like this one. She'd use the money she'd earned and saved for years, sewing prayer *kapps* and clothes for other church community members, and making craft items and selling them wherever she could. She also did mending for a few of the women who said they were too busy. It wouldn't matter if she didn't have a husband and children. She would focus on her dream and she would be happy. With the Lord's help, she'd find the peace and enjoyment in being a store owner—and she wouldn't let it upset her that her father never urged her to find a husband like he did with her sisters. He'd pushed her older sister, Nell, to find a husband first—which she did, although the fact that he was an *Englisher* had been a problem at first. Then, there was Meg. Three years younger than her, Meg was happily married to Peter Zook, a nice young man and member of their church community. As for her other younger sisters Ellie and Charlie, there was plenty of time for them to find sweethearts, although she'd witnessed firsthand the attention that the community boys gave them. She knew they would marry and have families of their own, even if she never did.

Which bought her thoughts back to Henry Yoder. The only man who had shown her kindness—for a little while anyway. His snarky attitude afterward just confirmed that she wasn't worth any man's attention.

She scowled. Not that she would ever like Henry Yoder. The man couldn't be trusted. She had forgiven him for what he'd done to Isaac. But forget? *Never.*

Leah wondered how long she should stay in the room. Was Henry upset enough to leave her there? To lock up the store and go home? And what would she do if he did? How would she get her horse and wagon? Were the pole-barn doors locked? Would she be able to slide them open if they weren't? Panic set in and she had trouble catching her breath. She recognized her symptoms as hyperventilation, having suffered from it once before. Yet, she was powerless to help herself.

"Leah, the rain's stopped." Henry entered as she struggled to slow her breathing. She heard him utter an exclamation and saw him rush out of the room. He returned within minutes with a paper bag. "Leah," he coaxed softly, "breathe into this."

She looked up with relief as she took it and held it over her nose and mouth. She closed her eyes and breathed deeply into the bag until she was able to draw a normal breath. She could sense Henry's presence, feel his concern. She was a terrible person. The man had been there for her twice, and she'd snapped at him like a shrew.

Slowly she opened her eyes and faced him. Henry studied her with concern, which eased when she pulled the bag from her mouth. He was taller than her by several inches. She looked up at him with remorse. "I'm sorry."

He frowned. "What for?"

"My behavior." For some reason, her voice was hoarse and she didn't know why.

The grin that curved up his mouth lit up his face and sky blue eyes. "Leah," he said, "I was trying to make you mad."

She jerked. *"What?"*

His lips shifted into a gentle smile. "While you were livid, you forgot about the storm."

Her anger left as quickly as it had come. "You knew I was terrified," she said softly.

"Ja."

She blushed. "I didn't want you to see."

The good humor left his expression. "I understand."

Leah stared at him and wondered if he *did* understand, but she didn't want to discuss her fear anymore, and she prayed and hoped that he would keep her weakness to himself. "You won't tell anyone?"

He appeared confused. "About—"

"That I'm a coward and deathly afraid of thunderstorms."

His eyes widened. "You're no coward, Leah. A coward wouldn't have run out into the storm to see her horse to safety."

Leah blinked, pleased by his words.

"I'll not say a word about today, Leah." Henry looked sad, and Leah struggled with the urge to do something to make his sadness go away. "No one will know that you spent any time here with me in the store. Your secret is safe."

And for some odd reason, Leah felt dejected as he preceded her out of the room, then out of the store… and as she watched him open the barn doors for her and waited for her to get into her wagon. As she steered her buggy home, the feeling intensified and tears stung her eyes. She had no idea why she was so emotional about taking shelter during a thunderstorm.

Henry stood near the barn and watched Leah leave. His thoughts were in turmoil. Everyone in the community had forgiven him for keeping silent except Leah Stoltzfus—and himself. Despite his hurt feelings, he liked being in Leah's company. She was a mystery that he wanted to unravel. It was true that he hadn't been back to her church community. His family had left after learning about Isaac's involvement in the vandalism to Whittier's Store. His father didn't want Isaac to be a bad influence, which made him feel worse. After he'd come forward and confessed and told the truth about

Isaac's innocence before Leah's church community, his parents had been so horrified by Henry's involvement that they'd felt compelled to stay with their new church district. Despite the new people he'd met, he missed his friends. Isaac had been more than generous in his forgiveness of him. They were close friends again, and Henry could never repay Isaac enough for thinking to protect him by accepting blame.

He'd wanted for a long time to return to the church community he'd been a part of for most of his life. He wanted to see the Lapps every Sunday, to spend more time with Isaac and his siblings, and the Zooks and all of the other families he'd known and cared about. After this afternoon he wanted to see and spend time with Leah again. One way or another he'd find a way to make her forgive him—and like him. There was something about the woman that made his heart race. She made him feel alive. From the moment he'd seen her outside the door, he'd known who she was. He was glad that he'd been there to make sure she was all right. He'd liked helping her, wished he could have done more.

Henry went back inside. He peeked into the storage room, saw the damp quilt that he'd placed around her shoulders and felt the kick to his belly caused by her absence. He'd caught her stroking the stitches along the pattern as if she appreciated the quilt and all the work that had gone into it. There was something about her expression that got to him. He wanted to learn all of her secrets. "I'm going to make you like me, Leah Stoltzfus, if it's the last thing I do."

He draped the damp quilt over the counter to dry, then flipped off the light and went back into the rear room to finish the store's bookkeeping. This building was the only one on the property with electricity. The church elders allowed it in certain businesses, although not in their homes and outbuildings. Cell phones were allowed for business use, but his parents were opposed to them so Yoder's General Store didn't have one. Henry knew that would have to change if they were ever to increase their business to include more of the English. Until then he'd keep his mouth shut and work in the store. He had a dream of his own and it wasn't to take over the family business. But he stifled that dream because he owed it to his parents for all the trouble he'd caused them. Now, with his father suddenly in the hospital and his mother spending her days at his bedside, it was up to him to make sure Yoder's General Store ran smoothly as usual.

Someday, if the Lord deemed it, he would have his choice of making a living—as a cabinetmaker. Not in competition with Noah Lapp, who had a good business crafting quality furniture. But similar to what Ethan Bontrager did for a living in New Holland, making kitchen cabinets, vanities and bookcases. He and Isaac had spent some time in Noah's furniture shop. He'd loved feeling the texture of the wood, instinctively knowing that he'd be good at cabinetry.

Henry grinned as he recalled Leah's reaction to his comment about her and Mary Bontrager. Isaac and he had never discussed Leah's friendship with Mary. He knew because he'd seen them together often enough when he'd attended church service or Visiting Sunday gatherings. Isaac and he had talked about Henry's secret desire for his future, and Isaac had mentioned that Mary Hershberger Bontrager's husband, Ethan, made cabinets for a living. His friend had suggested that Henry talk with Ethan about the business. Henry had planned to visit Ethan the next day, but then his father's recent heart attack had changed everything. He'd visited *Dat* in the hospital, where his parents had made him promise to run the store. Henry had agreed. Being a dutiful son was the least he could do for the parents who'd raised and loved him.

Unable to be or do what he wanted didn't mean he couldn't make the best out of a difficult situation. He'd keep the store open. *And I'll convince Leah to forgive me.* He smiled as he looked forward to the challenge.

Chapter Two

Her family was relieved to see Leah as she steered the wagon into the yard and parked it near the barn. They were all outside, as if hoping that the buggy sound they'd heard was her. She climbed down from the vehicle and faced them.

"Leah!" *Mam* said as she hurried forward, quickly followed by Ellie and Charlie. "I was worried that you'd been caught in the storm." Her eyes widened as she took in Leah's appearance—the damp state of her clothes, her missing prayer *kapp* and wet hair.

"*Ja*, I was caught at first but managed to find shelter." Leah smiled to reassure her and her sisters as she watched her father descend the front porch and approach more slowly. He looked more concerned than her mother. "As you can see, I'm fine." She met her father's gaze as he drew close. *"Dat."*

"Leah." He studied her as if gauging whether or not she was all right, then he seemed to let go of his worry. "I'm glad you're home."

"I am, too, *Dat*." She moved toward the house and

everyone fell into step with her. "I'm hungry, though. 'Tis been a long time since lunch."

"Supper is nearly ready," her mother said, moving ahead, apparently eager to get the meal on the table.

"We're having fried chicken," Charlie added with delight. She hurried to help her mother.

Leah turned to Ellie. "Were you caught in it?" she asked her sister.

"*Nay.* Got home just in the nick of time." Ellie eyed her carefully. "'Twas a bad one."

"*Ja,*" she agreed.

"Ellie, you should help your *mudder.*"

"*Ja, Dat.*" Leah watched her sister run into the house. She turned toward her father.

"*Dochter,*" he said.

"*Ja?*"

"Was it awful?"

She knew what he meant. He was asking how well she'd coped with her fear. He was the only one who knew of her phobia. He was the one who'd found her during a raging storm curled up in a ball in an open field, sobbing with terror as thunder crashed overhead and lightning flashed while it threatened to strike her. He'd picked her up and carried her to safety. Despite the fact they were walking through the storm to the nearest shelter in their barn, she'd felt safe and secure within his arms. She was three years old at the time. Her mother hadn't been home. *Mam* and her older sister, Nell, were at her grandparents' house. As young as she'd been, Leah had begged her father that no one learn of what happened. Her father had agreed readily. Her mother was with Meg, and he hadn't wanted to upset her. And so they'd both kept the knowledge—and Leah's subsequent fear of thunderstorms—to themselves. As far as she knew, she hid her fear well and her family still didn't know.

"Nay," she said and realized that she spoke the truth. "I did *gut*." Despite her initial terror, she'd weathered the storm better than usual—because of Henry Yoder. She felt worse than ever before for treating him badly.

Her father's expression cleared. "That's wonderful, Leah." His smile reached his eyes. "Let's go eat supper."

Surrounded by her parents and sisters at the dinner table, Leah felt the stress of being caught in the storm and her time spent with Henry dissipate. She smiled as she listened idly to her youngest sister Charlotte's conversation with Ellie.

"Visiting Day is at Aunt Katie and Uncle Samuel's," Charlie said. "Can we bring chowchow and apple pie?"

Ellie arched her eyebrows. "Why chowchow? I'm sure Aunt Katie has plenty."

Charlie frowned. "Who says she'll serve hers?" Then softly, as if voicing her thoughts, she murmured too quietly for the others to hear, except for Leah who sat next to her, "I want to bring something I made by myself."

Leah shot her a look and noted the wistfulness in Charlie's expression. She smiled in Ellie's direction. "I think it's a great idea for us to bring chowchow. The last batch was the best I've ever tasted." She could feel Charlie's gratitude in the release of tension in her sister's shoulders. "I'm sure Aunt Katie only brings hers out if no one else thinks to bring some."

"That's true," her mother said with a smile. "So, we'll bring chowchow, and I'll make the apple pie and some sweet-and-vinegar green beans. Any other ideas?"

"I'll make potato salad," Leah offered.

Ellie grinned. "I'll make a cake."

"I'll help you with the cake," Charlie offered, clearly happy that everyone had agreed that they should bring a bowl of her sweet-and-sour chowchow, a pickled mixture of the remainder of last summer's garden vegetables, a favorite among the members of their Amish community.

The next morning Leah worked to make German potato salad while Ellie and Charlie gathered the ingredients to make a cake and her mother rolled dough for an apple pie. She loved these times when the women in her family were all together in the kitchen, but she missed having her married sisters, Nell and Meg, with them.

As she carefully drained the hot water off the potatoes, Leah found her thoughts drifting to Henry and his kindness to her during yesterday's thunderstorm. The last thing she'd wanted to do was spend time with him, but he'd made it bearable. She'd found herself softening when he'd wrapped a quilt around her shoulders. Leah frowned. She didn't want to think of Henry. It bothered her that she'd been unable to get him out of her thoughts since she'd left the store.

Forcing Henry from her mind, she concentrated on enjoying the time with her mother and sisters while she made her potato salad and found happiness in the company of her family.

Sunday morning Leah got ready to spend Visiting Day at her Lapp relatives. Once she'd put aside thoughts of the storm—and Henry—the day spent with her mother and sisters baking and cooking was wonderful. Amish women weren't allowed to cook or do any work on Sundays, so it was important to make sure everything was done by Saturday afternoon. Leah had made two large bowls of German potato salad, a family favorite. Ellie and Charlie had baked two cakes, one chocolate and one carrot. *Mam* had baked the apple pie and made traditional sweet-and-sour green beans with sugar, vinegar and chopped pieces of cooked bacon. The green beans fixed this way were delicious cold as well as hot, so it was the perfect side dish to any Sunday meal.

Since Friday's thunderstorm, she'd been unable to keep Henry Yoder out of her mind. Would he be visiting with Isaac today? Her heart thumped hard at the thought. She wished she'd taken the extra time to thank him, as well as apologize for the way she'd been eager to get away from him. Thinking on it a lot since then, Leah realized that Henry made her nervous. No man ever affected her that way. She shouldn't continue to fret about it but found it difficult to stop.

It was a perfect spring day, with temperatures well into the upper seventies. As her father steered their family buggy close to the Samuel Lapp house, Leah noticed that everyone was outside enjoying the weather. Tables were set up on the back lawn and her male cousins were already playing baseball in the side yard. She felt a burst of excitement as she climbed out of the parked buggy and reached in to grab the two bowls of potato salad. It looked to be a good time spent with good people. Charlie and Ellie joined her as she watched the activity about the house.

"Do you think *Endie* Katie wants us to bring the food inside?" Charlie asked.

"Ja," Leah said. "'Tis too early for lunch and we didn't bring any breakfast foods."

"There's she is now!" Ellie exclaimed. "Let's ask her."

Mam and *Dat* appeared beside them as they headed to greet Leah's aunt. Her uncle Samuel came out of the house behind his wife, and Leah watched as they talked a moment. The affection between the two wasn't overt, but she could see the love they shared in the way they regarded each other—and the way her uncle placed a hand gently for a moment on her aunt's shoulder. Leah felt a little twinge of pain as she realized she wanted a relationship like they had. She wanted a husband and a family. She straightened her spine. If the Lord wanted her to marry, then she would. If not, then she must be content with only a craft business in her future. She'd find joy in her shop and be grateful for her loving family and her friends. She had no right to feel anything else.

"*Endie* Katie!" Charlie exclaimed with a grin as her aunt and uncle approached. "We've got apple pie, cake, chowchow, green beans, and Leah made her German potato salad!"

"So much food," Katie said, beaming. "Are you hoping to feed our entire community?"

When her aunt looked in her direction, Leah smiled. "Better too much than not enough."

"Do you want everything in the kitchen?" *Mam* asked.

"*Ja*, that would be *gut*." Katie turned to her brother. "*Hallo*, Arlin. I'm glad you're here."

Her *dat* eyed his sister with affection. "I wouldn't miss this." His voice softened. "I still thank the Lord that we moved home."

"*Ja*. Happiness is a fine place to live," Missy agreed. "I'm more than content to live here."

Her father shot his wife a grateful look. Leah loved

watching her parents together. There was so much love between her mother and father and her relatives with their spouses that she was pleased to be a part of the family. Not for the first time, she silently thanked the Lord for the blessings He'd given her throughout her life.

"Charlie!" a male voice called. "Want to play baseball?" It was their cousin Joseph Lapp. He tossed the ball back and forth between his hands. "I need someone *gut* on my team."

Charlie laughed. "Aren't you afraid I'll show you up?"

Joseph shot her a grin. "Not if you're on my team."

"Let me put these cakes inside the house and then I'll play."

Leah laughed when she heard Joseph's older brothers groan. "Not fair, Joseph. She's younger than us," Daniel complained.

On her way to the house, her youngest sister halted. "Already making excuses, cousin?"

The other members of Joseph's team chuckled. "Sounds about right, Daniel," Joseph said.

"Our teams will be even. You'll be able to play now." Joseph looked toward a spot out of Leah's sight.

She froze when she recognized the dark-haired man as he stepped into her view. *Henry Yoder.* She stared at him, and he locked gazes with her. She noted the upward quirk of his lips. Her face heated as she felt a sudden spirt of irritation. He hadn't come because he wanted to see her, had he? He arched an eyebrow as if reading her thoughts and she looked away. When she glanced back, she saw Isaac join him. The two men talked, and Isaac laughed at something Henry said.

He'd better not be talking about me!

Flushed with outrage, Leah continued to the house. Henry's presence made her feel unsettled. All thoughts of apologizing to him vanished. She scowled. She could hide in the house, but she was no fool. He'd know immediately why she was avoiding him, and as he'd told her she was no coward.

He knew when he heard Joseph call her sister Charlie's name that Leah would be close by. But seeing her again, despite the unhappiness in her expression as she glared at him, buoyed his spirits. He'd hoped she'd be here today, figured she would be since the Lapps were her family, but he couldn't be sure. He hid a grin. She was upset to see him. He must have affected her more than he'd realized.

"I don't think your cousin likes me," he said to Isaac.

Isaac frowned. "Which one?"

"Leah."

"*Nay*, not possible. Leah likes everyone. What makes you think she doesn't?"

Henry's gaze followed Leah as she headed toward the house. "She glares at me."

His friend laughed. "You're imagining things."

"*Nay.* She hasn't forgiven me for what I did to you."

Isaac frowned. "That doesn't sound like her."

"Look at her. See for yourself."

Leah had paused to glance back.

"She does look unhappy with you." Isaac grew thoughtful. "Interesting." He met Henry's gaze. "Ellie told me that Leah wants to open a craft shop. Maybe you could offer to help her. You know about running a store and keeping books. She might soften toward you while you teach her all you know."

Henry brightened and felt a sudden shifting inside of him. "That might work."

"But be careful how you ask her," Isaac warned. "Find time alone with her. Don't let anyone hear about your offer or she's liable to get mad and feel as if you're forcing her hand. Besides, not many people know about her store plans."

"I'll be careful."

"I know." Isaac grinned. "You want Leah to like you? This might just be the way to do it."

"What if she refuses my offer?"

"Then you try again later."

"I don't want to force her," Henry said.

"You won't force her. You'll make the offer, then step back. From what Ellie says, Leah wants to own a craft shop badly." Isaac glanced toward the gathering on the lawn. "The others are waiting. Ready to play ball?"

He nodded. As he joined the Lapp brothers and their friends for a baseball game, Henry wondered if Isaac was right. Would teaching Leah about running a store be the key to winning her friendship?

"Henry, you take left field," Joseph shouted from first base. "Charlie, you play short stop."

He nodded and hurried to take his position. There was nothing else to do right now but focus on the game. He'd figure out later what to do with Leah.

The baseball game was fun, with a lot of whooping and hollering as teammates ran around the bases. When he got up to bat, Henry hit a grand slam and sprinted around the bases, sending everyone before him home. As he slid onto home plate, Joseph was there to high-five him. Everyone on his team grinned while taunting those on the opposite side.

"I told you we needed him on our team," Joseph said to two of his brothers and Charlie.

Isaac grinned at him. "'Tis great to play ball together again."

"Are you up for another game?" Noah asked as he and Daniel joined them. Both brothers were on the other team along with the Peachy brothers and Peter Zook.

Joseph laughed. "'Tis lunchtime."

Henry glanced toward the tables that were set up in the yard. "*Ja*, the women are bringing out the food." He felt a rush of pleasure when he spied Leah among them. "Sorry, Noah," he said, unapologetic, as he watched her return to the house. "Food first. Whether or not we have another game will depend on how we feel afterward. Right, team?" He paused. "After all, we've already won. We've nothing to prove."

His teammates laughingly agreed. Henry grinned as they all headed toward the food table. Leah came out of the house with a bowl in each arm. She started forward when she must have heard their laughter. She glanced at him and froze. He slowed his steps. His grin stayed in place as he studied her. She seemed to tense up before she averted her gaze and continued toward the table. She set down the bowls and, without looking back, hurried inside.

The grin faded from Henry's lips. Getting Leah to forgive him wasn't going to be easy. He'd have to find a way to earn her trust first. Friends first, then forgiveness, he thought. Then maybe something more. He froze with shock. *Something more?*

"Hey, you coming?" Isaac asked. "I thought you were hungry."

He smiled at his friend. "I am."

"Let's go then."

The table was overflowing with food. Henry saw cold meats—roast beef, fried chicken and ham. There were a lot of dishes, including a large bowl of macaroni salad, two huge bowls of potato salad, vinegar green beans, dried-corn casserole and many other inviting sides. On a separate table were the desserts. He studied the pies, cakes and other mouthwatering sweets and was glad that Isaac had invited him. His family wasn't here. His mother and father had been invited, too, but even if they were ready to return to their former church district, his *dat's* hospital stay had made it impossible for them to attend. The fact that they probably wouldn't have come if his father had been well made him feel sad and guilty. He had done this to them. Because of what he'd done on *rumspringa*, he'd made it difficult for his parents to face all of these wonderful people.

He was glad that Isaac had invited him. Not only did he get to spend time with everyone, he was able to see Leah Stoltzfus again. Henry sighed as he followed the others to the food table. He could see her, but Leah avoided him like he suffered from the plague. He'd have to be patient. Leah would come out of the house eventually.

Ellen Lapp was among those serving the men and children. Isaac beamed at his wife and Henry gave her a tentative smile. "Henry!" she greeted. "I'm so glad you came."

He relaxed. "I'm happy that Isaac asked me."

"You don't need an invitation—ever," she assured him.

He felt warmth and a fluttering inside his chest. It had been Ellen who'd brought him to his senses and given him the courage to confess what he'd done first to Deacon Abram Peachy, then the rest of the church congregation. *"Danki,"* he whispered.

"Henry, you've got to try my wife's vanilla cream pie." Isaac gestured toward the dessert.

"After you both eat a *gut* meal first," Ellen said with a narrowed but teasing gaze at her husband. She held up a bowl. "German potato salad?" she offered them. "'Tis a favorite. Leah Stoltzfus made it."

Leah made it? He immediately held out his plate. "I don't know that I've ever tasted her potato salad before." As Ellen placed a large scoop on his plate, he discovered that Leah had come out of the house. She was staring at him, and he stared back unflinchingly and arched an eyebrow. She quickly looked away and strode over to where her mother and sisters were talking with Katie Lapp. He hid his amusement. Apparently, he continued to disturb her.

With loaded plate in hand, Henry moseyed on over to where the Stoltzfus women sat. He was eager to test his theory about Leah. *"Hallo.* The food looks *wunderbor,"* he said.

Missy, the girls' mother, smiled. "I'm happy you think so."

"I'm particularly eager to try the German potato salad," he commented with a glance in Leah's direction.

"Ja, 'tis one of our favorites," Ellie said. "I think you'll enjoy it." She flashed her sister a look. "Leah made it."

"Hmm. Can't wait to try it."

Leah eyed him politely. "I suppose you'll let me know whether or not you like it?"

"Absolutely." He smiled. "If you'll excuse me, Isaac

is waiting for me." He gestured toward the table filled with married Lapp brothers and their wives. He could sense Leah's gaze on him as he left.

"'Tis *gut* to see him back with us," he heard Missy say.

"Why?" Leah asked stiffly. "Did you miss him?"

"Leah!" her mother scolded.

As he continued toward Isaac's table, Henry couldn't hear Leah's response. But he was secretly pleased. Perhaps her mother could convince Leah that her reaction to him was unreasonable. He hoped so. He'd need her to unbend a little before he approached her with what he hoped was an offer she couldn't refuse. And he'd have to figure out a way to secure a few moments alone with her. He suffered a painful lurch in his belly. He had to do this right or he'd ruin all of his chances of winning the woman's friendship.

"Why would you say such a thing?" Ellie asked, curious.

Leah shrugged, unwilling to admit that she was attracted to Henry Yoder but was afraid to trust him. "Everyone has welcomed him with open arms. It bothers me after the way he hurt Isaac."

"That was a long time ago, Leah." *Mam* made a *tsk* sound with her tongue. "Henry Yoder is a *gut* man. It took a lot of courage to stand before our church congregation and confess. Isaac has forgiven him. Why shouldn't Henry be here? I'm just sorry that Margaret and Harry couldn't come, too."

Blushing, she agreed. "*Ja*. I'm sorry. I'm just feeling out of sorts."

"I'm not the one who deserves an apology." Her

mother eyed her with concern. "Are you ill, Leah? 'Tis not like you to be unkind."

"Ja," her sister Meg agreed. She had come with her husband, Peter, whom she'd married last November. "Out of all of us, you've the sweetest temperament."

"Maybe I am coming down with something," she mumbled. She felt guilty. Henry was a *gut* man, a kind man, and once again she'd behaved badly toward him. *Again.* But how could she apologize when just the thought made her insides churn with nervous apprehension?

"You'd better make sure you get enough rest, *dochter.* I know that you didn't sleep well last night. I heard you get up for a while before you went back to bed. Why can't you sleep?"

Leah shrugged. "I felt restless, so I went down and drank some hot milk." But she knew she'd gotten very little sleep since the day she'd found shelter with Henry in the store. Since then, she was unable to forget being the focus of his intense blue eyes.

"The men have their food," Ellie said. "Let's get ours."

As the Stoltzfus women went for their meal, Leah shot a glance toward Henry and her cousins' table. A frisson of sensation rippled down her spine as she caught Henry gazing at her with an odd look in his eyes. She stared back for a long moment and tried not to think about how handsome he was or that if circumstances had been different, she would have longed for his attention. She turned away deliberately, slowly, and followed her sisters to the food tables, pretending she didn't care that he was watching her. Inside she felt a jumble of nerves, but she wasn't about to let the man see how much he rattled her.

A short time after she finished eating her lunch, Leah had risen to help clean up when she caught sight of Henry's approach, his gaze focused on her. She stiffened even while her heart fluttered in appreciation of how handsome he was.

"Leah," he greeted softly. "May I have a word?"

"I'm cleaning up."

"I'll take care of this," Ellie offered as she grabbed the plates Leah held. She hurried away before Leah could object.

Leah shifted uncomfortably as she watched her sister stride away. She arched an eyebrow as she turned toward Henry. "Do you need me for something?"

His lips curved in a smile that stole her breath. "It's not what I need. It's about what I may be able to do for you." He paused. "Walk with me?" When she hesitated, he added softly, *"Please?"*

When he asked so nicely, how could she resist him? She nodded and fell into step beside him. Thoughts of an apology hovered in her mind.

They started toward the fields beyond the barn. Leah didn't look back, afraid to discover that others might be watching them. She experienced a tingling at her nape as they strolled some distance away from the gathering. She stopped, unwilling to go any farther.

"What do you want, Henry?"

He halted and turned her to face him. "I want to help you with your craft shop."

She gasped. "What? Who told you about it?"

"Isaac," he said calmly. "One of your sisters told him."

A ball of hurt fisted inside her chest. *"Ellie."*

Henry nodded. "Don't be angry with either one of

them. It came out accidentally when Isaac and Ellie were talking. Isaac mentioned it because he thought I could help you. I know what it takes to run a store—about inventory, purchasing, merchandise displays, bookkeeping…"

Leah knew she should be angry, but for some reason something in Henry's expression softened something inside of her. "I'm not ready to open a store just yet."

"Will you think about it when you do? Me helping you?"

"That's nice of you, Henry, but—"

"You don't trust me enough."

Leah shook her head because, for some reason, she trusted him in this. "'Tis not that. I don't have enough capital to look for a place yet."

"I understand." But something in his blue eyes had dimmed. He turned as if to head back toward the main yard.

She felt the uncontrollable urge to stop him. She grabbed his arm to halt him. "I'm telling the truth, Henry. I'll be happy to accept your help when the time is right."

Henry grinned, and Leah reeled back under the bright warmth in his eyes. "*Gut.* I'll be pleased to help you. And if you need assistance looking for a place when the time is right, I'm your man."

Leah felt her face heat. *I'm your man.* She had a sudden mental image of him working with her, smiling at her, making her feel special. She glanced away. "We should get back." She started to walk and he fell into step with her.

"Danki," he murmured as they entered the barnyard. She met his gaze. "For what?"

"For trusting me enough to accept my help," he whispered. Then, as if he'd sensed her unease, he left her, and she watched as he hurried toward the dessert table.

Shaken, Leah knew a strange yearning in her heart, one she didn't recognize. Still, she managed a smile as she rejoined her sisters where they sat drinking iced tea and sharing desserts.

Chapter Three

Monday morning Leah exited the house in good spirits. Ellie had been hired to houseclean for a new client who owned a huge five-bedroom residence. Because of the amount of work involved, her sister had requested her help. Leah was more than willing to work with Ellie. She'd put away the money for her shop. Since turning eighteen, she was allowed to keep all of her work earnings. Which was why she made it a point to help her parents as much as she could around the house and farm. It was her turn to feed the animals this morning, and she was happy to do it.

Her thoughts on the day ahead, she descended the porch steps and started forward, then halted abruptly. Her heart began to hammer hard as she stared at the man who stood several feet from her. "What are you doing here, Henry?"

He approached, and as he drew closer, she backed away until she was up against the bottom rung of the stairs. "Aren't you happy to see me?" A tiny smile curved up the corners of his mouth.

She sniffed, determined to keep him from realizing that she *was* glad to see him. "What do you think?"

His smile disappeared. "Contrary to what you might believe, I'm not stalking you."

She blushed. "I didn't say you were."

He folded his arms as he studied her. He wore a green shirt, navy tri-blend pants with black suspenders. A black-banded straw hat rested on his head, but he'd tipped back the wide brim. Beneath it, his sky blue eyes looked sapphire. "I'm here to help your father."

Leah blinked, tried to stay calm. "With what?"

Henry sighed heavily. "He wants to install a cabinet in one section of the barn to store things."

She gazed at him with suspicion. "My cousin invited you to Visiting Day, where my father just happened to ask you to install a cabinet for him, and all within four days of Friday's thunderstorm?"

He shrugged as if he didn't care whether or not she believed him. As if he was telling the truth. She frowned.

Her father came out of the house behind him. "Henry!" he exclaimed, and Leah immediately slipped past Henry before she looked back to watch the interaction between the two men. "Glad you could make it."

Leah experienced a burning in her stomach. Her *dat* seemed genuinely pleased to see him. The hot sensation intensified. Henry had told the truth. Why did she continually misjudge him?

Ashamed, she turned away, headed toward the barn to feed the animals. She started to hurry as it occurred to her that Henry and her father would be along soon. She fed all of the horses first, ensuring that each had fresh water and a bucket of feed. Later in the day, she'd return for their third feeding. Her sister Charlie would do the second one midday. She then went on to feed their dairy cows, bull, goats and sheep. She was outside with their hens and rooster when she heard voices from within the barn. When she was done throwing down chicken feed, she reluctantly returned to the outbuilding to put away the bucket. Their two cows needed to be milked, but she'd ask Charlie to do that for her. She had no desire to stay inside the barn as long as she had to share it with Henry Yoder.

Leah froze in the act of putting away the feed bucket. What was wrong with her? One minute she felt bad about the way she'd treated Henry, then in the next she was going out of her way to avoid him. She drew a cleansing breath. She wasn't going to run. She'd milk the cows before getting ready for work with Ellie. She wasn't going to let Henry's presence make her run scared.

Leah found the milk pails and went to Bessie first. Dragging over a stool, she sat down to milk her. The steady, rhythmic sound of milk against metal soothed her, and she became immersed in the farm chore. Once Bessie was milked, she moved on to Annabelle. The cow wasn't as cooperative as Bessie. The animal shifted restlessly and tried to kick her. She backed away before she was struck by the cow's hoof.

"*Nay*, you don't, you ornery critter!" She turned to get fresh hay and groaned when she saw Henry Yoder, who watched her with amusement.

"Having a bit of trouble, Leah?" he taunted, his voice deep and extremely male.

She glared at him as she lifted her chin. "Nothing I can't handle." Annabelle bumped up against her, nearly sending her sprawling. Henry's quick response to steady her made her grit her teeth.

"Need help?" he asked.

"Nay!" She was too aware of his strength as he released her.

He laughed. "Afraid I'll do it better and faster?"

"Go away," she said as she found fresh hay, which she tossed before Annabelle. The animal bent her head, content to eat. "Why are you here? I thought you were with my *vadder*." She pulled up the stool and started to milk Annabelle before she looked up at him.

He had taken off his hat and she could see the twinkle in his blue eyes. "I am," he said patiently. "He went into the house to fetch his drawings."

Leah frowned. "What drawings?" The sound of milk hitting the inside of the bucket wasn't as loud as her rapidly beating heart.

"Of the cabinet he wants me to build for him."

She paused in the act of milking. "Why would he want *you* to make him a cabinet?" Her voice sounded unnecessarily sharp. Contrite, she closed her eyes and drew a calming breath. Annabelle shifted uneasily, and Leah continued to milk her until the pail was nearly full.

"Because I like making them." He regarded her without warmth.

Leah studied him. She could see that her questioning his cabinetmaking abilities had upset him. "Have you made one before?" she said, softening her tone.

Henry nodded. *"Ja,* several."

She stifled a rude retort.

"I don't spend every minute in my parents' store," he added drily.

He'd aroused her curiosity. "Where does *Dat* want this cabinet?"

"Come with me," he invited.

Leah puckered her brow. Believing that she had little choice but to accompany him, she placed the filled milk pails into cold storage before she followed. She studied the back of his head and neck as he led the way through the barn and stopped at a familiar stall. She stared. It was the area that had housed Nell's dog, Jonas, and her cat, Maxie, then later the dog Peter Zook had given her sister Meg. Now the space was empty. *Why does* Dat *want a cabinet in here?*

She must have spoken the thought out loud. "Because he plans to get a dog," Henry said, shocking her. "With your sisters married and gone, he finds he's missing their animals. He thinks a cabinet will be a better place for dog food than on the shelf."

"*Dat* wants a dog?" she asked disbelievingly. Why hadn't her father told her?

Henry tilted his head as he regarded her. "You don't like dogs?"

She shook her head. "*Nay*—I'm mean—*ja*, I like dogs fine. I just didn't realize that my *vadder* did." Most Amish men wouldn't be willing to own a pet. Her sister Nell, who was married to a veterinarian, must have influenced her father more than she'd realized.

Before Henry could respond, her father returned, carrying a notepad. "Here you go. You can take this with you," he said as he tore off a page and handed it to Henry. He glanced at Leah briefly before turning back to the younger man.

Leah vaguely heard their discussion. She heard mention of wood and hinges and other stuff she couldn't comprehend. When the men's conversation ended, the barn became overwhelmingly quiet.

"*Dat?* You're going to get a dog?"

"I am." Arlin gazed at her with a silent look that warned her to mind her own business.

"Why didn't you tell me?" She fought back the hurt. It wasn't the first time she'd felt a little left out, set off from her family. She managed to smile. "What kind?"

Dat smiled and his demeanor changed from stern to little-boy excitement. "I don't know. What do you think?"

"I have no idea." She paused. "We could ask Nell. She'll recommend a good breed."

"I already asked her."

Nell knew. Who else? That feeling of being excluded rushed in again. She could feel Henry's gaze. Refusing to look at him, she addressed her father. "May I go with you when you pick one out?"

Her father beamed at her. "*Ja*, but I'd like to fix up the stall before I bring one home." He turned his attention to the space where the dog would be kept. "Jonas was happy here."

Leah nodded. Nell's rescue dog had been happy in these surroundings. "*Ja*, he was." She swung her gaze grudgingly toward Henry. He studied her with a thoughtful expression, and she feared that he could read the pain she'd tried to conceal while talking with her father.

"Leah!" Ellie's loud voice called from out in the yard.

"I've got to go," she said and spun around. She ran a few yards before she stopped. "See you later, *Dat*. Henry, you do a *gut* job with the cabinet, *ja*?" She softened the request with a slight curve of her lips.

Pleasure transformed Henry's features. "I will," he promised.

Leah trusted that he would. The warmth in his penetrating gaze had her scrambling to escape. She didn't want to feel anything for Henry Yoder—even the littlest, tiniest bit of warmth that settled within her chest and reached out in an unsuccessful attempt to capture her heart.

Henry watched Leah leave before turning back to Arlin. "She seems surprised that you want a dog."

Arlin had been studying his daughter as she left. He turned his focus on Henry. "She doesn't mind, though. All my *dechter* are animal lovers."

After a nod, Henry quietly studied the paper in his hands. "This looks simple enough. You want me to take down the shelf and put up a plain cabinet."

"I thought we could leave the shelf and install the cabinet to the left of it," the man said.

Henry eyed the wall space. "That would work. The dimensions for the cabinet are small."

The older man inclined his head. "Big enough, though. I'm getting a dog, not a herd of goats." He chuckled. "The two goats we have cause enough damage."

Henry didn't join in. He kept remembering the look of pain on Leah's face as she'd learned that her father hadn't bothered to include her in his plans. "When do you need this?"

"When can you get it done?"

He thought for a moment. His father was being discharged from the hospital that afternoon. He'd work in the store but figured his mother would want to spend time there. "I can have it done before Thursday."

Arlin looked surprised. *"Gut, gut."* The man headed toward the door and Henry fell into step beside him. "I was glad to see you back on Sunday." He hesitated. "I would have liked to see your *mam* and *dat*."

"Dat's been in the hospital. *Mam* has been spending all of her time there." Henry became quiet. "I've been running the store. My *vadder* will be released today. Maybe in a couple of weeks, they'll be able to come."

The older man regarded him with concern. "I didn't know about your *dat*." Arlin was too polite to ask, but Henry could see his curiosity.

"He had a heart attack, but his doctor says that there's no permanent damage."

"A wake-up call," Arlin said as they stepped out of the barn.

"Ja." He saw Ellie and Leah inside the buggy as Ellie steered the horse to head toward the street. He couldn't tear his attention away from the taller of the two blonde women who sat on the vehicle's passenger side.

"She can be stubborn," the man next to him murmured, catching Henry off guard. "Just like her mother."

Henry's gaze focused on Leah's father. "Who?" he asked, but he knew.

"Leah." The corners of his mouth bowed upward. "She's the sweetest and kindest of all of my *dechter*, but she can also be the most hardheaded."

"I've never known Missy to be hardheaded." Henry noted a strange look enter the man's expression and saw him stiffen.

"Leah hasn't welcomed you back to our church community, has she?" When Henry was too stunned to answer, the man continued, "Don't let it bother you. She'll get used to you soon enough."

"You think so?"

Arlin nodded. "*Ja.* 'Tis Leah. She's different than the others. I've never known her to be upset with anyone for long."

Henry took comfort from her father's belief that sooner or later Leah would accept him for the changed adult man that he'd become—and forget his foolish teenage mistakes.

His father was released from the hospital late Monday afternoon. Henry had worked on the cabinet an hour or two after the store closed. He stopped when his *dat* got home since he wanted to spend time with him and to assure his parents that the store had run smoothly with a steady flow of customers in their absence.

Henry got up extra early Tuesday morning and finished the cabinet. He had time to make a quick run to Arlin's to install it. While he drove his market wagon to the residence, he hoped to see Leah again. His heart raced at the prospect. As he pulled his vehicle into the driveway and parked near the barn, he caught a glimpse of the woman ever present in his thoughts at the clothesline, taking down laundry. She must have heard him arrive for she turned and glowered at him.

He climbed down from the wagon and reached into the back to retrieve the cabinet. He didn't realize that Leah had left the clothesline to approach until she stood within several feet of him. She watched silently as he carried the cabinet inside the barn. Henry set it in the designated stall, then left to get his tools. He accidentally bumped into Leah as she entered the barn. Instinctively, he reached out to steady her.

"Careful," he murmured. She smelled like vanilla and honey, a fragrance that would forever make him think of her. *Her soap?*

He saw her throat move as she swallowed when she stepped away. "You've finished it already?" She seemed skeptical.

"*Ja,*" he replied. "'Tis a simple design. *Gut* enough for a barn stall."

Her brow knit with confusion. "Where are you going?"

He hid his pleasure. It was as if she was afraid that he'd leave. "To get my tools." When red stained her cheeks, he realized that he'd guessed correctly. Hiding his joy, he swept past her on his way back to his wagon, where he retrieved everything he'd need for installation, including the cabinet doors, which he'd left off to make it easier for him to carry the unit. Leah hadn't moved from where he'd left her. He didn't say a word as he walked past her and into the stall.

Ignoring her, he pulled out his tape measure to gauge the distance between the small shelf to the wall corner. He'd crafted the cabinet to the right measurement. Feeling pleased, he placed two screws between his lips before he lifted the cabinet to where he wanted to secure it. Henry pulled his carpenter's pencil from behind his ear and marked within the predrilled holes before setting the unit down again. He grabbed his battery-operated screwdriver, picked up the cabinet, then screwed it into place. Once secure, he wordlessly reached for a door, which he installed before he secured the second one. When he was finished, he turned. Leah stood behind him, examining his work. She jumped back, startled as she met his gaze. He didn't say a word as he picked up his tools and headed outside.

"It looks *gut*," Leah said grudgingly as she followed him out of the barn.

He met her gaze to see if she was mocking him. She wasn't. She seemed genuinely impressed by what he'd done in so short a time. Her approval spiked his pleasure of standing in her company. "Basic and solid."

"You finished it," she said. "But it's not one that belongs in a kitchen. I think it's exactly what *Dat* had in mind."

"I just made it to look like your *vadder's* drawings."

She nodded. Her expression wasn't bitter or condemning. Henry felt his heart open like a blossom in the sun. He gazed at her a long time, then dragged his eyes away. He'd made some progress with Leah and he didn't want to press his luck. He climbed onto the wagon seat. "Show it to your *vadder* when he gets home, *ja*?"

"I will," she said.

"Take care, Leah." He turned the horse-drawn vehicle toward the main road. He flicked the leathers and his mare started forward when he heard her shout.

"Henry!"

He immediately drew in the reins to halt his horse.

She walked to his vehicle and gazed up at him. "I've decided... I'd like you to teach me about storekeeping."

He blinked, pleased. "You do?" When she nodded, he felt his heart rate accelerate. "*Gut*. There's a lot I can show you." He smiled. "Do you have a name for your shop?"

She shook her head. "I don't have a name because I don't have one yet."

"Think about a name. It will help you as you reach for your goal."

He heard her release a sharp breath. "I'll do that." She grew quiet. "I should go," she said. "I'll see you later, Henry."

"I want to know the name of your shop the next time I see you." His lips curved. "We can talk about your plans then."

"Sunday?" she asked, almost like an invitation.

He nodded. "I'll see you then."

When she beamed at him, he left with the mental image of her lovely face turned toward him, her gaze without censure. It wasn't forgiveness or friendship he'd seen in her blue eyes, but it was a start. He grinned. He couldn't wait to see her again. She'd become important to him. He attributed his anticipation to his interest in her as a woman and a prospective friend.

Leah groaned as Henry pulled his buggy onto the main road. What had she done? She'd been impressed by the cabinet he'd made, but was that any reason to ask the man if he was coming to their church service? Like she *wanted* him there?

She couldn't believe she'd been so impulsive. Why had she accepted his offer of assistance? Henry Yoder was trouble and she certainly didn't want or need it in her life. She had enough to contend with. Working with Ellie yesterday had been wonderful. They'd earned a great deal of money, and Leah was able to put a substantial amount away for her shop.

"I can do this. It will be business only," she murmured as she took down the laundry.

She exhaled with relief. She'd be polite, businesslike,

but she wouldn't give him any special attention. She would express her gratitude, of course. He was offering her his time, and she was thankful. A working relationship with him was nothing to be concerned about.

Her heart skipped a beat as she recalled his smile, the way the sunlight had reflected on the tiny golden streaks in his dark hair. Leah closed her eyes in shock. She was attracted to Henry Yoder. As long as she kept her distance emotionally from him, she would be fine.

"I'll not lose my heart to him," she whispered. And she found herself relaxing. She just had to remember that this was Henry Yoder, and she was interested only in opening a craft store.

She'd unpinned the last garment from the clothesline and headed back to the house. She smiled when she spied her father as he came home from a day spent with Horseshoe Joe Zook, Meg's father-in-law. *Dat* had been helping Joe with a home project. What, Leah had no idea.

"Dat," she greeted. "Henry was here. He installed the cabinet you ordered."

Her father looked surprised. "Already?"

She bobbed her head.

"How does it look?"

"Gut. 'Tis perfect for the barn."

He appeared pleased. "Come to take a look with me?"

Leah beamed. *"Ja.* Just let me put this inside," she said as she held up the laundry basket.

A few minutes later she followed her father into the stall. He went straight over to inspect the cabinet. She waited with rapid heartbeat for his reaction. Why, she didn't know. Certainly it wasn't because she worried that he wouldn't be pleased with Henry's work.

"Dat?" she murmured as he opened and closed the cabinet doors several times while he inspected every inch of the unit.

He closed the doors one last time, then turned to her—and smiled. *"Wunderbor,"* he pronounced. "When can you come with me to Nell's to look at some puppies?"

Leah grinned. "Tonight? After supper?" she suggested.

"After supper," her father agreed, then they headed toward to the house to see how long it would be before dinner.

She was excited about having a pet. Her spirits rose. It wasn't because her *dat* was pleased with Henry's cabinetwork, she thought. Or was it?

A mental image of Henry rose in her mind, making her uncomfortable. She wasn't attracted to him. She didn't like him. She sighed. His kindness stirred up feelings that she could control because they weren't real. *They can't be real.*

Leah became to wonder if she should forget about accepting Henry's offer to help. Surely, she could learn about storekeeping on her own. It would be much safer that way.

Chapter Four

Leah couldn't get Henry's offer of assistance out of her thoughts. Ever since she'd accepted it yesterday, she'd vacillated between telling him she'd changed her mind and letting her acceptance stand.

She was alone in the kitchen doing the breakfast dishes. Her mother was cleaning the upstairs and her father was out delivering his newly built wooden birdhouses to several shops in the Lancaster area. Ellie was on a housecleaning job and she wasn't sure where Charlie was, but it had to be elsewhere since Leah could always tell when her youngest sister was home. The girl was a whirlwind of activity and conversation one couldn't ignore.

She washed the dishes, then picked up one from the drain rack to dry with a clean tea towel. She gazed out the window as she dried each cup and dish and found comfort in the simple chore.

"Leah!" her mother called from upstairs. "Would you please take care of the animals?"

"Ja, Mam!" she called back.

Mam entered the kitchen a minute later as Leah put

away the last dish. "I sent Charlie to Katie's with our quilt squares."

"Too quiet for her to be here." Leah grinned. *Endie* Katie hosted their monthly quilting bee, and whenever there was a new quilt to be made, her aunt would sew the squares together, then ready the quilt to be hand stitched by the women who attended the gathering. Thoughts of quilts brought her right back to Henry, as anything crafty made her yearn to get her shop up and running. And Henry was going to help her.

Henry hadn't mentioned a time for them to meet. If he'd heard him right, she'd see him at church services. But what if he had changed his mind about teaching her? *I hope not.* She felt a painful wrenching in her midsection. Leah knew at that moment that she would let her acceptance of his offer stand. She prayed that he'd ready to teach her soon.

She hung up the dish towel. "You done upstairs?" she asked her mother as she headed toward the back door.

"*Nay.* I need to strip and wash the bedsheets."

"I can help with those," Leah offered.

But her mother shook her head. "No need. It won't take me long."

"I'll head out to the barn then. Call me if you change your mind."

Her mother's expression was warm and loving. "You're a *gut dochter*, Leah."

"You say that to all your *dechter*."

Mam laughed. "And each of you is special in your own way," she said as she headed toward the stairs.

With a smile lingering on her lips, Leah crossed the yard and entered the barn. The aroma of animal dung and straw hit her as she made her way toward the goats.

It was a scent that she was used to so she didn't mind. In fact, she found the familiarity of it soothing. The goats gravitated to her when they saw her.

"*Hallo* there, little ones. Hungry?" She opened the rear door of the barn that led to the pasture. Then she returned to release the latch on the goat stall and herded them outside. "Some lovely fresh grass for you to enjoy," she said fondly.

The small animals were quick to frolic about before stopping to graze. Leah filled the water trough near the fence, then returned to the barn to feed the horses before releasing them into the pasture with the goats. She fed the chickens, then went inside to feed their cows, and after that, she took care of their bull, Mortimer, and released him into a separate fenced area.

When all of the animals had been seen to, Leah meandered down the aisle to where their puppy would live once he was old enough to be parted from his mother. Her gaze settled on the cabinet Henry had crafted that hung on the far wall. She sighed. It looked good and it would work well for storage. She glanced down to where Nell's and then Meg's dogs had slept, saw matted bedding and frowned. Last evening when she'd come into the barn, she'd put down the fresh straw, but this morning it looked as if someone had lain there.

Her lips curved. Charlie. No doubt her sister had escaped here for a few moments to enjoy some privacy. Charlie was as excited as *Dat* about having a new pet. She could picture her little sister as Charlie lay back and stared at the barn rafters while she chewed on or fingered a piece of straw. Without thought, Leah retrieved a rake to fluff up the bedding before she put it away.

She wondered if her mother needed anything from the store. *Yoder's General Store.*

She exited the barn and stopped abruptly to avoid colliding into a solid male form. "Henry!" She gasped.

If he'd been startled by their near collision, Henry didn't show it. His mouth curved up slowly. His blue eyes warmed. "Leah, just the person I want to see."

She felt a fluttering in her chest. "I didn't expect you to visit today."

"I thought I'd stop by to see when you wanted to start storekeeping lessons. Didn't want to wait until Sunday." He shoved his straw hat back on his head, exposing more of his dark hair.

She felt the shock of looking closely into his blue eyes. Leah swallowed hard. The man was far too good-looking for her peace of mind. "I don't know. When's a *gut* time for you?"

"Tomorrow? Nine o'clock? *Mam's* working the store today." He smiled. "She brought my *vadder* with her. I'll be handling the store tomorrow. In between customers, I can show you our store account books. Go over some things that may help you." He gazed at her steadily as if trying to read her thoughts.

Tomorrow? She shifted as she found it difficult to breathe. "Can we go outside?" she asked huskily. It was strange standing in the door of the barn and she desperately needed the fresh air.

He nodded, stepped aside and gestured for her to precede him. Once they were both outside, he fell into step with her. Without a word, they headed toward the back of the property, around the fenced area and into the farm field, away from the road and the prying eyes of anyone who might drive by and see them together.

If he wondered why she chose this direction, Henry didn't mention it. Leah chanced a look at him and encountered the direct impact of his gaze. Her heart thumped hard. Twice. Three times. She glanced away. "I don't want you to feel obligated to do this for me. I know you sell crafts in your store and…"

He halted and she jolted when he placed a gentle hand on her shoulder. "Leah, I want to help you. As for the crafts in our store? They don't sell well there, because our focus is food and supplies and our customers are mostly members of our Amish community. But a craft shop like the one you want to open? It will draw business from two directions—from community members who will want you to sell their items to English residents of Happiness and to tourists who are visiting the area." He seemed taken back as he noted where he'd placed his hand. He quickly released her. "We need a craft store. Your shop will do well, I'm sure of it."

The earnestness in his expression moved her. "I hope you're right," she whispered. She continued to walk. She knew she should get back to the house, but for some reason she wanted to prolong her time with him. Considering how she'd felt about him before the day she'd taken refuge from the storm, she found her change of heart somewhat disturbing, as well as exciting. She still wasn't sure just how much she should trust him. *As long as I consider him a teacher and nothing more, there is no cause for me to worry.*

They walked until they reached the road that bordered the rear of the property. "This land is your *vadder's*?" Henry asked.

Leah nodded. "It used to belong to Aaron Troyer, but he decided to move closer to Lancaster City, where he runs his buggy-ride business. *Dat* bought it to add to the farm."

He nodded as if he knew of Aaron's business. "He does well with tourists."

"*Ja*, and he enjoys it. His sister, Martha, helps him." Leah frowned. "Sometimes I wonder…" She stopped as she realized that she shouldn't voice her thoughts, that she often wondered if Aaron wasn't lonely without a wife or family. He was in his late twenties or early thirties. He was a nice man, although she hadn't spent a lot of time in his company. She had no idea why she was now thinking of his personal business.

"You wonder what?" Henry stopped and faced her.

Leah shook her head. "'Tis nothing." She smiled up at him. "And none of my business." He frowned. She was grateful that he didn't push. "We should head back."

She turned and started forward. He halted her with a touch on her arm. She inhaled sharply as she gazed at him. "Is something wrong?"

He didn't say a word as he continued to study her. His perusal seemed almost like a caress, but that was only her imagination. There was nothing but polite concern in his expression. "What's bothering you?"

She tilted her head as she furrowed her brow. "Why do you ask?"

Henry gazed at the woman before him, feeling concern. He couldn't tell what she was thinking. He had a feeling that she was struggling with something, and all he wanted to do was help. He just hoped that the something wasn't *him*. "You still want me to teach you?"

Her gaze met his, then skittered away. "*Ja*, I can learn a lot from you."

"But?" he asked as his stomach burned. What if she'd changed her mind? He honestly wanted to help and spend time with her.

She met his regard head-on. "I just wonder if 'tis a *gut* idea. I feel like I'm taking advantage."

Stunned by her answer, he shook his head. "*Nay.* You forget this was *my* idea."

Leah seemed afraid to believe him. "Are you sure?"

His lips curved from a smile into a full-out grin. "Positive. If you'd like, you can help with customers."

He saw her relax and felt gratified. "*Danki,*" she murmured.

"I'm more than happy to help, Leah."

As they headed back toward the house, Henry felt the tension ease between them. He and Leah Stoltzfus would be spending a lot of time together. He hoped that she'd come to accept the man he'd become. That his mistake was a while ago should have made things easier for them, but he realized that when it came to family, it wasn't easier to forgive and forget despite the teachings of the Amish faith.

Leah accompanied him to his buggy. "I'll see you tomorrow," she said.

She stepped back to allow him room to climb into his vehicle. Her mother exited the house and approached.

"Who'll be hosting church service next?" he asked, figuring she would know. He'd forgotten to ask Isaac when he'd seen him last.

"We are," Missy said as she drew near. "The Kings were to host, but there's been a family emergency."

Henry frowned. "I hope it's nothing serious."

"I don't know. Mae and Amos had to leave for Ohio. I believe Mae's brother is ill."

"I'll keep everyone in my prayers," he said.

Missy nodded as if she approved. Henry glanced at Leah. "See you soon." He then waved at the two women as he steered his horse back to the road. He didn't look back until he reached the street. He wasn't surprised that the women had gone inside the house, although he realized how much he'd hoped that Leah would linger outside until he left.

As he headed back to the family store, he looked forward to the next morning. He was eager to show Leah how they kept their books. He hadn't mentioned the lessons to his parents, but he didn't see why they would think them a problem. He would show Leah a ledger page and explain about accounting columns and how to keep track of inventory, as well as accounts receivable and payable.

He was also eager for Sunday since it was to be held at the Arlin Stoltzfus farm. It would be wonderful seeing more of Leah's home and how she and her family related to each other. Henry was the youngest of three siblings. His eldest brother had chosen to leave the Amish life. His parents were upset by his choice, not because he'd done anything wrong by leaving when he had. He hadn't joined the church, so he was free to live an English life if he chose. His father and mother were upset because David had moved away and hadn't been home to visit in years and the last letter they'd received had been over ten months ago. Henry wondered how his older brother was faring. There were many years between them, so it seemed as if they'd grown up in different families. His sister, Ruth, was married and living in Ohio. Henry couldn't recall the last time he'd seen her. He had written to her recently to let her know about their father's hospital stay. If Ruth didn't come after receiving the news, then he didn't know how to convince her that it was well past the time for her to visit.

He thought of Leah, who was constantly in his thoughts. He was encouraged that she trusted him enough to allow him to help. He grinned as he flicked his horse's leathers and urged the animal into a fast trot toward home.

When he arrived, he went to the store first to check on his parents. Earlier, he'd talked with them about returning to their former community. They'd said they would think about it, and he'd had the impression that they were going to agree. He needed to make sure that they were still willing to go. If so, he could help his mother prepare her contribution to the midday meal that the church members enjoyed after service was finished.

He opened the door to the shop and stepped inside. It was bright outside and it took a minute for his eyes to adjust to the change in light. *"Mam?"*

"Henry!" she exclaimed as she caught sight of him. "I thought you were spending the day with Isaac."

"I did for a while, but he had work to finish and I do, too. I stopped by the Stoltzfuses. Do you remember the cabinet I was building? It was for Arlin. He wanted it for his barn."

His mother smiled but seemed preoccupied.

"Where's *Dat*? Isn't he here?"

"Nay, he was feeling tired so I sent him home to rest."

"Mam, do you think he's ill?"

"I don't know, but I think I'll ask to move up his doctor's appointment."

Henry thought his mother's decision wise. "Would

you like me to check on him? Or I can stay here if you'd like to go back to the house yourself."

"Would you go? I'd go myself but I'm expecting Alta Hershberger."

Alta Hershberger was the local busybody from their former Amish church community.

"I'll let you know if anything is wrong," he assured her. "I won't bother him if he's sleeping. He may be tired because of his medication."

"I hope that's all it is," his *mam* said with a look of worry.

Henry left the store and parked close to the house barnyard. *"Dat?"* he called not too loudly as he entered. If his father was awake, he'd be able to hear his call. If not, then his *dat* was probably asleep.

When there was no answer, he walked through the house to check each room until he found his father in the bedroom. He approached silently and was glad to see his *dat's* even and easy breathing as his parent slept. He left as quietly as he'd come and went into the kitchen for a glass of iced tea and a bite to eat. He'd bring his mother lunch while assuring her that *Dat* was resting comfortably. He made two ham-and-cheese sandwiches, then he headed back to the store down the lane from the house.

When he got back, he saw Alta Hershberger in conversation with his mother. He entered and greeted Alta with a smile. The woman looked at him speculatively, acknowledged his greeting, then abruptly turned back to his mother. He met his *mam's* gaze briefly, and the look in her eyes apologized for Alta's behavior. Henry went quietly into the back room where they often ate midday meals while at work. He set the sandwiches on the table, then went out front to grab two bottles of iced tea from the refrigerated display case. With a nod in Alta's direction, he returned to the back and waited for his mother.

He didn't have to wait too long. His mother entered moments later, saw the tea and sandwiches on the table and smiled. "How thoughtful!"

Henry's mouth curved. "I thought you might be hungry."

"I am." She pulled out a chair and sat. "I'm sorry about Alta."

"There's no need to apologize. Alta is Alta. She is who she is."

"She has a good heart."

He nodded. "But most of the time she hides it." He chuckled. "She doesn't bother me." He took a bite of his sandwich and watched his *mam* do the same. He felt happy when he saw his *mam's* enjoyment of the simple meal. "*Dat's* sleeping."

His mother frowned as she set down the sandwich. "I'm worried about him."

"He seems to be resting comfortably."

"But the doctor said there was no permanent damage to his heart. Why is he so tired?"

He pushed his mother's bottle of tea closer to her. "I don't know, but I agree that he should see the doctor." He thought of Sunday service and longed for assurances that his parents would be attending. "*Mam*, you'll come to church services at Arlin's *haus*, *ja*?"

She furrowed her brow. "I want to."

"Everyone has been asking after you." He reached for her hand. "*Mam*, please don't let my past mistakes keep you from your friends. I know you've made new ones in the new church district, but this community—

the Lapps, Stoltzfuses, Kings and others—miss you. They want to see you."

Her blue eyes glistened. "They do?"

"*Mam*, I know Alta can be difficult," he began.

She laughed. "As you said, Alta is Alta. She doesn't bother me."

"Then will you and *Dat* come?"

His mother nodded. "We'll be there."

He relaxed and smiled. *"Gut."* He took a bite of his sandwich, chewed and swallowed. "I thought I'd work in the store tomorrow so you'll be able to spend time with *Dat* and keep an eye on him."

Mam looked relieved. "That's a fine idea. *Danki*."

Henry grinned. "You're welcome." He picked up his iced tea and sipped. "I figured I'd help Isaac with the bench wagon Saturday."

"Tell him I said *hallo*."

Henry beamed at her. "I will." He suddenly had a lot to look forward to, starting with Leah's first store-keeping lesson tomorrow, then spending time helping Isaac on the Stoltzfus property on Saturday and returning again on Sunday for church services. He'd get to see Leah on three, maybe even four, occasions if he could convince her to return for lesson two on Friday, he thought with a rush of pleasure.

He couldn't wait.

Chapter Five

Leah woke up Thursday morning, eager to learn more about storekeeping from Henry. Her sister Ellie had asked her to help with a job late yesterday afternoon, and she'd been pleased for the work, for she had more earnings to add to her savings. She planned to accept any work Ellie offered her from now on while learning what she could whenever Henry was available to teach her. A general store wasn't the same as a craft shop, but surely the bookkeeping and ordering of merchandise would be similar. She showered, then donned a light purple dress with black apron and white prayer *kapp* over her hair. Figuring that she'd be on her feet helping him with customers, she put on comfortable black shoes that allowed her to stand for long periods of time.

"Morning, Leah," her mother greeted as Leah entered the kitchen for breakfast.

"*Gut* mornin', *Mam*. I'll plan to pick up a few things at Yoder's store this morning. Do you need anything?"

"That's nice of you, Leah." *Mam* turned and reached for a sheet of paper on the kitchen countertop. "I already have a list."

She took and studied it. She saw several items that made her wonder how soon her mother might want them. "*Mam*, I may stay awhile. Do you need these right away?"

"Whenever you get home will be fine, Leah. I'm off to help Josie Mast with her baking. Now that Ellen is married and out of the house, Josie feels that she needs someone to teach her to bake a pie without making a mess of it."

Leah chuckled. "I know she has trouble. Ellen confided in me about it. Josie is a fine cook, just not a *gut* baker." She grabbed a muffin from a plate, made a cup of tea and then sat down to enjoy both. "Where's Charlie?" she asked.

"Charlotte Peachy has asked her to help with the children today. She left about five minutes before you came down."

"The Peachy residence, eh?" She grinned at her mother. "I'm surprised she agreed to go. She's not overly fond of Nate."

Mam gave her a slow smile. "He's not going to be there."

"No wonder she agreed," Leah murmured.

It didn't take her long to eat her muffin and finish her tea. She rose and brought her dishes to the sink, where she washed and dried them before putting them away.

"Are you sure you've eaten enough?" her mother asked.

"I'll be fine. If I get hungry, I can always buy something to munch on at the store."

Mam nodded. "I'll see you later then. Give Harry and Margaret my best. And Henry, too."

The mention of Henry's name made her blush. "I

will." She felt suddenly nervous about the upcoming lesson.

Less than a half hour later, Leah steered her horse-drawn buggy into the parking area near Yoder's General Store. She got out of the vehicle, tied up her horse and went to the front store entrance. The door was unlocked and opened easily. "Henry?" she called.

He came out from the back, looking pleased to see her. He looked handsome in a green shirt and blue tri-blend pants held up with black suspenders. She admired his dark hair, for he always took off his hat inside.

"You came," he said as if he hadn't been sure she'd actually show. "Come around to the back." He jerked his head toward the rooms beyond the merchandise area.

Breath hitching, she followed him around the counter to the room where she and Henry had taken shelter during that terrible spring thunderstorm.

He led the way into another room that she hadn't noticed before. There was a desk and a large book, opened, with pages of columns and rows filled with figures and descriptions. A chair sat behind the desk, and she watched as Henry pulled another one next to it.

"I thought we'd start with bookkeeping," he said. His blue eyes regarded her with warmth. "'Tis always *gut* for a store owner to know how to manage her accounts." He pulled the chair out from under the desk. "Sit here."

Trying to calm the butterflies in her stomach, she sat where instructed. Henry shifted the other chair so that he could sit close to her. She immediately became aware of his clean masculine scent. He smelled of soap and cinnamon. As he sat beside her, she asked, "Are you baking cinnamon buns?"

He grinned, and she felt his good humor with a tingling right down to her toes. "*Mam* made them this morning. I've brought some down for us. Want one?"

She felt her face heat. "*Ja*, please."

Henry rose and left the room. He returned moments later with two cups of hot tea and a plate with four large cinnamon rolls. "Here you go."

"You made me tea," she said breathlessly.

"You like tea with two sugars but no milk," he replied as if proud that he'd remembered.

Startled that he knew, she accepted the cup with a nod of thanks. "You made the tea here?"

"I did." He shoved the plate of cinnamon rolls toward her. "Eat up. We've got a lot to cover, so you'd better enjoy them before we get busy."

Henry watched with enjoyment as Leah sipped at her tea between bites of cinnamon roll. He was glad she was here. He knew he needed to be careful with her. He didn't want to scare her off. She didn't trust him completely, and he didn't blame her. Still, it was a comfortable silence as they finished their breakfast. When they were done, he pulled the ledger book closer to her and began to explain the system of logging income and expenses.

"What is this?" she asked, pointing to a column that listed merchandise ordered from an out-of-state company.

"We order some of our stock locally and from Ohio, Indiana and West Virginia. Once we place an order, we write the quantity of items requested in this column, the cost in this column, and see this? This is where we list the date of the order. We also keep track of the day the items arrived, whether we received everything we requested and the date we paid the invoice. Lastly, we keep track of how many we sell so that we can figure out when to place the next order."

Leah studied the ledger page carefully. "Makes sense." She glanced toward him just as he leaned closer, and he found their faces close enough for him to see the deep blue flecks in her eyes. She had beautiful fair skin and a lovely pert nose. He saw her swallow thickly before she said, "I'll have to figure out how to stock my store. I hope to sell crafts from the women in our church community on consignment, but I also want to sell sewing supplies and other craft items that will appeal to tourists in our area." Her lips were pink and he stared at them before he quickly sat back and looked away.

"That's a sound idea." He rose, needing to put some distance between them before he said or did anything to upset her, which he'd immediately regret. He crossed the room, then faced her. "Have you given any thought to a name for your shop?"

She blinked. "I've had a few ideas, but they seem silly."

Bracing himself with his palms flat against the wall behind him, Henry leaned back and studied her. "Tell me."

"Second Sister's Crafts."

He smiled as he gazed at her. "I like it."

"Or Happiness Quilt and Craft Supplies."

"I like that one, too." He loved looking at her. Their eyes caught and held, and he fought the urge to look away. From a distance, he felt more in control of his emotions. Leah Stoltzfus was getting to him in a way he'd never expected. He longed for more than friendship from her. But that was impossible. The goal was to get her to forgive him and be his friend. He'd be polite and helpful, and make sure she couldn't read his thoughts—or his attraction to her. The room grew silent. Henry felt a rising tension. "Would you like more tea?" he asked, pushing himself from the wall.

She looked down briefly at her cup and nodded. "That would nice."

He stared at her intently a moment, unable to look away from her beautiful eyes and face, until he realized he'd made her uncomfortable. "I'll be right back," he murmured before heading into the front room. He checked the contents of the teakettle and realized there was enough water to heat back up. He set it on the propane single-burner unit they kept on the table behind the counter and turned it on. Henry looked down and saw that they needed more tea, so he went down one of the store aisles and grabbed a box of tea bags. The store entrance door opened just as he stepped behind the counter. He glanced back and felt a moment's dread when he realized that it was Alta Hershberger, the community busybody, who'd entered.

Hoping to alert Leah of potential trouble, he moved close toward the opening to the back room. "*Gut* morning, Alta!" he said loudly enough for Leah to hear. "What can I help you with this fine day?"

"Henry." The woman narrowed her gaze as she studied him. "Have you been staying out of trouble?"

Henry stiffened but managed to smile. "*Ja*, I've learned my lesson." Some imp inside of him said, "And you?"

Alta sniffed. "As if I would do something so outrageous to be considered trouble."

He barely managed not to grit his teeth. "May I help you find something?"

Suddenly all business, she moved closer to the counter. "I have a list," she said, shoving it in his direction.

Henry studied the paper and nearly groaned. The list looked a mile long, and it appeared that now that she saw he was here, she expected him to pull all the merchandise for her. And since some of the items sported different brands, he had a feeling that whatever one he picked for her wouldn't meet her expectations. With a sigh, he grabbed a handbasket and started down the first aisle.

The teakettle whistled, drawing Alta's attention. "You're making tea?" she asked. "*Gut.* I'd like a cup."

Fighting irritation because he was here, after all, to help their store customers, even one as contrary as Alta Hershberger, he smiled as he came around to the back of the counter where he set down the basket to prepare the woman a cup of tea. He poured water into a clean cup, added a tea bag from the box he'd taken from the shelf, then set it on the counter before her. "Sugar? Milk?"

"Sugar," she said with a raised eyebrow as she studied the tea bag. "Lots of it. This kind can be bitter."

"Ja," he agreed pleasantly as he set the sugar bowl and a clean spoon before her.

"Do you have a chair?"

"I'll get you one." Henry was eager to go into the back and see Leah in case she hadn't heard him and didn't know of Alta's presence in the store. The last thing he wanted was for the woman to find out that Leah was in the back room. He entered the room where she'd sat at the desk only to find it empty. His heart lurched and he placed a hand over his burning stomach. Leah was gone. She hadn't waited for him to return.

He grabbed the chair he'd been sitting in only moments ago and brought it out for Alta.

"Here you go."

To his shock, her expression softened and she smiled at him with approval.

The front door opened again. "*Gut* morning!" the newcomer said. Henry was stunned to Leah acting as if she'd just arrived with list in hand. "Nice day for shopping, isn't it?" Her eyes fell on Alta and Leah beamed at her. "You had the same idea as my *mudder*!" Her gaze shifted to Henry, but there was nothing in it to give away her thoughts. He couldn't help feel pleased that she hadn't left. She must have heeded his warning and found this entrance the best solution to a possible bad situation.

She approached where Henry stood and Alta was seated. "Henry, I'm sorry to bother you on a day that you're busy, but *Mam* asked that I pick up a few things for her. When you're done with Alta, do you think you could help me?"

He kept his features polite as he nodded. "It will take me a few minutes. Alta is having tea. Would you like a cup?"

"*Ja*, that would be wonderful," she said, and a quick glimmer of amusement flickered in her blue eyes. His mood lightened. "But I'll make it…if it's *oll recht*," she added.

His smile was genuine. "Feel free."

"Use lots of sugar," Alta grumbled as Leah skirted the counter to the teakettle.

"Cups are below." Henry had moved back into the

first aisle where he began to assemble Alta's grocery order. He took his time, making sure he got everything on Alta's list. He questioned her on a few things, and she seemed to approve of his diligence in getting the correct items.

He no longer minded Alta's presence, because Leah had stayed and was making herself at home. Soon the older woman would finish her tea, pay for her order and leave. And Leah would still be here. *She had stayed. Thanks be to God.*

Three hours later Henry was alone in the store, cleaning the teacups left behind by Alta Hershberger and Leah. The morning—the day—hadn't turned out as he'd hoped. After he'd filled Alta's order, he'd started on Leah's but, instead of leaving as expected, Alta had stayed for another cup of tea. When he was done with Leah's order, there was nothing for her to do but leave. The woman had taken it as a given that Leah would want to continue their conversation outside. Unfortunately, Leah hadn't come back into the store, and Henry began to wonder if she'd ever return. He wanted badly to work with her and be her friend. He had to fight his rising feelings for her. There'd be only heartbreak if he gave in to them.

It was one o'clock in the afternoon. Leah and Alta had been gone for over two hours. Only two other customers had come into the shop, but, unlike, Alta they grabbed the items they wanted from the shelves without help. Henry had smiled and made polite conversation, even answering questions about his *dat's* health. Everyone was glad that his father was home and recovering, and they commended him for stepping in to keep the store running.

Henry had work to do in the back. He needed to note what had been sold in the last month and make a list of what to order. Gazing at the front door, he got an idea. He walked to the last aisle, where he grabbed a small goat's bell. Then he secured it to the inside of the entrance so that he would hear if anyone came in. After opening and shutting the door a few times, he was pleased that the bell alert would work. Then he turned with a heavy sigh toward the back room, wondering when he could approach Leah about her next lesson. He sincerely hoped that Alta's appearance hadn't convinced her that it would be wiser if she didn't come. He liked having Leah in the store with him. He liked sitting close and explaining all the columns and rows in the accounts ledger book. He prayed that this morning wouldn't be the last time that Leah allowed him to help her.

Henry got down to the business of the account books when he heard the bell on the front door, signaling someone had entered. He pushed back his chair and stood. He had started toward the store area when a figure blocked the doorway.

"I thought she'd never leave," Leah said with a smile.

He experienced a lightness that came only in her presence. "I figured you went home."

She stepped back as he continued toward the front. "I did, but only to bring *Mam's* groceries home. I'd always planned to come back." A concerned look came over her pretty features. "I'm sorry. Is this a bad time?"

He shook his head. He was happy to see her. "This is the perfect time." He grinned. "Want a soda?"

Her lips twitched. "What, no offer of tea?"

Arching an eyebrow, he asked, "Would you rather have tea?"

"*Nay,* I had enough just waiting for Alta to leave. Once I realized that she wasn't going to go without me, I gave up and followed her outside." She reached to adjust her prayer *kapp.* "I came back as fast as I could, but Alta—she kept me outside talking for over an hour."

"*Ach nay!* I'm sorry for that."

Leah laughed. "It was fine. I didn't give her anything to natter about. She filled me in about everyone's business, then left after making sure I drove my buggy toward home. She followed me."

He reached into the store's refrigerated case for two sodas. "Cola or root beer?"

"Root beer," she said.

He opened a bottle of root beer and handed it to her. She accepted it with a nod of thanks. "I'm glad you came back."

"I'd hoped to make things easier for you," she murmured. She glanced about the store. "Can we work out here? In case someone else comes? Will you let me wait on customers? I'd like to help."

"You would?" He thought her truly an amazing woman.

"*Ja,* it will be a *gut* experience," she said. Her eyes settled on the front entrance. "I like the bell you put on the door."

"Some might think it too fancy, but I thought it necessary to know when someone comes while I'm working in the back." He grinned. "When *we're* working in the back."

"Does Alta come in often?"

"At least once a week."

"So she won't be back until next week."

"I can't guarantee it, but I don't think she will." He

couldn't take his eyes off her. "What do you want to learn next?"

"Can we go back to the ledger book?"

"I'll get it," he said. "I think it's a wise idea to work out here. We can use the table behind the counter." He studied the space. "You won't be able to sit, though. Do you mind standing while we work?"

"Does a rooster crow?" she replied with laughter in her eyes and her tone.

He chuckled, delighted. "I believe it does."

"I don't mind," she assured him.

The afternoon flew by quickly for Henry as Leah listened to him explain how his mother had organized the accounts. "I made a few changes that seem to work better," he said. "Fortunately, *Mam* agrees."

When it came time for Leah to leave, Henry broached the subject of looking for a craft store location.

"I don't know," Leah hedged worriedly. "Isn't it too early to look?"

"Not if you can find a place you can afford. You said you'd been saving for years. As long as you have enough for a security deposit, if necessary, and the first two months' rent."

"But I'll need merchandise."

"You can start with the women in the community. I'm sure they have crafts they'd like to sell."

Leah looked thoughtful. "That's what I'd hoped for." She smiled. "We can go. You'll come, *ja*?"

He felt his lips curve. Considering how she'd felt about him, he felt grateful that she trusted him enough to want him to come. "I wouldn't have it any other way." He was embarrassed when she raised her eyebrows. He knew he had no right to assume that she'd want his help in this, but he really wanted to accompany her as she checked out different places to rent. "Sorry."

Her laughter rang out, surprising him. "I won't go unless you come with me, Henry. I really could use your help."

"And I honestly want to help you," he said, unable to tamp down the happiness her admission caused. He had to remind himself that this was business with her, nothing more. "When?"

"How about tomorrow morning?"

"I'll come for you," Henry suggested.

She bobbed her head. "Nine?"

"See you then," he promised.

Chapter Six

❧

Friday morning Leah found herself alone in the house. Everyone in her family had someplace to go, including her, but it was only eight in the morning so she had time to do a few chores before Henry's arrival. Grabbing a broom and dust rag, she decided to start upstairs. It would be one less thing for her mother to do later.

The day was warm and balmy. The first thing she did was open the windows to allow in the fresh air. She checked each of the bedrooms to ensure that the beds were made. If not, then she knew that she'd have time to strip off and launder the sheets. She cleaned Ellie's room first, then moved on to Charlie's. She had already tidied her own room earlier, so after she finished with her youngest sisters' bedchambers, she entered her parents' room.

Her *mam* had already made the bed and opened the bedroom windows. Leah dusted the top of the small chest of drawers and the low wooden chest at the end of the bed. When she was done, she grabbed the broom and swept the floor, reaching under the bed for any dust that may have settled. As she pushed the corn bristles farther underneath, she felt the broom bump into something hard. She crouched down and was surprised to discover a heavy-duty cardboard box. Odd, she thought, that her mother didn't store whatever was in the box in the wooden chest at the end of their bed. She used the broom to push the box out from underneath the bed frame. Then she leaned the broom in the corner and picked up the box. Curious, she lifted the lid and looked inside.

The first thing she saw were several school papers from her and each of her sisters. She smiled, remembering when she had done hers. She'd been learning English and the teacher in Ohio had made her students write English words several times until they remembered the meanings, the spellings and the pronunciations as they said the words aloud.

She was overwhelmed with fond memories as she dug deeper into the box's contents. There was her sister Nell's birth certificate—and there was Meg's, Ellie's and Charlie's. Curious to see her own, Leah flipped through other papers until she spied hers near the bottom of the box. She pulled out the certificate and stared. It wasn't her birth certificate. It was another document with her name and her parents' names. Adoption papers. Leah gasped and felt an immediate sense of betrayal. Her parents' names were listed as the adoptive parents of a baby girl named Leah.

The words blurred as she realized what her parents had been keeping from her. She wasn't a Stoltzfus sister but some girl without a real mother and father. Her eyes overflowed with tears. Somewhere in the back of her mind she acknowledged that Arlin and Missy Stoltzfus had been good to her, that they must care for her a great deal if they had been willing to bring her into their home. *They felt sorry for me.*

But where did she come from? How did she end up being placed with this particular family? She experienced a shaft of pain when she thought of her sisters, who weren't really her sisters.

Why, Dat? *Why,* Mam? *Why didn't you tell me?*

She wasn't a Stoltzfus daughter. She'd sometimes felt as if she didn't belong. *Not sisters,* she thought with a sob. *Not blood.* And hadn't she wondered why her parents never encouraged her to marry like they did the others?

Sobbing, she put the papers back in the order she'd found them and shoved the box back under the bed. Then she swept the rest of the floor with tears running down her face. When she was done, she put away the broom and escaped to the barn where she could cry in earnest. She didn't want any Stoltzfus family member to see her tears. She didn't know what to do. *I don't belong here. Who am I? Do I have any relatives who want to know me?*

Didn't her real mother want her? What about her father? Had he rejected her, too?

She ran through the barn, slipped out the back exit, then slid down the wall to her knees, where she continued to cry as her heart broke. She cried until there was no more tears, until she felt numb inside. Leah got up and went back into the barn. Without thought, she headed toward the front of the barn and found herself in the stall which would house the new dog. As planned, she and her father had visited Nell and James to take a look at a litter of puppies. They had picked out a cute little mixed-breed puppy, but her sister wanted to ensure that the puppy had his vaccinations before releasing him into their care. Nell had promised to bring the little dog by today. Dat *will be excited to see him!* As she entered the stall, she felt tears well up again.

Not my vadder. *Not my sister. Not my dog.*

Hugging herself with her arms, Leah slunk down to sit on the fresh bed of straw and sobbed loudly.

Henry was happy. He looked forward to spending the day with Leah. While he knew he should be careful about keeping himself emotionally protected from heartbreak, he couldn't help his rising spirits as he steered his horse toward the Stoltzfus residence.

No doubt, he'd see her family. Had she told them where they were going and why? Did they know of her wish to open a craft store, which she was closer to achieving? He knew that her sister Ellie was aware, for she'd told Isaac and Isaac had told him. But what of the others? Did they know? *They must.* Why else would she tell him that he could pick her up at her house? She wouldn't want them to think that they were seeing each other. His spirits dampened slightly as the truth—the reality—of their working relationship reminded him that while polite and even friendly toward him, Leah still didn't think much of him as a person.

The Stoltzfus residence loomed ahead, and he clenched his stomach. Henry slowed his horse, then steered him off the road onto Arlin's property. There were no buggies in the yard. Was that why Leah had allowed him to come? The notion hurt but he shouldn't have been surprised.

He tied up his horse and approached the house. He knocked on the back door and waited. If the Stoltzfus family were anything like his, they would spend a great deal of their time in the kitchen. There was no answer. He frowned. Had Leah gone out with her sisters? Had she forgotten that they were to meet this morning, that she'd agreed that he would accompany her to look for a store location?

He knocked again. When no one came after a few minutes, he headed toward the front door in case there was someone in that part of the house. He experienced a burning in his chest when it became clear that there was no one inside. He left the front of the house for his buggy. He had stepped up to climb inside when his gaze fell on the open doors of the barn. He knew a sudden lurch of fear. Leah clearly had been happy to learn everything he had to teach her. Surely, she hadn't forgotten their excursion.

He hurried toward the barn. Henry stepped inside and thought he heard a noise. A loud, strangled sound. Was an animal in trouble? A weight settled deeply inside his chest. Or was it Leah who was hurt?

He glanced in each stall as he moved farther into the barn. He heard a sob and he realized that it was coming from inside the stall where he'd installed the cabinet. He didn't see anyone at first, but then the heartbreaking sound of crying had him opening the stall door. And then he saw her. And she was clearly in a lot of pain. He rushed to hunker down at her side. "Leah, did you hurt yourself?"

At first, it seemed as if she hadn't heard him or realized that he was there. She was bent over, clutching her stomach, bawling.

"Leah." He touched her arm. She jerked back instinctively and lifted her head. She gazed at him for a long moment, then resumed crying.

He shifted to sit beside her. "Leah, tell me what's wrong. Maybe I can help you."

"I can't go with you," she finally whimpered. "Go home. I can't go right now."

"Talk to me. What is it?"

She leaned back, met his gaze. "I…"

"You can tell me. I won't tell anyone. You have my word." He prayed that she trusted him enough to confide in him.

"I was cleaning this morning," she began as she wiped her eyes. "Everyone had someplace to be, so I thought I'd help *Mam* and do some of the housework that needed to be done." She took a long shuddering breath before continuing. "I was cleaning my parents' room. I found a box under their bed." She met his gaze briefly, her eyes were filled with tears, before she looked away. "I was curious," she admitted, "so I took a look inside. I was happy to find school papers for me and my sisters." Her face crumpled at the word *sisters*, before she continued. "There were birth certificates inside for all my sisters, but not for me. But do you know what I found?"

Henry held her gaze, feeling tenderness toward Leah. He reached for her hand, and the fact that she didn't pull away told him how much something had hurt her.

"Adoption papers," she said, tears streaming down her cheeks. *"Mine."* She sniffed. "I'm not Arlin and Missy's daughter. I don't know who I am. I'm not a real part of the family."

"Leah," he whispered, aching for her, feeling suspiciously close to tears. "You are part of the family. I know that your parents love you."

"They're not my parents."

"They are your adoptive parents. They chose to keep you. That's something, isn't it?"

She shook her head as a spark of anger lit her glistening blue eyes. "*Nay*, 'tis not. They never told me. Maybe if I had known, this would be easier, but they kept it a secret from me. My sisters..." Her voice caught and he could tell that she couldn't go on.

"Love you," he said. His breath hitched. "*Your family* loves you."

"But that's just it—they aren't my family."

Henry opened his mouth to object, then decided to keep silent. Leah was feeling emotional and with good reason. All he could do was to be there for her. *So much for keeping my distance.* Studying her upturned, tear-streaked pretty face, he felt the strongest urge to take her into his arms. But he didn't have the right and he knew that she wouldn't welcome his embrace.

"Leah," he began carefully.

"I need to know who my parents are," she cried. "Why they abandoned me! How I ended up here. I need to know, Henry. *I have to know!*"

He nodded. "I understand," he said. "I'd want the truth if it were me."

Her expression softened. "You would?"

"*Ja*, of course, I would, Leah, but—" He saw her look down at the hand that held hers and he quickly withdrew. "But you should talk with your parents—your adoptive parents," he corrected when her eyes hardened. "Question them. I know it hurts, but talk with them alone when you have the chance. I'm sure they'll be able to make you feel better about..."

"My adoption," she finished for him. He was glad to see that her features had relaxed again, as if her resolve to learn the truth from Arlin and Missy Stoltzfus had promised the hope of understanding.

"Shall we look at store locations? I don't want to push you," Henry said, "but today's search can help to keep you busy and perhaps make you feel better until they come home." He didn't make the mistake of saying *your family* or *adoptive parents*. Leah didn't need the reminder that might make her cry again. He rose to his feet and held out his hand to her. She gazed at it a moment before grasping his fingers. He quickly pulled her to stand beside him.

He smiled at her. "I have three places I'd like to show you." He didn't release her hand as he led her from the barn, then stopped to gaze at her. To his surprise she didn't pull away.

"You do?" She was close enough for him to see the dark blue flecks in her bright azure eyes. She wore a spring-green dress, which strengthened rather than distracted from the blue in her irises.

He was overly conscious of her nearness…her clean familiar scent of vanilla and honey soap laced pleasantly with her sweet-smelling shampoo. Her blond hair looked golden in the morning sunshine. Her lashes were dark for someone who was blonde. There were traces of tears on those eyelashes and drying remnants on her lovely smooth cheeks. He realized he was staring when he felt her shift uncomfortably. With an inward sigh, he let go of her fingers. "*Ja*. I can take you other places as well, but let's start with these three. *Oll recht?*" She swayed toward him and he gently grasped her shoulders. "Are you feeling well enough?"

"I'm fine," she assured him. "I'd like to go."

She didn't object when he helped her into the buggy.

He shouldn't be happy at the sign that they were becoming friends, but he couldn't help himself.

Leah sat beside Henry as he drove his buggy to a second potential store location. The first stop seemed promising at first. It was on the main road through Happiness, down from Whittier's Store; only this building was farther out from her Amish community than she would have liked. Still, it remained a good possibility until they spoke with the English owner. Not only did the store need a lot of repair work, the owner, a Mr. Terence Brown, was asking too much for rent.

She climbed into the vehicle without a word. Henry got in beside her and flicked the leathers to head to the next location. "He wants too much money," he finally said after a few minutes of silence during the ride.

"Ja." She didn't look at him. The day had begun with anticipation and excitement which had suddenly turned dark when she'd discovered her adoption papers in her parents' room.

"We'll find you a better place."

She faced him, then bobbed her head.

"Don't think about it, Leah," he urged as if reading her mind about her adoption. "There will be time to talk with them later."

She released a sharp breath. "I know that, but—"

He reached across the wooden seat for her hand, interweaving his fingers through hers. His hand was warm and hard and strong. Her heart started to beat harder as she met his gaze. He was a handsome man. His blue eyes were filled with tenderness and compassion. His dark brown hair curled slightly beneath his black-banded straw hat. He wore a burgundy shirt with black tri-blend denim pants held up with black suspenders. The fact that she found him attractive frightened her. She trusted him to help her with the store, but she couldn't allow herself to think of anything more.

The fact that Isaac was friends again with Henry wasn't enough for her to entrust him with her heart.

"Danki for your concern," she murmured as she pulled her hand away. She immediately suffered from the loss of contact. She looked out the window, anywhere but at him. Leah could sense his regard, his disappointment, but she had to protect herself. Just because it looked as if she'd be an old maid without a family didn't meant she should grab the first man who paid her any attention.

"Leah."

She shot him a quick look. The sadness in his blue eyes was nearly her undoing. She didn't want to hurt him. She studied him for a long moment, then attempted to smile at him. When his expression brightened a little, she realized that her smile must have appeared genuine. Her caution nearly sifted away with the breeze.

"Danki," she heard him murmur moments later.

Studying the passing scenery out her side window, Leah closed her eyes. She hoped everything would be all right, but she didn't hold much hope that she'd ever feel the same way about her family and her home.

Ten minutes later, Henry steered the carriage into a paved parking lot near a small brick building which housed two different businesses. He got out, tied up his horse, then came around the vehicle to help.

Leah stared at the building and became aware of Henry's hand extended to assist her. She hesitated, unsure whether or not to touch those masculine fingers again. Then she recalled how nice it had felt to have him hold her hand earlier. She reached out to grab his hand and he helped her down. She felt an odd, disquieting disappointment when he released her quickly, as if he'd been burned by her touch. She shifted her gaze to the building and her surroundings. *Henry has been nothing but kind to me.* Why was she stressing over a simple offer of help? It wasn't as if he'd asked to be more than a teacher or a friend. But despite her resolve to be careful, she knew that a friendship was developing between them. While she cherished it, she also held herself back. Something had changed since this morning when he'd found her crying in the barn. She wasn't sure exactly what the shift between them meant yet.

Henry didn't say a word as together they approached the front door of the store that was empty. The entrance door opened as they drew near. A young woman in her early to midtwenties waited for them. "Sarah Richardson?" he asked.

"Yes, come in." The woman was a pretty *Englisher* wearing a long blue skirt with a white short-sleeved blouse. Leah saw the way Henry studied her and she felt jealous, which upset her since jealousy was a sin. And she didn't want to feel too much for Henry.

Sarah Richardson held the door open and Henry waited for Leah to precede him inside. Leah looked about the floor space, which appeared too small for what she had in mind.

"I apologize for the condition. My aunt used this space for a used bookstore." Sarah's brown eyes filled with sadness. "She passed away recently, and being her only relative, I'm in charge of her estate."

"I remember her store," Leah said. She softened her

expression. "I'm sorry for your loss." She turned back to examine the interior critically. She'd never been inside. "How much space is there in the back?"

Sarah seemed surprised that Leah had asked and not Henry. Leah looked at him, saw the amused twinkle in his blue eyes and the slight upward tilt of his beautiful male mouth.

"I'm the one looking to rent store space," Leah explained. "For a craft shop."

Sarah pulled her gaze from Henry to stare at her. "There's a fair amount of space in the back. Would you like to see?"

Leah nodded. She tried to picture crafts and supplies on shelves and on the floor in this building, but something was lacking. The space just wasn't right for her. Still, she wanted to see the back. Perhaps if the back room was large enough, she could have a wall moved back to create a larger merchandise area.

She trailed behind Sarah, aware of Henry following closely. Leah felt a tingling at the back of her neck, overly aware of his penetrating gaze on her. She halted to glance back, then was disappointed when she realized that he'd been studying Sarah and not her.

Leah perused the rear work area and was pleased to see that it was much larger than she'd expected. This store could work if Sarah was willing to renovate the store space. "This is a lot of space back here. Would you be willing to move this wall back a little to allow for a larger front merchandise area?"

Sarah's mouth dropped open. "You want to move a wall? Are you kidding me?"

Stiffening, Leah said, "No, I'm serious. You have more space back here than in the storefront. I need more space for merchandise." She paused. "I think you'll find others will feel the same way."

The woman, to her credit, appeared to give the matter some thought. "I'll have to look into this further and get back with you."

"How much are you asking for rent?"

Sarah named a figure that could be doable, but there was a lot to consider before Leah agreed.

"Leah," Henry said softly. "We should go. 'Tis getting late and we have one other place to see today."

Meeting his gaze, she nodded before turning toward Sarah. "Thank you for your time."

"Is there a way for me to reach you? In the event, that I'm willing to move the wall?"

Henry handed the woman a paper with a name and phone number. "That's the number for Whittier's Store. Leave a message with Bob that you need to speak with Leah and she'll call you back."

The *Englisher* accepted the phone number, then walked with them to the front entrance. "Thank you for coming," she said pleasantly.

Henry spoke up before Leah had a chance. "We appreciate your time."

Thoughtful, Leah walked to the buggy in silence. She quickly climbed in before Henry could extend an assisting hand. She knew she shouldn't be feeling annoyed or ungrateful that he'd spoken up on her behalf, but her world was turned upside down and she needed to take charge, at least, in the one aspect of her life that she could—her craft store.

She waited while Henry untied his horse, then climbed in next to her. He didn't say a word as he grabbed the leathers and steered the horse back onto the main road. They had one more stop to make, but Leah was no longer in the mood. She felt testy and could no longer put her upcoming talk with her adoptive parents from her mind.

"Henry, please take me home."

She felt him stiffen before he glanced in her direction. Her gaze pleaded for understanding. "Please, Henry."

He regarded her a long moment, his expression unreadable, before he gave a nod. Within minutes, Leah saw the house ahead and the buggy in their driveway. Her adoptive parents were home, and most likely her sisters were there, too. "Stop!" she cried urgently.

He drew sharply on the reins. "What's wrong?" He gazed at her, clearly wondering about her outburst.

"Would you let me out here? My parents are home."

He appeared hurt for a brief moment, a look that was gone so quickly she couldn't be sure she hadn't imagined it.

"I'll be in touch." Her lip quivered and she started to shake. "Wish me luck," she whispered.

His expression softened. "You don't need luck, Leah," he said. "Just be honest and ask what you need to know."

"I—" She paused, warmed by his understanding. "May I come by next Tuesday?" She bit her lip. "The store?"

He shook his head regretfully. "I don't know if I'll be at the store. I've got other work to do and *Mam* wants to work."

She nodded. Was he telling the truth about having other plans? Or did he just not want to see her again?

With a murmur of thanks, Leah climbed out of the carriage and walked toward the house. Alone on the road, she looked back in time to see Henry turn the buggy around and head home. *I've upset him*, she realized. She might have even made him angry. But she was so hurt and confused by the discovery of her adoption papers that she couldn't think straight. Yet, right after that thought, she couldn't stop the niggle of concern that Henry might be upset and not want to see her again.

She reached the barnyard within minutes, just as Charlie came bounding out the back door. Her youngest sister spied her and ran in her direction. "Leah! Everyone's been wondering where you went."

Leah managed a smile. "I had an errand to run."

"Where?"

"Nowhere important," she answered vaguely. "*Mam* and *Dat* inside?"

Charlie nodded. "*Mam's* making a late lunch. We all just got back. Ellie should be home soon, too."

She gazed at the house. "And *Dat*?"

Her sister beamed at her. "He's in the barn with the puppy."

Leah felt herself soften. "Nell brought him," she murmured. "I thought he was too young."

"*Nay*, James thought he'd be fine. And Nell didn't bring him. *Dat* picked him up from their *haus*."

"Is he alone?"

Charlie looked at her strangely. "*Ja*. Why?"

"Nothing. I thought he might want some time alone with the new dog before I barge in to take a look."

"*Dat* won't mind if you visit Jeremiah."

"Jeremiah?" Leah arched an eyebrow.

"*Ja*. I think 'tis a *gut* name, don't you?"

"Let me guess. You came up with it."

Her sister shrugged. "Maybe, but *Dat* seemed to think it a fine name for our new member of our animal family."

The mention of family darkened the light in Leah's heart. "I think I'll go inside to see if *Mam* needs help with lunch." Then, without waiting for Charlie's reaction, Leah escaped into the house, asked Missy if she needed assistance, then when Missy said no, she hurried to her room to catch her breath and compose herself. Until she had a private moment to discuss what she'd found, she would have to act naturally around her adoptive family. No matter how hard it would be to do so.

Leah stood at her window, staring outside, wondering how she would broach the subject of her adoption. She had a lump in her throat, and her eyes were moist from her recent bout with tears. But she was no longer crying and she wouldn't again. This evening she would have to find the time to talk with her parents alone.

"Leah." Charlie stepped inside the room. "Lunch is ready."

She turned from the view and managed to smile. "I'll be right down."

Her sister hesitated. "You're upset about something."

Leah shook her head. "I'm fine."

"You seem pensive. As if something is weighing on your mind."

"You don't have to worry about me, Charlie." Her sister's concern made Leah's smile more genuine.

Charlie studied her a moment, then nodded. "Come downstairs. Before Ellie plows through the meal to get to the dessert." She started toward the door. "I made a chocolate cake," she said over her shoulder.

"We can't have her eating all the cake now, can we?" Leah said, unable to keep from being amused at the younger woman.

They ate sandwiches and salads for the midday meal.

When they were done, Charlie proudly brought out the cake she'd baked. The family ate amid conversation, laughter and grins. Leah was quieter than usual but no one seemed to notice. She knew that at some point today she'd have to confront her adoptive parents and get answers to the serious questions and concerns that she had.

Ellie had gone back to work. She had another cleaning job to do. Although it wasn't a particularly large one, she'd asked Leah if she wanted to help since she knew that Leah was working to save money.

"Can't this afternoon," Leah had said with a smile before Ellie left. "I have a few things I need to do today."

Charlie had been asked by their cousin Jedidiah if she'd help out his wife, Sarah, today. She'd met him as on her way home from the Abram Peachy residence earlier. Sarah was pregnant with her third child, and she needed Charlie's help with the other children since she wasn't feeling well lately.

With both sisters gone, Leah was finally able to talk with her parents alone.

"*Mam. Dat.* May I speak with you?" she asked grimly.

Arlin, who'd been heading for the back door, returned to sit at the head of the kitchen table. "What's on your mind, *dochter*?"

His use of *daughter* had her closing her eyes in pain.

"Leah," Missy said as she sat near her husband and across from Leah. "What's happened?" She gazed at her with concern.

Her heart started to pound as she eyed the two people who, she'd thought, were her parents. "I was cleaning your room this morning, and I found something under your bed."

* * *

After he'd dropped off Leah, Henry headed toward home. It hurt him that she didn't want her family to see them together. It was as if she were ashamed of him. Did she regard him so poorly that she was afraid to let her family know of their working relationship? Or was it because her parents didn't know that she wanted to own a craft business?

"'Tis a *gut* thing she doesn't know how I'm starting to feel toward her," he murmured. The store loomed up ahead. His mother had brought his father with her to work this morning. Before he'd left earlier, he'd helped his *dat* get settled in a chair by the front counter. He'd also made sure that there was a more comfortable chair in the back room for when his father became too tired to deal with customers. Henry had planned to drive past and up toward the barn where he usually worked on his cabinets, but concern for his parents had him parking close to the store. He tied up his horse before he went inside. He saw his mother behind the counter. Next to her, where others could see him, sat his father. He appeared happy to be in the store, his eyes clear and his expression bright. Charlotte Peachy was paying for her purchases and she and his parents were having a conversation. Charlotte had been a kind girl when younger, and she hadn't changed. After his parents acknowledged him as he approached, the deacon's wife turned to grin at him.

"Henry!" she greeted with a warm smile. "I was catching up with your *eldre*. I'm glad your *dat* is doing well." Her eyes met his father's for a heartbeat before she shifted her gaze back to him. "I was just telling them how glad I am that they'll be returning to our church community. We've missed all of you. I know that Isaac is happy to have you back. And Ellen can't say enough *gut* things about you." She picked up her bag of groceries, then turned to face him. "I heard, from Arlin, that you made him a cabinet. I was wondering if you'd be willing to stop by. I have a small job I hope you'll be interested in."

His parents looked at him approvingly. Henry nodded. "When would you like me to come?" he asked, his gaze meeting those of his parents to ensure that he hadn't misread their expressions. His *mam* was smiling at him, while his *dat* beamed, clearly pleased.

"Next Tuesday? Around two?"

"I'll be there," Henry told her. He experienced a burst of excitement as he watched Charlotte leave. He faced his parents. "Do you need anything from the *haus*? I thought I'd work a bit in the barn."

"Go ahead," his father said. "We have everything we could possibly need right here in the store."

Henry went into the barn, stared at a project he'd been working on as a surprise for Isaac and Ellen, and tried to forget the pain he'd felt in knowing that Leah didn't want her family to know that they'd spent time together.

Chapter Seven

Leah sat across from her parents, her eyes dry, as she'd explained about the papers she'd found that morning. "You adopted me, and you never told me." She saw Missy and Arlin exchange horrified, guilty looks. "I want to know who my parents are. I want to know how I came to be in your care. I want to know why you hid the fact that I'm not your *dochter*!"

"Leah, you *are* our daughter," her mother said. "We love you."

"Leah—" Her father stood, paced about the room. "You know we love you. We didn't tell you because you are *our* daughter. You must know we think of you as our own."

"Do you know how it felt to learn about it in that way? Maybe I shouldn't have looked inside the box, but I didn't think there was really anything to hide. I saw all the papers we'd done in school. Then I found your daughters' birth certificates and wondered if mine was in the pile. So I dug a little deeper and that's when I found the adoption papers." She blinked against tears.

"Who am I?" she whispered. "What happened to my parents? They didn't want me?"

"Nay!" Missy cried as she shoved back her chair. "It wasn't that."

"Missy," her husband warned.

Leah blinked back tears. "Why won't you tell me?"

Arlin gazed at her kindly. "We can't," he said softly.

"Can't?" she cried. "Or won't?"

"Both." He grabbed his hat from a wall peg and opened the back door.

"You're just going to leave without giving me any answers?"

"I can't tell you what you want to know." Suddenly stoic, he shoved his hat on his head and exited the house, leaving Leah alone with Missy.

Despite her determination not to cry, Leah felt tears running down her cheeks as she turned toward her adoptive mother. *"Mam?"*

But Missy looked away. "I'm sorry. We can't," she breathed as she stared at her. "I have things to do. Leah, we love you. I hope you believe us and accept that we want only what's best for you." Then she left the room, and Leah could hear the sound of her footsteps on the wooden stairs as she went up to the second floor. No doubt to hide the box that Leah had found, so she'd have no other opportunity to look at it again and maybe discover some pertinent information she might have missed.

Left alone in the kitchen without answers, she was overwhelmed with grief. She felt betrayed. Her parents were not hers at all, but some strangers who had taken her in to live with them. She recalled how they'd pressed their daughter Nell to marry, how pleased they'd been when Meg had fallen in love and wedded Peter Zook. They had even talked about Ellie and Charlie marrying someday, but never her. Which was why she'd decided that they didn't care whether or not she married. As if she wasn't good enough to be a man's wife and mother to his children.

Leah had to get out of the house. She needed to talk with Henry. He was the only one besides Missy and Arlin who knew what she'd found. She ran outside, relieved to see that the pony cart was in the yard. Within minutes, she was headed to Yoder's General Store. Henry would understand. He would figure out a way to help her. She bit her lip. *I hope.*

When she pulled her vehicle into the store parking lot, she noticed that there were no other buggies around. She tied up her horse, got out and headed inside. Henry had said that his mother was working in the store today. Perhaps Henry decided to help her after he'd dropped her off.

She felt a wave of remorse. When she'd seen that her parents were home, she'd ordered Henry to stop and let her out. Had he understood why? Because she was nervous about confronting her adoptive parents? A knot formed in her belly. Did he think otherwise? She hoped he didn't believe that she was ashamed to be seen with him. But with her other worries, it didn't seem like the best time to tell her adoptive parents why she'd been out riding with him.

Concern made her feel jittery as she fingered the doorknob to the front entrance. She heard the bell on the door jingle as she pulled it open and stepped inside. Henry's mother had allowed the goat bell to remain on the door, believing her son's idea to be a good one.

There was no one near the counter. Leah saw a chair beside it and wondered if that wasn't where Henry's father had sat while his wife, Margaret, had waited on customers. She frowned. Where was she? She hoped that Harry hadn't had a relapse.

"Hallo?" she called out as she moved closer to the counter. "Is anyone here?"

A figure came out from the back room. "Leah!" It was Henry's mother. "I'm sorry, I didn't hear the bell."

Leah glanced at the chair. "Is Harry *oll recht*?"

"He's fine." Margaret smiled, which reassured her. "I sent him up to the *haus* to rest." She tilted her head as she studied her, perhaps noting Leah's tension. "What can I get you?"

Leah thought quickly for something that was needed at home until she began to wonder if she could remain with the Stoltzfuses now that she knew the truth. Her mind went blank. "I'm not here to shop," she admitted honestly. "I was looking for Henry. Is he around?"

"He's up at the *haus* with Harry."

"I see." She wouldn't disturb him then. Besides, it wasn't as if she had the right to seek his help. They were just learning to become friends. "I don't want to bother him. I should go."

"Wait!" Margaret called as Leah started toward the door. "Why don't you go up and see him? I'm sure he'll be pleased to see you."

Leah froze. What was she doing? Coming to talk with Henry? She suddenly regretted seeking him out, especially after the way she'd treated him initially. "'Tis nothing important. I'll talk with him another time."

"I'm about to close the store. Are you sure you won't come up to the *haus* with me?"

"Nay." She managed to smile. She turned to leave, then paused. "I'm glad Harry is doing well." She hurried from the store, climbed into the cart and left. She'd driven a mile or more down the road when she heard the sound of another horse-drawn vehicle behind her.

"Leah!" It was Henry.

She slowed her horse and pulled it safely onto the shoulder of the road. Henry waved as he steered his buggy past her before he parked his wagon in front of her cart.

"Henry." She met his gaze and hid the fact that she was glad to see him, even though the knowledge that his mother must have told him embarrassed her.

He climbed out and approached. "You should have come up to the *haus*."

She felt a lump rise in her throat. "You were with your *vadder*. I didn't want to bother you."

He studied her a moment. "You're no bother," he said. He frowned. "Did you talk to them?"

She was unable to meet his gaze.

"Leah." The fact that he could tell she was upset should have bothered her, but it didn't.

"Ja, I spoke with my parents," she confessed, her eyes locking with his. The memory of their discussion, or lack thereof, made her choke up. "It didn't go well," she whispered. The understanding in his expression nearly made her cry.

He held out his hand. "Let's go for a walk," he urged.

She looked at their vehicles. "We can't leave our buggies here."

"We'll pull in behind Millie Mast's bakery. She won't mind. We can take a short walk from there." The look in his sky blue eyes was warm and encouraging. "The horses will be fine. There's a hitching post in the back."

Leah stared back at him a long moment, then gave a nod. They climbed into their vehicles, and she followed Henry down the road until they reached the bakery. She was familiar with the place. Her brother-in-law James had lived in an apartment above the bakery when he'd been operating his veterinary clinic—before he'd joined the Amish church and married Nell. Now she believed Andrew Brighton, James's friend from veterinary school, lived there. He'd taken over the clinic while James kept his work helping animals within their community. He gave medical care to English farmers' animals as well, when they needed him and if they couldn't get a hold of Drew.

Leah pulled her cart into the lot behind Henry's wagon, then tied up her horse next to his. "Where would you like to walk?" She suddenly felt shy. Could she do this? Tell him about her conversation with her parents? And, most important, could she trust him? For some strange reason, she knew she could.

"We don't have to walk," he said. "Look. There's a bench over there."

She glanced over. Sure enough there was a wooden bench under a shade tree. It must be new since she didn't remember seeing it the last time she'd bought something from Millie's bakery.

The bench looked inviting, but still she hesitated.

"Leah?" He held out his hand, and, heart racing hard, she paused for a just a second to stare at it before she took it. The warmth of his fingers clasping hers soothed her.

She sat on the bench and Henry settled next to her. Without releasing her hand.

She was quiet a long moment, unable to speak as she fought tears. *Nay!* she thought. She wouldn't cry. She couldn't cry and explain what happened. Henry squeezed her hand and she looked at him. His expression encouraged, his smile was gentle. He was so handsome he stole her breath, but the thought was fleeting, for, as hard as this would be, she had to tell someone. She wanted to tell him.

Leah closed her eyes briefly. "They won't say," she blurted out.

Henry felt his heart break for Leah as he glimpsed the tears in her eyes. "Won't say what?" he asked.

She pulled away and stood. "They won't tell me anything about my birth parents. They said they love me and basically that I should accept that." She sniffed and tears escaped to trail down her smooth cheeks as she faced him. "*Dat* walked out of the *haus* in the middle of the conversation." She met his gaze, her blue eyes glistening. "*Mam* said she had work to do and left."

He wanted to rise and take her into his arms to comfort her but didn't. "I'm sorry," he whispered.

She tried to smile but failed. "I don't know what to do. I want to know. I *have* to know."

Henry nodded. "Give them time. What if legally they can't tell you. They might have to get permission first."

"But it's my life. I'm an adult and old enough to know." She returned to her seat beside him.

He reached for her hand and was glad when she didn't pull away but turned her palm up and laced her fingers with his. "Do you think 'tis because they want to protect you? I believe that they love you as their own.

I've seen the love in Arlin's eyes—a *vadder's* love for his *dochter*."

She withdrew her hand and rose. He fought the feeling of hurt at the distance. "This is hard for me. I know in my heart that they love me. They wouldn't have cared for me all these years, but…" She paced a few steps and paused, then returned and sat down again. "It still hurts," she whispered.

"I know." He softened his expression as he felt the strongest urge offer comfort her, to confront Arlin and Missy and demand answers. But he couldn't, of course. The only thing he could do was be there for her, to listen and be a sympathetic ear. "I'd wait a day or two, then ask again. Make them see how important this is to you." When she shot him a hopeful look, he added, "I think it would be worth taking the chance, don't you?"

Looking relieved, she bobbed her head.

He smiled at her. "Would you like a soda or—" he grinned "—a cup of tea?"

To his amazement, she laughed. "Hot tea?"

He stood, reached to help her rise. It seemed natural when she followed his lead. "Is there any other kind of tea?" He glanced toward the bakery. "And I'd like to buy you a cupcake."

"I wouldn't mind a chocolate one."

They headed toward the bakery, where he ordered two chocolate cupcakes and hot tea. When they got their order, they returned to the bench to enjoy the snack. Henry took a bite of the delicious chocolate cake and made a sound of pleasure. "These are *gut*," he said. "So what are you going to do?"

He watched her swallow a mouthful of cake before

she answered. "I'm going to take your advice. Wait for a while, then ask again."

"Gut." He eyed her with approval as he popped the last of his cupcake into his mouth and swallowed. "Want to keep looking for a place of your store?"

Leah was thoughtful for several moments. "I'd like that."

Henry beamed at her, overjoyed at the prospect of more time with her. "When?"

"Monday?"

He agreed. "I'll wait for you at the store."

"Henry," she began, looking apologetic. "I'm sorry." She bit her lip. "For not asking you to come in with me when we reached the *haus*. I realized afterward what you must have thought after I asked you to stop and let me out. But it wasn't because I was uncomfortable to be seen with you. It was because…" She inhaled sharply before continuing. "When I saw my parents, all I could think of was that I wasn't their daughter and it hurt."

"I understand," he said. And he truly did. She'd been overwhelmed after learning of her adoption and worried about confronting her parents. The fact that she had come to the store later to talk with him, that she had confided in him with her secret fears made him feel a whole lot better. And it meant a lot to him that she'd decided to take his advice and wait before talking about her adoption with Missy and Arlin.

With both cupcakes consumed, they went their separate ways after setting up a time to go store hunting again on Monday morning, which would work out fine since he promised to go to the Peachy residence about a job on Tuesday. Henry smiled as he watched Leah's departure. All he'd ever wanted was for her to accept him as someone other than the one who had betrayed her cousin. The fact that she'd turned to him today was an indication that she had begun to regard him as a friend. *Thanks be to God.*

Leah decided that she couldn't go store hunting with Henry on Monday. The more she thought about what she'd told him, the more she felt embarrassed, and she felt it would be wise to put some distance between them. Not that she was afraid he'd break her confidence. He'd promised to keep her secret, and she believed him. But there was no reason to look for a location when the last thing on her mind at this point was her opening a craft shop. So Leah debated about writing him a note and asking her sister Ellie to deliver it for her, but she realized that she should tell him in person this weekend when she saw him. She tried not to feel bad that she'd let Henry down by canceling their plans. It was only hours since she'd approached her adoptive parents with the knowledge of her adoption. She figured next week would be enough time passed for her to ask them again about her birth parents. Unfortunately, Missy and Arlin Stoltzfus clearly didn't want to talk. Since Leah had brought up the subject, they continued to keep their distance. With a sound of frustration, Leah went to check on their new dog in his barn stall. She wanted to visit with the little one, hoping she'd feel better rather than out of sorts.

It was already getting dark. With a flashlight in hand, she pulled open the one side of barn doors, then entered and headed toward Jeremiah's area. She peeked in, expecting to see the puppy curled up and sleeping. She froze and gasped. What she hadn't expected was to find that he wasn't alone. A young girl lay next to the little dog. An *Englisher* by the looks of her. She appeared to be in her teens. She lay, curled on her side with Jeremiah snuggled against her. As if sensing a presence, the girl's eyes suddenly opened. When she saw Leah, she quickly scrambled to her feet, her movements waking up Jeremiah.

"I'm sorry," the teenager said. "I know I shouldn't be here." Eyeing Leah warily, she edged toward the stall door. "I was tired and fell asleep. I'll just be on my way."

Her shock dissipated. "Who are you?" Leah asked.

"It doesn't matter," she murmured. "Can't I just go? *Please*. I promise I won't bother you again."

It was then that Leah realized from her rumpled clothes, dirty face and frightened expression that the girl was a runaway. "I can help you."

The young *Englisher* shook her head no. "I'm fine. I shouldn't have come here." She paused. "But I was so tired and thought only to lie down for a minute."

"Where do you live?" Leah asked. The stark terror that entered the girl's eyes and the way she hugged herself with her arms told her that the girl had escaped from a bad home situation. "You're safe here."

The girl stared as if debating whether or not to believe her. "Jess," she murmured. "My name's Jessica."

"Are you hungry, Jess?" Leah asked gently.

"I have to leave—"

Leah stepped back to allow the girl to exit the stall. "Go ahead. But if you're hungry, I can grab you some snacks from the house."

Jess stepped out of the stall, making sure she closed the door so that Jeremiah wouldn't escape. "Everyone is inside. If I hurry, I can get you food to take with you before you go." She hesitated. "Or you could stay the night and leave first thing. I won't tell anyone."

The girl frowned. "I don't know…"

"It's up to you. I won't force you." She sensed the moment when Jess started to lower her guard and relax. "Do you want something to eat?"

"I can't stay."

"You don't have to," Leah assured her. "You can leave while I go inside if you want, but I hope you'll wait for me." She smiled. "I'll be quick."

Jess nodded. "Okay."

Leah ran out of the barn and hurried into the house. Fortunately, there was no one in kitchen. She grabbed cookies and an apple, then added a few slices of bread and cheese. It wasn't much, but she'd bet that it was more than Jess had eaten in a while. She found a plastic bag and stuffed the food inside, then reached for a can of soda, the kind her sister Charlie preferred. On impulse, she stuck a flashlight in the bag before she rushed back to the barn. She must have made noise as she approached, because the girl gasped, spun and looked terrified until she recognized Leah.

"I put a few things in here for you," she said as she offered Jess the bag. "There's a flashlight in there, too."

She saw Jess blink back tears. "Thank you."

"Sleep. Just leave at dawn. If you come back to sleep again, make sure you come after dark and enter through the back door." Leah regarded her with compassion. "That's how you got in, isn't it?" The girl nodded. "I'm Leah Stoltzfus."

Jess gazed at her a long moment. "Thank you, Leah." A horse snorted in a nearby stall, startling her.

"Take care of yourself, Jess," Leah said softly. "If you ever need help, come find me."

"I can't stay. I need to go," Jess cried. With the bag clutched tightly against her, she fled past Leah as if she were being chased by wolves.

Leah fought the urge to run after her or to watch which direction she'd taken. The girl needed sleep and she was in serious trouble. While she would have liked nothing more than to run after her, Leah hung back. She entered Jeremiah's stall and hunkered down in the straw beside him. The puppy, who'd been whimpering since he'd woken up, quieted when she sat and pulled him onto her lap. As she ran her fingers through the dog's fur, she thought of Jess and wondered if the girl had slept here previously without discovery. She had believed that Charlie had been the one who'd messed up the straw after she'd put in a fresh bed before Jeremiah's arrival.

What if it had been Jess? What if she'd slept more than one night here? And if she had, what made her risk discovery by sleeping here during the day?

She spent several minutes running her fingers through Jeremiah's fur. After he fell asleep, she carefully moved their puppy onto his new bed. As she left the barn, she saw and she heard a buggy approaching along the dirt lane from the main road. Who could it be at this hour?

Was it the church bench wagon? Jess had left just in time. As thoughts of the girl entered her mind, Leah hesitated. Considering what the girl had suffered, she realized that she shouldn't be upset that she was adopted. Her adoptive parents had given her a good, loving home. They didn't deserve for her to hurt them by continuing to bring up her past.

Leah sighed. She only wanted to have a sense of who she was. And what had happened to her birth parents. What was wrong with that?

Henry steered his horse down the lane leading to the Arlin Stoltzfus residence. He probably shouldn't have come. It was late. But he wanted to see Leah. He was worried about her and needed to make sure she was all right.

What if she just doesn't want to see me?

He felt a burning in his stomach. He'd thought they'd become friends. What if she had changed her mind about him? What if she no longer trusted him? If she regretted confiding in him? A shaft of pain enveloped him at the thought.

He saw the beam of a flashlight as someone exited the barn as he drove past the house. The person moved and he recognized Leah in the flash of light. She stared at his buggy, but he was unable to gauge her reaction to his visit. He parked and got out of the vehicle. "Leah."

She closed her eyes and released a sharp breath. "Henry, it's late," she said quietly. "I didn't expect to see you."

He approached, stopping within a few feet of her, and studied her with concern. The golden glow of the light softened her face, making her appear extremely vulnerable. "I know. I'm sorry if I'm intruding but I wanted to make sure you were *oll recht*."

"That's kind of you."

Henry continued to enjoy the sight of her. She didn't seem overly upset that he'd come…unless she was good at hiding her feelings. "What is going on?" he asked worriedly.

She shot a look toward the house. "Nothing." She bit her lip.

"Have they said anything?"

"*Nay*, I thought I'd try talking with them again next week." Her blue eyes filled with hurt. "They are avoiding me." Her voice lowered. "Except for supper, after which, they left the room so they didn't have to be alone with me."

Henry regarded her with compassion. "They are afraid to talk about it."

"*Ja.*" She stepped away from the barn.

He noticed that her hair and skin appeared more golden in the flashlight's beam. "Is there anything I can do?"

She shook her head and gazed at him through worried eyes. "I was going to send you a note. About next week. Then I thought I'd tell you in person. I think it's wise if I put any store plans on hold."

He stared at her, noting her discomfort. "You want to forget about our lessons and looking for a location." He was more than a little disappointed. He'd been looking forward to spending more time with her. "I see," he murmured. "I hope you'll ask for my help when you're ready to begin again."

When she didn't immediately agree, Henry felt his spirits sink to an all-time low.

"I should go," he said. It was clear that Leah was tired of his company, had changed her mind about their working arrangement. She didn't say a word as he climbed into his buggy.

He was stunned when she approached his buggy window. "Henry," she began, "will I see you on Sunday?"

His heart, which had picked up its pace when she approached, slowed. "*Ja*, my *dat* is well enough for church service." He picked up the reins and clicked his tongue to get his vehicle moving. "Take care, Leah. I'll see you then." He steered the horse toward the road and had traveled several yards when he heard Leah calling him. He quickly drew up on the leathers, then stuck his head out the window to see her running toward him. "Leah?" he asked with concern.

"I wanted to thank you for all you've done for me," she said softly.

"I haven't done anything—"

"Henry," she interrupted. "You've done more than you know, and I appreciate it."

Why was she thanking him now? He hadn't done anything. Was it because she no longer needed—or wanted—his help? Was this, in essence, a goodbye? "I didn't do anything."

"You're wrong! You sheltered me during the storm… and you taught me a lot about bookkeeping."

"Not that much, Leah," he said. "There's much more for you to learn."

"I know, but I just can't right now."

He understood the silent message. She didn't want to work with him. "I'll see you at church service." Then he flicked the leathers and headed for home.

He'd steered his horse about a mile down the road when a car came up from behind him and slowed. Henry glanced over and suffered a moment of dread.

"Henry Yoder," a male voice mocked with a cruel expression. "You and me need to talk." Then the *Eng-*

lisher pulled his car over to block off his escape, and Henry had no choice but to park on the side of the road and face his former friend. The same man who threatened to hurt his family and Isaac if Henry told the truth to the authorities about who had vandalized Whittier's Store that night years before.

"Brad Smith," he greeted, hiding his misgivings. "What are you doing out of jail?"

The man's expression hardened. "Aren't you happy to see an old friend?"

Chapter Eight

Midday Saturday was a flurry of activity in the Arlin Stoltzfus household. Leah, her mother and sisters had cleaned the day before. This morning, they put a roast in to cook and made a few dishes to add to the midday meal that everyone would partake of after church service the next day. Her uncle and male cousins had arrived a short time ago with the bench wagon. The men were clearing the furniture from the great room in readiness for the church benches.

Leah checked on the roast beef in the oven before she poured four glasses of iced tea for the men and then went into the great room to see how they were making out. Many of the benches were already set in place. She smiled at her uncle as she extended the tray of glasses toward him. Samuel Lapp accepted one with a nod of thanks. "Looks *gut*."

Her father approached from the other side of the room. *"Wunderbor, dochter. Danki."*

She grinned, happy with his pleasure. "Where's Isaac?"

"He's outside, waiting for Henry," her cousin Daniel said as he accepted a glass of tea. "Not sure what's taking him so long."

"Henry's coming?" Hearing mention of Henry made her heart skip a beat. He hadn't mentioned that he'd be coming today.

"*Ja*, he'll be helping with the benches."

Leah nodded. She wanted to talk with her cousin before Henry arrived. Leah smiled at Daniel before she went outside. "Isaac."

Her cousin Isaac turned from the bench wagon. He had slid out two benches and was reaching inside for another. "Leah!" His eyes lit up as he studied her.

"I thought you might be thirsty."

He smiled. "I am. *Danki*."

She nodded, then watched as he took a large swallow of the cold tea. "You told Henry about my hope of opening a craft shop," she accused mildly.

He froze in the act of taking another drink to eye her over the glass. "*Ja*, I thought he could help you."

She inclined her head. "I accepted his offer of help, and I already had my first lesson."

Her cousin's brow cleared. "*Gut*. That's *gut*."

"Ellie shouldn't have told you."

He shot her a surprised look. "She didn't run to tell me, Leah. It simply came up in conversation. No one else knows."

Leah scowled. "Except Henry."

"But you accepted his help."

"*Ja*, I did but—" How could she tell him that she'd put her plans on hold without telling him why? That she was upset to learn she'd been adopted?

"Leah, if the end result worked out, why are you

worrying? What do you have against Henry Yoder?" he asked, clearly puzzled.

She said the first thing that came to mind. "He hurt you." She set the tea tray on the empty side of the wagon. "You suffered because of him."

"Henry apologized and we're fine. If I can forgive him, why can't you?"

"I have forgiven him," she mumbled, sincere. Spending time in his company had made her see him for the kind man he actually was. She had skipped out on their recent plans to find her a place for her store, and she felt terrible about it. And she'd been thinking way too much about him... She wanted to know what had happened that night. The Henry she'd come to know didn't seem like the kind of man who destroyed other people's property, especially a friend's.

Isaac leaned against the back of the wagon. "There is more to what happened at the store that night."

"What happened?" Leah asked, intrigued.

Isaac shook his head. "Not my story to tell." He took another gulp of tea, then lowered his glass.

A buggy drove into the yard, drawing her attention. She felt nervous suddenly. It was Henry, come to help set up the church benches.

"I wouldn't suggest asking him about it, Leah," her cousin warned softly as Henry got out of his vehicle and waved. "It's still a painful subject for him. He doesn't need you digging into his thoughts. If he wants to tell you what happened that night at Whittier's Store, he will, but it will come from him when the time is right and not before." He steadily held her gaze.

She released a breath. "I understand," she said softly.

Her cousin grinned at her before they both turned to greet Henry.

"Isaac," Henry said as he approached. "Leah." His voice had turned noticeably cool.

Leah frowned. Their discussion last night had clearly upset him. Was he upset because she'd put off her lessons? Last night he hadn't seemed to be. He'd said he understood.

He stared at her without a word. Leah shifted uncomfortably, wishing she could turn back the clock and change how things stood between them.

Obviously uncomfortable with the sudden tension between her and his friend, Isaac cleared his throat. "Come on, Henry. These benches won't get into the house by themselves."

Leah started toward the house, then stopped to watch as each man lifted a wooden church bench from the wagon. Her attention was drawn immediately to Henry. She couldn't help but notice the play of arm muscles below his shirt's short sleeves. When he turned to set the bench down, he looked surprised to see her, as if wondering why she hadn't gone into the house. Blushing, she quickly looked away and hurried inside.

She was in the great room when she felt Henry's presence as soon as he entered. He carried the bench under one arm. There was a light sheen of perspiration on his forehead, and the dampness caused a lock of dark hair to curl. He barely looked at her as he set the bench next to another to finish one church row. As he turned to leave, he locked gazes with her, and she felt the intensity of his look ripple along her spine.

"Is there something you need?" she asked.

A shutter came over his expression. *"Nay."* He sighed.

"Henry, what's wrong? I can tell something is bothering you."

He shrugged. "Nothing for you—or anyone—to worry about." Then he left to get another church bench.

She was ready with glasses of iced tea and lunch when the men were done setting up the benches and had gone outside to enjoy the balmy day. She fought to hold her hand steady as she handed Henry one of the glasses.

Henry held her gaze as he took it from her. *"Danki,* Leah."

She nodded, then gave him his sandwich and quickly turned away to give Isaac and the others theirs. She could sense Henry's eyes on her as she returned to the house.

Her mother was in the kitchen as she entered. "Everyone get what they need?"

"Ja, although I think *Dat* will want some cookies," Leah replied with a smile.

"Here," *Mam* said as she held out a plate of cookies. "Take these out to them. I'm sure your *vadder* isn't the only who'll be interested in something sweet."

Leah felt heat surge in her belly as she carried the plate outside and heard the murmurs of pleasure when the men saw the cookies. "Everyone have enough iced tea?" she asked as she set it down on the tail end of the bench wagon. Surrounded by men, she was only conscious of Henry's nearness. "Another sandwich?" She glanced at each of them, surprised to find Henry's lips curved in a funny little smile.

"These are fine," he assured her, and the others immediately agreed.

Feeling her face warm, she murmured something appropriate and started to leave.

"Leah." Henry had followed her.

"Something I can help you with?" She glanced back quickly, glad to see that none of the others had noticed, except for Isaac, who wore a grin. She returned her attention to Henry.

"I just wanted to thank you again for lunch," he said, his expression unreadable.

"You're *willkoom*." She became flustered when he stared at her without moving. "Henry?" She wanted to repair their budding friendship. She hated the sudden tension that had cropped up since he'd arrived this morning.

"I'll see you at church service tomorrow."

She managed a polite smile. Her mouth felt stiff and unnatural. "I'll see you then." She turned.

"Leah."

Heart racing, she faced him. *"Ja?"*

He studied her and his eyes softened. "I know you wanted to put your plans on hold, but would it hurt to take a ride with me to see what other buildings might be available?" He paused. "For future reference."

"Nay, I suppose not." She missed spending time with him. Here was her chance.

"Will you come with me next week? Monday?"

She nodded. "Nine o'clock?"

"Ja, nine will be fine." He reached out to brush back a lock of hair that had escaped from beneath its pins. Her heart fluttered. "I'll come for you."

"Oll recht."

"Leah, don't you be canceling on me."

She blushed. This man had gone out of his way to help her, she had to remember that. "I'm sorry."

"Leah, I already said that there is nothing to be sorry for."

"I'll see you tomorrow then."

"Ja." Pleasure flickered in his gaze and was gone. He inclined his head, then left.

As she went inside, Leah realized that she was suddenly looking forward to the next two days. Tomorrow she'd see Henry at church service and then on Monday he'd be driving her around the county. She grinned. Despite her initial reservations, he was glad he'd come today and she was eager to see him again. What was it about Henry that he could so easily change her mind?

Sunday morning Henry and his family didn't come to church service. Disappointed and a bit miffed, Leah struggled to pay attention to Preacher Levi's sermon. Her thoughts went from anger to worry to fear as she began to wonder why Henry hadn't come. *Something must have happened.*

Directly after the service came to a close, she went to Isaac to ask if he'd heard from his friend.

"Nay," Isaac told her when she managed to find a moment alone with him. "He told me he'd be here."

"I'm worried," she admitted.

Isaac's gaze reflected her concern. "I'll stop by his *haus* later to see if he is *oll recht*."

Leah wanted to go, but didn't know if it was right for her to ask. Until she recalled the kindness Henry had shown her—first the day of the storm and then later with his offer to teach her about storekeeping. "May I come with you?"

"Ja," her cousin said without hesitation.

Later that afternoon, after the midday meal, Leah accompanied Isaac as he steered his buggy toward the Harry Yoder residence. Less than a half hour later, her cousin drove the vehicle into the Yoder yard, past the store and toward the house farther up the lane. There was a buggy parked near the house. Leah frowned. Had Henry simply changed his mind about coming today?

She and Isaac got out of the carriage and approached the house. They exchanged glances before Isaac knocked on the rear entrance door. They waited for someone to answer but when no one came, Isaac knocked hard on the wood with his fist.

"I don't think they're home," Leah said before Isaac could voice the same thought. "I hope nothing's bad happened."

Isaac's expression held concern. "Doesn't look like they went to a church service," he replied as he gestured toward the family buggy in the yard.

"Where could they have gone?"

"Maybe something happened with Henry's *vadder.*"

"How can we find out?"

"Call the hospital?" Isaac gazed at the house with worry.

"Should we go to Whittier's Store?"

"Ja." her cousin urged. "We can use Bob's phone. He may have heard if anything bad happened."

Leah climbed into the passenger side while Isaac hopped into the driver's seat and picked up the reins. Her cousin urged his horse into a canter in the direction of Whittier's Store. It seemed ironic, somehow, that the first place they went after Henry's strange absence would be Whittier's Store, the scene of the criminal vandalism that had caused problems for Isaac when he'd come onto the property to find Henry and their English friends spray-painting the exterior of the building. That night the culprits had fled, leaving Isaac to take the blame.

Isaac pulled into the lot and parked. He got out, tied his horse to a hitching post and gestured for Leah to follow him as he entered into the store.

Bob Whittier arched his brows when he saw them. "Shouldn't you be at church?"

"Service is over. We were hoping to use your phone," Leah told him.

"Henry Yoder and his family were to attend service with us today, but we haven't seen nor heard from them. We checked the house. There is no one home, yet their buggy was in the yard. Have you heard anything?"

The look in Bob's face made Leah's stomach burn. "Yes, I'm afraid so. I'm in the ambulance corps. Yesterday I heard a call to the Yoder residence on my scanner. Someone was rushed to the hospital."

"Do you know who?" Isaac asked with concern.

"I'm sorry, I don't. We don't discuss names or conditions on the radio after the initial call."

Leah grew increasingly worried. She felt terrible. She'd been silently condemning him for not keeping his word, and he could be seriously hurt. "Which hospital?" she asked.

"Lancaster General."

She was familiar with the place. It was the same hospital her sister Meg had been in after she and Reuben Miller had suffered a buggy accident. "May we use your phone? I'll pay."

The man looked offended. "Feel free, but I'll not be taking your money under the circumstances."

She held his gaze a moment, then nodded. "Isaac?"

Her cousin took the hint. "Thank you. I'll make the call."

Leah hovered nearby and listened while Isaac spoke with someone on the other end of the line.

"I'm calling to see if Henry Yoder is there. I understand a family member was brought in by ambulance yesterday." Isaac paused to listen. "He is? Can you put me through to his room?... What?... Is there anyone in the family who I can talk with?... Fine. I'll wait." He met her gaze while he was on hold, his expression grim. "'Tis Henry who's in the hospital."

The burn in her stomach intensified as she waited for someone to come back on the line. Isaac frowned. "*Hallo?* Henry! Are you *oll recht*? They said it was you in the hospital! Oh, *ja*, that's right. Your father's given name is Henry, too." He listened quietly while Henry apparently told him what had occurred. "I'm sorry to hear that. Is it bad?" Her cousin exhaled sharply. "We'll keep Harry in our prayers." He paused. "Henry, Leah is here with me. *Ja*, I will."

He met her gaze and held out the phone receiver to her. "Henry wants to talk with you."

She swallowed hard as she moved closer and accepted the phone receiver. "Henry?" she greeted tentatively.

"Leah! I'm sorry. I know we made plans for tomorrow, but I won't be able to make it. My *dat* suffered another heart attack." He sounded choked up as he continued. "We don't know the extent of the damage yet, but it doesn't look good."

"Henry," she whispered, aching for him. "I'm sorry. Is there anything I can do?"

He grew quiet. It must have been only a few seconds, but it seemed much longer before he spoke again. "I wish... I could see you. I was looking forward to spending time with you tomorrow."

"We'll have time for that when your *vadder* is better."

A hesitation. "*Ja.* Plenty of time." She heard an odd strangled sound from his end of the line. "May I talk with Isaac again?" he asked.

"Ja." Feeling slightly hurt by his desire to get off the phone with her, Leah said, "I'll keep your *dat* and your *mam* and you in my prayers, Henry. Stay strong."

She heard warmth in his tone as he said, *"Danki.* I will."

Leah handed the phone to Isaac. After a quick glance at Bob, she stepped outside for some fresh air, hoping to calm herself. She wished she could do something to help him. She wanted to see him. Isaac came out of the store seconds later and eyed her with a knowing look. "Bob is calling someone to take us to the hospital."

She glanced at him with surprise. "Now?"

Her cousin nodded. "He's also going to get word to our families where we've gone."

He paused to gaze at her steadily. "You want to go, *ja*?"

Overcome with relief, she nodded. "I want to go," she admitted softly.

Isaac smiled. "'Tis *oll recht*, Leah. I understand how you feel. Henry's a *gut* man. You may think you know what happened that night, but you don't."

She knew he was referring to that night years ago when Whittier's Store had been vandalized. "And you still won't tell me," she said with resignation.

"*Nay*, I won't."

Bob Whittier stuck his head out the door. "Rick Martin is coming to take you to the hospital."

Leah turned to him with a smile. "Thank you."

"My pleasure. Please let Henry and his family know that I'm thinking about them."

She blinked, surprised by his request. "I will." Then Bob disappeared back into his store.

She faced her cousin. "He holds no ill will toward Henry—or you."

"*Nay*, he doesn't, and that tells you something about the situation, doesn't it?"

She gazed at him irritably without replying. At that moment, Rick Martin, an *Englisher* who often helped out members of their Amish community whenever they needed a ride, pulled up before them.

Leah greeted Rick as she got into the back while Isaac climbed into the front seat. As she stared out the car window during the ride to the hospital, she couldn't stop thinking about Henry. Would he be pleased to see her?

Chapter Nine

Henry sat in the chair next to the bed, gazing at his ill father, listening to the *beep, beep, beep* of the heart monitor. His *dat* looked pale. An IV drip was attached to his left arm and he lay as still as death. If it weren't for the rhythmic heart sound, he might have thought his father had died. He sensed movement on the other side of his parent's bed. He glanced over and saw his mother stir in her chair. She had fallen asleep and he hadn't the heart to wake her. They'd been at the hospital since late yesterday afternoon after his father had cried out and gripped his chest, and Henry had known that he'd suffered a second heart attack, this one much worse than the first one.

He rose from his seat and skirted the hospital bed, coming to stand at his mother's side. He placed a hand gently on her shoulder. "*Mam*, may I get you something to eat or drink?" he said softly. "You need to keep up your strength."

Mam released a shuddering sigh. "I could use a cup of tea."

Henry lightly squeezed his mother's shoulder. "I'll

get it and come right back." He hunkered down so that he could directly meet her gaze. "He's going to be fine."

He saw her swallow hard. "I hope so."

"He will," he insisted. He stood and smiled at her tenderly. "I'll be right back."

She acknowledged his comment with a nod, and he left the room and headed for the elevator. He, too, needed something to keep up his strength. Henry rode the elevator toward the lower level, where the cafeteria was located. He had a lot on his mind, with his father's illness. The elevator stopped and, without thought, he got off, only to realize that he had stepped out on the wrong floor.

"Henry!" a familiar male voice called, and he saw Isaac and Leah. He felt a punch of gladness in his chest.

He managed a smile as he approached and met them halfway. "'Tis *gut* to see you, Isaac." His gaze settled on Leah. His voice softened. "Leah. *Danki* for coming."

"Are you *oll recht*?" Leah asked with genuine concern.

Henry shrugged. "Better than my *dat*." He was tired, but seeing the two of them had raised his spirits.

"You look about ready to drop," Isaac commented. "Were you headed home?"

He shook his head, aware of Leah's study of him. "I'm going downstairs for something to eat."

"May we come with you?" Leah asked shyly.

His heart melted as he met her gaze. "I'd like that." She looked pretty in her Sunday-best royal blue dress with white prayer *kapp*, cape and apron. Her garment's blue fabric accentuated the blue of her eyes, making them shimmer.

"Is he doing any better?" Isaac asked as they stepped into the elevator.

"I don't know," Henry admitted. "The doctor hasn't given us an update." He ran a hand through his dark hair. He was exhausted and so was his mother. He needed food quickly to keep up his strength. Since they'd arrived, he hadn't left his father's bedside, but he knew that he and his mother couldn't continue without eating. It was bad enough that he'd barely slept.

"I'm sure you'll hear something soon," Isaac said encouragingly.

He was startled when Leah touched his arm. "Henry," she murmured, "is there anything we can do?" She quickly drew back when he halted and faced her. "We saw your buggy at the house. I can take care of your horses for you."

His heart fluttered, then beat harder. "You would do that for me?"

She looked puzzled. "Of course. You've been…" Her voice trailed off as she looked away as if embarrassed.

"That's a fine idea," Isaac said. "Henry, Leah will care for your horses until you get home."

Henry studied her, liking what he saw, grateful that she was willing to step in and help when he needed her. "I'd appreciate it, but our neighbor is seeing to them today." He felt something spark between him and Leah, an odd awareness that tightened his chest and made her blush and avert her gaze.

The elevator stopped. They got out and entered the cafeteria. "What would you like?" Henry asked. "Coffee and a sandwich? My treat." He was eager to show his appreciation of their visit.

"We ate before we came," Leah replied.

"A cup of tea? You're not going to allow me to eat alone?"

Amusement lit up her gaze, and he recalled the tea they enjoyed on the day of Alta Hershberger's visit to the store. "A cup of tea then."

"I'll have a soda," Isaac said. "But I'm paying, not you. Please, Henry, let me buy today."

His eyes stung and he blinked several times as he looked at his friend.

Isaac studied him thoughtfully. "Don't even think about paying me back."

Despite the circumstances, Henry laughed. "I'm glad you're here." He turned to Leah. "Both of you."

He ate his sandwich quickly while Leah drank her tea and Isaac his soda. When he was finished, Henry stood, eager to return to his father's room. "I have to get back."

"We'll come with you," Isaac said.

He was pleased when Isaac and Leah followed him into the elevator. He wasn't sure how many visitors his *dat* was allowed to have, but Henry decided that he would insist that Isaac and Leah stay if anyone tried to convince them to leave. He really wanted his friends with him—Isaac, his closest friend—and Leah, a woman who was quickly becoming to mean the world to him. His mother, he knew, would be happy for the distraction of their visit. He glanced toward his best friend who had insisted on carrying his mother's tea. Leah held a bag of chocolate-chip cookies that Isaac had insisted on buying while Henry carried the roast-turkey sandwich he'd decided his mother needed to eat.

The ride up in the elevator was made in silence. Henry stared at the lit floor numbers that flashed above the door. He felt Leah's gaze while they waited to reach the third floor. He glanced in her direction as the elevator eased to a stop. She blushed but didn't look away, and the tenderness in her expression made his breath hitch.

"Room 322," he said softly as he headed in the right direction. Henry grew worried as he neared the door until he peeked inside and saw his mother was still where he'd left her, seated in the chair by his father's bedside. He looked at the bed and was relieved to see that his father's eyes were open. His *dat* looked tired, but the fact that he was awake gave Henry hope.

"Dat!" he said with a grin. "You're awake. How are you feeling?"

"Tired but alive," his father grumbled, and Henry's grin widened.

"Mam, I've brought you a turkey sandwich…and a couple of friends have stopped by to say *hallo*." He turned as Isaac and Leah entered the room.

"Isaac!" his mother exclaimed. "'Tis *gut* to see you." She turned to her husband. "Harry, look who's come!"

To Henry's relief, a small smile settled on his father's lips. "Isaac," he said warmly. "Who's that with you? Is that Ellen?"

"Nay, Harry," Isaac said. "'Tis Leah, my cousin."

Leah smiled as she approached the man's bed. "I'm glad to see you're awake," she said.

"You're Arlin's daughter," his father said.

"Ja, second eldest." Her smile dimmed. "I'm sorry you're not feeling well."

"I'll live," the older man said. "At least, the doctor says so."

"Dat," Henry breathed with joy. "How bad is the damage?"

"There's some, but not as bad as we feared," his mother said, answering for him, "and with a change in heart medication, he should do well."

"Thanks be to God," Henry said. He felt the tension in his shoulders drain away.

"He'll have to stay another couple of days," *Mam* said. "I want to stay but you should go home, *soohn.*"

Henry shook his head. "I'm staying."

"But the horses…"

"I'll care for them," Leah said.

"Anything you need?" Isaac asked after a glance at the wall clock. "A change of clothes?"

"Nay, I grabbed some things before we left the house." He focused his gaze on Leah. "I'll send word when we're home."

She bobbed her head, then turned her attention to the man in the hospital bed. "Harry, I hope you feel better soon."

Henry watched her as she and Isaac left, overjoyed that she had come, wishing that he could have spent more time with her.

Just over a week later, Henry saw his father settled in a chair in their family's great room before he entered the kitchen to check on his mother. *"Mam,* would you like me to open the store today?"

His mother turned from the dishes in the sink. *"Ja,* I think I should stay here with your *dat.*"

He inclined his head. "Is there anything you need?"

His *mam* smiled as she shook her head. *"Nay.* We'll be fine."

He saw a good opening to talk about an important matter. "I know that you and *Dat* never wanted a cell phone, but after what happened, don't you think it would be wise to have one? We can't always rely on our neighbors to get us help."

"I agree."

"*Dat* will argue against one."

"I'll talk with your *vadder*. Twice he's been in the hospital. I'll convince him that it's time."

"And 'tis *gut* for business." Henry grabbed a key from a wall peg. "I need to run an errand, but I'll open the store." He turned to leave.

"Henry."

He faced her. *"Ja?"*

"Danki for all you've done."

He shifted uncomfortably. "I've not done anything another son wouldn't do for his parents." His mother gave him an affectionate smile. He smiled back, then headed toward the door. He meant what he'd said. He loved his parents. They'd stood by him when things got tough. It was always right that he would do the same for them.

"You're a *gut* man, Henry."

He swallowed hard. "I've got to run, but I'll be back."

"Maybe you can look into buying us a cell phone," his mother said softly.

Henry grinned. "I can do that."

"A plain phone—nothing fancy."

He chuckled. *"Ja,* I'll find us a plain phone."

He left the house and drove his buggy to the Stoltzfus residence. He had promised to tell Leah when his father had come home. The doctor had released *Dat* later than either his mother or he had expected. *Dat* had a follow-up appointment soon. Henry would offer to take him, but he had a feeling that his mother would want to be the one to drive his father to make sure she received specific instructions on his care.

The day was unseasonably warm for a week into summer. It felt more like late in the season with the rise in temperature and humidity. Still Henry didn't mind. His father was home, and he was grateful that his parent was alive. And he was happy that he would soon see Leah. He hadn't been able to meet with her again last week, but she'd understood. It had been sweet of her and Isaac to visit and for Leah to care for the horses while they were gone.

The concern for him on Leah's face had warmed his heart. He spurred his horse into a canter in his eagerness to see her again. His decision to visit Leah first thing had come to him during the night. His time working in the store would be the perfect opportunity to resume her storekeeping lessons.

The Arlin Stoltzfus residence loomed ahead. A sudden case of nerves unsettled his stomach as he steered his horse onto the driveway and drove toward the house. He parked the buggy close to the barn and got out. Would Leah be pleased to see him? He swallowed against a suddenly dry throat as he approached the residence. He halted when he caught sight of someone at the clothesline in the backyard. The woman was young and blonde. Leah? Or Ellie?

He watched as she lifted a wet garment from the laundry basket near her feet before she pinned it to the line. *Leah*. He could tell it was her by the way she moved. He'd always been overly aware of Leah Stoltzfus.

He headed in her direction. "Leah!"

"Henry!" She eyed him shyly as he approached.

"My *dat* is home from the hospital."

"Is he doing well?"

He nodded. "We brought him home late yesterday."

She smiled. "I'm so glad." She held his gaze. "You must be relieved."

"*Ja*, his doctor is pleased with his recovery. 'Tis been a long few days."

Concern filled her blue eyes. "Are you *oll recht*?"

I am now. He was startled by how much he enjoyed being in her company. "I'm fine. I wanted to let you know that we were home. Thanks for taking care of our horses. I see that you fed them before we got up this morning." Her smile confirmed it. "I'll be working in the store this afternoon. Would you like to resume your lessons?" His heart accelerated at the prospect of spending time with her.

Her features filled with regret. "I would have liked to, but I have to houseclean with Ellie."

Henry felt something wither inside of him. "Just let me know when."

Leah tilted her head as she looked up at him. "We're not cleaning our *haus*, Henry. I'll be helping to clean for one of Ellie's English customers. This particular *haus* is huge and she needs it done quickly and efficiently before the owners get home from work."

Henry closed his eyes briefly. *Thanks be to God.* "Tomorrow then?"

"In the morning?"

"*Ja*." His heart filled with joy when she agreed. He reined in his happiness. Fortunately, Leah didn't appear to notice his eagerness to work with her again. "I can come for you." He paused. "If you want, we can check out a location first before we head to the store."

She hesitated. "Are you sure you can get away?"

"*Ja, Mam* wants to open and work for an hour or two. *Dat* is going to sit and watch her." He shifted a few feet closer. "Leah—"

She pinned her father's shirt to the line. *"Ja?"*

"Danki."

She faced him, her brow furrowed. "For?"

"Coming to see us. For checking on the horses. It was *gut* to see you—and Isaac," he added quickly. "It had been a difficult day. Your visit cheered up not only me but *Mam* and *Dat*, too."

She beamed at him, and he felt her smile radiate over him like a bright burst of much-needed sunshine. "I'm glad we could come."

Silence reigned and the moment grew awkward. "I should go," he said. "I know you have things to do, and I need to get back and open the store." He turned to leave.

"Henry."

He swung back.

"I'll see you tomorrow."

"Nine o'clock." He held her gaze a moment longer before he turned and headed back to his buggy, aware that she had gone back to work and wasn't watching him as he would have liked. He sighed. His feelings were one-sided. Still, he had tomorrow to look forward to. Once he opened the store, he would see what he could do to prepare for Leah's next lesson. He climbed into his vehicle, grabbed the reins and, with a flick of the leathers, drove toward the road. Henry glanced over his shoulder and felt an infusion of warmth when he saw

Leah, with the empty basket in her arms, staring in his direction as he departed. He grinned with satisfaction.

"Can I get you anything?" Henry asked after he'd helped to see his father settled in a chair by the front counter in the store. His parents had decided to spend the day rather than just the morning.

"We are fine, Henry," *Mam* assured him.

"We have a store filled with anything we could possibly need," his father added.

"Are you feeling well, *Dat*?"

"I'm fine, *soohn*, but your *mudder* insists that I stay in this chair. I told her I would sit today, but that tomorrow would be a different story. I have plenty of energy with this new medicine, and I need to exercise." He glanced at his wife. "Doctor's orders."

Henry laughed. "I'll be back to relieve you a little later."

"No need. We'll manage," his mother said. "Take some time for yourself today. You've earned it."

Satisfied that his parents were happy to be left alone for the day, Henry got into his buggy and drove to pick up Leah.

Leah was waiting for him as he pulled into the yard. She smiled as she approached. "*Hallo*, Henry."

"Leah." He felt his breath quicken at the sight of her. He helped her into his buggy, then climbed in. He studied her with a smile. "*Mam's* working all day. If you still want to come, I thought we'd ride around and see if we see anything interesting." He paused. "Do you want to go or stay since we can't use the store?"

"'Tis too nice of a day to be inside," she replied. "I'd like to go."

Henry experienced a rush of pleasure.

The afternoon flew by quickly as they drove through the area, looking for potential locations for her craft shop. They stopped for lunch in a local diner before they continued their search. They didn't see any building worth looking at, but Leah didn't seem to mind, and Henry was glad. He was happy to simply enjoy her company as they discussed the area, the sights and the neighbors in their community. All too soon for Henry, it was time to take Leah home.

"I enjoyed our ride," Leah said after he'd hurried around to help her step down from his vehicle.

"I did, too," Henry admitted huskily. "I'm sorry we didn't find anything worth consideration. I should have gone out ahead of time to look for places to show you."

"*Nay*, Henry. There is no rush. Remember, I wanted to put my plans on hold. It was fun searching the area, but I'm not worried. Eventually, when I'm ready, I'll find something."

He nodded. "When can I see you again?" He stiffened when he realized what he'd said.

"Sunday?" she said.

He relaxed when he saw the teasing twinkle in her blue eyes. "*Ja*, no doubt." He smiled. "Service is at Abram Peachy's?"

"It is."

"I'll see you then." He climbed into his buggy and, with a wave, left. He'd wanted nothing more than to stay and talk with Leah longer, but he was afraid that she'd discover that he had deep feelings for her...and the last thing he wanted to do was to scare her away.

He'd steered his horse about a mile down the road

when a car came up from behind him and slowed. Henry glanced over and sighed. *Not again.*

"Henry," a male voice sang with a cruel expression. "Whatcha doing?" The *Englisher* pulled his car off the road, and Henry had no other choice but to face him.

"Brad," he greeted pleasantly. "We meet again. What do you want?" Why wouldn't man leave him alone?

The man looked amused. "I thought we'd visit awhile."

Henry stared at him calmly, but inside his heart started to hammer hard. The man was nothing but trouble. Years before, Isaac and he had been too young and inexperienced to recognize Brad for the cruel bully he was. If they had, they would have avoided Brad and his English friends instead of befriending them. Unfortunately, he and Brad Smith shared a past, and there was nothing Henry could do about it, except refuse to let the man intimidate him a second time.

Chapter Ten

Sunday morning Leah sat in the back of the family buggy with her sisters. She had yet to ask her parents about her adoption again. Partly because they were talking again, and she didn't want to do anything that would make things difficult and tense between her and Missy and Arlin. After meeting Jess in the barn, she realized how lucky she was to have adoptive parents who'd cared for her. As her father steered the buggy toward the Abram Peachy residence, where church service would be held, Leah wondered how Jess was faring. She'd seen no evidence of the girl's return. She sighed. She hoped Jess was all right. She was worried about her. She should have done more and offered the girl a safe haven, perhaps consulted with one of the church elders.

I don't know her situation, but it doesn't mean I couldn't have done more for her. She sighed. Jess would have run away as fast as she could if Leah had tried to do anything more. Leah prayed that the girl would return if she was in trouble.

She got the sudden urge to see Henry. She had enjoyed her outing with him. She reminded herself to be cautious with her heart. The Henry Yoder she was beginning to know wasn't the kind of man who would hurt anyone intentionally. She'd trusted him enough to confide in him. It might have been impulsive to tell him the secret of her adoption, but she didn't regret talking with him.

The Yoders would be attending today's service. Leah recognized the rush of anticipation as pleasure at the thought of spending time with him.

Leah felt butterflies in her stomach as her father turned onto Abram Peachy's property.

After *Dat* parked their buggy, she scrambled out of the vehicle after her sisters and waved to her cousin Isaac and his wife, Ellen. With the cake she'd baked in her arms, she approached them. "*Hallo*, cousins."

Ellen beamed at her. "Leah, 'tis wonderful to see you. You're looking well."

"You are, too," Leah replied with a smile. She glanced past the couple for any sign of Henry.

"Looking for someone, Leah?" Isaac said with amusement.

She raised her eyebrows and answered truthfully. "I'm looking for Henry. I need to talk with him."

Her honesty surprised her cousin. His teasing twinkle vanished. "He's not here yet. I talked with him yesterday and he said his parents were coming, too."

"I'll look for him after service." She held up her plate. "I need to put this cake inside."

The benches in Abram Peachy's great room were set up in sections, one section for women and children and the others for the men and older boys. Abram was a church elder and deacon. The family of his wife, Charlotte King Peachy, were neighbors of her aunt Katie and uncle Samuel.

There was no sign of Henry as she took a seat in the women's section of the congregation. Leah watched as her sisters and their husbands came in and sat down. Nell grinned as she sat next to her, and Leah, pleased to see her sister, returned her grin. Sarah, her cousin Jedidiah's wife, grabbed a seat on the bench directly in front of them with her two children. Her cousin Noah's wife, Rachel, murmured a greeting as she and her daughter, Susanna, sat on Leah's other side.

Leah leaned over to ruffle Susanna's hair before she sat back. Her pulse rate changed as Henry and his parents entered the room. Her gaze locked with Henry's. She nodded a greeting with the hope that he'd approach her after the service.

Preacher Levi Stoltzfus entered the pulpit area. Everyone stood, opened the *Ausbund*, the book of hymns, and began to sing. Afterward, Levi began to speak. Everyone was silent as they listened, including the youngest members of their Amish community. Deacon Abram rose and said a few words. The service was interspersed with hymns and sermons until church ended and everyone stood to leave the room. The men grabbed benches to bring outside to use as seats for the midday meal. The women headed toward the kitchen to get the food. Leah pitched in to help take out cold food dishes and paper plates with plastic utensils.

The weather was perfect for eating outside. The men set the benches near tables made from plywood laid across wooden sawhorses. A separate table was created to hold food. Leah went back and forth to the house until all the family food donations had been put out for the community. To drink, there were pitchers of iced tea and lemonade and several bottles of soda. Their young children had the choice of milk or juice.

The women waited until the men were seated before they served them. The conversation at the table was of crops, animals, weather and local businesses. Henry sat beside his father, who looked well despite his recent hospital stay. Margaret fixed a plate of food for her husband and son before she went to get her own meal. During the colder months, when forced to eat inside, the men would eat first, then give their seats to their women and children. Leah loved this time of year best. The good weather allowed for enough table room for families to eat together.

She glanced toward her adoptive mother and felt a catch in her throat. This woman had mothered her since she was a baby. Leah knew that she had no reason to complain. Missy might not be her birth mother, but she had raised and loved her. If it wasn't for her deep-seated desire to know the truth—no matter how painful—Leah would have allowed the matter of her adoption to rest. Were her parents afraid that the truth would hurt more than help her?

Nell and Meg were filling plates for themselves and their husbands when Leah approached. "Are you certain you have enough to eat?" she teased as she grabbed a paper plate for herself.

Meg stared at the overfilled plate she'd fixed for Peter. She looked amused when she met Leah's gaze. "Too much?"

Nell considered the plate Meg held carefully. "I don't know. Maybe you should add a piece of cake."

"Peter needs a separate plate for dessert."

Leah chuckled. "Meg, 'tis *gut* to see you," she said sincerely. "You, too, Nell. I've missed you both. Everything seems different now that you're married and out of the *haus*."

"What about you?" Meg asked. "No beau or potential husband?"

"As if I could pick and choose whom to marry," Leah said with a sigh.

"Are you *oll recht*, Leah?" Nell studied her with concern.

"Ja." Leah managed a smile. "Trying to decide on the chocolate cake or the vanilla cream pie for dessert."

She followed her sisters to their family table. As she approached, she and her *dat* exchanged looks. She smiled shyly as she took the seat directly across from him. "A beautiful day for a meal outside. I'm glad to be here," she murmured and was rewarded with the look of pleasure in her mother's expression.

"Leah."

She recognized the male voice immediately. She faced him with a smile. "Henry."

"When you're done, do you have a minute to talk?"

She felt a burning in her stomach at his unreadable expression. *"Ja.* Just give me a few minutes."

He appeared serious as he inclined his head. "I'll be with my *eldre* until you're ready."

When she faced them, she saw her family's curiosity. "Business," she explained, although she was afraid that it wasn't business he wanted to discuss with her.

She finished her meal, then threw away her trash. Henry was seated with his parents in the next row of tables. She hesitated before approaching. Had some-

thing happened since they last saw each other? Why
was she so worried?

Because I like him—maybe too much. She started
toward the table. Henry saw her and stood, murmured
something to his parents and came to meet her.

"You wanted to talk with me?" she asked, her heart
thumping hard. His features were stiff, almost angry.
She didn't understand, because that wasn't the Henry
she knew. That man had only ever been kind to her.

"Let's walk this way," he said abruptly, then started
toward the road before making a right onto the front
farm field of Abram Peachy's property.

Leah was aware that he purposely kept his distance
as they walked side by side. It was as if they'd never
worked together or become friends. *Friends.* Was he
worried that she saw him as more than a friend? She
was attracted to him, but she'd been polite and she
hoped she'd done nothing to make him think that their
working relationship was anything other than friendship. So she missed him when she wasn't with him.
She'd given him a glimpse of her vulnerable side and
questioned the wisdom of it since she'd cried and he'd
tried to make her feel better. And he'd offered her good
advice. A knot of pain formed in her chest. Yes, she
longed for more than friendship from Henry Yoder, but
she had no plans for telling him.

Her throat tightened and he remained tensely silent.
Unable to stand it any longer, she stopped and face him.
"Henry." She felt him stiffen as he halted and met her
gaze. "Have I done something to offend you?"

"Nay," he said.

"Then what?" Panic set in. Was Henry ill? What
could have happened to make him study her so seri-

ously? She stared into his blue eyes and knew. "You don't want to help me anymore."

His expression softened. "I can't work with you," he said huskily. "Not right now."

She blanched. "I see."

"I'm going to be busy over the next couple of weeks, and I needed to let you know. To explain."

"I understand." But she didn't and turned so he couldn't see her tears.

He gently touched her arm, and she closed her eyes with longing and a world of hurt. "Leah," he whispered. "I'm sorry."

She hardened her heart and faced him defiantly. "I've heard no explanation."

He opened his mouth, then closed it. "You have a lot on your mind with Missy and Arlin, and I have to worry about my *vadder*."

Her insides softened at the mention of his father. "Is Harry *oll recht*? He seems well enough."

He refused to meet her gaze. "He's been having a *gut* week, but I worry that he'll suffer a relapse."

Leah narrowed her eyes. "I see." The sudden impression that he wasn't telling the whole truth struck her hard, because she'd come to expect better from him.

Harry Yoder wasn't the reason that Henry no longer wanted to work with her. Unless it was because he'd had enough of her and wanted to ease back from their friendship until it was over.

She nearly gasped at the pain. She blinked rapidly and was able to control her tears.

"Leah."

She managed to smile. "I understand, Henry. I do." She drew a calming breath. "*Danki* for all that you've taught me. You're a great teacher." She glanced back toward the table area where her family and friends would be enjoying dessert. "We should head back. I want a piece of chocolate cake before it's gone."

She felt his stare but she didn't look at him until, after a long silent moment, he seemed to demand it of her. She gazed up to see a something like regret flicker in his blue eyes. "I wouldn't mind a slice myself," he said. His smile was slight, missing his usual gorgeous good humor.

"Then we'd better hurry. Noah is here, and he's bound to jump in and eat our share if we don't claim it."

Tension hung between as they approached the community area. Leah immediately walked to the dessert table and picked up a plate. Aware that Henry had left her, she turned to see that he'd rejoined his family. She fought back tears as she cut a generous piece of chocolate cake. For once, her cousin Noah hadn't returned for more. Her dessert plate blurred as she headed slowly toward her family's table. Until Henry stepped into her path and blocked her. She gaped at him. "May I sit with you?" he asked.

She stared at him in shock and couldn't help the sudden rising surge of hope. Maybe he liked her a little. She nodded, and he led her to an empty table, vacated by her cousins, who were playing ball on the back lawn. Without looking at him, Leah slid her legs under the table as she sat down.

Henry didn't say a word but seemed more at ease. "The cake looks delicious," he finally said, drawing her glance.

Her heart beat wildly as she met his gaze. "I like chocolate."

His lips curved crookedly. "Me, too." He'd taken a couple of brownies and a small piece of the chocolate cake Leah had baked yesterday. Holding her gaze captive, he didn't look away. "Leah," he began. He shifted uncomfortably. "I…like you."

Her pulse raced. "I like you, too," she admitted softly.

He looked away. "I don't know what to do," he murmured.

She wrinkled her brow. "I don't understand."

He sighed. "I can't spend time with you, but I'd like to."

Leah was surprised to see real regret in his expression. "Henry—"

"I want to see you, Leah, but… I can't explain why I can't." She saw herself mirrored in his blue eyes. "But I'd like to spend today with you."

Henry gazed at the woman before him and experienced a pain so intense in the region of his heart that it nearly stole his breath. He wanted nothing more than to be with Leah, but how could he after Brad's threats to harm anyone he cared about? The *Englisher* was angry. He'd had nothing to do with the man's time in jail, but Brad was determined to blame someone for his troubles—and unfortunately, he'd chosen Henry. If only Isaac and he had stayed away from the *Englisher*. Newly on *rumspringa*, they'd become caught up in the excitement of having English friends. Until they discovered, after it was too late, that Brad had no conscience. The man had enjoyed defacing Whittier's Store and taken great pleasure when Henry had become upset and tried to stop him. Yesterday wasn't the first time that Brad had threatened his family and friends. Henry hadn't done the crime, but it had felt as if he had, for he was ashamed that he hadn't been brave enough to come forward with the truth—even after Isaac was blamed—because he'd been afraid of the *Englisher*.

Later, when Brad was in jail and no longer a threat, Henry had finally confessed. A visit by Isaac's sweetheart, Ellen Mast, had influenced his decision to come forward. His silence had destroyed his best friend's reputation. Isaac hadn't denied the wrongdoing to protect him, and Henry had suffered with guilt, even after he'd stood up before his church district and told the truth. Although forgiven, Henry hadn't been able to forgive himself until recently, when Leah's forgiveness had soothed his guilt-ridden soul. Since then, he had discovered his life was a blessing while he enjoyed every moment with Leah Stoltzfus.

Now, with Brad's recent threats hanging over his head, Henry had no choice but to distance himself from her for her protection when all he wanted to do was to hang on tight. *Lord, please help me to let her go to keep her safe.*

Brad mustn't learn about his friendship with Leah. If he didn't, things would be fine. Henry wanted the gift of today and then he'd step away. He'd find a way to ease back without hurting her. The distance would devastate him, for he would suffer forever with his longing for her. If he could figure out a way to eliminate the threat one day, he'd seek Leah's forgiveness and beg her to take him back.

"Leah?" He shifted as he stared at her. "You haven't answered me. May I spend the rest of the day with you?"

Dark lashes blinked across bright blue eyes as she

bobbed her head. "Would you like more dessert?" she asked.

He grinned. "I wouldn't mind. You?"

Her lips curved in a teasing smile. "Maybe."

As he gazed at her, he knew that he wouldn't be able to stay away from her. As long as he could have her and keep her safe. They could spend Sundays together, he thought. He doubted Brad would seek him out on church or Visiting Days. Henry became overwhelmed with a sudden rush of warmth and tenderness, laced with extreme excitement, that he might not have to keep his distance from Leah on Sundays.

He watched as she cut two pieces of apple pie, He had to find a way to keep Leah in his life. Was Brad Smith really a threat? If he hurt anyone, the *Englisher* would end up in jail again, the last place Brad wanted to be.

Overjoyed, Henry beamed at Leah with warmth as she handed him his plate. "*Danki*, Leah." He was surprised when she blushed. Her pink cheeks and shy smile made his heart pound and fill up with hope. He sent up a silent prayer, asking the Lord for Leah and him to have a future together, that Leah would love him as he loved her. *Please, Lord.* He wouldn't tell her of his love, not until he knew if she shared his feelings. He would enjoy her company and enjoy their growing friendship, and he'd continue to pray that their relationship would become something more…and permanent.

Chapter Eleven

Henry was stocking the shelves with merchandise when he heard the bell on the entrance door. He glanced over and was pleasantly surprised to see Leah Stoltzfus.

"*Hallo*, Henry," she greeted.

His pulse rate shot up as she smiled at him warmly. "Leah. I didn't expect to see you today." She looked pretty in a lavender dress with matching cape and apron. Her white prayer *kapp* covered most of her blond hair without a strand out of place.

She held up a grocery list. "*Mam* needed a few items, so I offered to shop for her." She approached, and he watched her with no small amount of interest.

"Anything I can help with?" he asked softly.

Leah froze as she came within a few feet of him, as if she'd suddenly sensed something strong between them. "*Nay*, the list isn't too long." She turned away quickly, apparently eager to put distance between them.

He rushed after her, gently grabbed hold of her arm. "Leah."

She stiffened but met his gaze. He smiled to assure her that he was still the same man who'd taught her the basics of bookkeeping and storekeeping—her friend. "Would you like a cup of tea?"

The offer drew a reluctant smile. "Black tea with sugar? Lots of sugar?"

"If you'd like." He grinned. The awkwardness had dissipated. "I'll put on the hot water."

"I'll wander around the store while I wait."

Henry nodded and went behind the counter to brew the tea while he prayed that the easy camaraderie between them would remain and Leah would stay to visit for a while. When the tea was ready, he joined her on the other side of the counter with the two cups. "Here you are."

She accepted the cup with a murmur of thanks. "Your *mam* took the day off?"

His stomach lurched as he swallowed a sip of tea. "She took *Dat* for his follow-up doctor's appointment." Had she been disappointed to find him here instead of his mother? "How long is your *mudder's* list?"

"Not too long." She pulled the list from where she'd tucked it beneath the waistband of her apron and glanced over it. "Eight items."

"Are you sure you don't want me to help?" he asked with the hope that she'd say that she was in no hurry to shop and leave.

"*Danki*, but *nay*. I'll find them when I'm ready." Her blue eyes regarded him with a twinkle. "I'm enjoying my tea. I'm in no rush to check out."

Thank You, Lord, Henry thought.

Suddenly she frowned. "I don't mean to keep you from working."

"Leah," he said quietly, "I'm not worried about the store. I'd much rather spend this time with you." He

eyed her carefully and was rewarded when she blushed.
Did she feel it, too—the attraction, the camaraderie and
warmth? He was thoughtful. "How about a cookie to
go with your tea?"

"Chocolate?"

"If you'd like." He liked how her blue eyes shim-
mered with good humor.

She suddenly looked uncertain. "*Nay*, but *danki*. I
should finish *Mam's* shopping and get home."

Her reluctance warmed his heart. "Will you…shop
again?"

Leah grinned. "*Ja*, I like shopping here."

He couldn't help but grin back at her. He walked
with her through the store, despite her initial refusal of
his help, and worked with her to collect the items she
needed. He followed her back to the counter where he
rang up her merchandise, mostly food and bakery items.
He grabbed a wrapped chocolate-chip cookie and put
it in her bag. "For you." He eyed her shyly, hoping that
she wouldn't refuse the treat. "For later, when you're
hungry."

She chuckled. "I love chocolate-chip cookies."

His chest swelled with love. He then walked with her
to the door and to her buggy. "How are things going
with your parents? Have they told you anything about
your adoption?"

"*Nay,*" she confessed with a sadness that made him
regret bringing up the painful topic.

"I'm sorry."

"Don't be. You've been…"

He arched an eyebrow.

"…helpful," she ended with a teasing twinkle that
caused him to laugh out loud.

If she could laugh about it, he thought, maybe things would get better for her.

He helped her into her buggy. "I'll see you Sunday at the William Masts'." The family would be hosting Visiting Sunday for family and a few friends, including Henry and his parents.

Leah smiled, looking flushed, as she agreed before she steered her horse out of the parking lot.

Henry had turned back to the store when he heard a car engine roar up from behind him. He spun and felt the drop in his stomach when he recognized the driver.

The *Englisher* rolled down the side window. "Henry."

"What do you want now, Brad?" He was glad that Leah had left. If she had been here… Henry felt a chill.

"Just thought I'd stop for a quick chat with an old *friend*."

"I can't stay to talk with you. I've got work to do."

Anger flashed across the *Englisher's* blunt features. He drew a sharp breath. "Guess we all got to make a living, huh?"

Henry nodded, unwilling to look away, because he didn't trust him.

"Can't stay, either. Mom's making me my favorite dinner."

"That's nice." He remembered how much the man's mother had favored her son over her daughter. Isaac had told him how Brad's sister, Nancy, had run away from home to seek refuge from her abusive brother, abuse that their mother refused to believe had occurred. Isaac had taken the girl to Abram Peachy, their deacon, who had made sure Nancy had a safe haven in a new home.

With a wave and a nasty snicker, Brad drove his car out of the lot. Henry had never been so happy to see him leave. *Please, Lord, keep Leah safe. And please protect my family and friends from Brad Smith.*

Henry woke in the middle of the night, wondering how he could help Leah find out about the circumstances of her adoption and what he could do to ensure that Brad Smith no longer had the power to disrupt the life of anyone he cared about. Missy Stoltzfus's parents lived in Ohio. He could visit them and find out what they knew. Did they know anything about Leah's birth parents?

He'd leave on Monday after Visiting Day. He could hire a driver or take the bus, then return as soon as he could. Leah wanted to know who her birth parents were. He would help her discover the truth. And while he was at it, he'd figure out a way to get Brad Smith out of his life once and for all. With a decision made, Henry exhaled softly and felt his eyelids droop closed.

Sunday couldn't come fast enough for Leah, who was eager to see Henry again. She had no reason to visit the store again. Her mother didn't need supplies, and she didn't want to appear forward and stop by simply to say *hallo*. Visiting Sunday was at William and Josie Mast's house, her cousin Isaac's in-laws. Upon arrival, Leah saw the Lapp clan in the yard with the women setting up for breakfast. She climbed down from the carriage with her egg casserole and looked for Henry. Her breath caught when she spied him chatting with Abram Peachy's eldest daughter, Mary Elizabeth. She experienced a sharp pain in her chest as he laughed at something the young woman had said. Then, as if sensing that she was there, he looked her way, excused himself quickly and hurried in her direction.

He grinned as he reached her. "Leah!" His look of pleasure filled her with happiness. "May I carry your dish for you?"

She shook her head as she beamed at him. "*Danki*, I can manage. I'm only taking it as far as there." She gestured toward the outside food table. She was surprised to see his cheeks redden with embarrassment. Henry was handsome and adorable, and her love-stricken heart started to pound hard. "'Tis egg casserole. Do you like egg casserole?" she asked in an attempt to get past the awkward moment.

He nodded. "Love it. Especially if it has cheese in it."

Leah affected a frown. "Mine doesn't have cheese."

Henry blinked as if he didn't know how to reply. "I like it without cheese."

She laughed. "I'm teasing you, Henry. *Ja*, it has cheese. What would an egg casserole be without lots of cheddar cheese?"

His face fell. "Oh, cheddar."

"You don't like cheddar." She was disappointed.

He burst out laughing. "Of course I like cheddar cheese." He eyed her with amusement. "I can tease, too."

As they grinned at each other, Leah felt her insides warm with affection. "Let me set this down."

To her surprise, he followed her. She didn't mind. There was something about being in his company that thrilled her. As she slid him a quick glance, she remembered how she had once regarded him and wondered how she could have ever thought ill of him. So he'd made a mistake. Everyone did at one time or another. And she knew Henry was genuinely sorry for his.

"Would you like to take a walk?" he asked, drawing her gaze.

"We haven't had breakfast." Still, she wanted to go now, even if it would seem odd if they disappeared without eating.

"After we eat then?" His blue eyes seemed to plead.

She nodded, moved by the fond look in his expression. "After breakfast," she agreed.

The day already showed signs of being Leah's best day ever. She ate breakfast with her family, whose table was next to Henry's so she and he basically sat side by side, and she loved every minute. A warning rose in her mind to protect her heart; she ignored it, as she already loved Henry and there was nothing she could do about it. She didn't tell him—and wouldn't—because while they were friends who clearly enjoyed each other's company, it was too soon for love. *Although I've known him for many years.* She'd thought she'd be spending her life with only her craft shop for company. She was scared to hope for marriage. Even her adoptive parents hadn't expected it of her. Did they know something about her, something horrible, that would prevent her from having a husband and children? She gasped. Maybe she couldn't have children!

Ellie, Charlie and Nell laughed at something James Pierce, Nell's husband, said. Leah saw a small smile curve her father's lips, and she realized how much she missed their close relationship. Aware of her gaze, he looked at her, and she fought back tears as she gave him a genuine smile. Something shifted in his expression, and she clearly saw his love and affection for her—

his daughter. Her mother said something to him, and he turned to her. Leah inhaled sharply and wondered why she'd fought so hard to learn the truth about her birth parents. Did it matter who they were when she had a family who loved her? Her sisters didn't know the circumstances of her birth. What would they say if they knew?

She felt a warm hand entwine fingers with hers below the table. She shot Henry a glance to see his compassion and warmth…and an emotion she couldn't read.

Henry bent close and whispered in her ear, "We've eaten. Ready for our walk?"

Leah nodded. She rose with her used paper plate in hand and wandered to the trash can to throw it out. Some of her Lapp cousins had already risen and chatted nearby. She smiled at them and meandered toward the barn. She walked to the back of the building and waited for Henry to come. It seemed the best way to go for a walk without raising eyebrows. She didn't have long to wait. Henry approached from the other side of the barn and would have frightened her by his approach, except that she sensed him coming.

She turned as he rounded the corner. "Henry."

He regarded her warmly. "*Danki* for coming. We won't go far."

Henry led the way and headed to the back of Abram Peachy's property. "I don't think anyone saw me leave." Leah halted. "I'm sorry. I didn't think…"

"Leah," he said as he reached for her hand. "I wanted this time alone with you. 'Tis no one's business if we want to walk together."

She swallowed hard, disappointed.

"Not that I would care if everyone knew," he added, brightening her mood.

"You wouldn't?" she whispered.

In answer, he entwined his fingers with hers and gave them a little squeeze. "You're beautiful."

She blushed. "Henry."

"I mean it, Leah. I've always thought you so."

Leah stopped and faced him, eager to read his expression. She could tell that he told her the truth, and the knowledge startled as much as pleased her. "I don't know what to say."

He regarded her silently, his blue eyes filled with warmth and caring. "Then don't say anything. Let's walk."

And so they did. They started out in silence and soon relaxed enough to have a conversation about what they saw. The colorful array of summer wildflowers reminded them that the season was upon them. With Henry by her side, Leah appreciated the varied colored blossoms in white, yellow, purple and gold. The sun felt warm on her face and a light breeze caressed her skin, but it was the touch of Henry's hand against hers that gave her the most pleasure.

Neither spoke, as if the company of each other was enough. Time seemed to stand still until Leah realized how long they'd been gone and became afraid that someone would look for them.

"We should get back." She didn't want to end or ruin the moment but knew it was past time. She caught him studying her. "What?"

Henry shook his head. "You're right. We should get back." He, too, seemed reluctant to leave, which gave her hope.

As they walked back, Henry released her hand, but he continually brushed shoulders with her. Once they reached the barn, he stopped, gently grasped her arms and turned her to face him. "I enjoyed our walk."

She inclined her head. "Me, too."

"It will be lunchtime before we know it."

"Ja."

"I have to leave soon after lunch," he said as they continued. *"Dat* still gets tired."

Silently Leah continued on.

"Leah."

She halted and met his gaze.

"I want to help you. May I?"

She frowned. "I don't understand."

"To learn the truth about your parents."

"I'm fine, Henry. I'm letting it go." She would try to, at least. She wanted to forget about the circumstances of her birth. And she would. She firmed her lips. "Henry, do you think there is a reason they won't tell me? Like something bad about my real parents?"

He furrowed his brows. "Why would you think that?"

"Because my parents have never encouraged me to marry like they have my sisters."

He shook his head. "I doubt that, Leah. They might have been more careful of you because they wanted you to choose for yourself."

"But if they considered me their *dochter*, wouldn't they treat me the same?"

Henry seemed to give the matter some thought. "There is nothing wrong with you," he said. "Arlin and Missy may love you too much to push. Maybe they were afraid that you would be upset with them if they did."

Leah stared at him. "Why would I be upset?"

His lips curved up slightly. "If they'd urged you to find a husband before your younger sisters were allowed to wed, how would that make you feel?"

She blinked. "I don't know."

"There is nothing wrong with you, Leah Stoltzfus." He caught her hand, gave it a squeeze before releasing it.

At the barn, Henry and she parted ways, each returning the way they'd come—from opposite sides of the building. As she headed toward the gathering, Leah saw Ellie wave at her and she waved back. Henry was nowhere in sight as she joined her sister and went into the house with her to bring out food. Ellie didn't say a word about the length of time she and Henry had been gone and she was grateful for her sister's apparent lack of interest. It was only as the two of them left the house with plates in hand that Ellie turned to her with a secretive smile.

"So how was your walk with Henry Yoder?"

Leah gasped.

"That *gut, ja*?" Ellie laughed.

"Does everyone know?"

"Not everyone," her sister said. "Just Isaac, Ellen and me noticed."

"You won't say anything?"

Ellie regarded her worriedly. "Why not?"

"I don't know if it means anything. Henry has been teaching me about storekeeping, and—"

"Storekeeping?" Ellie chuckled. "Leah, that man doesn't look like he has storekeeping on his mind when he looks at you."

Chapter Twelve

Henry put his small suitcase into the car waiting in the yard. "I'll be back in a day or so," he told his parents.

"Check out that vendor while you're there, *ja*?" his *mam* said.

"I will." He'd decided the trip to Ohio could be used for three purposes—to visit the company they often ordered merchandise from, to speak with Leah's adoptive grandparents and to figure out what to do about his ongoing problem with Brad Smith. He'd be staying with his sister, an added bonus. He'd called the phone she used to take calls and asked if he could stay, then left the store's new cell phone number. Less than an hour later, Ruth had called back and told him she'd be pleased to have him stay with her.

He turned to his father. "*Dat*, take care and don't overdo it," he said softly.

Harry Yoder grimaced. "I'm fine."

"I know you are, but I feel better saying it to you with the hope that you'll actually take heed."

His *dat* chuckled. "I'm getting stronger every day, enough to keep your *mudder* company in the store."

I can live with that. "I'll see you soon. Anything you'd like me to bring back?"

"Your sister and her family?" his mother said with a wry smile. Her expression sobered. "You've got the quilt I made for her?"

"Have it."

"And the cookies I baked?"

"Have those, too, *Mam.*" He reached out and hugged his mother. To his surprise, she pulled him in tight. When she released him, he met his father's gaze. "Bye, *Dat.*"

More reserved than his wife, his father dipped his head in acknowledgment. "I'll call the cell when I get there, so you won't worry," Henry said.

He climbed into the front seat of the car. He knew the hired driver and figured he'd appreciate the company. He lifted a hand to wave to his parents as Timothy Trader drove out of the yard. Henry thought about what might lie ahead and realized that he already missed Leah more than he'd ever dreamed possible.

Leah went into the barn to feed the animals. She heard barking and decided to visit briefly with Jeremiah, their new puppy, before continuing with her chores. The first thing she noticed as she entered the stall was that someone had fed Jeremiah and filled his water bowl. She frowned. Her father hadn't been out to the barn yet, and she knew that her mother and sisters hadn't stepped outside. *Had Jess come back last night to sleep?*

She stared at the tamped straw as she bent to ruffle Jeremiah's fur. An idea came to her on how to help Jess if she came back, and it involved leaving food in a place that only the girl could find. Leah smiled as she took care of the other animals.

When she was done, Leah headed to the house. She froze at the sight of a large commercial van with a huge circular object on the roof. Her mother and father were in the yard, talking with two men who stood beside the vehicle.

One man spied her. "Is that her? Is that *his* daughter?"

"That is Leah and she is *our* daughter," she heard her father said tightly. "One of five." She quickly approached to stand by her parents.

"Leah, go into the *haus*," her father ordered.

Her heart beat wildly in her throat as she immediately obeyed.

"You need to leave," she heard her father say. "Ours is a quiet community. You have no right to be here. You don't belong, and I don't know where you got your information, but our daughters are ours—and no one else's."

She entered the kitchen and saw her two sisters at the window. "What's happening?" Leah suspected the men were here to talk with the adopted daughter of Arlin and Missy Stoltzfus. Her.

"I don't know. *Dat* told us to stay in the *haus*."

Leah joined them at the window. *Dat* and *Mam* were coming inside. The men hadn't left and *Dat's* expression was grim.

Charlie approached them first as they entered. "Why are those men here?"

"They have the mistaken impression that one of you is the daughter of a celebrity." Her father frowned. "I have no idea why."

"Will they leave?" Leah asked. She felt the constriction in her chest tighten.

"I hope so," *Mam* said. "What should we do?"

"Ignore them," *Dat* said. "Eventually they'll grow tired of waiting and go."

Ellie stared outside. "Doesn't look like they plan to leave anytime soon." She faced her parents. "What if they stay the night? I have to work tomorrow. How can I leave if they're still out there in the morning?"

"Let's not worry until it happens," her father said reasonably.

It was early in the day. How would they manage their daily lives if they couldn't go outside for fear that they would be accosted by an English news reporter with a camera and a microphone?

Leah put on a pot of coffee. "Anyone for a piece of pie?"

"I am," Charlie said, and the rest of the family echoed her response.

They sat, drank coffee and ate pie while they talked about what they'd do in the event the news van remained on the property.

"I can call the police on my cell phone," Ellie suggested.

"Not yet," *Dat* said. "Let's ignore them and maybe they will leave us in peace."

Her sisters helped Leah clean up while her parents stayed at the kitchen table. Ellie excused herself to go upstairs and call her client on today's schedule. Charlie decided to put in a load of laundry. Leah remained behind to dry the dishes and put them away while her parents grew silent at the table behind her.

When she was done, she hesitated. She wanted to ask them if the reporters were here for her. She kept her mouth shut, unwilling to cause friction between her parents and her. She started to leave the room.

"Leah," her father said. "Would you come and sit? 'Tis time we told you what you've wanted to know."

Swallowing against a suddenly dry throat, Leah sat across from her parents.

"Leah," Missy began, "please know that we love you, and we want only the best for you."

"I love you," Leah said sincerely.

Her mother smiled, but her father's expression was unreadable.

"'Tis true that we adopted you when you were an infant," *Dat* said. "We thought it best to keep the truth from you because we wanted a normal life for you." He waited for Leah's nod before he continued. "You may not be our daughter by birth, but you are ours—never doubt that. You are a part of this family." He exchanged a brief, warm look with his wife. "Your mother was Missy's sister. She got pregnant during her senior year of high school. She couldn't take care of you, so she brought you to us—and we were thrilled."

"You're my aunt and uncle?" she whispered, floored by the knowledge.

"We were until we held you in our arms and took you for our own. From the first moment I laid eyes on you, I loved you," her father confessed huskily.

Tears filled Leah's eyes. Her father wasn't usually verbal with his affection, and she was deeply moved. "Who is my birth father?"

"He was Christine's high school sweetheart. He loved her. She never told him about you because Jason had big dreams. Chris loved him and didn't want to interfere with his plans. She never told him that she was carrying his child. If he'd known, he would have insisted on marrying her. She let him go, then after you were born, she brought you to us."

"May I see my birth mother? Meet her?"

Pain flickered across her mother's features. "'Tis not possible." She drew a sharp breath as if bracing herself for what she must reveal. "Your mother was killed in a car accident two months after you were born." Tears welled in her eyes. "Before she died, she frequently came to see you, but as your aunt not your mother. She wanted you to be happy, and we promised we'd take *gut* care of you." She sniffed. "We tried."

"You've always taken *gut* care of me," Leah said huskily. A tear escaped to trail down her cheek. "And my father?"

"He doesn't know about you," *Dat* said. "At least, we don't think he does, but now that those news people are outside, we've wondered…"

Leah frowned. "Why would those reporters care who my birth father is?"

"Your father's name is Jason Kingsley. He left home for a career in music. We don't know if he made it, so we can't be sure," her father explained. "Those men outside are looking for Derek Rhoades's daughter. The man is a musician, a singer and a rock star. We can't be certain, but it's possible that Derek Rhoades is the name Jason took for his music career."

Her pulse rate jacked up as Leah tried to process what her parents had told her. "He's not Amish?"

Mam shook her head. "I didn't grow up Amish, Leah. I chose to join the Amish church after I fell in love with your *vadder*." Her face was soft as she regarded her husband lovingly.

"So what will we do if they won't leave?" Leah asked as she glanced toward the window.

"We ignore them for as long as we can. You are our daughter—and no one else's. They have no proof that you are anyone else." To her surprise, her father reached across the table to clasp her hand. "I know you are mad at us, but I hope you still trust us."

"I trust you," she murmured. "And I'm not angry with you. I know you did what you thought was best, what my birth mother wanted you to do." She paused. "Was she kind? Your sister, Christine?"

Mam's expression filled with sadness. "She was a sweet girl who was desperately in love with her boy-friend. She sacrificed her happiness so that Jason could have the life he wanted. If that isn't kind…"

"'Tis more than kind," Leah whispered. She stood and peered out the window. "They're still there."

"They'll grow tired," *Dat* assured her.

"What if our faces make English TV news? What if Derek Rhoades believes the gossip and shows up?" she asked.

Her father stood. "Then we will deal with him when he does."

How? Leah wondered. *"Oll recht."* She hesitated, then asked, "What will you tell my sisters?"

"The truth," *Mam* said.

"Then they'll know I'm not their real sister."

"You are their sister, and they will be the first to say so."

Ellie and Charlie entered the room with identical confused expressions. "Why isn't Leah our sister?" Charlie asked *Mam*.

"Because I'm adopted," Leah said quietly.

"So?" Ellie's smile was warm as she gazed at Leah. "You *are* my sister."

"And *mine*," Charlie added.

Tears rushed to her eyes again. "But you don't know the circumstances…"

"We don't have to know. We love you," Ellie said.

Leah narrowed her gaze as she stared at her. "You overheard us."

Her sister shrugged. "Some of what you said but not all."

"Enough to know why that news van is camped outside our *haus*," her father said in a scolding tone.

Ellie shrugged. "Wouldn't matter if we hadn't eavesdropped, although that wasn't why we came back." She grinned. "We were hungry for sweets. We want coffee cake."

Missy laughed. "I should have known."

Her sisters joined them at the table, and the family decided to ignore the media and simply enjoy one another's company.

An hour later Leah peeked outside and cheered. "They're gone. The van and the reporters have left!"

"Thanks be to *God*," her father said, and they all echoed his prayer.

Two hours later, the newsmen returned, but there were three vehicles instead of one, and more men with cameras.

Leah saw them first. "*Dat!* The *Englishers* are back!"

Henry stood on the front porch of his sister and her husband's home and said his goodbyes. "You'll think about coming home for a visit?" he asked Ruth. "*Mam* and *Dat* miss you. We all do."

Ruth exchanged glances with her husband, John, who nodded. "I didn't know that *Dat* had a heart attack," she murmured with concern. She'd been upset to find out that Henry had written her and she'd never received his letter.

"He had two," Henry replied, "but he's doing well, especially since the doctor changed his medicine." He paused to study his sister. "They didn't want to worry you."

She sighed, because she understood her father. "But if he hadn't made it…"

"I'll make sure to call you if anything happens again."

She was only slightly mollified. "I'll call the store to let you know when we plan to come."

"Soon, I hope."

"Within the month," John said. "Hopefully within the next two weeks."

Henry smiled. "I enjoyed my visit. *Danki* for having me."

"As short as it was," Ruth complained.

"I need to get back." He'd decided that business was all he would do. Visiting Leah's grandparents would be the last thing she'd want, and he realized that he'd be breaking his promise about keeping her secret. He was ready to go home and see her. On the way here, he'd thought long and hard about what to do with Brad Smith. He decided that the next time he encountered the man, he would stand up to the *Englisher* no matter the consequences.

Henry looked down at the four boys who stood near their parents. "Bye, nephews. Be *gut* for your *mudder*."

"*Onkel* Henry, when can we see you again?" asked little Caleb, the youngest son at five years old.

"Soon," he promised with a grin for his sister, who tried to hide a smile.

Harley, who was a year older than Caleb, said, "When we come, can we see your store?"

Henry nodded. "You may, but the store isn't mine. It belongs to your *grossmammi* and *grossdaddi*."

"Where do you work then?" Caleb piped up.

"I help out in the store and—"

"Then the store is yours, too!" Harley insisted.

Henry laughed. "I guess so." He studied his sister's two older boys thoughtfully. "I like to build things. I can show you when you come," he told Aaron, aged eight, and John Junior, aged ten. "Would you like that?"

The boys bobbed their heads. With a sigh, he met his sister's gaze. "I have to go. I'll see you within the month." To his surprise, Ruth gave him a hug. Henry exchanged handshakes with his brother-in-law. "Take care. And *danki* for caring for my sister and nephews."

John's blue eyes twinkled. "They're not too much work."

Ruth gasped with outrage and tapped her husband on the arm, and Henry cracked up, with John quickly joining in the laughter.

Henry climbed into the hired car, waved and was soon on his way home. He missed the warmth of Leah's blue eyes and sweet smile. He hadn't been gone long so he doubted that she knew he'd gone away. Especially since it was Tuesday and the last time he'd spent time with her was Sunday.

It was a five-hour car's ride from Charm, Ohio, where his sister and her family lived, to his home in

Happiness, Pennsylvania. It was early morning, and he should get back to his Amish community by two thirty in the afternoon at the latest. The first thing he'd do, once he dropped off his suitcase and spoke with his parents, would be to drive over to see Leah.

His heart beat rapidly at the thought. His stomach felt as if it was filled with fluttering butterflies. He was so eager to see Leah again that he'd head to wherever she'd gone if she wasn't at home.

Chapter Thirteen

"There have been news vans outside the Arlin Stoltzfus place since yesterday morning," Henry's mother said.

"News vans? Why?" Henry felt a lurch in his chest. He was worried about Leah. What had happened to bring the attention of English television?

"They claim one of the Stoltzfus girls is the daughter of someone famous. A singer-musician by the name of Derek Rhoades."

His heart raced, but he didn't let on that he had his suspicions, for it would mean giving away Leah's secrets. "Which daughter?"

Mam shook her head. "I don't know. It's not right. We all know that every one of those girls belong to Missy and Arlin. They all look like them."

Henry agreed. Leah had found proof of her adoption, but she did look like her adoptive parents, especially Missy. "Has anyone been able to get through to the *haus*?"

"*Nay*, the news people are like vultures, waiting to pounce on anyone who goes in or out. Noah Lapp drove by and was stopped by one. That's how he learned what was going on."

"This must be difficult for them," he said softly.

His mother regarded him with a knowing look. "You're worried about Leah."

He opened his mouth to deny it but found himself telling the truth. "*Ja.* I wish I could help her. Be there with her."

"You could try," she suggested. "Sneak in from the road at the back of the property."

Henry firmed his resolution. "I'll go now."

"Not until you've eaten," *Mam* insisted. "You've been traveling for hours. 'Tis late and you haven't had lunch."

"*Mam.*"

"*Henry.*" Her voice was firm and final. "I'd like to send supplies with you. I'm sure they have plenty of food, but it will make me feel better if you bring more. If you're staying there with her, you'll need to eat."

Within a half hour later, Henry drove his buggy to the Adam Troyer residence, which was located down the road from the Stoltzfus dwelling. He parked in the barnyard, then stopped for a brief word with Adam about leaving his vehicle before he headed on foot toward Leah's house. He cut through from the back of Arlin's property as his mother suggested. He kept hidden so that he could check out the situation without anyone catching sight of him. He made an effort to stay low as he ran from one bush or tree to another toward the house. He froze when he caught sight of several large news vehicles with round disks on their roofs parked in Arlin's driveway. The *Englishers* congregated in the yard. Some stood with large cameras ready to film anyone exiting the house. Others owned small handheld devices with the hope of taking photos of members of the Stoltzfus family. As he watched from behind a honeysuckle bush, he saw Arlin exit the house onto the porch.

"I told you that there is no one here of interest. I don't know where you got your information, but the girls inside the *haus* are my daughters. You are bothering my family and scaring my girls. You need to leave immediately. If you don't, we'll call the police."

"With what?" one man taunted. "You don't have a phone."

Henry's heart started to beat hard when Leah stepped out onto the porch to stand next to her father. She looked beautiful and upset…and very pale. He longed to go to her, call out to her, but remained still and silent. "We have a cell phone," she said loudly. "Our church elders have allowed it."

One man raised a camera to take a photo.

"Nay," she cried as she blocked her face with her hand to stop him from taking her picture. "'Tis forbidden to have our pictures taken. Go away!"

"Maybe we should leave," said a young man to the older one with the camera. "These people don't lie. They're telling the truth. We should leave them in peace."

The cameraman glared at him. "All people lie under the right circumstances."

"Leah, go inside," Arlin ordered.

Once Arlin and Leah had gone inside, Henry slipped away. To get caught outside their house would only draw more attention to the family. He would go home and return after dark. Surely, the news people would be long gone by then.

But first he would head to the store and, using their

new cell phone, call the police. Someone needed to order those awful reporters away. Maybe the police would order them gone, and the men would listen.

"*Dat*, what are we going to do?" Leah cried. "Maybe I should give them an interview."

"*Nay*," her father said. "You are my daughter. We don't even know who Derek Rhoades is. And they don't know that you are adopted. We need to keep the secret, or they will never leave us alone."

"But Derek Rhoades could be Jason Kingsley, *ja*?" she asked quietly as she fought back panic.

"'Tis possible, but not likely."

"If you go outside again, then I'll go with you. If you tell them you're adopted, then I will, too," Charlie said with a fierceness that startled Leah.

"Me, too," Ellie added with determination. "And I'll call Nell and Meg to say the same."

"Why would you do that?" Leah's eyes swam with tears. She wished Henry was here. He had the habit of making her feel good about herself.

"Because we are sisters…always have been and always will be."

She wiped her wet cheeks with the back of her hand. "But it will ruin your life."

"It will ruin yours if we don't stick together." Ellie moved to the window and stared outside. "I say we ignore them. If you go, then we will, too, but why should we give those awful people what they want?"

"Exactly," *Dat* said. "Stay inside. If they don't leave soon, Ellie, use your phone to call the police." Ellie nodded.

"I'm going upstairs to watch them from our bedroom window," Charlie declared. "Anyone want to come with me?"

"I will," Ellie said with a quick look in Leah's direction before they left.

Soon Leah and her parents were alone. "I'm sorry," Leah said. "I love you, and I'd give anything to stop this intrusion into our lives."

In a move that caused Leah a rush of emotion, her father encircled her with strong arms. He gave her a firm hug before releasing her. "I have loved you since the first time I saw you. I'd do anything for you as I would for any of my *dechter*. Don't worry. I'll take care of this."

"This isn't a thunderstorm, *Dat*," she whispered, referring to the time he'd rescued her when she was a young child.

"*Nay*, thunderstorms are more frightening," he answered and then grinned.

Leah chuckled through her tears. How could she not when her father was beaming at her. Concern made her look toward her mother. *"Mam."*

"I've known, Leah," her mother confessed. "About your fear of thunderstorms, but your *vadder* didn't tell me. I agree with him. This is easy compared to knowing your daughter is afraid and not being able to acknowledge it or do anything about it."

Leah gave her a sad half smile. "I'd like to be upstairs with Ellie and Charlie."

Her father nodded. "Don't worry, Leah. With God's help, we will get through this."

She hurried up the steps and entered Ellie's bedroom. "What are they doing?"

"Nothing," Ellie said with a grim face. "Absolutely nothing. They won't leave."

"Maybe this has gone on long enough," Charlie said. "You should call 911, Ellie."

Ellie picked her phone up from the windowsill and flipped it open. "*Ach nay*, I can't make the call," she cried. "The battery is dead!"

"Can't you charge it?" Charlie asked, clearly without a clue about the charging of cell phones.

"Where?" Ellie challenged. "I need electricity. I usually plug it in to charge wherever I'm working, but since I couldn't clean *haus* today…"

Leah gave her a reassuring smile. "'Tis fine, Ellie. We'll manage. I'm sure they'll leave us alone eventually."

Ellie looked dismayed as Charlie stared out the window. Her sisters wanted to go out, but they were forced to stay inside.

"I'm sorry," Leah told them.

"You have nothing to apologize for, Leah," her sisters uttered simultaneously.

As she stared into the yard, Leah's longing for Henry grew. Her sisters now knew about her adoption, but it was Henry she'd confided in…trusted. He had a way about him that soothed her and made her feel better.

She frowned. *Where is he? Surely, he's heard about the news crews staking out the* haus. Was he afraid to get involved? Had she been wrong about him? To believe that he cared enough to come when she needed him? Not that she had sent him a message, but she'd caught sight of her cousins Noah and Isaac, who'd driven by the property separately. Isaac would have hurried to tell Henry, wouldn't he?

Why isn't he here?

* * *

Henry waited until it was night before heading back to the Stoltzfus family. He'd explained his intent to Adam Troyer. He parked in the Troyer yard again and walked to Leah's. It was easier for him to approach the house in the dark. He caught sight of a light in the driveway to the house, but it was clear that all but one vehicle remained with a crew who were either too stubborn or they didn't care about consequences should the police return to discover them still on the premises.

He crept closer, keeping an eye on the crew and the front porch. Which door should he try? Would they answer and let him in? He moved carefully as he debated where to go when he heard someone call out.

"*Hey, you!* I want to talk with you! What do you know about the Stoltzfus sisters?"

Henry shot out into the night, eager to escape. He had the darkness and his knowledge of the property in his favor as he fled. It was only as he reached the road that he realized they could easily drive around and find him. He kept off the street, choosing instead to run across neighboring land until he reached the Troyers. He knocked on Adam's door.

"Please stay inside," he told the man. "The reporters saw me. I escaped, but they may knock on your door. It would be best if you don't open it."

Adam nodded. "What are you going to do?"

"I'll wait a few minutes, and if they don't come, I'll drive home. This has gone on long enough. Tomorrow I'm calling the police again. Those men need to leave the family alone."

"May the Lord be with you."

"*Danki* for your help, Adam."

The man smiled. "I will see you on Sunday if not before. Feel free to park here whenever you need to."

Henry nodded his thanks. "Do James and Nell know what's going on?" he asked, referring to Leah's sister and her husband, James, who was Adam's stepson.

"I don't know. Please call them. James has a phone."

Henry left a short while later, after he felt sure that no one had followed him. He decided to go to the store and call the police again. There was no sense waiting until the morning. The officer who took the call assured him that someone would be out to the property this evening.

After he hung up the phone, he realized that the only thing he could do at this moment was head up to the house.

The next morning, after a fitful night's sleep, Henry returned to the Arlin Stoltzfus property and was pleased to see that the reporters finally had left. With a sense of satisfaction, he approached the house but took the precaution of advancing from the back of the property. He knocked on the back door and Missy Stoltzfus answered it.

"Is Leah home?" Henry asked. "I was wondering if I could see her."

"I'm afraid she's sleeping. She's had a rough couple of days."

"Will you tell her that I stopped by?"

Missy smiled. "Of course."

"*Danki.*" He returned her smile. "I'll stop by later if you think she'll be awake."

Missy retied her apron strings. "I can't promise but feel free."

Henry turned away. He halted and faced her again, but Leah's mother had already shut the door. He was eager to see Leah and disappointed that she wasn't available, but he understood. These last days must have been awful for her. There was so much he wanted to tell her. Like how much he loved her. He prayed that she returned his love.

He came back in the afternoon, but this time it was Arlin who answered the door. "*Hallo*, Arlin. Is Leah awake? I know she's had a difficult time."

Arlin stepped back and gestured for him to enter. While Leah's father's disappeared to find her, Henry enjoyed the warm coziness of their family kitchen. There was something delicious smelling baking in the oven. He was admiring his surroundings when Arlin returned. "I'm sorry, Henry, but Leah still isn't ready to see anyone."

Henry experienced a tightening in his chest. "Do you know when she'll be ready for visitors?"

The man shook his head. "I'll tell her to contact you when she is."

He left then, feeling as if she knew he was there and had decided to avoid him. Why? Had he done something wrong? He'd tried to help her by calling the police. He'd done the best he could under the circumstances. He'd tried to get through to her, but the reporters had made it impossible to get to the house without being accosted by them.

Henry decided he would return again and again until Leah agreed to talk with him. If she didn't want to see him again, she'd have to tell him to his face. The notion made his stomach burn.

He climbed into his buggy and drove home. He'd driven only a mile or so when a car pulled up alongside him. He ignored it and kept driving, shaken to see Brad Smith, who laughed and waved at him before he sped off.

The next morning, he went to the Stoltzfus residence. When her sister Ellie tried to put him off, Henry couldn't stop himself from pushing inside.

"Please," he begged. "I need to see her. I have to see Leah."

Ellie stared at him a long moment and something softened in her expression. "I'll get her," she said quietly.

Leah mended clothes as she sat by the window in her room. She'd witnessed Henry's arrival and told Ellie that she didn't want to see him. He looked so handsome that he stole her breath. He wore no hat, and his dark hair was tousled as if he'd run his fingers through it. The depth of her feelings for him scared her. *He didn't come when I needed him.* How could she rely on a man who stayed away because it was inconvenient for him to deal with the reporters?

She set aside the mended shirt and dropped her head into her hands. She loved Henry, and she shouldn't. She needed to keep distance between them so that she could get over her love for him.

Ellie appeared in her doorway. "Henry refuses leave. He says he needs to talk with you."

"Ellie."

"I think you should see him, Leah. Find out what

he has to say." Her sister stared. "He seems desperate to see you."

"I thought he would come when the reporters were here," she confessed softly. "I needed him and I thought he would come but he didn't."

"Maybe he didn't know what was happening," her sister reasoned.

"How could he not? Everyone else in our community knew. Word spreads quickly throughout our community. And the media was here long enough."

"You need to come down. If you have something to say to him, then say it. If you don't want to see him again, you need to tell him face-to-face."

Leah stood. "Fine." She brushed down the folds of her pale blue dress, checked to make sure her prayer *kapp* was on straight, then went downstairs to see the one person she feared seeing the most because of her overwhelming love for him. Henry Yoder was the only man who had ever made her feel feminine and vulnerable...and alive.

She entered the kitchen to find him standing near the back door with his hat in his hands.

"Leah." Henry gazed at her with longing in his blue eyes, and Leah felt her heart skip a beat before it settled into a rapid, steady rhythm. "Are you *oll recht*?"

His look of tenderness nearly undid her. She fought against the weakness and pretended to be strong. "I'm fine, Henry. I'm surprised to see you here. Why have you come?"

"I wanted—needed—to see you, Leah." A small smile curved his lips. "I've missed you."

She looked away, unwilling to fall for this. He was

the only person who had the power to hurt her. "I thought you'd come sooner."

"I tried," he admitted. "I couldn't get near the *haus*."

"You mean you didn't try hard enough."

He slowly approached. "Leah, I did try."

She narrowed her gaze. "I don't believe you." She'd needed him and he hadn't been there for her. "I think you should leave."

Henry shook his head. "Please, Leah. I'd like to explain. *Please*. I was out of town for a night. I didn't know what happened until I returned. I tried to get to you immediately…"

Skeptical, Leah folded her arms across her chest and stared. "You need to go, Henry. I don't want to talk now. I'm tired and I need peace. I'm not up for a discussion with you." When he slumped as if in defeat, she firmed her resolve to prevent herself from running to him and begging him to love her as much as she loved him.

"May I come by tomorrow? Can we talk then?" he asked quietly.

She shook her head. "I don't think that's wise."

"Why not?"

"We worked together such a short time, Henry. Why would you think that I'd want or need to see you again?" Her chest tightened as she uttered the falsehood. She prayed for God's forgiveness.

A flash of pain darkened his blue eyes, then was gone so quickly that she thought she'd imagined the change. "I won't bother you again, Leah." He turned and opened the door. "I care for you, Leah," he said without facing her. "A great deal. I… I thought we'd become friends, and I'd hoped for more." He was silent for several seconds but didn't turn. Yet, he still didn't leave. "Take care of yourself." His voice was husky and thick with emotion.

Then Henry Yoder walked out of the house and possibly out of her life, and Leah knew that she'd never be the same again.

Chapter Fourteen

He'd wanted to be there for her. Hadn't he tried to get to her? And he'd done what he could to help. He'd called the police twice. As he left the Stoltzfus property, Henry felt terrible. Leah was mad at him and told him she never wanted to see him again. He grew thoughtful as he steered his buggy home. *Why is she so angry?*

As he entered the house minutes later, Henry saw his mother.

"You went to see Leah?" she asked knowingly.

"Ja."

"How did it go?"

Henry shook his head. "Not well. She's upset with me. She asked me to leave."

"Why?"

"Something about not being there for her," he mumbled.

"You tried to see her. Called the police to help."

"I know, but she didn't want to listen." He paused. "I don't know what to do."

"You love her," his *mam* said softly.

He met her glance, then looked away. *"Ja,* I do."

"Then you need to keep trying. She's had a rough time. Maybe she just needs to rest."

Henry met his mother's gaze with a feeling of hope. "Do you think so?"

Mam inclined her head. "I've seen the way she looks at you."

"How?"

"Like she cares for you. She may be scared, Henry. Leah has never had a sweetheart. And I suspect she feels the same way that you do, but she's afraid to trust her feelings for you."

He froze with disbelief. Could it be true? Did she care for him but was afraid to give in to her feelings? Was she so frightened of getting hurt that she'd chosen to withdraw from him?

He smiled. He'd never hurt Leah. In fact, the only thing he wanted to do was love and care for her…and protect her. No matter what she'd said, he wouldn't—couldn't—stay away from her, not if there was a chance that he might have her in his life forever. *As my wife.*

Henry sighed. He would see Leah again and he would convince her that they were meant to be together. They had become friends during their working relationship and his feelings for her had grown. *I love her.* Now he had to get her to admit that their love should be given a chance. He'd give her until this afternoon before approaching her again. He said so to his mother.

"Do you think that's wise?" she asked with concern.

"I have to see her, *Mam.* I don't think I can wait until tomorrow."

She looked as if she understood. "I have to visit Katie Lapp at three. I'll drop you off on my way, then pick you up on my way home."

"I can walk," he said with a smile. "'It isn't too terribly far, and if she rejects me again, I'll need the exercise to think about what to do next.'"

What have I done? Leah sat up in bed, horrified that she'd sent Henry away. She'd been tired and frustrated—and angry with what had happened. How had the reporters found out that one of them was adopted? Who had dug deep enough to bring more than four news companies to the front of their house?

She wanted to see Henry and apologize. She rose from bed and got ready to leave for Yoder's Store. She recalled the quick flash of hurt she'd seen in his eyes and felt her chest constrict with pain.

She checked to make sure that her hair was neatly pinned and tucked up under her prayer *kapp*. She wore her light blue dress and looked to make sure it wasn't soiled or wrinkled. Satisfied with her appearance, she headed downstairs, wondering why she cared how she looked. She'd never given in to vanity before, and it bothered her that she had now. *I want to look nice for Henry.* Would he forgive her?

Leah entered the kitchen and froze at the sight of strange men seated with her mother and father at the kitchen table. When her parents saw her, their expressions filled with concern. As she turned to study the two men, she found her gaze held by the man who was so handsome that she was taken aback.

"I'm sorry, I didn't mean to disturb you," she said as she turned away.

"Sit down, Leah," her *dat* said quietly. She obeyed, choosing to sit next to her mother. "Leah, this is Derek Rhoades and his manager, John Markinson."

"Hello, Leah," Derek said. It was his looks that first caught her attention.

"Why are you here?" she asked, suddenly feeling shaky.

"To apologize for all the problems you'd had with the press."

"I see."

"And to meet my daughter for the first time."

She blinked with shock. "Your daughter?" she replied huskily. She looked to her mother for confirmation.

Mam dipped her head. "Derek's real name is Jason Kingsley."

Leah stared at her biological father. Her heart beat hard as she tried to study him objectively. "Why now?"

Derek seemed taken aback by the question, then he laughed. "You are just like your mother," he murmured, clearly pleased.

"My mother is sitting beside me." She exchanged glances with Missy, whose eyes had filled with tears.

"I know." Derek's voice became soft. He gave her a sad smile before he turned to Missy. "You've done an amazing job with her."

"We love her," her *dat* said, and Leah reached under the table to squeeze his hand. He seemed shocked, but then he met her gaze with his love for her shining in his brown eyes.

"I'm not here to interfere," her biological father said. "I just found out about you a week ago. As much as I wanted to meet you, I was going to stay away." He frowned. "I don't know how the information leaked to the press, but I'm sorry it did. It wasn't my intention to hurt you and…your family."

Leah eyed him closely, noting the tired lines about his eyes, the dark shadows that told her that he hadn't slept in several days. "Did you love my birth mother?"

He rubbed the back of his neck. "Yes, I did, and I was foolish enough to believe that my music career should come first, so I left." Pain flashed in his blue eyes. "Chris encouraged me to go. She said she was proud of me for chasing my dream." He released a shaky breath. "We kept in touch during those first months I was gone. Then suddenly I didn't hear from her, and I admit I was so caught up in the growing success of my band and career that time seemed to get away from me. The next time I tried to call her, I learned that her phone had been disconnected. I wrote but never heard, so I figured she'd moved on with someone else."

Listening quietly, Leah felt an odd mixture of sympathy and dismay for a young couple who had loved and lost. "She never told you about me."

Derek shook his head. "No. I learned what happened to Christine only recently after I hired a private investigator to find her. That's when I learned about the car accident—" he blinked rapidly, clearly overcome with emotion "—and that she'd had a child eight months after I'd left. I knew her child was mine. Chris and I were exclusive." When Leah arched an eyebrow in question, he tried to smile before he said, "We were in love and saw only each other."

She nodded. She waited a moment, then asked, "What do you want from me?"

The man opened his mouth to answer, but his manager beside him replied for him. "He came to apologize about the barrage of media. He wants you to live happily and in peace."

Leah felt a rush of emotion as she thought of Henry Yoder. She could be happy with Henry and she always felt peaceful in his company. "Thank you," she said sincerely.

Derek beamed at her. "I've given your parents my private cell phone number. Should you ever have trouble again, please let me know. I'll put a stop to it."

"You can do that?"

"Yes." His tone was clipped, determined.

She studied him with fresh eyes and saw what her birth mother, Christine, had seen in him. And it wasn't just because of his looks. If this man had chosen a different path, then she would have had a different life with a different father and mother. She glanced at her *mam* and *dat*, and was glad that her life had ended up this way. "I'm sorry for your loss," she said, referring to Christine. Her birth mother, Missy's sister, might have died right after she was born, but he'd just learned of her death and his loss was still new and raw.

Her birth father appeared surprised, but then he understood. "Thank you," he whispered. He took one last sip from the coffee that her mother had fixed for him, then stood. "We should go."

Leah rose, as did her parents. "It was nice to meet you. To know the truth," she said as she accompanied him toward the door.

He stopped and faced her. "Leah, should you or your family ever need anything—anything at all—please call me. I'll always be happy to help my daughter and her loving family."

"Thank you," she said politely, trying not to feel more for this man who was her birth father. Now that she'd met him and understood the circumstances surrounding her adoption, she felt satisfied and more eager to see Henry.

Derek raised his hand as if to touch her cheek but then promptly dropped it, as if realizing how wrong the action would be, especially to a woman who had been raised and still was a member of an Amish community. He shifted his gaze to Missy. "Thank you." He turned to Arlin and held out his hand. "Thank you for loving her." He spun back to open the door and stepped outside. Leah heard him curse beneath his breath.

"Stay inside," he ordered.

It was a lovely day as Henry started the two-mile walk that would bring him to Leah. The sun was warm, but a summer breeze kept it from being too hot or humid. He stayed just off the shoulder of the road. He knew that cars often sped by and he didn't want to take any chances. With Leah in his life, he had too much to live for. He passed a yard where the scent of honeysuckle reached out to tease his nose. He smiled and picked up his pace. He wanted—needed—to see Leah, and now he wished he'd waited for his mother to drive him so he could get to her faster.

He heard a car come up from behind him but paid it no mind and moved farther off the road. It was only when the driver pulled his car to block Henry's path that he looked up, startled. He groaned as he watched Brad Smith get out of his vehicle. The last person he needed to see right now was the *Englisher*. He'd already made up his mind to stand up to Brad, and he would.

"Henry," Brad said in a taunting voice. "Enjoying your walk?"

He shrugged. "It's a nice day for one." He gazed at the man and sighed. "What do you want, Brad?"

"A little payback."

Henry frowned. "For what?"

"For my years spent in prison."

"I didn't put you there. You went a long time after that night at Whittier's Store." He stared. "Might have something to do with your sister?"

Brad bristled. "What do you know about my sister? Do you know where she is?"

"No." He didn't move, although he longed to push past the man so that he could get to Leah.

"I don't believe it. Tell me where she is."

"I told you I don't know where she is."

"Then you'll pay."

The hit came out of nowhere. Pain lanced Henry's check as he fell to the ground. He scrambled to his feet and was promptly slugged again. He didn't fight. It was against the *Ordnung*, so he took the man's punches to his head, his shoulder, his stomach, and he fell to his knees, gasping for breath.

"Stop!" a familiar male voice demanded. Henry could barely make out his friend Jeff Martin's image as it wavered before him. The Englisher and his father often gave rides to members of his community. "Get away from him!"

Brad stepped back, held up his hands. "I don't want no trouble," he complained.

"Yet you're beating on a man who won't fight back," Jeff said. "Henry's faith won't allow him to hit you back, you coward!"

Henry felt a gentle hand help him to his feet.

"Are you all right?" Jeff asked softly.

"I'm fine." But he felt woozy and he teetered on his feet as he stood.

Immediately Jeff slipped his arm around Henry's waist to support him. "I'm taking you to the hospital."

"*Nay!* I need to go to Leah's. I need to see her."

"But you're hurt badly. You can see her after you've received medical attention."

But Henry continued to shake his head. Every movement intensified his pain, but he didn't care. No one would keep him from seeing Leah Stoltzfus. "I'll go after I see her. I need to see her. *Please.*"

"Leah Stoltzfus?"

"Yes," Henry whispered.

"I'll drive you." Jeff said "But then I'll be driving you to the hospital with no arguments."

Henry managed to smile although he had a cut lip, and all of his injuries throbbed terribly. "Thank you."

"Don't thank me. I'm not doing you a favor by waiting."

A police siren heralded the arrival of the authorities, who caught Brad as he tried to leave, but his car wouldn't start.

"Finally," Jeff said with satisfaction. Henry heard Brad's loud complaints interspersed with whining as he was pulled from his vehicle and shoved into the back of the police car. "Thank you, Officer," he called loudly.

"He won't bother anyone again," the uniformed policeman said. "The fellow has an outstanding arrest warrant."

Henry sighed with relief. "I hope he is put away longer than the last time."

A second officer stood back from Brad's vehicle and held up a clear bag filled with a white substance. "There will be extra charges filed against him. He won't walk anytime soon."

The officers left as Jeff gently helped Henry into the front seat of his SUV. "I still think you should go right to the hospital."

"No. Need to see Leah," he said. His pain was intense, but he fought back the darkness. He needed Leah. Had to make her understand. "Leah," he murmured as Jeff drove fast toward the Stoltzfus residence.

Chapter Fifteen

Leah heard Derek's sharp command, and after he and his manager stepped outside, she opened the door to see what was happening. She gasped. News vans filled with reporters were back, camped out on the edge of their property, apparently having learned of the celebrity's visit.

"Derek!" one man cried. "Come to see your daughter?"

"I came to apologize to this good family for your interference. If you think it's anything else, then you're mistaken."

"So you don't have a daughter who lives here?" another reporter called out. There was a cameraman beside him filming the encounter.

"The daughters in the house are Arlin and Missy Stoltzfus's," Derek replied politely. "So I'd thank you to stop filming on this property. Amish aren't allowed to have their photos taken. It's against their religion and a breach of their way of life." When the cameraman kept filming, he turned on the charm. "Please," he asked nicely.

The man lowered the camera and Derek flashed him

a smile. "What are you doing in town then?" the reporter asked.

"I'm on tour. I was in the area and I'd heard what happened so I came."

"That's it?" a woman said with a snarky tone of disbelief.

Derek ramped up his famous charm. "Maybe. Maybe not. But it's not in this house." He hinted that there was another more personal reason for him to be in Lancaster County.

Sensing a diffusing of interest in her family, Leah stepped out onto the porch. Her parents and sisters quickly followed suit. She gazed at the news crews and her breath constricted. She wanted them to leave. She wanted to find Henry.

Derek and his manager were talking with the media. Derek was telling them about the fine women who lived in this part of Pennsylvania, and Leah saw how enthralled the media was with him. He was something to behold, Leah realized. All charm, dark good looks and charisma.

A car honked as it pulled onto the lawn to get past the news vehicles. Leah looked at the car with recognition. It was Jeff Martin. The man and his father often gave rides to the members of her community. She wondered what he was doing there and why the fanfare until her heart gave a lurch as she spied the man in the front passenger seat. Henry Yoder. She stared, fascinated, until Jeff got out and hurried to the other side of the car. Frowning, Leah watched as he reached in to assist Henry out of the vehicle. Leah took one look at the man she loved and gasped. He was injured. She got a quick glimpse of his bloody face and he could barely stand.

She glanced at Derek, who was still close enough to hear her gasp. He encouraged her with his gaze, then he quickly led the media away from her, grabbing the media's focus as he headed toward the news vans.

Henry had his head bent with his hat pulled low to hide his face as he approached. She shot a look toward Derek and his manager, who were surrounded by the media. She faced Henry with concern. He was struggling as he tried to get to her. With a whimper of remorse, Leah ran to him.

She halted within a few feet of him and examined him thoroughly, noting the injuries to his poor face and neck, and the bruises on his lower arms. Where else was he injured? "What happened?" she asked softly with concern.

After hearing her voice, Henry raised his head until their gazes locked. "I have to talk with you."

She inhaled sharply. There was more blood on his face than she'd realized. A laceration across his left cheek. There was a darkening bruise around his right eye.

"I have to talk with you, too," she replied with the tears in her eyes. "Henry," she whispered. "You're hurt."

"I'll live."

"Not if I don't get you to the hospital soon," Jeff said darkly.

Leah eyed Jeff. "Why is Henry here then?"

"He wouldn't go," Jeff explained quietly, "until he had a chance to see you."

Her attention shifted to the man she loved. "Henry, about this morning…"

"Leah," he murmured as he swayed on his feet. "I love you. I know you don't want to see me, but I want a chance to change your mind. I need you in my life…"

"Henry," she admitted, "I love you, too." But he hadn't heard her, for he'd slumped to the ground, unconscious. *"Henry,"* she cried. "Jeff!"

"Get in the car," Jeff told her gently as he examined Henry with a concerned look. "I'm taking him to the hospital, and he'll want you to be there."

She nodded, then ran to her parents. "*Mam. Dat.* Henry..." She choked up, unable to continue.

"Go," her father said as if he correctly understood the situation. "We'll come when we can."

Jeff had put Henry onto the back seat, and Leah climbed in next to him. The *Englisher* had taken off Henry's hat, and Leah had the strongest urge to stroke Henry's soft dark hair, but she was afraid she'd hurt him. She picked up his hand, which seemed to be one of the few spots that were injury-free. *Because he didn't fight back.* She wove her fingers through his and stroked his hand with her thumb.

As his car sped toward the hospital, Jeff told her what had happened, ending with Brad being hauled away by police and Henry's insistence that he had to see her. Emotionally spent, Leah closed her eyes as she prayed hard and silently that Henry would recover fully.

He loves me. She continued to pray. *Please take care of him, Lord.* He'd insisted on seeing her before seeking medical attention. The idea was foolish and humbling. She realized just how much he cared for her, and she never stopped praying so that she could tell Henry as well as show him again and again just how much he meant to her.

Henry came to with a groan. He hurt all over. He didn't know where he was, but then the *beep, beep, beep* of a heart monitor made him realize he was in the hospital. And then it all came back to him. His encounter with Brad Smith, Jeff's arrival at a time when Henry had begun to wonder if the man would kill him before he was through. His hazy visit with Leah.

"Leah," he murmured.

"I'm right here," she assured him. "I'm not going anywhere."

He felt a light touch on his right hand and he opened his eyes. The sight of her beautiful face brought him to tears. "Leah, you're here," he whispered. The knowledge that she was close made him happy. He felt himself relax, then promptly fell asleep again.

When he awoke next, he was more alert. He glanced toward his right and saw Leah seated in a chair close to his bed. She was slumped against his mattress, her hand still holding his.

"You're awake," his mother said in a soft voice. "How are you feeling?"

"Sore."

She inclined her head. "I'll get the nurse. Maybe she can give you something for the pain."

He shook his head and winced at the painful movement. "Not yet. I don't want to sleep again." He glanced down with love at the woman who slept at his side. When he lifted his gaze again, it was to see his mother's warm expression and the knowledge that she was pleased and approved of the woman he loved. "How long has she been here?"

"All night. Since you were brought in yesterday afternoon."

Henry frowned. "She must be exhausted."

His mother smiled. "She wouldn't leave your side."

She moved closer so that she could talk more quietly without waking up Leah. "She loves you. She's *gut* for you."

He gazed at his *mam* with the truth of his heart in his eyes. "Where's *Dat*?" he asked, needing to change the subject before he bawled like a baby.

"He went downstairs for coffee." She moved up toward his head. "Are you hungry?"

"Nay," he said softly. Leah murmured in her sleep, then shifted before she came abruptly awake. "Henry," she whispered, then she sat back and looked up at him, startled yet pleased to see him awake. "Henry, I've been so worried about you."

"So much that you were able to sleep." He gave her a teasing half grin, then gasped at the searing pain in his cheek.

"I haven't slept the whole time!" she insisted but then saw from his mother's expression what Henry had tried to do. To put aside her fear and concern for him by showing that he could joke with her as he fought pain. "Oh, you!"

"Henry," Arlin greeted as he and Missy entered his hospital room. "You're awake. That's *gut*." His voice was gruff, filled with concern.

Henry looked from one to the other before returning his attention to the woman he loved. "They were here yesterday and came back today," Leah said.

"We're glad you're on the mend," Missy said.

"Me, too." He switched positions of his and Leah's fingers so that it was he who caressed the back of her hand.

"Henry." Another man stepped forward. Henry had never met him before, so he eyed him with confusion.

"Do you need anything?" the man said. "If you need anything at all, ask."

Henry glanced from the handsome *Englisher* who looked somehow similar to Leah, the woman he loved. His eyes widened. "Leah."

"Henry, this is Derek Rhoades, my birth father. Derek, meet Henry Yoder, the man I hope to marry someday."

Marry someday. Leah's words formed in his brain, and it was all Henry could process. He gazed at her, then at the man, and he drew a sharp breath. Pain shot through his ribs, overwhelming him, and his vision blurred.

"Henry." He heard Leah's voice from a distance. *"Henry!"*

And then Henry heard no more as his world receded, then went dark.

He woke again to the sound of a distressed feminine voice followed by assurances in deep male tones. He opened his eyes to see Leah talking anxiously with a tall *Englisher* while another one, a man who looked familiar, spoke with his and Leah's parents.

"Leah," he called out to her, his voice weak to his ears.

She spun and rushed to his side. "Henry, are you *oll recht*? You passed out and scared me."

"I'm sorry," he apologized.

The tall English man, who wore a doctor's white lab coat approached the bed. "Pain got too much for you," he said with a look of compassion. "You've two broken ribs. The pain can be unbearable enough to make you pass out. And we've been concerned because of your concussion." He bent close to examine him, telling him to look one way, then another, as he shone a light into his eyes. He studied the cut on Henry's cheek before he stepped back. "You'll live. Although I don't expect it wise to run up against another fist anytime soon," he joked.

Henry controlled his smile into a small crooked tilt of his lips. "Thank you, Doc."

The man faced the others. "I'm going to discharge him tomorrow morning. I think he'll feel much better recuperating at home."

The other *Englisher* stepped forward. "Is there anything he'll he need once he's home?"

"Her." The doctor smiled as he pointed toward Leah, who gazed raptly at Henry while she shifted closely toward the bed.

The dark-haired *Englisher* smirked. "Not mine to give, but you can ask her father," he said, shifting his gaze toward Arlin.

"We'll take care of him," Arlin said with determination and a warm look toward Henry, who felt his spirits rise.

The tall handsome man nodded, then approached the side of the bed where Leah stood. "At first, I thought Leah's introduction to me caused you to pass out." He gave him a crooked smile. "Until Dr. Morgan explained everything to us." He smiled at Henry. "I'm Derek Rhoades, also known as Jason Kingsley. Leah's birth father."

Henry's gaze flew to Leah, whose gaze remained locked on him. "You discovered the truth."

She nodded. "*Ja.* I know everything."

Henry studied her face and realized that she was fine with what she'd learned. He waved her closer until she'd bent close with her ear turned to hear his quiet words, meant only for her. "I love you, Leah Stoltzfus."

She pulled back and beamed at him.

"And that would be my cue to leave," Derek said with a chuckle. The man addressed everyone in the room, including Leah, before returning to Henry's side. "You're a lucky man, Henry."

"I know."

The man's expression turned serious. "Take care of her."

"I will. I promise."

Then Derek left, and their parents followed him, leaving Leah alone with Henry.

"Don't you want to see Derek off?"

She shook her head. "I'd rather be with you," she murmured, and to his surprise, she reached across his pillow to tenderly run her fingers through his hair.

He lifted a hand to caress her raised arm. "You need to go home and rest."

She scowled at him. "I don't want to leave."

"I'm not going anywhere until tomorrow morning. I'm going to need you rested and refreshed then."

"Are you saying that I look bad?"

"*Nay*, never that. You'll always look beautiful to me."

She sighed heavily, but there was a glimmer of happiness in her pretty blue eyes. "I'll go, but I'll be back first thing."

"Fine." He lowered his hand and closed his eyes, as their conversation had tired him. She stood close and continued to run her fingers through his hair. He breathed a happy a sigh. "Go home, Leah. I love you."

"I love you, too," she whispered. Then he heard her leave, and he pressed the nurse call button. He was ready for his medicine that would help him sleep. He needed to heal quickly. There was so much he wanted to do with Leah. So much he wanted to say. And there were plans to be made.

"See you tomorrow, *soohn*," his father said quietly a few minutes later. Henry opened his eyes, managed a tiny smile and nod. Then he fell asleep and dreamed pleasantly of Leah and the house they would live in and the babies they would have together.

Chapter Sixteen

Henry sat on the front porch of his family home and stared at the yard. He was on the mend, but his parents insisted he continue to rest and recuperate. He was feeling edgy. He hadn't seen Leah in several days, and he wanted nothing more than to go to her. But wouldn't she visit him if she loved him, as she'd claimed? Had something changed in their relationship? Something he wasn't aware of?

According to his mother, his black eye had faded to a soft yellow. He'd gone back to the doctor yesterday and learned that his cheek was healing nicely. The man had inspected his stitches and he was pleased with the look of the wound.

Where was Leah? Why wasn't she here? Henry scowled as he rose from his chair. If he could just get to his buggy before his parents saw him. It wasn't a long drive to the Stoltzfus residence. He'd be fine.

Movement in the yard heralded the return of his mother. Henry quickly plopped back into the chair, unwilling to openly disobey her order to rest and stay put, but he needed to go.

He waited for her to climb the porch steps before he spoke.

"I don't know why I have to sit here all day. I need to go out for a while." He needed to see Leah, to ensure that she really loved him the way he loved her.

"Your ribs aren't fully healed," Mam pointed out sternly.

"The doctor taped them up after x-raying them again yesterday. I can get around just fine. Please," he pleaded. "Let me take the buggy."

"Leah still hasn't been by to visit?"

He felt glum as he shook his head. "That's why I have to go. I have to make sure that nothing's changed between us."

"Henry."

"*Mam*, please. I haven't been anywhere. I haven't been to church services, and you wouldn't let me go to the Lapps' for Visiting Sunday."

His mother studied him thoughtfully. "She'll come to you when she's ready."

"I don't understand," he said. "Ready for what?" He experienced a clenching in his belly, a pain more powerful than his broken rib or cut cheek. "She's changed her mind and she is trying to find a nice way to let me down."

Mam shrugged. "You'll know soon enough," she said cryptically.

He must have looked devastated, because she approached him and placed a hand on his shoulder. "Trust in the Lord," she said. "If you and she are meant to be, you will be."

He glanced away as he fisted his hands in his lap. "I have to do something. Sitting here by myself is slowly killing me." He rose and, taller than her, he looked down to capture her gaze. "I'm going to the barn."

"The horses have been fed and watered."

"I'm not going for the horses," he said as he continued on his way. He felt fine, he assured himself. The slight twinge in his midsection was merely an inconvenience, nothing more.

"Henry."

"I'm sorry, *Mam*, but I have to do something." It might as well be something to keep his hands and, hopefully, his mind busy.

She kept silent then, but he could sense her disapproving gaze as he crossed the yard and entered the section of the barn where he built cabinets. He saw a project he'd started before he'd gotten injured. The free-standing combination cabinet and chest of drawers had been ordered for Barbara Martin, Rick Martin's wife and Jeff's mother. Rick had commissioned the work as a surprise for their wedding anniversary. He thought a moment, trying to recall the deadline Rick had given him. Neither Rick nor Jeff had stopped by to see the progress of the project, but Henry figured it was because both men were aware of his injuries and didn't want to rush him.

He picked up a drawer he'd made, eyed the size and shape of it, and knew he still had three more to make to finish the lower chest portion of the cabinet. He eyed the wood he'd selected for the work, picked up a medium-sized length, then promptly put it down as he realized that his parents were right. He wasn't up to doing anything but sitting inside or on the front porch. He wouldn't mind it if he had someone to keep him company. Actually, only one specific person to keep him company. *Leah Stoltzfus.*

Henry walked out of the barn and headed back to his chair on the porch. The sight of Leah Stoltzfus in the yard talking with his mother gave him pause.

"Henry," his mother said. The young woman turned around, and Henry was more than a little disappointed. It wasn't Leah in the yard; it was her sister Ellie, the other blonde Stoltzfus sister.

His steps slowed as he made his way back to the porch. To his surprise, Ellie followed him and waited until he was seated before moving to stand before him. Henry looked up into her eyes and then promptly shut them. He didn't want Ellie's visit. He wanted Leah.

"Henry," the young woman said. "Leah wanted me to give you this."

His eyes opened and he tried to read her expression before he glanced down at what she held. "She's been... ah...busy lately, and she wanted you to know that she was thinking about you."

She thrust a ceramic plate at him, then turned to leave. "She'll be by as soon as she can."

He couldn't answer her. His attention was caught at the chocolate-chip cookie on the plate. It was shaped in a heart and painted with icing. He read the words *Leah loves Henry* and felt the flutter in the region of his heart. A big smile stretched across his face.

"Ellie," he called to Leah's sister. She stopped as she was about to climb into her buggy. "Tell her I feel the same way about her."

Ellie's grin was sweet. "You'll have to tell you yourself the next time you see her."

"And when will that be?"

She shrugged. "I don't know."

Henry sighed. "I'll wait for her."

Ellie boosted herself into the buggy's driver seat. "That, I'll tell her." And then she left, leaving Henry with a renewal of hope and the anticipation of seeing Leah again.

An hour after Ellie's departure, another buggy approached down the drive and pulled close to the house. Henry, still seated on the front porch, stared at the buggy as Leah climbed out and approached. She carried a bag and a large dish.

He gazed at her. "What have you got there?"

She froze, as if something in his tone had upset her. "I brought you lunch."

"Why?"

"Because you have to eat." She appeared hesitant.

"*Mam* has food in the house."

"I thought you'd like to sit and eat with me."

"I'm already sitting."

Leah nodded. She was even more beautiful than he'd remembered. He wanted her with him until his last breath. "If I'm bothering you, I can go," she whispered, looking hurt.

"Don't you dare," he said huskily. "I need you to come here and sit by me as much as I need air." He regarded her with warmth, and her face cleared of worry, making her appear even more radiant. She sat next to him in silence, opened the bag on her lap and pulled out two more chocolate-chip cookies with icing messages.

He gazed into her eyes, then at her mouth, before studying what she held. He read *I miss you* on one cookie and *You're the only one for me* on the other. She looked embarrassed as she then pulled out two sandwiches made with fresh turkey. Henry studied the cookies, then the sandwich she gave him. "I only need those," he said, focusing his eyes briefly on the cookies before lifting to caress her with his gaze.

She didn't look away. "I'm sorry I haven't been by."

He swallowed hard. "Why haven't you?"

"I needed to find a place for my craft shop."

Hurt, he stared at her. "You didn't wait for me."

She shook her head.

"Why not?"

"You were recovering." She glanced at him shyly. "I know you told me you love me, but you were hurt and ill…and I wasn't sure."

"Yet, you made me cookies," he said.

He saw her hand tremble as she tucked back a lock of her hair. "I'm sorry. I don't know much about having a beau since I've never had one."

"And you never will," Henry said fiercely, which made Leah jerk with shock.

She stared at him with a tormented expression. "I see."

"*Nay*, you don't, Leah, because you don't need a beau. I have more in mind for you." He smiled when she blushed. He reached to grasp her hand. "I want to wed you, Leah Stoltzfus." He rose and with a grimace dropped down to one knee. "Leah, will you marry me? Be my love and my safe haven. Will you let me care for you, protect you and keep you forever?"

He heard her sob and saw tears fill her eyes. He stiffened with the belief that his proposal was unwelcome. "*Ja*, Henry Yoder," she breathed. "I'd love nothing more than to be your wife."

Still holding on to her hand, Henry climbed awkwardly to his feet, ignoring the twinge of pain left from his injured ribs. *"Praise the Lord!"* he shouted, overjoyed. He glanced over to see that her father had joined her mother in the yard, and both of them looked pleased as they gazed at the two of them.

Henry grabbed Leah's other hand so that he held each of her hands in one of his. "I love you desperately." He watched her features soften with love and her blue eyes shine with happy tears.

She sniffed. "I love you more."

He chuckled as he gazed at her with emotion. "Never, Leah. I'll always love you more." He inhaled sharply, then released the breath. *"Much more."*

Epilogue

Leah stood in her wedding dress in a room filled with women. Her dress was an azure blue, made for her by her mother. Three of her Lapp cousins' wives studied her with pleased expressions.

"It looks lovely," Rachel, her cousin Noah's wife, said. "The color's wonderful on you, Leah."

The other Lapp women agreed. Sarah and Annie beamed at her while her mother adjusted the white cape and apron and Ellie walked around to study Leah from every angle.

"Are you ready?" Ellie said.

"*Ja*, more than ever." Leah grinned. "I love him and can't wait to be his wife."

"On that note, I think 'tis time for us to leave," Sarah said with a chuckle, drawing her two sisters-in-law out of Leah's bedroom. "We'll see you at the church gathering."

The only ones left in the room were Ellie and *Mam*. Charlie had been up earlier, given her a hug, then promptly raced downstairs to help with last-minute details for the reception back at the house after the wedding ceremony.

"Is my hair *oll recht*?" Leah asked her mother. She was nervous, not a bad nervous, more like a tingling, warm, heightened anticipation of becoming Henry Yoder's wife.

It was early, before dawn. Leah had been amazed when the Lapp women arrived to help with the wedding feast before coming to her room to make sure she had everything she needed.

"Leah." Her mother's voice was hushed, reverent.

Leah met her gaze and saw tears in her *mam's* eyes. "What's wrong?"

Mam shook her head. "Nothing. Only that I'm going to miss having you at home."

She smiled. "We won't be far, and we'll come to visit often. So often that you'll get sick and tired of seeing us. And you can come to us. I'll make supper and when we have children, we'll want you to babysit and mother them." She bit her lip as she was overcome with emotion. "I love you. You've done so much for me."

"Nay," Mam whispered. "Not true. Loving you was easy, Leah. You were the sweetest and kindest little girl…and the loveliest young woman. I love you."

The two women hugged briefly. Ellie stood by with tears in her eyes.

Ready to wed the man she loved, Leah climbed into the buggy that would take her to the Lapps, where the church service and ceremony were to be held. It was a Tuesday. The November day promised to be clear if a bit chilly. Her cousin Isaac was driving while his wife, Ellen, sat next to him in the front seat. In the middle bench seat sat her older sister, Nell, and her brother-in-law James. Leah was with Henry in the vehicle's very back seat.

Henry clasped her hand and give it a reassuring squeeze. Leah met his loving gaze and couldn't stop the grin that settled on her lips. "You look beautiful, Leah," he whispered for her ears alone.

"I've never known anyone more handsome—inside and out." She chuckled when he arched his brows in puzzlement. "You're a wonderful man, Henry Yoder," she explained. "That's all I'm saying."

Then it was Henry's grin that lit up the back seat.

The church congregation had gathered in the Samuel Lapp residence. Henry's sister, Ruth, and family were among them. Even his brother, David, had arrived to surprise and please Henry and his parents. The front set of benches were for Henry and Leah in the center and their attendants on both sides of them.

Bishop John Fisher stood and asked Henry and Leah to step outside the room. He, Preacher Levi and the deacon, Abram Peachy, alternately spoke about marriage and their earthy duties as a couple and their responsibilities that the two of them would share in raising children. Leah blushed but nodded as she and Henry agreed with what was expected of them. Through the talk, they could hear the congregation singing wedding hymns from the *Ausbund*, the Amish book of hymns.

"Let's go back," the bishop said.

Leah felt the wonder of love as she accepted Henry as her husband. Henry was clearly more than happy to take her to be his wife. After a long sermon, Henry and she were called to step forward and asked to recite their vows as responses to a series of questions. Bishop John spoke without written word, straight from the heart and with the Lord's help.

"Are you willing to wed as God in the beginning ordained and commanded?" the bishop asked.

"Yes," Henry and Leah answered together.

"Henry, are you confident that God has chosen this sister to be your wedded wife?"

"Yes," Henry said with a glow in his eyes as he gazed at her.

"Leah, are you confident that God has chosen this brother to be your wedded husband?"

"Yes," Leah said as she beamed at Henry with greatly felt joy.

"Henry, do you promise before God and this church that you will never more depart from her, that you will care for and cherish her, even if bodily sickness comes to her or under any circumstances which a Christian husband is responsible to care for, until our dear God will again separate you from each other?"

"Yes."

Bishop John Fisher asked her and Henry to clasp hands before he gave the blessing over their marriage. Then the bishop pronounced them husband and wife.

Isaac and Ellen quickly pulled the newlyweds toward the carriage for the ride to the reception in the Arlin Stoltzfus home. Nell and James got into the seat in the middle, and Nell glanced back at them with a huge grin. "Welcome to the family, Henry."

Henry stared at his new sister-in-law and had never been happier than he was at that moment. "*Danki.* I'm pleased to be a member of your family," he murmured. As the others faced the front, he slipped his arm around

Leah's shoulders and pulled her to his side. "Mrs. Yoder, I love you."

Leah gazed at him, enrapt. "I like the sound of that. Mrs. Yoder, Mr. Yoder." She studied him silently. "I love you."

"Gut." He leaned close and kissed near her ear. "We're going to have many happy years together." He refused to let go of her, and he saw that she was pleased by his close proximity.

"We're almost there," Isaac called back. "Are you ready?"

The couple would be seated in the *eck*, one corner of the tables set up to form the shape of a squared-off U, with their attendants seated beside them.

"Will you mind living in the Yoder *haus*?" Henry asked his wife softly. His parents had decided to retire. They had given the store space over to Leah for her craft shop, which she decided to call Yoder's Country Crafts and Supplies. Harry and Margaret Yoder had moved into the *dawdi haus* in the back of the property, leaving the big house for Henry and Leah.

"I will love living in the Yoder big *haus*," she replied quietly. "I'm happy to live anyplace where you are." She bit her lip, and Henry felt the strongest urge to kiss her.

She was his wife, so he gave in to the feeling. "Leah," he breathed. When she turned to him, he kissed her and smiled when he saw her pink cheeks, bright eyes and the pretty curve of her lips afterward. "Wife."

"Husband." She leaned in closer. "Forever."

"Amen. *Forever*," Henry whispered right before he stole another kiss from her.

* * * * *

WE HOPE YOU
ENJOYED THIS

LOVE INSPIRED®

BOOK.

If you were **inspired** by this

uplifting, **heartwarming** romance,

be sure to look for all six Love

Inspired® books every month.

Love Inspired®

www.LoveInspired.com

Love Inspired

Save $1.00

on the purchase of ANY
Love Inspired® or
Love Inspired® Suspense book.

Available wherever books are sold,
including most bookstores, supermarkets,
drugstores and discount stores.

Save $1.00

on the purchase of ANY Love Inspired® or Love Inspired® Suspense book.

Coupon valid until October 31, 2019.
Redeemable at participating retail outlets in the U.S. and Canada only.
Limit one coupon per customer.

52616440

Canadian Retailers: Harlequin Enterprises Limited will pay the face value of this coupon plus 10.25¢ if submitted by customer for this product only. Any other use constitutes fraud. Coupon is nonassignable. Void if taxed, prohibited or restricted by law. Consumer must pay any government taxes. Void if copied. Inmar Promotional Services ("IPS") customers submit coupons and proof of sales to Harlequin Enterprises Limited, P.O. Box 31000, Scarborough, ON M1R 0E7, Canada. Non-IPS retailer—for reimbursement submit coupons and proof of sales directly to Harlequin Enterprises Limited, Retail Marketing Department, Bay Adelaide Centre, East Tower, 22 Adelaide Street West, 40th Floor, Toronto, Ontario M5H 4E3, Canada.

U.S. Retailers: Harlequin Enterprises Limited will pay the face value of this coupon plus 8¢ if submitted by customer for this product only. Any other use constitutes fraud. Coupon is nonassignable. Void if taxed, prohibited or restricted by law. Consumer must pay any government taxes. Void if copied. For reimbursement submit coupons and proof of sales directly to Harlequin Enterprises, Ltd 482, NCH Marketing Services, P.O. Box 880001, El Paso, TX 88588-0001, U.S.A. Cash value 1/100 cents.

5 65373 00076 2 (8100)0 12427

® and ™ are trademarks owned and used by the trademark owner and/or its licensee.

© 2019 Harlequin Enterprises Limited

LICOUP47012

Paralyzed veteran Eve Vincent is happy with the life she's built for herself at Mercy Ranch—until her ex-fiancé shows up with a baby. Their best friends died and named Eve and Ethan Forester as guardians. But can they put their differences aside and build a future together?

Read on for a sneak preview of
Her Oklahoma Rancher *by Brenda Minton,*
available June 2019 from Love Inspired!

"I'm sorry, Eve, but I had to do something to make you see how important this is. We can't just walk away from her. It might not be what we signed on for and I feel like I'm the last person who should be raising this little girl, but James and Hanna trusted us."

"But there is no *us*," she said with a lift of her chin, but he could see pain reflected in her dark eyes.

The pain he saw didn't bother him as much as what he didn't see in her eyes, in her expression. He didn't see the person he used to know, the woman he'd planned to marry.

He had noticed the same yesterday, and he guessed that was why he'd left Tori with her. He'd been sitting there looking at a woman he used to think he knew better than he knew himself, and he hadn't recognized her.

"There is no *us*, but we still exist, you and me, and Tori needs us." He said it softly because the little girl in his arms seemed to be drifting off, even with the occasional sob.

"There has to be another option. I obviously can't do this. Last night was proof."

"Last night meant nothing. You've always managed, Eve. You're strong and capable."

"Before, Ethan. I was that person before. This is me now, and I can't."

"I guess you have changed. I've never heard you say you can't do anything."

He sat down on a nearby chair. Isaac had left. The woman named Sierra had also disappeared. They were alone. When had they last been alone? The night he proposed? It had been the night she left for Afghanistan. He'd taken her to dinner in San Antonio and they'd walked along the riverfront surrounded by people, music and twinkling lights.

He'd dropped to one knee there in front of strangers passing by, seeing the sights. Dozens had stopped to watch as she cried and said yes. Later they'd made the drive to the airport, his ring glistening on her finger, planning a wedding that would never happen.

"Ethan?" Her voice was soft, quiet, questioning.

He glanced down at the little girl in his arms.

"What other option is there, Eve? Should we turn her over to the state, let her take her chances with whoever they choose? Should we find some distant relative? What do you recommend?"

He leaned back in the chair and studied her face, her expression. She was everything familiar. His childhood friend. The person he'd loved. *Had* loved. Past tense. The woman he'd wanted to spend his life with had been someone else, someone who never backed down. She looked as tough, as stubborn as ever, but there was something fragile in her expression.

Something in her expression made him recheck his feelings. He'd been bucked off horses, trampled by a bull, broken his arm jumping dirt bikes. She'd been his only broken heart. He didn't want another one.

Don't miss
Her Oklahoma Rancher *by Brenda Minton,*
available June 2019 wherever
Love Inspired® books and ebooks are sold.

www.LoveInspired.com